daughter's keeper

ayelet waldman

SOURCEBOOKS LANDMARK™
AN IMPRINT OF SOURCEBOOKS, INC.®
NAPERVILLE, ILLINOIS

Published by Sourcebooks, Inc.
P.O. Box 4410, Naperville, Illinois 60567-4410
(630) 961-3900
FAX: (630) 961-2168
www.sourcebooks.com

Library of Congress Cataloging-in-Publication Data

Waldman, Ayelet.
Daughter's keeper / Ayelet Waldman.
p. cm.
ISBN 1-4022-0313-6 (alk. paper)
1. Mothers and daughters—Fiction. 2. Women prisoners—Fiction.
3.Drug traffic—Fiction. I. Title.
PS3573.A42124D38 2003
813'.54—dc21
2003004763

Printed and bound in the United States of America
BG   10 9 8 7 6 5 4 3 2

In memory of Amanda Davis

part one

part one

They were obviously mother and daughter: the expression on the young woman's face gave them away. She wore the peculiarly adolescent scowl that—after they reach the age of seventeen or eighteen and their disdain for the world gives way, again, to a sense of possibility—young women reserve only for their mothers. The mother studied the menu, ignoring her daughter's expression. Perhaps she was so accustomed to the girl's sneer that it was no longer even remarkable to her.

"What's good?" Elaine asked, her voice high and cheerful and false.

"Everything," Olivia said, though it wasn't true. The pupusas—fat pats of corn meal stuffed with cheese and meat and fried in lard on the grill—were good. Nothing else was.

Elaine glanced around the room. It was small and unremarkable, with an open kitchen on one end where two women scooped handfuls of dough out of a large, white plastic bucket, mashed them with their palms, and lay them on a sizzling griddle. They knew exactly how much dough they needed, pinching off the excess with a practiced twist and tossing it back in the bucket. There were only a few tables and three cracked, red vinyl booths that looked like they'd been ripped out of a defunct diner and propped along the wall. Elaine and Olivia sat in the middle booth. The only other patrons were a family sitting at the large table in the middle of the restaurant.

"What's that they're eating?" Elaine pointed to the family. The father, a small man whose weather-beaten face peered out from under a straw cowboy hat, distributed a steaming pupusa to each of his four young children. His wife, also tiny but rounder and younger-looking, poured Coke out of a single can into six plastic cups. She smiled as her children gulped greedily at their drinks, her large white teeth splayed like a fan of playing cards in her broad, cheerful mouth.

"Mom, you're pointing," Olivia said. "Pupusas. That's the specialty. They're like fried tamales or stuffed tacos. Like that."

"Sounds great. That's what I'll have." Elaine put down her menu and tucked her hair behind her ear with a small, square hand. She was a pretty woman, although as she aged fewer and fewer people noticed. Her carefully highlighted brown hair shone with the glints of red that had once appeared naturally whenever she went out in the sun. Fine tracings inched out from the corners of her eyes and the top of her upper lip, and the line of her jaw had the slightest hint of heaviness. She looked younger than her forty-nine years, though not by much.

They sat in silence until a young man in a spattered apron came to the table. Olivia placed their order in rapid Spanish. Her accent was perfect, Elaine noted, maybe even a little too perfect, like reporters on public radio who pronounce the names of Latin American capitals with an ostentatious correctitude.

"I'm always amazed at how good your Spanish is."

The girl blushed and smiled. Elaine knew how proud Olivia was of her proficiency. She had started studying the language in the third grade. Her elementary school class had been given the option of learning either French or Spanish, and even at the age of eight Olivia had expressed derision of those who did not choose to study the language of California's laborer class. She had gotten the same straight *A*s in Spanish as she had in all of her other classes, but they seemed to come effortlessly, without the grueling hours of preparation her success in other subjects cost her.

"This is such an interesting restaurant," Elaine said. "Do you come here often?"

At the other table, one of the children spilled her Coke, and the father jumped back to avoid the spreading pool of liquid. The mother dabbed at it with a single, white napkin.

"*Interesting,*" Olivia said. The edge of disgust in her voice caused them both to wince. "Jorge and I eat here a couple of times a week. The men on his corner all come here."

"His corner?"

"You know, where he waits for work. The day-laborer corner. Where the men wait all day for construction work or gardening." Olivia paused and picked the wrapping off a straw. She slurped at her tamarind soda. And then, almost as if she couldn't help herself, as if she were being forced against her will to hurt her mother's feelings, she continued, "Sometimes rich Berkeley matrons pick them up to clean out their garages."

Elaine blushed, feeling first precisely the sense of shame her daughter had intended and then a flash of irritation. She was irritated at herself for letting her daughter poke at a guilty conscience she wasn't even sure she possessed, but mostly she was angry at Olivia, who surely knew exactly how hard-won Elaine's financial security was.

Elaine owned the same small College Avenue drugstore where she had taken her first job as a pharmacist twenty years before, when Olivia was a very little girl. The drugstore, like so many businesses in the city of Berkeley, was less a modern profit-making venture than an homage to nostalgia—an opportunity for the citizens to express, with the very act of filling their prescriptions for Celebrex, Viagra, and Zoloft, of buying their toothbrushes, foot powders, and feminine hygiene products, their commitment to an ideal of community, of small-town neighborliness that has all but disappeared from the landscape of contemporary American society. At the front of the pharmacy was a bona fide 1930s soda fountain. Black-and-white tiled, chrome-plated, and absolutely authentic. Elaine counted pills and poured liquids to the whir and hum of the Oster milk shake machine. She knew her customer's names, the particulars of their diagnoses, and the precise quality of their aches and pains. She put aside samples of Bag Balm for older women with unusually dry skin and stocked fine-milled soap for those with delicate noses. She knew when it was time to order a breast pump for a pregnant customer and was the sole confidant of many whose ailments were too embarrassing or too indicative of a creeping advanced age to be confessed to the world at large.

Her business was steady and her customers loyal, and as the years passed she had made the drugstore more and more profitable. But no one could ever have considered her wealthy. Not even Olivia.

"So Jorge is still doing day-laborer work? He hasn't found a steady job yet?"

"God, Mom." Olivia gave her head a shake. "That is such a shitty thing to say."

"What? What did I say? I just asked if he'd found work. I didn't mean anything by it."

"Of course he hasn't found a regular job. Do you know how hard it is for illegals to get decent jobs? He's lucky if he can get picked up a couple of days a week. It's not like he's not trying. He waits on that fucking corner every fucking day."

Elaine flinched at her daughter's profanity. "I didn't mean it as a criticism," she said. "Really. I was just asking. I'm sorry."

The girl just shrugged her shoulders. "Whatever."

Olivia was twenty-two years old, although she looked much younger. As a little girl, she had been beautiful, rosy-cheeked and blond-ringleted. Today she wore baggy jeans and a ragged green sweatshirt that had been washed so often that its zipper arced in waves from her neck to her waist. Her best feature remained her hair, which hung, an unwashed mass of blond, brown, and red kinky curls, down to the middle of her back. She'd swept part of it off her face and clipped it back with a chipped tortoise-shell barrette.

Elaine adored Olivia's hair. As a baby, Olivia had been entirely bald, then, suddenly, around her second birthday, she sprouted a head full of blond corkscrew curls—show-stopping curls. The kind of curls that old women in the supermarket couldn't keep themselves from reaching out and touching. Elaine had always been disappointed by her own lank hair, so when confronted with the beauty of Olivia's, she had spent far more money than was sensible on things like barrettes, hair elastics, scrunchies, headbands, combs, and leave-in conditioners. Every morning from the time Olivia was a toddler, Elaine sprayed the little girl's hair with Johnson's No More Tears and slowly, painstakingly combed it out, careful not to tear or pull. In the winter, when the dryness of the heat blown through the house made Olivia's hair hang limp and almost dull, Elaine labored over it with gel, foam, spray, lotion, or mousse—to give it the bounce, shine, volume, or whatever else the product promised. Her attendance to Olivia's curls was the only physical contact with her daughter that gave them both unalloyed pleasure, that was not fraught with Elaine's discomfort at her daughter's voracious neediness. Olivia had a way of draping herself over her mother, crawling into her lap to be kissed, that left Elaine feeling uneasy, trapped by the longing that flowed palpably from her daughter with her clinging limbs and searching lips. Yet, when the girl sat, still and quiet, as Elaine pulled the hairbrush gently through her hair, they were both at ease. The ritual went on well into high school. When, at last, at age fifteen, Olivia declared that she wanted to care for her own hair, Elaine felt bereft.

Olivia reached into her scuffed leather satchel and pulled out a brown paper bag. "Here, I got you something."

"Really?" Elaine smiled in surprise. She reached across the table and took the bag. "What is it?"

"Nothing, really. I picked it up at the Frida Kahlo show at the Oakland Museum. It's just a silly little thing."

Elaine opened the bag and pulled out a manila envelope with a portrait of the stern-faced artist on the front. She smiled uncertainly. "Are these *paper dolls*?"

Olivia shrugged. "Yeah. They reminded me of that time when I had mono, remember? In fourth grade? My eyes were so blurry I couldn't read. Remember you cut out paper dolls for me and colored them to look like famous women? You did Martha Washington and Joan of Arc. Gertrude Stein. Barbra Streisand. Lieutenant Uhura from *Star Trek*."

Elaine smiled uncertainly. "I remember you were home for almost three weeks. What a nightmare that was. That was the year before I bought the store, and I ended up using up all of my vacation time—every last minute of it. I remember thinking that if you didn't get better, I was going to lose my job."

"But you don't remember the dolls? You cut them out of computer paper, the kind that was like one continuous page? And then you colored them in? You started to color Uhura's face black, but I made you use the brown pencil instead? Remember?"

Olivia sounded almost desperate, and Elaine felt a familiar tug of guilt. "Oh right," she said. "Of course. The paper dolls. I remember."

They were so random, these accidents of memory. The events in Olivia's life that Elaine had consciously tried to freeze in the remembered record of the girl's childhood invariably disappeared. Long forgotten were the trips to Disneyland, the evenings spent suffering, frozen-bottomed, through interminable Ice Capades shows. Olivia could no longer execute a competent plié or call to mind her basic chords and five-finger variations. Had there not been a pinchpot to testify to its occurrence, the ceramics class would have faded entirely from memory. Yet the moments recalled with precision and an almost eerie detail were ridiculously haphazard—a long-ago trip to Costco in a borrowed minivan had assumed near-mythic importance, and the time the sprinklers flooded the yard was, for no reason at all, indelibly seared in Olivia's mind. It seemed to Elaine that Olivia's chosen recollections were always of accidents or mistakes, of times the girl had been ill or hurt, or when Elaine's desperation to fill the empty hours had resulted not in a day made pleasant by successful planning but rather in one made miserable by an argument or some other mishap or misadventure. Her daughter's memories were, Elaine felt, without fail testament only to her own failures as a mother.

"Anyway," Olivia said, looking neither at her mother nor at the dolls but rather at her own hands. "I just thought they were cute."

"They are. Who should I give them to? Most of my friends' little girls are sort of beyond paper dolls." As soon as the words escaped from her lips, Elaine realized that she'd made a mistake. Olivia had intended the gift to be for her.

"They're stupid. I know. They just made me think of those other ones," Olivia said. She took a gulp from her drink. "Anyway, Mom." Her voice dropped to a mumble. "I have a favor to ask of you."

Elaine sighed. She had feared this was coming, from the first moment she heard Olivia's voice on the telephone inviting her out to lunch. She smoothed her hair back behind her ear and waited for the inevitable.

Olivia blushed and vigorously stirred her straw around her soda glass, clinking the ice cubes against each other. "I was hoping you might be able to make me a loan. Just a small loan."

"I just lent you three hundred dollars two months ago," Elaine said, her voice neutral. "You haven't even begun to pay that back."

The girl, who wore thrift shop clothing and often seemed to subsist on a diet of rice and beans, displayed an inexhaustible need for cash. When Olivia had dropped out of college, over her mother's vigorous objections, Elaine expressed her disappointment, her disgust with Olivia's heedlessness, by refusing to support her any longer. Over time, however, Elaine's resolve weakened, and she had begun loaning Olivia money, though she kept a scrupulous account of what she dispensed and generally made sure that Olivia paid back each loan before getting more.

Elaine turned over the packet of dolls and looked at the artist's mustachioed face. She began calculating how much she could give her daughter. It was not merely a question of what she could afford, or of what she was willing to spare from her own carefully apportioned budget. She wanted to be sure that the sum she bestowed, while enough to satisfy whatever emergency had inspired the request, would not be so much as to leave Olivia with the impression that Elaine approved of her choices.

"I'm going to pay you back," Olivia said. "I promise. It's just hard right now."

"Is there a problem at work?"

"No. Not really. I mean, I'm doing okay. Tips are good. And I like a couple of the other waitresses. I'm trying to convince them to help me set up a union. We don't have any kind of health insurance and no paid vacation time. There are waitresses there who've been working for, like, seven years without a week off." For the first time since they'd sat down together at the restaurant, Olivia's voice lost its listless tone and grew animated, even passionate.

Elaine shook her head. "Oh, Olivia."

"What?"

"Nothing. I don't know. It's just…you shouldn't make your bosses angry."

"Why not? They can't fire me." She leaned back, crossed her arms in front of her chest, and glared at her mother.

"Can't they? I mean, you don't have a contract or anything, do you?"

"Mother, they can't fire you for starting a union. I'll file a grievance with the NLRB and sue them."

The two fell silent.

Finally Olivia, her voice drained of its spirit, said, "It's just hard trying to support two people on a waitress's salary."

Elaine turned the packet of dolls face down with a firm snap. "I'm sorry, Olivia. I know that you're having a difficult time. However, I think I've made my position clear on this issue."

"Right. I don't even know why I asked. Forget it." Olivia reached across the table and grabbed the packet of paper dolls. She got up and went over to the family at the center table. She kneeled down next to one of the little girls.

"*Para ti*," she said, handing her the packet.

The girl's eyes widened, and her parents looked confused.

"It's okay," Olivia said. She cupped the girl's cheek in her palm and smiled gently at her.

The little girl looked over at her father, who shrugged, then nodded. Only then did she tear open the packet. She pulled out the paper dolls and looked at them, uncertainly. "*Gracias,*" she murmured, and then, as if to reassure Olivia, smiled broadly.

Children liked Olivia, they always had. And she liked them. For a long while Elaine had assumed she wouldn't have to worry about her daughter, that Olivia would always spend her weekends and vacations baby-sitting for families in the neighborhood rather than out getting in trouble with kids her own age. She'd been a highly sought-after sitter—her New Year's Eve sleepovers were the stuff of legend in the Elmwood, the part of Berkeley where they lived. Neighbors and pharmacy customers still reminded Elaine about it—more than one couple remembered those years as the last they'd been able to celebrate the holiday without their children. Of course that had ended when Olivia had discovered boys—or rather, when they discovered her. Even after she'd begun dating, though, Olivia remained in close touch with the neighborhood kids. Almost every weekend morning a child or two would ring the front door, and Olivia would sit on the porch with them, feeding them cookies or popcorn. They would submit, for her inevitable approval, especially well-done homework assignments, rollerblading tricks, and newly acquired puppies. To this day, half the holiday cards that filled Elaine's mailbox every December were from local families and were addressed to her daughter alone.

Elaine sighed. She peeked out of the front window of the restaurant at her car, a three-year-old Honda Accord parked across the street. Not for the first time, Elaine regretted the color. She had bought it off the lot, and gotten a good deal, but had almost immediately been embarrassed by the obviousness, the ostentation of a cherry-red car. In this neighborhood, it seemed worse than ever. She had followed Olivia's directions here, growing more and more nervous as she drove out of the parts of Oakland that she recognized. Elaine had never been to Fruitvale. The closest she'd come was reading the exit sign as she whizzed past on her way to the Oakland airport or down to the Peninsula.

Driving along Fruitvale Avenue, Elaine had battled the overwhelming urge to lock her doors. She knew Olivia would think she was being racist, but the groups of young men with slicked-back hair and baggy pants standing on the corners struck her as menacing. She had parked across the street from the restaurant and sat in her car for a moment, wondering if she should snap the anti-theft club in place over her steering wheel. She felt a vague sense of embarrassment; she didn't want to hurt the feelings of anyone who might be passing. She also knew that the sight of the bright red club would enrage her daughter and prove to Olivia that her mother was, after all, an incurable bourgeois bigot. Finally, Elaine left the club on the floor in the backseat. It wasn't until she got out of her car and walked to the restaurant that she noticed that all the other cars were clubbed.

After a moment or two, their food arrived and, with relief, Elaine busied herself with her pupusas, dipping them in salsa, blowing on the steaming dough, and tearing off small bites with her meticulously whitened teeth. "These *are* terrific," she said. "What a find! They should write about this place in the *Oakland Tribune* or something. They're always on the lookout for little out-of-the-way places like this."

"It's only out-of-the-way if you don't live here," Olivia said.

Olivia pulled out of her parking space and stopped at the light. She looked into her rearview mirror and watched Elaine cross the street and get into her car. She had chosen the restaurant especially to oblige her mother to drive to a section of Oakland that she would otherwise never have entered. It was part of the campaign in which Olivia had been engaged since she was a teenager—to shake Elaine out of her myopia, to force her to confront and understand the desperate circumstances in which people lived just a few miles from the stuccoed mansions of the Berkeley Hills and the gracious brown-shingled homes of the Elmwood.

Only once she saw that Elaine was safely in her car did Olivia turn her attention back to the street before her. It was, after all, a lousy neighborhood, and she didn't want anything to happen to her mother. While she drove home, Olivia thought, not for the first time, that Elaine looked worn, almost old. She used to think her mother pretty, but now she saw only Elaine's sagging skin, the blue-tinted pouches under her eyes, the false brightness of her colored hair, and they made her impatient. Aging seemed, to Olivia, to be another of her mother's irritating habits, like the slurping sound she made when she drank her morning cup of Earl Grey, or the fastidious grimace she wore when filing her nails.

Olivia and Jorge lived off Park Boulevard, in a part of Oakland notable only for the ethnic diversity of its inhabitants.

Other neighborhoods in the city were segregated with an apartheid-like efficiency that confused Olivia. How did everyone know exactly where to live—exactly on which corner the line of demarcation was drawn? Olivia liked her block's rainbow-coalition flavor. At least she liked it in theory. In practice, nobody talked much to anybody else, and her attempts at neighborliness had gone ignored, by and large.

As she walked down the long narrow alley that led back to her small apartment tucked behind a three-story building in what had once been a garage, Olivia held her breath. The young black man in one of the front apartments had just brought home a rottweiler puppy, and while Olivia knew she should be grateful to him for cleaning up after his dog, the stench of feces coming from the garbage bins was unbearable. She and Jorge had stopped opening their front window and had taken to burning incense, a smell she found just barely more acceptable than dog shit.

Jorge was lying on the living room couch, his legs stretched out in front of him. One toe poked through the white sock on his left foot. On the television, men kicked a ball back and forth. Sometimes it seemed to Olivia that an endless loop of a single *futbol* game played day and night on Spanish-language television. The teams were indistinguishable from one another, and no one ever scored, but Jorge never grew tired of watching.

"Hey, little mother, give me a kiss," he said in Spanish. Nine months in the United States had taught Jorge barely enough English to order a cup of coffee—not surprising since he almost never needed to speak the language. He and Olivia spoke only Spanish together, as they always had. The men who hired him gave whatever instructions were necessary in the same language, and the other workers were all, of course, from Mexico or Central America. Olivia supposed she could have been better about introducing him to her Anglo friends, putting them both into situations where he would have been forced to listen to and speak some English, but the few times they'd gotten together with her girlfriends had been more or less disasters. Jorge had nothing at all in common with the young law students and software designers her friends were dating. He sat silently through a number of dinners, smiling politely except when someone directed a question directly at him. Then he looked at Olivia, stricken, and she quickly deflected the conversation away. She had been more relieved than sorry when the invitations stopped coming.

Olivia bent over and planted a kiss on the tip of Jorge's hooked nose. He grabbed her around the waist and dragged her onto the couch, on top of him. He reached a hand down the seat of her pants and grabbed her butt.

"Mmm," he said, squeezing her.

Olivia smiled, pleased as always at the obvious pleasure Jorge took in the parts of her that she had used to think of as too fat—ugly even. It was hard not to love a man who frequently commented that no ass that could fit into just two hands was worth grabbing.

"So, how's *Mamá*?" Jorge asked.

Olivia burrowed down into the couch. "Same as always. I took her to Paco's and she was scared out of her mind. Not that she'd ever say."

"Did she give you the money?"

Olivia shook her head. She had hated asking her mother for money. She hated letting Elaine know that they weren't getting by, and most of all she hated giving Elaine the opportunity to comment on how she lived and what she did. Olivia couldn't remember a time when she hadn't resented Elaine's perennial disapproval. It seemed to her that from the first time she had made an independent decision or formed an opinion of her own, her mother had found it wanting in some way.

Olivia felt everything passionately, and her mother, she believed, felt nothing with any kind of ardor. Olivia followed the compass of her heart, trusting that what moved her, what inspired her, would point her toward the true North. Elaine carefully considered, thoughtfully evaluated, and most often, to her daughter's disgust, decided to do nothing at all. This difference in the fundamental nature of their personalities was apparent from the time Olivia was a very little girl. Elaine would take her shopping for shoes, and Olivia would spot a pair of red, sparkly, magic slippers, the perfect shoes to skip down the yellow brick road. Olivia would cling to the ridiculous, lovely shoes as her mother fitted her with brown Oxfords, white sneakers, and plain black Mary Janes. When Elaine finally chose the most sensible, most comfortable, longest-lasting shoe, Olivia invariably wept—never once, in all the years, had she anticipated the denial of the object of her adoration.

When she was grown, and no longer subject to her mother's prohibitions and demands, Olivia followed her own enthusiasms. What she cared about was something she defined loosely as freedom and equality, and her intent was to work in some way to better the lot of others; she just wasn't sure how. She was waiting tables while she tried to figure it out. Rejecting the goal of professional achievement that her mother wanted for her meant that Olivia was constantly short of cash, which explained why she'd ended up doing something she found as repellent as asking for money. She didn't want to rely on Elaine to bail her out, but sometimes it was unavoidable. Nonetheless, the request was always an exercise in humiliation, particularly when it was rebuffed.

"It doesn't matter," Jorge said.

"Was there anything in the classifieds today?"

He shrugged and focused intently on the television.

Olivia raised herself up on one hand. "Did you even look?"

"What's the point?" he said, not taking his eyes off the flickering screen. "None of those places are going to hire an illegal who speaks no English. Why should I bother calling, just to have them tell me no?"

"Well, what about the corner?" she asked. "Wasn't there any day work today?"

Jorge stiffened for a moment and then shrugged his shoulders. "No. I got sick of standing out there. I came home."

She stared at him for a moment, doing her best to restrain her irritation. She reminded herself to be understanding; he was trying, after all. At least she hoped he was. "It'll be okay. I'm working tonight. It's Saturday; tips will be good."

He jerked himself up into a sitting position and said, "It's not okay. I am the man. *I* should work."

Relieved that he had woken from his torpor, Olivia kissed him on his hollow cheek. "What difference does it make? As long as we can pay the rent."

Jorge shoved Olivia to one side and sat up. His sharp Mayan features were grim, and his face was stone-like. "It makes a difference."

She hadn't meant to hurt him. She'd been thoughtless, but that was only because she was so tired and depressed after lunch with her mother. "I know. I know it does."

"You don't know what this is like for me. You don't know. I stand every day on that corner like some…like some goddamn *campesino*. I went to university for almost two years! I am not just a back for a white son of a bitch to load up. I was a student. A *student*. Do you know what that means?" He was shouting.

"I know," she said.

"You!" He waved a dismissive hand at her. "What do you know? You know nothing. You quit university like it was nothing. Like it meant nothing."

Olivia blushed at Jorge's disgust. He was the first in his family to graduate from high school and had reveled in his life as a student. When his political activities had gotten him expelled from the university, he had been devastated.

"It's just different here," Olivia said.

He looked at her and shook his head. "I know it's different. Mother of God, I know just how different it is. In Mexico I was something. A leader. Here, I'm nothing. I came here to be with you, because I love you, and I am nothing here. Just another brown man on a corner."

Olivia stroked Jorge's face. "Oh, *mi vida*. I know how hard this is for you. I know that you are doing your best. It's not your fault," she murmured.

He shook off her hand, got up, and walked across the floor to the bathroom. He slammed the door behind him, and the flimsy walls of the house shook.

Olivia reached for the remote and turned off the television. She leaned back on the couch and sighed. They had had this fight before. They both knew that there was one simple way to give Jorge the immigration status he needed to get off the street corner and find a legitimate job or go to school. But Olivia couldn't bring herself to do it.

When Jorge had first shown up on her doorstep, just a few months after she had met him and left him in San Miguel de Allende, Mexico, she had felt a sinking in the pit of her stomach. She was sure that he expected her to marry him. After all, the man had borrowed the entire contents of his parents' bank account, paid it to a "coyote," and crawled across the border for her. He had spent three days traversing the Arizona desert without food or water and another two in the back of a truck heading north through California to Oakland, just to be with her.

But Olivia refused to consider marriage, even a civil marriage with the acknowledged goal of getting a green card and nothing more. Perhaps it was because her mother had married her father so casually, almost blithely—they'd met and married in two months. Eight months later, Olivia was born, and by the time she could say the word *daddy* there was no one around to whom the word applied. When she was about five years old, she had suddenly understood that she was different from other children.

She was the only one who didn't have even a father she saw on alternate weekends. She announced to her mother that when she got married it was going to be forever. She had meant it then, and nothing in her life up until now had convinced her to change her mind.

A marriage of convenience with Jorge was out of the question, and, although she didn't often admit this to herself and certainly never said as much to him, nothing about their relationship made her think that it was destined to be permanent. Olivia and Jorge's affair in Mexico had been intense but brief. Although she had wept when she left him at the airport, part of her had boarded that plane eagerly, glad to be going home and returning to her real life. If she imagined any continuation of their romance, it was of intense and longing letters that would gradually grow shorter and less ardent, and finally trail off completely. His would take up residence, with all the other letters and cards she'd saved from the time she was a little girl, in the fragrant cedar box she'd made in woodshop in seventh grade, and she would take them out from time to time and remember with a shiver of nostalgic pleasure the time she'd had a Mexican lover. It had never occurred to her that he would come to Oakland.

Jorge banged around in the bathroom for a few minutes, and then Olivia heard the sound of the shower running. She got up off the couch, stripped off her jeans and sweatshirt and navy blue panties with the little anchor on the side, and walked into the bathroom. She slid open the cracked glass shower door and stepped into the steam.

"*Hola*," she said.

Jorge looked at her for a moment and then drew her close. She leaned against the ropy cable of his arm and raised her face, keeping her eyes shut against the spray of the shower. He kissed her softly and she parted her lips, teasing his tongue with hers. He laughed, and bit her gently. She leaned back against the tile wall, and raised one leg onto the side of the tub. He slipped inside her and wrapped his arms around her back.

"*Te quiero*," he murmured.

She leaned her head back against the tile and moaned softly, mostly just to tell him that it felt good. Then she said, "Don't come inside."

When he was done, she soaped his body gently and rinsed him under the cooling stream. As the water poured off the flat plane of Jorge's hairless belly, Olivia pressed herself against him. For a brief moment, she allowed herself to imagine the possibility of marrying him, of making love with him like this for the rest of her life. The fantasy gave her neither pleasure nor dread, and she found it easy to push it from her mind. She kissed him once and then got out of the shower, leaving him behind in the cooling stream.

Olivia had planned on falling in love *with* Mexico, not *in* Mexico. Inspired by the poetry of Octavio Paz and the paintings of Rivera and Siqueiros, she had dropped out of UC Santa Cruz and caught a bus for Mexico City. Her plan had not been particularly well thought out.

At school Olivia belonged to organizations with names like Diversity NOW!, Students United for Peace, and Women Take Back the Night. She demonstrated on behalf of bilingual education, affirmative action, and an end to the death penalty. She drove up the coast with a dozen of her friends to link arms around an ancient redwood and protect it from the jagged teeth of the chain saw. It had never occurred to her to wonder if her nearly compulsive compassion for the poor and downtrodden had as its genesis her unfulfilled longing to be mothered herself.

Olivia had imagined that Santa Cruz would be a laboratory for her political activism. She was certain that the university, with its reputation for counterculturalism, would teach her how to harness her inchoate caring and passionate need to help someone, somewhere, and direct it into action that would profoundly change the world. Instead, she found a place where students and faculty talked endlessly about social justice in class and out, where meeting after meeting was held about Latin America's disappearing rain forest and North America's deepening racism. But, to Olivia, with her boundless energy and her desperate desire to *do* something, it all seemed like just so much talk. So, after three semesters, she packed a single small backpack and caught a bus for the border. She intended to travel to Chiapas and offer her services to the indigenous people's revolution. She had no idea what those services might entail, but she imagined that she would tend to the sick and the hungry, march with the outraged and the angry, and inspire the poor and the tired. Where she would live, what she would eat, even how she would contact the people she so desperately wanted to save were problems Olivia did not stop to contemplate.

She never made it to Chiapas. A pair of German backpackers who had relieved her unexpected loneliness on the bus convinced her to join them in San Miguel de Allende. The tall, gangly women with barking laughs and bright blond hair tangled on their legs fascinated Olivia. They were potters on their way to study ceramics at the *Instituto Allende*, a college of arts and language, and Olivia thought they might be lesbians. Her initial feelings of anxiety and forlornness upon leaving the United States had surprised her with their intensity, and the idea of following two cheerful artists rather than her own poorly planned agenda was too attractive to resist.

The tiny colonial city, with its cobblestone streets, thickly stuccoed houses, and Indians in *tipica* costumes of brightly embroidered fabrics, was exactly the Mexico Olivia had been looking for. While her German friends threw their pots and mixed their glazes, Olivia wandered the streets in a state of perpetual enchantment. Her feet slid confidently over the cobblestones as if they'd never felt asphalt and concrete. Her half-Jewish, entirely nonreligious soul shivered with delight whenever she ducked into one of the many churches and dropped coins in the offering baskets for *La Guadalupana*, the gentle virgin whose graceful image adorned places of worship, municipal buildings, key chains, and shopping bags throughout the city. One Sunday morning she joined a line of penitent Catholics, following their lead, kneeling when they knelt, mumbling the words of the prayers in her perfect Spanish and finally, thrillingly, accepting the flavorless body of Christ onto her tongue. In the market, Olivia chattered to the vendors and gleefully gobbled *taquitos*, fresh mangoes, and strange Mexican candies that tasted like fiery bits of paper. She bought filigreed silver earrings and crudely painted wooden turtles with bouncing heads that fit in the palm of her hand. She drank coffee in the *Jardín*, the main square, in the shade of the gazebo and watched the peddlers hawk their *churros*, balloons, and toys made from cut soda cans.

Olivia enrolled in a Spanish language and literature class at the *Instituto,* so she could make use of the school's family placement program. She moved out of her cheap hotel and into the spare room of a little house on the outskirts of the city. The young couple who the school administrator insisted on calling her "host parents" were no more than a few years older than she was. He drove a truck, and she took in sewing and cared for their three children. The family of five slept in a single room, on a long bed made of three or four cots pushed together. Olivia slept in a small, dark bedroom off the kitchen. She woke early in the morning to the sounds of the roosters living in a cage under her window, and ate a simple breakfast of eggs and tortillas served by her sleepy "mother" who refused, despite Olivia's entreaties, to join her in her meal. Olivia returned in the evenings after her classes, ate with the family, and then watched

Univision, a child perched on either knee. She was absolutely content—in love with the city, with the country, and with her own sense of belonging.

One afternoon six weeks after she'd arrived in San Miguel, Olivia noticed banners hanging from the street lamps and across the busy boulevards. The signs announced the commencement of the annual *Celebración de Resistencia: Indígena y Popular*. She followed them to a soccer field in the center of town and found it teeming with students in jeans and T-shirts emblazoned with American brand names, and Indian men in straw cowboy hats, their wives and daughters wrapped in scarves and skirts made of gaily colored woven fabric. They were all gathered in front of a stage that had been assembled in front of one of the goal posts, and Olivia joined the throngs, pushing her way up to the front of the crowd. For the next three hours, she listened to speeches about the rights of indigenous peoples throughout Latin America. She applauded loudly when the others did, even when she wasn't quite sure what it was the speakers had said.

Finally, as the light began to fade, a young man took the podium. He was a handsome man, although not unusually so. His face had the sharp angles and broad planes common to the Indians, but his nose was large and hooked, not flat. He wore his black hair a little long, to his collar, and he stood taller than most of the other men on the stage. His jeans were new and pressed, and his shirt was embroidered with tiny birds. Olivia wondered who had done that for him—his mother? Sister? Wife? He didn't lecture like those who had stood before him. Instead, he raised his voice in a shout and his hand in a fist.

"*El pueblo, unido, jamás será vencido,*" he bellowed, and the crowd soon joined him. The young man swept Olivia up in the embrace of his cry, and she raised her voice along with the rest. The evening ended with them all shouting to the night that the people, united, would never be defeated. Olivia trembled with the sense that she had finally found a goal worthy of her resolve and a man worthy of her desire. She stayed on the soccer field long after the crowd had dispersed and the cool night's breeze had begun to blow. She sat, perched on the edge of the bleachers, and watched the speakers embrace one another and head off down the darkened streets. Finally, shivering, she rose to leave. She picked her way through the detritus of soda cans, paper wrappings, and banana leaves and peels that had been left by the crowd. Suddenly, she caught her foot in a rut in the field and stumbled. A hand steadied her, and she looked up into the thickly lashed eyes of the young man whose voice had inspired the crowd and had set her heart aflutter.

"Be careful," he said, softly, in Spanish.

"Thank you," Olivia replied in the same language and righted herself. She took a tentative step and winced as though she felt a twinge in her ankle.

"Are you hurt?" he asked.

Olivia, surprised at the ease with which she had assumed the role of damsel in distress, quickly answered, "No, no. I'm fine."

"Are you North American?" Olivia heard the sound of laughing and only then noticed the other two young men standing behind the one whose hand still rested on hers. He leaned over and punched one of his friends in the arm. Then he whispered something in a rapid slang that Olivia couldn't understand. The other two boys laughed again and walked away, whistling over their shoulders. The young man led Olivia back to the bleachers, and she limped alongside of him, careful to continue her pantomime of injury.

"Are you a tourist?" he asked, once she'd sat down.

"No. I mean, I'm from the United States, but I'm a student. At the *Instituto*."

"You speak Spanish well. Your accent is very good." He sat down on the bench next to her.

"Thank you."

"What's your name?"

"Olivia," she said.

"Olivia," he repeated.

"What is *your* name?"

"Jorge. Jorge Luís Rodriguez Hernandez."

"I enjoyed your speech."

The young man shrugged and leaned back on one arm, forcing her to turn slightly to look at him. He had a narrow line of an upper lip, but the lower was wide and full and looked soft, like a baby's. "It was just a chant," he said. "Not a speech. I've given speeches at the University. Lots of them."

"Are *you* a student?"

"Yes," he said, and his pride was obvious. "I study politics at the University of Guanajuato. Have you been to Guanajuato?"

Olivia shook her head. "No. Not yet."

"You should go. It's a beautiful city. A real city, not like this tiny little town." He waved his hand derisively at the now entirely empty field and the shuttered stores behind it.

"Is that where you live? Are you from Guanajuato?"

He shook his head. "No, I'm from San Miguel. My family is here. But I've been at the University now for almost two years."

Olivia was conscious of the heat of Jorge's body. He sat close to her, almost touching, and she felt her leg ache to inch closer to his.

"I came today for the conference," he said. "Did you hear the speeches?"

"Yes, they were wonderful."

Jorge shook his head in exaggerated woe. "Old men. All of them. What do they know of the struggles of the youth movement or the Indians? But, still, their voices are better than nothing."

"Are you involved in the…in the movement?" Olivia asked, not sure what movement she was talking about.

"I am a cell leader for the Guanajuato Student Revolutionary Union," Jorge said, with just the faintest tinge of haughtiness in his voice.

Olivia's breath quickened in her chest, and she smiled. It was as though everything in her life—her love of Spanish, her commitment to social change, her itchy traveling feet—had been designed to lead her precisely to this dusty field, to this dark night, and to this young man wearing a shirt embroidered with birds.

They talked for a long while. He told her about the guerilla theater his student group performed in the streets of Guanajuato and of the letters they wrote to the president of Mexico in support of the Indians in Chiapas. She shared with him her plans to travel to the violence-torn area and offer herself as a laborer for the revolution, and although his lips twitched in a smile, he told her he was impressed with her courage. Finally, as the night grew colder, he reached an arm around her. "You're shivering," he murmured.

Olivia didn't reply. She leaned her head back and felt his smooth, hairless forearm on the back of her neck. She closed her eyes and wasn't surprised to feel his mouth on hers. She parted her lips softly. His tongue darted into her mouth. He tasted faintly tangy and sharp, like nothing she had ever tasted before. He tasted like Mexico. They kissed, and then, finally, Olivia said, "I have to go." But she didn't move.

"I'll walk with you. Where are you staying?"

She told him the address of her host family, and they walked there together, his arm wrapped tightly around her waist, and their footsteps echoing loudly on the empty cobblestone streets.

Olivia looked up at the colonial houses lining the blocks. The street lamps cast pools of orange light along the walls, and the heavy night sky flickered with stars. In the distance, the bells of a hundred churches began to clang and jangle with the tolling of the hour.

"It's so beautiful here," Olivia said.

"Yes, beautiful," Jorge said and pressed his lips to hers. She stumbled over a broken cobblestone, and he caught her in his arms.

Jorge watched Olivia rub the rough towel across her body. She bent over to dry her legs, and he stared at her round bottom, its cleft revealing a hint of the reddish-gold pubic hair that still made him catch his breath with desire whenever he saw it. His penis, which had never quite softened, stirred, and he resisted the urge to stroke himself. Instead, he ducked his head under the water, shuddering against the cold. It had taken him no time at all to grow accustomed to hot showers. In his family's home there was no hot water in the shower, nor anywhere else in the house. They would no sooner have wasted money heating their bath water than they would have burned dollar bills for fuel.

Jorge's family was not poor, exactly, but his father, Juan Carlos, had always had to work not one but two jobs in order to provide for the seven children his wife, Araceli, bore him. His industrious nature might have inched the family more surely up the ladder toward the middle class had he not taken just as seriously his obligation to support his mistress and their four children. It was this combination of dependability and profligacy that was Juan Carlos's undoing. The money he earned would have allowed a single family some modicum of security and perhaps the barest hint of luxury. It barely kept two fed and clothed.

Araceli ran a small market out of the front room of their house. From the time they were able to walk and talk, the Rodriguez children were expected to help her in the store, stacking cans of chipotle chilis and Nestle Table Cream, bags of Flor de Mayo and Maizena flour drink powder, jars of El Pollo Cuckoo and Barbacoa. They packed customers' purchases into crinkly plastic bags, swept and mopped up spills, and wiped away the dust churned up by the cars passing over the dirt road in front of the open door of the market. When he was a student at university, Jorge's father had gotten him hired onto the construction sites where he was the foreman. Jorge had lugged pieces of wood, stone, and brick, and fetched tools and water for the carpenters and masons. His days in Oakland were, in fact, the only ones in his life when he hadn't had a steady job, and the shame of his sloth was like bitter lemon on his tongue.

He watched Olivia wrap herself in the old flannel bathrobe she still wore, despite the beautiful, slippery satin one he'd bought her with the proceeds of one of his few days at work. He'd taken the BART all the way to Target in El Cerrito and had spent almost an hour sifting through bits of gossamer and lace until he found one in the precise shade of periwinkle blue of her eyes. He'd anticipated her squeal of delight in such minute detail that he knew her actual response was doomed to disappoint him, but it had been so muted, and her shiver when she'd slipped the glossy fabric over her shoulders so obvious, that he hadn't been surprised to find the robe shoved into a corner of her lingerie drawer, underneath the panties and bras she wore only when it had been too long since they'd visited the Laundromat. No, he hadn't been surprised, but he *had* been angry. He had taken the robe from its hiding place, ironed it precisely, just as he had seen his mother do to all his clothes, even his T-shirts and underwear, and hung it on a hanger on the back of the bathroom door. When she saw it there, Olivia had blushed and explained that it was too cold in the dank apartment for such a beautiful, light garment, but that she promised that as soon as the weather turned, she would wear it. She hadn't done so yet, and Jorge was sure he could see the robe hanging more limply every day, the blue fading to the flat gray of a foggy Oakland summer sky, and dust gathering on its shoulders.

Like most of her friends, neighbors, and fellow Californians, Elaine had been born someplace else—Bergen County, New

Jersey, in her case, not far from the Paterson Falls. She had grown up in a small suburb a short commute from the city, although neither of her parents ever actually spent hours on the buses or trains going into Manhattan. Her father was a printer in a shop in Paterson, her mother stayed home. Elaine grew up the only child of quiet, middle-class Jews in a quiet, middle-class Jewish town. The only thing that made her different from all the other Jewish girls growing up in the identical houses on the identical blocks was her father's vague past as a not-particularly-active member of the Communist Party—although the truth was that there were probably other ex-Party apparatchiks in the neighborhood. Many of the middle-aged women manning the voting booths and the men managing the local silk mills and small businesses might have spent evenings, when they were young, in stuffy union halls listening to Earl Browder revile the pointlessness of the New Deal and sing the praises of Soviet Socialism. Then they had children, grew more conservative and afraid, and worried less about redistributing the wealth and more about paying the mortgage.

The month after she graduated from Douglass College, Elaine had surprised her parents and herself by packing her belongings into a VW Fastback and heading out for California. She was young, only twenty years old, but it was already 1970, and Elaine was terrified that if she didn't get to San Francisco soon, it would all be over without her.

As it turned out, she had missed most of it.

Elaine lived for a while in an all-woman vegan commune in Haight Ashbury. They grew pot in their backyard and smoked it every night, but there was a desperate edge to their hedonism, as if each was afraid that the others would figure out that she was not really having the fun she claimed. Elaine had unremarkable sex with many of the men who passed through the house for much the same reason: because she'd come to California expecting free love and debauchery, and their joyless coupling seemed as close as she was going to get to what she'd been imagining, sitting in her organic chemistry and European history classes back in New Brunswick.

By the time Elaine met Olivia's father, she was living on her own in a small apartment in Cole Valley, near enough to the Haight to feel a part of the scene if it ever woke up again, but somewhere quiet and, most importantly, clean. He was just a guy, a lot like the other dozen or so guys she had been with over the past few years, although he stayed a little longer than most. Long enough, at least, to get her pregnant. They were married at City Hall, and he stuck around until Olivia was almost six months old. It wasn't a particularly dramatic leave-taking. They didn't scream or yell; he didn't even walk out the door for a pack of cigarettes and never return. One day he simply told Elaine that he wasn't cut out to be a husband and father and asked her if she'd be able to manage on her own. She said she would, and he left, taking with him their stash of marijuana and the Smith Corona typewriter her parents had given her as a graduation present.

The truth, however, was that she really couldn't manage. She felt totally lost in the face of the unremittingness of Olivia. No matter how many diapers Elaine changed, the baby dirtied more. No matter how many bananas she pureed or bowls of cereal she mixed, the next day the baby was still hungry. Elaine had never realized that it was possible to feel stretched so thin, worked so hard, and yet at the same time—there was no other possible word for it—so bored. She found Olivia tedious. And to her surprise, considering the fact that she was never alone, she was achingly lonely.

One morning Elaine dragged herself out of bed to the sounds of Olivia's wails, just as she had every morning for the past seven months. She staggered over to the crib and reached out her arms. Her hands stopped just before they touched her daughter's squirming body, and she stared into the crib as though she'd never seen the baby before. Olivia's face was red and sodden with tears and mucus. A few strands of thin, damp hair clung to her skull, and her hands waved desperately in the air. Elaine couldn't bring herself to touch her. The baby's cries grated in her ears like the voracious squawk of a carrion bird. She gagged at the stench of urine that just the day before had been so familiar as to be innocuous. She stared at her daughter, feeling nothing more or less than a mild revulsion.

She backed slowly away from the crib and out of the bedroom, closing the door gently behind her. Then she walked down the hall to the kitchen and put the teakettle on the stove. As she turned on the burner, she stopped before she heard the click of the igniter, and concentrated on the hiss of the gas, blocking out the baby's cries. Elaine stood there for a very long time, until the stench of gas made her gag. Then she twisted the dial to the "light" position. A huge, bright blossom of flame momentarily burst into bloom. An acrid smell filled her nostrils. Only then did she realize that the apartment was absolutely silent. She inched down the hall and froze in front of the bedroom door with her hand on the knob, wondering if she would find her daughter still breathing.

Olivia was lying in her crib, her fist balled and shoved into her mouth. Her eyes were wide open, and her chest heaved with silent gasps. She blinked when she saw her mother, but did not begin to cry until Elaine had picked her up and clasped her to her chest. Then the baby began to weep, but quietly and monotonously, without any of the urgency with which she had greeted the day. Elaine changed Olivia's drenched diaper and clothes and put the baby to her breast. She lowered herself onto the bed and, glancing into the mirror over her dresser, saw the source of the burnt smell that had filled her kitchen: the flame had singed her eyebrows off.

Esther Goodman, who had never flown in her life and had seen only the parts of America that lay between Fairlawn, New

Jersey, and the condominium complex in Pembroke Pines, Florida, where the Goodmans spent the winter, responded to her daughter's hysterical phone call by boarding a plane to San Francisco. She brought with her a present from Elaine's father, Saul—money. Money for a bigger apartment, money for Elaine to go back to school. Esther stayed four months, leaving only when Elaine was enrolled in a pharmacist's program at UCSF and Olivia was happily in day care.

By the time Olivia was four years old, Elaine was safely employed at the drugstore in the Elmwood. She had a decent salary, the beginnings of a retirement account, and a little house just a few blocks from where she worked. The only reminders of that morning when she had confronted the limits of her capacity to love her child were the bare patches of skin that she was obliged, for the rest of her life, to fill in with the strokes of an eyebrow pencil.

Elaine pulled into the driveway of her bungalow and paused in the car for a minute, enjoying the sight of the bougainvillea spilling over the roof of the garage. She'd planted it when she'd first bought the house, and it had grown with satisfying quickness, spreading a blanket of purple and red over the plain white stucco. She'd added a jasmine bush a few years ago, and that too was growing well. She liked plants that climbed and covered and gave a house a look of permanence, of being a part of the topography of the neighborhood.

Elaine unlocked the front door and slipped out of her sandals, lining them up squarely under the bench in the hall, where they joined the others: two pairs of comfortable leather flats for work, a pair of sneakers, a man's loafers with worn heels, and snazzy teal Nikes with bright orange laces. There was also a pile of Lonely Planet and Insight guides tumbled on the bench. She flipped one over. Morocco and Northern Africa. She groaned.

Elaine went on vacation every year with Arthur Roth, the man with whom she had been living for the past five years. As with so many other aspects of their life together, they had a system. They took turns choosing the destination. Elaine's choices were generally lovely but unexciting: two weeks bicycling through Italy, a week at a cooking school in the Loire Valley, and a couple of weeks one summer speculating about the depths of the Norwegian fjords. Arthur had taken them trekking to the Annapurna base camp, through the remains of the Brazilian rain forest, island hopping in Thailand. It was his turn to decide this year, and he had been debating between another excursion to the Third World and a long camping trip through the English countryside. Elaine had so hoped that they would be going to the Cotswalds.

"Hi!" Elaine called. "You home?"

Arthur came out of the kitchen, wiping his hands on a dishtowel. He was wearing running shorts and a Cal sweatshirt. His long skinny legs were covered in dark hair, except across the front of his thighs where the hair seemed to have rubbed off, leaving a smooth expanse of white skin. He had a bald head and a large nose, and, although he wasn't quite handsome, he was one of those men who photographed well. Whenever Arthur heard the click of a shutter, his face froze into a wide grin that made him appear more cheerful and easygoing than he was.

He crossed the hall and kissed her on the cheek. "Hey fiancée. How are you? I'm making Caprese salad. Want some?"

Elaine smiled. She still wasn't used to the idea that they were going to get married. Truth be told, they had been together so long without even considering marriage that she didn't really believe it would happen. "Are the tomatoes ripe already?" she asked.

"A few were. And I got some of that nice organic buffalo mozzarella from the Berkeley Bowl. You hungry?"

"I wish I were. Olivia schlepped me out to some godforsaken restaurant, in *Fruitvale* of all places. I ate something called *papooses*,

I think. Fried tortillas stuffed with mystery meat. Pure lard and totally disgusting." Elaine wasn't sure why she was lying. The pupusas had been delicious—she'd even considering bringing some home. It was just one of the things they did, she and Arthur—they complained about Olivia, rolled their eyes at her excesses and dramatics. Having been forced to drive out to the far end of town to eat a hideous meal made for a better story than the truth.

"Keep me company while I eat," Arthur said over his shoulder as he walked back into the kitchen. The makings of the salad were spread across the tiled counter. After the first time that Elaine had cooked for him, the couple had once again worked out an arrangement. He cooked, and she cleaned. He took gourmet cooking classes at Sur La Table, the chi-chi kitchen store down on Fourth Street, and her skills were limited to boiling water and dumping jarred sauce into a pan.

Elaine put her purse in its place on the shelf next to the fridge and rolled up her sleeves. While Arthur sat at the kitchen table, sopping up olive oil with crusty bread, she rinsed off the cutting board, put the knife in the dishwasher, and put the basil in the fridge. She found a bright-colored Deruta bowl from their trip to Umbria and placed the remaining tomatoes in it, being careful not to bruise them. Finally, she wiped down the counters with 409 and a paper towel and sat down next to Arthur.

"How's Livvy?"

"Fine. Same as always. Now she's going to organize a union at the restaurant where she works."

Arthur gave a short bark of laughter. "Leave it to Olivia. That's another job that won't last long."

"You would not believe how the girl is living. The restaurant was about half a notch above a taco truck. And she tells me Jorge is standing on street corners, begging for work."

Arthur shook his head. "Well, maybe he'll get picked up and deported."

"We can always dream," Elaine said and then grimaced. "We're *so* bad."

"Were you right? Did she want money?"

Elaine nodded and picked a dripping tomato off of Arthur's plate. "These are delicious," she said, slurping up the tangy pulp.

He wiped the oil from her fingertips with his napkin. "Much better than last year's, I think. You didn't let her browbeat you, did you?"

"No. I told her if she wants to go back to school I'll pay for that, but otherwise I'm not willing to support her." Elaine rested her head in her hands. "But now, of course, I'm feeling guilty. As usual."

Arthur reached across the table and squeezed her arm. "Don't. Your instincts were absolutely right. You can help her more by forcing her to stand on her own two feet. She's got to confront the results of her own decisions."

"You're right. I know you are. Anyway, I'm certainly not going to support *him*."

"Absolutely not! Just because Olivia's letting him freeload off of her doesn't mean you should."

One of the things Elaine liked most about Arthur was the way he made her feel that she wasn't as insufficient a mother as she sometimes feared. Whenever a conflict arose between mother and daughter, Arthur was squarely on her side. Without his support, she would never have developed the fortitude and resolve that Olivia's challenging adolescence had demanded.

"You've got those 'spent the day with Olivia' blues, again," Arthur said, sympathetically.

"I'm all right."

"Don't beat yourself up, Elaine. It's not like you can even afford to give her any money right now, not if we plan on buying the condo this year."

For the past four winters, Elaine and Arthur had rented a condominium in South Lake Tahoe. They'd gone up almost every weekend there was snow and had tried to take an entire week at least once during ski season. Arthur had introduced Elaine to the sport, and although she wasn't as fanatical as he was, she did enjoy it, particularly the quiet of an early morning on top of the mountain, right after a new snowfall. After over a year of saving, they finally had enough money to put a down payment on a place of their own.

"You're right. I know you're right," Elaine said.

"I have an idea. Let's go for a bike ride. We could head up to Inspiration Point."

"Okay."

"And maybe catch a movie tonight?"

"Sounds great." Elaine did her best to shake off the mood of lassitude and mild depression that usually followed time spent with Olivia. "Let me put on some sweats."

While she was changing her clothes, Arthur came into the bedroom. He lay on the bed and watched her carefully fold her black slacks over a hanger. She hung up her white cotton sweater, sniffing the armpits before deciding that it was clean enough for another wearing.

"You make me so hot when you do that," Arthur said.

Elaine laughed and pitched a pair of sweat socks at him. "Shut up."

"Have you given any more thought to Morocco?"

She sat down on the bed. "Can I afford it? You just said that I need everything for my share of the down payment."

"I wasn't including your travel costs; those are a separate line on the budget. I ran the numbers. You'll be fine." Arthur was an accountant, a partner in a firm in downtown Oakland. Although he and Elaine kept their finances strictly segregated, he had taken over the management of her money. It was a huge relief to her not to have to think about how much to save each month and what she could and could not afford. Arthur uttered the magic words, and Elaine rested easy, knowing that the numbers had been run, even if she wasn't at all sure what that meant.

"I don't know, Arthur. I'm not sure I'm up to another bout of Giardia."

"Hey, don't knock intestinal amoebas. You came home from Nepal sixteen pounds thinner than when you left!" He reached over and pinched her thigh. She slapped his hand away.

"Still, *Morocco?*"

"It's gorgeous, Elaine. Really beautiful. And it's hardly adventure travel. It's almost Spain. Anyway, you got sick on every one of our other trips, and you loved every minute of them."

Elaine had not, in fact, enjoyed their excursions to wild, untrammeled locales, but she never would have admitted that to Arthur. To Arthur, she was his partner, his equal—like him, she would not cringe from the snapping jaws of a caiman in the Amazon or collapse under the weight of a heavy backpack in the shadow of Kilimanjaro. No one before him had ever thought Elaine courageous or adventuresome, and she reveled in his image of her. Olivia, Elaine knew, considered her an abject coward. Doubtless, she had forced Elaine to drive to that awful Oakland neighborhood just to scare her.

"I just don't know, Arthur. Can we talk about it later?" Elaine said, pulling a sweatshirt over her head and tugging some thick socks onto her tiny feet.

Arthur hoisted Elaine's bike down from the rack attached to the back of his lovingly maintained1989 Saab convertible. He checked the air pressure in the tires, made sure the seat was securely locked, and tested the brakes a few times. Only then did he hand the bike to Elaine. She mounted, and he tugged at her helmet. She always clipped it too loosely, and he tightened the strap just a bit. She stuck her tongue out and gagged dramatically.

"Very funny. It won't do you any good if it falls off."

"I know," she said. "I was just kidding." She raised her face to him, and he buzzed her on the lips.

"I'll bet there's good biking in Morocco," he said, only half in jest.

She smiled, but it seemed a bit stiff, and he wondered if he'd pushed it too far. She set off up the hill. He watched her go for a moment, then turned back to the rack and unloaded his own bike. Arthur rode much more quickly than Elaine, and they liked for her to get a bit of a head start. While he ran his standard equipment check, he debated whether or not to apologize once he caught up to her. He was sure they'd end up going to Morocco. It was, after all, his year, and his turn to decide. Still, it didn't make sense to force the issue. She would come around soon enough. She always did.

Arthur and Elaine had met when he filled a prescription at the College Avenue drugstore. He had never shopped there before. While he wasn't a man who minded spending money on certain unique and particular luxuries, it made no sense at all to him to pay more for the same product just for the experience of buying it in a boutique rather than in a chain store. He purchased his books at Barnes & Noble, his toilet paper at Costco, and his medicine at Payless. On that day, however, the pain of a migraine had caused his vision to double, and he didn't think it was a good idea to get behind the wheel of his car. He walked from his duplex apartment off Ashby Avenue to the local pharmacy, covering his eyes against the agonizing glare of the sun. He pushed his prescription for Maxalt across the counter at Elaine, and she looked him up and down appraisingly. After a moment, she came out from behind the counter and led him to a stool at the soda fountain.

An hour later, the pills she'd pressed into his palm had taken effect, his eyes had cleared, the pain in his head had abated, and he was enjoying his first egg cream in thirty years. He went back to the counter to buy some Lactaid and to thank Elaine. In what he later realized was decidedly uncharacteristic fashion, she ignored the pile of prescriptions waiting to be filled and directed her assistant to handle the incoming phone calls and waiting customers. Arthur and Elaine talked for almost half an hour. He gave her advice on the tax consequences of her recent purchase of the drugstore. She suggested a beta blocker for his headaches. By the time he left, he had her home phone number in his pocket.

Their relationship, now in its eighth year, was every bit as satisfying as Arthur could have hoped it would be. When they had met, he was only just beginning to be interested in finding a serious girlfriend, having finally shaken off the effects of the disastrous end of his marriage. Arthur's wife had been a free spirit, a woman who called herself a poet although she never wrote, who contrasted her own artistic sensibilities with his more prosaic ones. Their marriage collapsed when their two children were still very young, but she had already managed to engender in them something akin to her own disdain for their father. Putting three thousand miles between the three of them and himself had seemed a good first step in recovering his equilibrium. Ten years of casual relationships and devotion to his career had done the rest.

Elaine couldn't have been more different than his ex-wife. Like Arthur, Elaine was cautious and deliberate, thoughtful and circumspect. She took care with everything—her work, her home, the words she used and the tone in which she spoke them. He found her consideration of him tremendously erotic, and her comfortable, stable life enormously attractive. He felt lucky to have found someone so compatible on every level—practically, intellectually, and especially sexually. They were even now, so many years after they'd first begun the exploration of one another's bodies, still discovering uncharted territory. They traveled together beautifully and had combined their lives effortlessly.

The only wrinkle was Olivia. For the first three years of his relationship with Elaine, Arthur had done his best to remain nothing more than a vague avuncular presence in the girl's life. When confronted with any difficulty between mother and daughter, he simply left the house. With Elaine, he was absolutely sympathetic and understanding. He viewed his role as being to support her decisions and take her side, and he did that admirably. With Olivia he was distant, albeit friendly. From the very beginning, he assured her that she did not need to fear that he would try to act like a father to her. Every so often, it occurred to him that this kind of male presence was exactly what Olivia lacked in her life, and he wondered if she might not have welcomed a more paternal role on his part. He always pushed such thoughts from his mind, however. The three weeks a year he spent with his own children more than satisfied any fatherly urges he had.

Once Arthur moved into Elaine's house, however, he could no longer be quite as benign and remote. He could not simply absent himself from the house whenever things grew tense, nor did he think Elaine would have wanted him to do that. She needed him there for moral support, and he continued to provide it—bolstering her and maintaining a united front against Olivia's adolescence. There were inevitable difficulties but very few explosions, and those Olivia still directed solely at her mother. Still, none of them could ever figure out exactly how to function as the makeshift family they found themselves, and they lived in a kind of uneasy truce. Once Olivia finally left for college, Arthur and Elaine had together heaved a relieved sigh and begun their real life together—a life characterized by companionable contentment and made exciting with the spice of travel and sex.

Arthur leapt on his bicycle and pedaled off after Elaine. He caught up quickly, even though she was pumping her legs vigorously as she sped down a short slope in the path. He smiled. The way Elaine invariably used the descents to gather speed to propel her up the inclines pleased him.

"Hey, beautiful," he said as he coasted up alongside her.

She huffed a quick breath and bore down on her pedals.

"I'm sorry about harping on the Morocco thing. I was just all charged up—you know how guidebooks always do that to me."

"It's okay." She was breathing hard from the effort of the ride.

"No, really. If you want to go somewhere else, we can. We can do that Cotswalds hike if you want. I'm sure it'll be beautiful." Of course he wasn't sure of that at all. In fact, he was fairly certain he'd find it tedious and disappointing—as bad as one of Elaine's choices.

Elaine shrugged and peddled faster. With a smooth pump of his left foot, Arthur easily caught up to her. She didn't look at him, and pointedly ignoring the injustice of what she'd now forced him to offer, he said, "We can swap. You decide this year. I'll make you go to Morocco next year. But I'm warning you, I may be on to something else by then. I know a great hotel in downtown Ouagadougou."

Elaine laughed, finally, and Arthur relaxed. She reached out her hand, and he grabbed it. They pedaled like that for a moment, side by side, fingers entangled. Then his momentum pushed him forward, and their arms extended farther and farther apart, until they finally broke away from one another.

"Hey!" he heard her call.

He turned his head in time to see her wave.

"To hell with England—I'm dying to go to Morocco!" she shouted as the distance between them grew wider.

Arthur smiled and spun his bike around. Within moments he was next to her again. He modulated his speed, and they rode close together, evenly matched, to the top of the next hill.

Jorge woke with a start, as he always did. Olivia was the only person whose bed he had shared since he moved out of his mother's when he was ten years old, and in the first moments of consciousness, he often thought himself back there, nestled in the warmth of Araceli's embrace. It was the difference between

Olivia's body and his mother's that caused him to jump. Olivia's spine pressed against his belly like a pearl necklace, each vertebrae a separate globe. His mother's bones were thickly covered by smooth, sleek flesh, like a seal floating next to him in the warm sea of her bed.

The one overwhelming similarity was the feeling he had now, the same one that had plagued him as a child: that he was a guest in another's bed. He had known when he was young that he shared his mother's warmth on sufferance, that sooner or later he, like his brothers before him, would be exiled to a cot in the outer room. Now, this bed, this room and everything in it belonged to Olivia. The pillows they shared had been hers since she was a child. They covered themselves with the patchwork quilt her grandmother had made for her thirteenth birthday. Even the furniture was either discarded from Elaine's house or purchased with the fruits of Olivia's labor. Her income paid the rent, the utilities, the grocery bills, and even purchased the cigarettes he smoked. The air was redolent with her employment; the stench of food permeated her apron and work clothes and hung like a miasma of purposeful occupation over the entire apartment. He felt like something worse than a guest; he felt like a parasite feeding off of her industry. But all that was about to change.

Jorge slid his leg along Olivia's, and the stubble on her shin scratched him gently. He did it again, enjoying the prickling sensation. The first time he had seen Olivia shave her legs he had been astonished, nearly flummoxed by the sight. It had simply never occurred to him that women did that. His mother and sisters had legs covered in dark fur and seemed a different species than women like Olivia, whose smooth hairlessness he had believed to be a natural condition. He had at first been disappointed to find out that it was as contrived as the cherry lips women painted on their faces or the black of their eyelashes. He began watching women more closely, comparing those he met, even the ones he saw in the street, to the woman who he was still astonished to find sleeping next to him. He had come to realize that Olivia was less a creation of makeup and illusion than most women, and he liked this about her.

Careful not to wake her, he stroked her hip with the palm of his hand. She didn't stir. He reached his arm all the way around her belly and drew her back and buttocks in close to him. She murmured and pressed against him. He leaned his face against the back of her neck, inhaling the slightly sour perfume of her hair. Jorge could not quite believe that he was permitted these everyday intimacies. Olivia was not his first, but she was the only one whose body was laid open to him, whose curves and crevasses he was allowed, even expected, to explore. And yet, despite this familiarity, she was a stranger to him. Her body was receptive, available, but her mind was shut tight. He rarely knew what she was thinking, had little access to her emotions, goals, or fears. And the truth was, this did not bother him much. Olivia was so foreign to him, so different from what he knew and recognized, that it would have seemed more bizarre to understand her than it was to find her entirely opaque. It was not just the difference in their backgrounds, the fact that they had no shared cultural context, no common first language. It was her very femaleness that moved her beyond the range of his comprehension.

He heaved himself out of bed. He had plans today. For the first time since he'd arrived in the United States, there was something he had to do, some place he had to go. The thought energized him, and he dressed quickly. After today, things would be different. Tonight he would come home to this bed and sleep in it as one who had a right. He would never again fear exile to another, colder place.

Once the door closed behind Jorge, Olivia stretched and rolled out of bed. She had only been pretending to sleep. She simply could not muster, so early in the morning, the energy to face the misery of Jorge's day, standing on the corner, waiting for a job that never came. She was disgusted with her selfishness and wished she had risen with him, cooked him breakfast, sent him out the door with a kiss.

She went to the bathroom and washed herself in the tub, standing over the faucet. She quickly rinsed the evidence of the night's lovemaking from her legs and belly and splashed water over her face. She didn't bother showering—in a few hours she'd be bathed in the sour stink of other people's food. Olivia pulled a clean pair of panties and a bra from the pile of laundered clothes permanently ensconced in the one armchair in the living room, and tugged on the shirt and pants she'd worn the day before. She was just pouring water into her tea cup when the telephone rang.

"Olivia, *que tal*, it's Gabriel, from the restaurant." Gabriel's accent was different than Jorge's and most of the other Spanish speakers Olivia knew. He insisted on speaking English, but the Cuban lilt was unmistakable.

She had no idea why the bartender would be calling her. They weren't friends, although she appreciated that he was always nice to Jorge. When Jorge would come early to pick her up from work, he would wait at the bar and, if the managers weren't around, Gabriel would give him a free beer.

"Hey. What's up?" she asked.

"Can I speak to your *esposo*?"

"We're not married, and he's not home."

"Okay, listen, *hombre*, take this message, okay?"

"Okay." She dug around the kitchen drawer for a pencil and some paper. She found a menu from a Chinese takeout and prepared to write on that.

"Tell Jorge that the dudes have got the *lana*."

"What?" Olivia could barely hear Gabriel's voice over the music in the background. It sounded like he was calling her from the bar.

"Just write it down. Tell him that as soon as he's got the shit, he should call me. Let me give you my pager number in case he lost it."

The tip of Olivia's pencil broke, and she realized that she'd ground it into the scrap of paper. "Gabriel, what's going on? Are you and Jorge doing some kind of deal?"

"Hey, I'm not getting in between the lovers, man. You want to know what your *hombre* is doing, you ask him yourself. Just give him the message, okay?"

Olivia slowly hung up the phone. She must have misunderstood the message. She knew that Gabriel did a little dealing. She'd heard he sold ecstasy and methamphetamine to a couple of the waitresses who were into the rave scene. They swore that his stuff was the best they'd ever had. Olivia herself had shared a joint with him one night after a particularly hard shift. But it didn't make any sense at all that Jorge would be involved with him. Jorge never did drugs. In fact, he'd been furious with Olivia for smoking pot with Gabriel and had made her swear never to touch the stuff again.

Olivia stood, holding the telephone in her hand. She was suddenly aware of a clammy sensation in her armpits.

When Jorge came home a few hours later, he was accompanied by a man Olivia had never seen before. He was older, also Mexican, wearing spotlessly clean jeans with an ironed crease down the middle. Long hairs curled from a large mole in the center of his cheek, and he kept his sunglasses on, even in the house.

Olivia was sitting on the sofa, holding the well-worn copy of *Dagon and Other Macabre Tales* by H.P. Lovecraft that she'd taken from her mother's bookshelf when she was nine and had kept with her ever since. Because Elaine never evinced any interest at all in horror, Olivia assumed the book had belonged to her father, and she turned to it whenever she felt herself missing the man she had never known. It was hard to imagine what kind of man would enjoy a story about a giant fish god preparing to devour humanity, but Olivia comforted herself with familiarity, if not insight.

Jorge paused in the doorway for a moment, obviously surprised to see her. He was wearing a pair of pants she'd never seen before—army green and slung low on his hips. He had unlaced his white sneakers, and the tongues lolled like a dog's. Since when had he begun dressing like this? He came over and gave her a kiss. "*Hola, mami.*" he said. "Aren't you supposed to be at work?"

"I swapped shifts. Who's your friend?"

Jorge's jaw tightened, but he smiled and said, "Oreste, Olivia. Olivia, Oreste."

"Good to meet you," Oreste muttered, staring down at his shoes, pale-gray lace-ups that might have been made of leather, but looked more like vinyl, or even plastic. Olivia said nothing, she just looked at Jorge and raised her eyebrows slightly. He stared back at her for a moment and then turned to the other man.

"*Hombre*, the woman isn't feeling well. I'd better stay in and take care of her."

The other man nodded. "Okay. We'll talk tomorrow. We'll set it all up then. No rush."

After Oreste left, Olivia glared at Jorge. She kept her voice calm and flat. "Are you doing some kind of drug deal with Gabriel Contreras?"

Jorge smiled, and, for a moment, Olivia thought he was about to reassure her. Instead, he leaned over and stroked her chin with the tips of his fingers. "This is none of your business," he said.

Olivia jerked her face away from him. "How can you say this isn't my *business!* You could get *arrested.* You could get *deported!* If they deport you for doing drugs, you'll never be allowed back in the country. Of course this is my goddamn business!"

Even as her cry rang in her ears, Olivia realized, with a sense of shame so profound it was almost frightening, that she *wanted* Jorge to be deported. She wanted him to go away, to go home, no longer to hang around her neck like a millstone of unsought responsibility. Horrified, she grabbed his hand and squeezed, as if to prove, more to herself than to him, that she cared what happened to him, that she wanted him there, that she loved him.

Jorge stood very still for a moment, then he sat down next to her. "Don't get so excited, Olivia. This is no big deal. Really."

Olivia leaned back heavily into the sofa cushion. She felt exhausted by the discussion before they'd even had it. How could she explain to this man for whom all of the United States seemed like one vast scam, one that other, bolder men knew how to work, that there were some things he just couldn't do?

"What's going on?" she said. "Just tell me what's going on."

For a while Jorge was quiet. Then he began to tell her about the humiliation of standing on the corner, day after day, sometimes getting picked to work, more often being passed over. She had heard this all before, but when she tried to tell him that, he hushed her and talked on.

"They drive up in their trucks and look us over like we're cattle or pigs. And you can't just stand there, waiting. You have to rush the truck and beg for work, because if you don't, they choose someone else. If you don't look eager, they won't hire you. The worst is that that's not even enough for them. You must look eager and willing to work, and you must also grovel. Yes boss, no boss. Otherwise they pick someone else, someone who kisses their asses."

"I know, *papi*, I know," Olivia said, reaching her arms around him.

He shook her off. "You *don't* know. You can't know. You've never had to feel that humiliation. You've never had to beg for work. You've never had to smile that pathetic *campesino* smile."

"I have to suck up to customers every day. I know exactly what it's like."

"It's not the same. You know the worst, Olivia? The worst is when I *do* get the job. When they *do* choose me. Because when I jump into the back of the pickup, I look behind me at the men standing there, the ones who got left behind. And maybe one has six kids back in Guatemala who will go hungry this week because I'm taking the job that would have let him send them money. And another one has a sick wife who won't see the doctor because the money to pay the bill is going to end up in my pocket, not his."

Jorge told her that a few weeks before, when he'd come by the restaurant late one night to pick her up, he'd confided in Gabriel about his difficulties finding work. Gabriel listened and sympathized. He had come to America on the Mariel boatlift, and he, too, had had problems finding a job. Then he told Jorge about two friends of his, *gringos*, who were willing to pay top dollar for methamphetamine. The problem was, the guys couldn't find anyone to buy from. Gabriel told Jorge that Mexicans had taken over the meth market and the old biker sources in the desert were starting to dry up. He said if Jorge could find someone, or even someone who knew someone, with connections, the two of them could make some easy money. The *gringos* wanted about five thousand dollars' worth. At a 50 percent markup, Gabriel and Jorge would clear a nice profit.

"But, Jorge, you don't know any drug dealers. You don't know anybody like that!" Olivia said.

"I don't, but who knows who knows, you know?" Jorge smiled. "I just started asking around, and one of the guys I met on that gardening job last month, he introduced me to Oreste. Oreste's been around. He knows some guys who are connected to the Mexican Mafia. They bring the crank in from Tijuana."

Olivia shook her head, wondering how the man who had laboriously copied Pablo Neruda poems onto blue paper with purple marker and decorated them with cutouts of little white doves for her could have become someone who so casually discussed the Mexican Mafia and methamphetamine connections.

"You'll get caught."

"Nobody's going to get caught. It's all between friends, you know? Gabriel's friends, my friends."

"You didn't even know this Oreste until two minutes ago. He's not your friend."

Jorge stroked her hair and began unbuttoning her shirt. "Don't worry, *mamacita*. I'm not going to touch the stuff. I'm just going to introduce some people. That's all. Look, I'm a man, Olivia. It's a man's job to care for his woman. That's all I'm doing, caring for you."

As he slid her shirt open, he began to kiss her between her breasts. She sighed, wanting to argue with him, but she understood how emasculated he felt. A while ago, he had started secretly taking money out of her wallet, and while at first she'd been angry, she soon realized that he was trying only to save himself the humiliation of asking, so she forced herself not to mind. What was hers was his. That was the way it was supposed to be when you lived with someone, when you were in love.

She leaned back in his arms, not giving up, just, for the moment, giving in.

The first time Olivia and Jorge had made love it had been in a motel on the outskirts of San Miguel. She had paid for the room. They'd been meeting every evening for a couple of weeks, after she finished her Spanish classes. He hadn't gone back to Guanajuato after the conference. Instead, he spent his days at the *Universidad del Valle de Mexico*, the private secondary school and college in town, trying to organize the students there into a union. She would find him waiting for her outside of the *Instituto Allende* where her classes were, leaning against the wall, usually with one or two of his friends. Then they would all go back to the *Universidad* for a meeting or a rally. That was what charmed Olivia most about Jorge: his politics and his politicking. A state university student on scholarship, he nonetheless managed to inspire the private school students, most of whom had previously been concerned only with maximizing their earning potential. Jorge taught them to care for *el pueblo* and *la lucha*. He organized demonstrations in support of the Indians of Chiapas and against the government's brutal quelling of their rebellion. He convinced the students to paint murals of Che Guevara on the school's walls and to boycott classes taught by any professor not sympathetic to their cause.

Olivia was enchanted by it all. She adored the banners and the pamphlets and the earnest conversation that she could just barely understand. Jorge's poems about freedom and liberty and the color of her eyes swept her along in a tide of something part love, part politics—the combination so heady, it did her in.

One evening, after hours of impassioned but seemingly fruitless debate, Jorge stood up in front of a gathering of twenty or thirty student leaders, and, quoting Marx, Castro, and Public Enemy, begged them to strike like their comrades at Mexico City's public university. The students of *Universidad del Valle de Mexico* were afraid that their private institution could and would expel them. Jorge convinced them that it wasn't enough to speak sympathetically of rebellion. They had to act. By the end of his oration, they voted overwhelmingly to strike.

That night, Olivia walked with the boy she imagined to be a young García Lorca down the *Avenida de Zacatecas* and out to the main road. They found a motel—the kind of place where cars drove into private carports in front of each individual room and their drivers pulled shut the flimsy metal doors behind them, hiding them from view.

When they checked in, the old woman at the counter asked if they were staying the night or *un rato*—a little while. Before

Olivia could buy them an entire night on the sour sheets and thin foam mattress, Jorge muttered, "*Solo rato,*" and took the key.

Unlike their necking, which had been languid and passionate, night after night on a bench in the park or in doorways along the street, the first time they made love was rushed and almost grim. When they walked into the dank little room, Jorge undressed quickly, motioning her to do the same. Olivia, who, despite the evidence of poetry and white doves, had more of a sense of romance than her lover, could have ignored the forty-peso room and imagined them in a canopy bed with an entire lifetime to spend in each other's arms. Jorge, it seemed, could not. He tore the wrapper off of a condom, entered her roughly without any preamble, and came almost instantly. He was dressed again before she'd even had a chance to inhale. They walked back the way they came, holding hands, but only because that was the way they'd walked there, and the contrast of not touching would have been too stark. He left her at her room, and she didn't see him again until the next afternoon, when she found him waiting in his usual spot outside the *Instituto*, a bouquet of purple irises in his arms.

That night marked what might have been the end of Olivia's infatuation with Jorge. Her disappointment with their lovemaking seeped into the rest of her relationship with him, and although she continued to echo his words of love and devotion, part of her felt like a fraud. She could not bear the thought of herself as a dilettante who casually took up with a Mexican man in a kind of excess of touristic fervor—too many of the American girls she met in Mexico seemed to have a travel checklist: see the sights, eat the food, sleep with the men—but at the same time her attempts to imagine a future with Jorge failed her and ultimately inspired her escape back home. When he had arrived in California, his skin caked with grime, his hair stiff with dust, and his pockets emptied by the "coyote," she had pushed all doubts out of her mind. He had sacrificed too much to follow her, and there was no longer room for ambivalence.

Olivia was a good waitress. She wasn't particularly interested in food, and she never knew what wine went with what dish, but she was attentive to and friendly with her customers, complimenting their choices and encouraging them to try a piece of flourless chocolate cake or an appetizer of sautéed calamari. While her solicitude came naturally to her, she was competent and amiable because she got better tips that way, not because she liked her customers. She came close to hating them at times, particularly late at night when groups of men, liberated from their decency by the absence of their wives and girlfriends, made jokes that they mistakenly believed were beyond her comprehension and grabbed her ass.

By 11:30 at night, Olivia's smile was so tight it hurt. After she pulled off her white apron and bundled it into her bag, she had to grip her cheeks with her hands and massage her face back into something resembling a human expression. She dug her hands into her pockets and pulled out the wadded bills. Ninety dollars. Pretty good. Enough to pay the electric bill.

Jorge was waiting at the bar, deep in conversation with Gabriel. The two men had hair identical in color—a deep, shiny black. The physical similarity ended there, however. Whereas Jorge was thin and sharp-faced, Gabriel, although not particularly tall, was massive. He had the over-developed biceps and chest of a man who earns his muscles lifting free-weights and the handles of Nautilus machines. He didn't look particularly strong, just large, as though his muscles were carved out of soap. His hair was clipped short, and he wore a row of earrings in one ear. If she hadn't heard stories in the waitresses' changing room of his sexual escapades, Olivia would have assumed he was gay. As it was, between the wife who occasionally showed up at the restaurant and the various waitresses he bedded, it was unlikely he would have had the time or the energy to have sex with a man, even if so inclined.

Olivia put her arms around Jorge's waist. She leaned against his back, feeling the cool slickness of his windbreaker against her cheeks. He spun around on his stool and kissed her quickly on the mouth. Turning back to Gabriel, he said, "Okay, call them now and we'll be there in twenty minutes."

"We'll be where?" Olivia said, as they left the restaurant and crossed the parking lot toward the car. "I don't want to go anywhere. I've been working since 4:30."

"Don't worry, *chica*. It'll just take a minute."

Olivia stopped in front of her car and threw her purse on the hood. It landed with a thud. "Jorge, what's going on? Where are we going?"

"It's nothing, Olivia. Don't worry. We're just going to make a stop. Two stops. But it'll be fast, I promise. You won't even have to get out of the car."

"Jorge, is this the deal? Are you out of your mind? Do you really expect me to go along with you while you do a drug deal?"

He leaned against the car and said beseechingly, "Look, it's no big deal. You're just going to wait in the car."

"No!"

"Okay, *mami*. But I need the car."

"Fine. Just drop me off at home before you go."

"I can't. You heard me tell Gabriel I'd be there in twenty minutes. I don't have time to drop you off. You're going to have to take a bus or something."

Olivia groaned, imagining the long, late-night bus ride. She hadn't any idea which bus to take, or even if they were still running this late at night. She considered the dent a cab ride would make in her night's earnings. She'd probably lose half, at least. Maybe even more. She looked around the parking lot to see if any of the other girls were still there, but they'd all run for home as soon as they'd cleaned up their stations and zeroed out their tabs. She knew the manager was still there, and she considered, just for a second, asking him for a ride. But what would she say? "Can you drive me home? My boyfriend needs my car to do his meth deal."

"This sucks," she said in English.

"*Cómo?*"

"*Nada.*" She reached for her bag and dug around for the keys. She tossed them to him. "You drive."

Jorge handed the keys back to her. "I don't want to have to park. I'm just going to pull up in front and jump out of the car. You have to drive."

She shook her head in disgust, although she was relieved that he didn't expect her to do anything other than wait for him in the car. She unlocked the doors and got into the driver's seat, throwing her bag in the back. Jorge sat next to her, jiggling his leg and tapping his knee with his fingers. He flipped open the mirror on the visor and smoothed back his hair.

"Put your seat belt on," she said.

He leaned back in his seat, still tapping nervously. "Don't worry about it."

"Jorge, you have to wear a seat belt. Do you want some cop stopping us while we're on our way to do your drug deal?"

He reached back for the seat belt.

She pulled out of the parking lot and followed his directions to a small house in South Oakland.

"Wait for me here. Don't turn off the engine," he said.

Olivia sat in the car, listening to the idle. The street was empty and quiet. The houses were small bungalows, most with wrought iron gates on the windows and doors. The house into which Jorge had disappeared was painted a pale color; she couldn't make it out in the dark. Its front lawn had been covered over in cement that was probably painted grass-green. There was a tricycle lying on its side in the driveway, missing one of its rear wheels. Along the side of the house, a clothesline drooped under the weight of sheets snapping in the night breeze.

Olivia turned on the radio. She punched the buttons, stopping finally on a station playing *bolero* music. Jorge would hate it, preferring as he did *Norteno* bands likes Los Tigres del Norte. But Olivia loved old scratchy records with the quavering voices of *boleristas* like Amparo Montes and Toña La Negra, singing about *desesperación del amor* and *almas solas*.

She jumped as Jorge jerked open the car door. He was holding a small cardboard container, about the size of two shoeboxes. He laid it gently in the well of the passenger seat and got in the car. Then, with an almost childish grimace, he buckled his seat belt.

Olivia's stomach lurched with dread. "What's that?" she whispered.

"You know what it is."

"I thought your job was just to introduce people! I thought you weren't even going to be touching the stuff!" Her fingers gripped the steering wheel so tightly she could see her knuckles glow white in the dark of the car. She kept her eyes on Jorge's face, afraid even to look at the box under his feet.

"I'm the one everybody trusts," Jorge said. "Oreste knows me, Gabriel knows me. It only makes sense for me to do the delivery. I just drop this off and pick up the money. That's it."

The back of Olivia's neck prickled, and she whipped her head around, terrified someone was watching her.

"Oh, God," she whispered.

Jorge hit his knees with his hands, obviously impatient with her anxiety. He seemed to feel none of it himself. On the contrary, he looked excited, almost happy. "Let's just drop this off, okay? Then I'll take you home. I'll deliver the money myself."

Once again she followed Jorge's directions to another house. She was so frightened she didn't even notice the route they took. The numbers on the digital clock on the dashboard seemed to be frozen, refusing to move while she waited alone in the car. She tried to listen to the radio, but the sound of her heart beating in her chest drowned out the music.

Suddenly, in her rearview mirror, Olivia saw the bright lights of a car driving up the block. She began to whimper, and by the time it had passed her and continued on its way, she was crying. It felt like hours before Jorge returned, and she almost left without him. When he finally opened the car door and leapt in beside her, she slammed the gear shift into drive and spun away, blindly driving down street after street until she reached a landmark she recognized. She kept her eyes glued to the road in front of her, refusing to look at Jorge or at the brown paper bag he held in his lap. She slowed down only when she was within a block or two of home. She pulled up in front of their apartment building and wrenched her house key off the ring. She grabbed her bag, jumped out of the car, and ran down the alley to their apartment.

Olivia gagged as she ran by the garbage bins and made it only as far as the kitchen sink, where she vomited again and again until her chest heaved dryly and nothing more came up.

She leaned her forehead against the cool metal of the sink and breathed deeply, willing her stomach to cease its anguished roiling. Finally, when she was able, she stood up and walked into the bathroom. She stripped off her clothes and stood under the hot shower until her breasts and belly were seared bright red.

She crawled into bed, pulled the thick comforter over her head, and buried her face in the soft pillow. Within moments she fell deeply asleep. She didn't hear Jorge come in hours later and didn't even shift in the bed when he lay down next to her. The next morning he was gone again. She took another message for him, writing out the details Gabriel gave her. Where. When. She did her best to put out of her mind what it was that her boyfriend was doing—how he was earning the money he imagined he needed to support her.

Olivia wished she had somewhere to go, something to do, but it was her day off. She cleaned the apartment, more because she needed to keep busy than because it was dirty. She was down on her knees, scrubbing at brown rust stains under the lip of the toilet, when she heard a faint moaning. Her bathroom window faced the alley leading toward the street, or she never would have heard the noise. Olivia opened the smoked glass window, jerked at the warped sash. She stuck her head out of the window and saw an elderly woman backed up against the rear of the apartment building. Her arms were spread wide and her fingers were scrabbling at the clapboard. A small black dog stood on its hind legs, its front paws leaving muddy prints on the woman's faded housedress.

"Don't be afraid! I'll be right there!" Olivia shouted.

She ran through her apartment and out the front door. By the time Olivia reached her, the woman had begun to slide down the side of the building, her breath coming in shallow gasps and her eyes wild with fear. It was the rottweiler puppy. Olivia scooped up the dog just as it began licking at the old woman's face. She held the dog in one arm and gripped the woman around the waist with her other. She tried to lift her to her feet, but quickly realized that she wasn't strong enough to do that one-handed. Instead, she lowered her gently to the ground until the woman sat propped up against the wall, her legs stuck out straight ahead of her like the ribs of a broken umbrella.

"Are you okay?" Olivia asked.

The woman didn't answer. The dog gave a sudden wriggle, and Olivia looked down at it. He barked happily, and she scratched his ears. Then she stormed across the alley and pounded on the door of the apartment where his owner lived. When no one answered, she knocked even harder. The door finally opened, and the young man who she had seen walking the dog peered out, his hair standing up on his head in wiry spikes.

"Wassup?" he said, rubbing the sleep out of his eyes.

"Your dog nearly killed someone, that's 'wassup'!" Olivia shoved the puppy into the man's arms.

"He just a puppy, he can't kill no one."

"Yeah? Well he nearly scared that woman to death." Olivia waved in the direction of the old woman. The man's defensive grimace disappeared, and his face sagged.

"She all right?" He began to walk toward the woman but stopped at Olivia's warning hand.

"Leave her alone. I'll take care of it. You just keep your dog inside where he belongs." She spun on her heel and ran back to the woman who had, by now, begun to breath more normally. "Are you all right? Do you need me to take you to the doctor? Should I call an ambulance for you?" Olivia helped her to her feet. Gnarled blue veins buckled the ashy white skin of the woman's twig-like legs, and her hand was a dry claw in Olivia's.

"Should I call 9-1-1?" Olivia asked.

"No, no," the woman muttered in a vaguely European accent. "I'm fine. Fine. I am only afraid of dogs. Nothing happened. Only I am so stupid. Afraid of a little dog." She wiped ineffectually at the paw prints mixing curiously with the faded pattern of teapots and cups on her dress. "Can you only help me to my house? Please?" She pointed to the rear door of the building.

"Of course! Of course." Olivia helped her inside and up the short flight of stairs to her apartment. "Are you sure you don't need a doctor? Is there someone I can call for you?"

The woman shook her head. "My daughter, she'll be here soon. She comes for lunch. She'll be here soon. It's all right."

She unlocked the door to her apartment using the key hanging around her neck and opened it only enough to slip inside. The door slammed behind her, and Olivia was alone in the hall.

When Jorge came home later in the day, Olivia began to tell him what had happened, about the woman's terror when confronted with the overly friendly puppy, and about how furious Olivia had been at the dog's owner. But Jorge cut her off.

"Did Gabriel call?" he asked.

She glared at him, and then wordlessly handed him the slip of paper on which she'd written the message from Gabriel. He took it, crammed it into his pocket, and tried to kiss her. She turned her head away.

"Come on, baby," he said in English, grabbing her up in his arms.

This was the first time Jorge had ever said anything like this to her. He only rarely used English phrases and words, and then with a kind of hesitant self-consciousness that had always charmed her. This sudden ease with an endearment never before part of their repertoire made her inexplicably angry. She twisted out from under his arms.

"*Mi amor*," he said, softly, and reached out again. She began to shrug his hand away, but he rested it so gently, so tentatively, that she could not bear to refuse him. In a low, earnest voice, he promised her that as soon as he got the second half of his money, he would wash his hands of Gabriel.

She gave in. He steered her to their bed, all the while whispering how much he loved her, how beautiful she was. She lay back on the pillowy down comforter, its striped duvet cover worn slick and feather-soft, and closed her eyes. She opened them to find him waving in front of her the wad of cash he'd brought home the night before and stuffed under the mattress of their bed. It was as if he thought the money were Spanish Fly or rhino horn—that the mere sight of it would make her voracious with desire. She looked at it for a moment, despite herself, because she'd never seen so many bills in one place. Then she rolled on her stomach and buried her head in her hands. Jorge kissed her unresponsive neck for a while and then gave up. He stretched out next to her, and the two of them lay there, silently.

After a while she turned to him. "I'm going out. Do you need the car?"

He shook his head. "Oreste is picking me up this time. I told him I didn't want to use your car again."

As if that made it all right. As if it were the use of her car to which she objected.

When Olivia was fourteen years old, in her first days in high school, her position on the rungs of the ladder of teenage popularity, always somewhat tenuous, had plummeted to the depths of her worst fears. Before then—before the advent of lockers and homerooms, of training bras and boy-craziness, Olivia had been surrounded by a group of girls whose loyal friendship she had always found somewhat surprising. None of these children whom she had known since their first days together in kindergarten was her best friend—she had never had one of those. Still, those girls, even while paired off in their own impenetrable couples, included her in their afterschool activities, sleepover parties, and birthday trips to the Oakland Zoo, the Discovery Museum, the teddy bear factory.

All that changed abruptly when they abandoned the ivy-covered haven and familiar worn blacktop of middle school for the squat brick buildings and bald playing fields of the high school. It was as if on the first day of school each child had been handed a list of names, a strict inventory of students ranked from most to least popular. While invisible, these rosters were absolutely immutable and utterly clear. For whatever reason—because of her lack of a father, of the familiarity of her mother to many of the children who had bought or even stolen candy from the pharmacy, of the precise tidiness of the clothing Elaine purchased for her at the beginning of every school year, or, most likely of all, because of her nearly palpable insecurity—Olivia found herself ranked some notches lower than the girls whom she'd always thought of as her friends.

One day in algebra class, Deirdre Black had punted a small football of a note onto Olivia's desk. Olivia had unfolded the paper to find a message written by the other girl on behalf of their entire small circle of friends. The note informed Olivia that the girls had had a meeting about her. They had decided that she was "ruining their reputation," that they could no longer *afford* to be her friends, and that she was not to sit with them in the lunchroom ever again "as long as we all shall live." The note was illustrated with Deirdre's signature doodle—a kitten's bewhiskered face. The girl had added a single fat tear under one of the cat's heavily lashed eyes.

Olivia stared at the paper, her face flushed, and her eyes burning with the acid sting of humiliated, and humiliating, tears. When she finally mustered the courage to look at Deirdre, she found the other girl smiling faintly and studiously copying the equation from the blackboard. Without really expecting to, Olivia lurched to her feet, scooped up her books, and ran from the classroom, ignoring the teacher's cry of protest. She burst through the doors of the school and out onto the street, not even bothering to be relieved that there was no hall monitor to object to her escape. She ran all the way up to College Avenue, the stitch in her side forcing her to limp the last few yards.

The pharmacy was quiet when Olivia lurched through the doors. She found Elaine alone behind the counter and ducked underneath it, flinging herself at her mother's body. She wrapped her arms around Elaine's slender waist and howled.

Elaine's own cry was more muted, but she was still, quite obviously, terrified. "What? What happened? Olivia? Olivia?"

Olivia poured out the story of her mortification, so wrapped up in her own misery and pain that she didn't notice as her mother's body stiffened. Finally, when she'd hiccuped out the last of her tale, she looked up into her mother's face. Elaine's jaw was tight, and her eyes were dull with disgust.

"You ran away from school because some girl wrote you a *note*? For God's sake, Olivia. This is the silliest thing you've ever done."

Olivia dropped her arms, and opened her mouth to protest, to explain to her mother the extent of her shame, the impossibility of her ever walking through the doors of Berkeley High again. Elaine's raised hand silenced her. Olivia stood by as her mother shrugged off her white coat and hung it on its hook. She followed her mother out the front door, waiting while Elaine meticulously adjusted the hands of the clock on the sign indicating when she'd return.

Olivia stopped crying long before they reached the school building. Her reddened eyes were dry when they entered the principal's office, and dry when her mother apologized on her behalf. By the time the principal instructed her to report to the detention room that day and every day for the rest of the week, the possibility of her seared, parched eyes shedding tears, then or ever again, seemed entirely remote.

After Olivia left Jorge and went outside, she felt a surprising, overwhelming urge to be with her mother. She wanted once again to be five years old, sitting at the soda fountain, spinning on her stool and drinking a milk shake. As a little girl, Olivia had felt proud of Elaine, glad to belong to the woman whom so many people trusted with their secrets, with their health, with their very lives. She would watch her mother behind the counter, looking so serious in her white coat, dispensing pills and reassuring pats on the hand. When the two of them watched *It's a Wonderful Life* at Christmas, they clucked their tongues reprovingly at the drunken pharmacist who killed the child in the world in which George Bailey had never been born. They both knew that Elaine would never ever have made such a mistake.

And so, long after the day in high school when it become clear that comfort was not likely to be forthcoming, Olivia sought it anyway.

Elaine leaned on the worn wooden counter, one hand stuffed into the pocket of her white coat, the other holding a medicine bottle. She nodded and smiled, doing her best not to let her mind wander as the tiny elderly woman in the nubbly pink sweater chatted on about her granddaughter's new baby. It was hard, at the end of a long day of dispensing medications and advice, of pretending interest and concern in the minutiae of her customers' lives, to keep her mask of polite attentiveness from slipping.

Finally, the woman's conversation wound down, and she piled her purchases on the counter. In addition to the vial of Metoprolol, she bought a tube of Anusol and a package of extra large Band-Aids. Elaine rang up her purchases and placed everything in a brown paper bag.

"Lots of water with that pill, Mrs. Hellwig."

"I will. A full glass. Or maybe juice. Does juice work?" She sounded worried.

"Juice is fine," Elaine said in the reassuring tone she'd perfected over the years.

The woman made her methodical way out of the store, and Elaine watched her, noticing how her gnarled toes poked out of the front of her beige sandals. Elaine eased a foot out of her plain, black ballerina flat. Reassured that her own toes had not yet grown knobby from corns, ingrown toenails, and a career spent standing behind a counter, and somewhat disgusted with her foolish vanity, she turned back to her work. She still had a pile of prescriptions to fill before the store closed at six.

Elaine worked steadily for a while, counting out pills, measuring liquids, and typing information into the computer to be printed out on labels for the small amber bottles. She restocked her shelves with more of the blister packs of Claritin Reditabs that flew out of the store. Finally she called in her nightly order to her wholesaler. When she heard the bell ringing over the door by the soda fountain, she raised her eyes and met Olivia's.

"Honey!" Elaine called, her voice betraying her surprise at seeing her daughter.

Olivia waved and motioned to the stools at the soda fountain. "Can I get a milk shake? Are you closing?"

"Just about. I'll join you in two shakes." Elaine said. "Get it? Shakes?"

Olivia replied with a sad, crooked little smile.

Elaine leafed through the remaining prescriptions, pulling only those that she knew needed to be filled for first thing in the morning. She worked quickly and finished just as Ralph, the soda jerk, was locking the front door. She took off her white coat and hung it on its hook behind the counter. She picked up her purse and walked through the store, and, recalling the paper dolls, stopped in one of the aisles to choose a small, sweet-smelling box from the rows of soaps.

Elaine perched on the stool next to Olivia. "Hi, honey, how's the shake?"

Olivia slurped through her straw. "Delectable, as usual. Ralph, you jerk a mean soda."

The heavyset man smiled and continued to rinse cups and spoons in the sink. Ralph Shockwell loved her daughter with a ferocity that Elaine had always felt owed something to his intellectual and emotional limitations. Olivia was quite simply Ralph's favorite person and had been ever since she was a little girl. Something about their relationship made Elaine uncomfortable. There wasn't anything even remotely sexual between them—Ralph wouldn't have been capable of that, and Olivia would never have considered it. It was more that Elaine felt that Ralph's devotion had so little to do with who Olivia really was. He felt that she was perfect, that she could do no wrong. While

Elaine was not the type to complain about her daughter to anyone, other than to Arthur, and she certainly would never have confided in Ralph, that he would immediately have taken Olivia's side in any altercation bothered her.

Elaine knew, of course, that Ralph's attachment was understandable. He had been a regular customer at the soda fountain when Olivia was a little girl. He came in every day for lunch and lingered late into the afternoon. It was Olivia who had convinced Elaine to hire him to run it when the former manager had quit. This was before Elaine had bought the pharmacy, but even then she knew that the nostalgic appeal of the soda fountain was an important part of the store's attraction, and she hadn't wanted to risk its success on someone like Ralph, who if not mentally retarded, was certainly pathologically shy, maybe even autistic. But every day after school, for as long as anyone could remember, Olivia had sat on the stool next to Ralph's at the fountain. She had drawn him pictures and offered him the remains of her pieces of pie. He had brought her coloring books and crayons and carried in his wallet the fourth-grade photograph she'd given him.

Olivia had begged her mother to give Ralph a chance, and Elaine, much to her own surprise, had done so. It had been a resounding success. Ralph had expanded the menu and the counter, added a couple of tables and a daily soup choice. And then, when the Carters had offered Elaine the chance to buy the business, it was only because of Ralph that she was able to afford it. Ralph had been squirreling away his wages and the money he received from SSI. He had enough to buy the soda fountain. With that paid for, the money Elaine had been saving since she began work was enough to cover the rest of the pharmacy. So it was that Olivia's insistence and Ralph's devotion had paid for Elaine's independence. In moments of uncharacteristic introspection, she wondered if the debt she owed them was, more than anything else, the thing that bothered her about their relationship.

Elaine handed Olivia the box of soap she'd taken off the shelf. "Look, sweetie. It's rose and oatmeal. All organic. I thought you might like it."

"Thanks, Mom," Olivia said, smelling the soap and slipping it into the pocket of her overalls.

"Can you come to dinner?" Elaine asked. "I marinated some shrimp, and Arthur's making a zucchini soup." She didn't expect Olivia to accept; she could count on one hand the times that Olivia had dined with them since she'd left home four years before.

"Yeah. Okay. That'll be great."

"Great." Elaine said, worrying now that she had not bought enough shrimp.

"Wanna sip?" Olivia offered. "It's really good. It's got extra malt."

"No thanks, honey. Arthur and I are in training. He's registered us for a 10K in two weeks, and we're trying to make ourselves lean, mean running machines."

Olivia shrugged her shoulders and slurped noisily.

"Is everything okay?" Elaine asked.

Olivia shrugged her shoulders again. Elaine knew she should press the girl, but she couldn't bring herself to. Maybe she would have more energy once they'd gotten home and she'd sat down, had a glass of wine.

Olivia finished her shake and unsuccessfully tried to pay Ralph for it. When she asked for her check, he just ignored her, singing loudly along with the ABBA tape he'd put on as soon as he'd locked the doors. Olivia left him a tip the size of the bill she would have paid, and the two women walked together out the door of the drugstore.

"Where's your car?" Elaine asked.

"Up the block. But let's walk."

The two ambled slowly up the quiet residential streets leading from College Avenue to Elaine's house, playing a game that used to amuse them for hours when Olivia was a child.

"That's my house." Elaine pointed at a large, turreted Victorian. "Except I'm going to paint it in shades of green. You can have the room in the tower."

"That's *my* house," Olivia said. The one she chose was a massive Berkeley brown shingle with a redwood tree in the yard and a white picket fence. "Except I'm going to tear down that stupid looking fence. Maybe put in a redwood one, instead."

"Redwood? Is that ecologically sound?" Elaine teased.

Olivia blushed and smiled. "Recycled."

Elaine smiled back. "Of course. Which is my room?"

"You're in the in-law unit over the garage. You can't stay in the main house because Jorge and I have so many children. We've filled all nine bedrooms with babies."

Elaine tried, unsuccessfully, to smile. She hated the idea of Olivia marrying Jorge. She imagined a different life for her daughter than one spent supporting an uneducated husband who couldn't even speak English. She imagined a boyfriend who'd gone to college and even law school or medical school. One who would encourage Olivia to go back to UC Santa Cruz and get her degree. Elaine was fully aware of how ironic it was that she, who had left her parents in search of a long-over summer of love and produced for them a grandchild with no father whatsoever, should have such banal ambitions for her daughter. Elaine had come to believe, however, that happiness just might lie in banality and convention. There was a reason those were the choices most people made.

A large pot simmering pungently on the stove testified to the fact that Arthur had come and gone.

"He must be out running," Elaine said, putting her purse away and pulling the shrimp out of the fridge. Surreptitiously, she counted them. There were enough. Just.

"Didn't he used to run in the morning?" Olivia climbed up on the kitchen stool and leaned against the counter, propping her chin in her hands. She had eaten breakfast perched on this stool from the time they had moved to this house when she was four and a half years old until the day she had left for college.

"Yes, but since he's started working only part-time, he likes to run twice a day." Elaine pulled open a kitchen drawer and took out a package of bamboo skewers. She began spearing the shrimp, one by one.

Olivia reached for a skewer. "I can't *imagine* Arthur not working ten hours a day. Who ever heard of a part-time accountant?"

"Put four or five on each skewer. Lots of accountants work part-time. Most of the women in his firm work part-time when they have new babies."

"Is there something you guys aren't telling me?"

Elaine looked up, startled. "What do you mean?"

"Jeez, Mom. It's a joke. Like do you have a new baby. Get it?"

Elaine smiled. "Oh. Right. Ha." She paused, holding a shrimp in one hand, the marinade running down her arm, perilously close to her sleeve. She dropped it and wiped her arm on a paper towel. "There *is* something, actually, Olivia."

Elaine hadn't meant to tell Olivia for a while. She hadn't told anyone yet. She was waiting to see who Arthur told, but so far, he'd kept mum.

"What?"

"It's nothing really. Just, well, Arthur and I have been talking about getting married."

Olivia looked up at her mother, startled. Her face flushed and it looked as though she would cry. "What are you talking about? Arthur doesn't *believe* in marriage. *You* don't believe in marriage."

Elaine opened her mouth to reply but then snapped it shut. She turned to a cabinet and got out a bag of rice. She carefully measured two cupfuls and poured them into the rice cooker sitting on the counter. She added water and plugged it in. Only then did she speak. "Arthur and I never said we didn't believe in marriage. It's just that neither of us had a particularly good experience with it the first time around. Now that Arthur's kids have finished college and he has no more child-support obligations, he feels more comfortable with the idea."

"Yeah, well how do *you* feel, Mom? Do *you* feel comfortable with the idea?"

Elaine, to her chagrin, felt herself beginning to blush. "I think I do, yes. We've been together quite some time and…" Her voice trailed off.

Olivia wiped her hands on a paper towel and leaned her chin back in her palms. "Well, then, great. It's kind of a coincidence."

"What is?"

"Your getting married."

"Why is that a coincidence?"

"Because Jorge and I are thinking about it, too."

Elaine froze, the pan full of skewered shrimp in her hand. "Oh, Olivia."

"What? You can get married and I can't?"

Elaine put the pan down on the counter and looked closely at her daughter. She didn't think Olivia was serious. The girl had that same defiant, closed-mouth scowl she always had when she was saying something designed to upset her mother. Elaine knew, however, that unless she pretended to believe her, Olivia would be furious. Worse, she might even do it, for no other reason than to prove that she had meant what she said.

"It's not that, honey. But Arthur and I have been together a long time. And we're older than you. You're still so young. You're younger than I was when I married your father."

"Yeah, well, it's not like there's any other way to get a green card."

"Is that what this is about? Isn't there *some* other way for Jorge to get papers? Maybe you can talk to an immigration lawyer before you do something so…so drastic. I'm sure Arthur knows somebody. He knows so many lawyers."

Olivia slumped over her stool as though she had deflated. "I'm not going to do anything drastic, Mom. It's just, he's my boyfriend. Shouldn't I be willing to marry him, I mean, if that's what it takes to keep him here?"

Elaine stared at the top of Olivia's bent head, automatically cataloging all the colors of her hair, as she had done since the blond had turned into a veritable rainbow when Olivia was in grade school. Olivia was asking for her advice, something she never did. And Elaine had no idea what to say.

"Just don't do anything rash, honey," she murmured.

Arthur swallowed his disappointment when he saw Olivia sitting at the kitchen counter he'd come to think of as his own. It wasn't that he didn't like her; they had always gotten along. When her mother wasn't around, that is. With Elaine there, Olivia turned into a caricature of a bratty adolescent. She whined and pouted and treated her mother like a sheet-draped member of the KKK who needed to be reeducated and dissociated from her reactionary politics. What bothered him more than Olivia's behavior, however, was how Elaine responded to it. Even with him there as a bulwark against her daughter's criticisms and condemnations, Elaine seemed unable not to take them to heart. It wasn't that she became emotional or exhibited her hurt feelings in any way— that wasn't something she would ever do. Instead, she shut down. Normally cool and even-tempered, she turned frosty and remote. That coldness remained long after Olivia had gotten over whatever had inspired her outburst. Olivia would turn to Elaine as if nothing had happened, only to be rejected. It was as if despite the lifetime they'd spent solely wrapped up in one another, Olivia didn't know Elaine at all. She never could seem to understand that merely because her mother didn't express her hurt like she herself did, with loud bursts of rage and bombastic expressions of pain, that didn't mean she didn't feel it. It was only with Arthur that Elaine permitted herself the barest expression of her emotions, and even then it was a constricted articulation, invariably more about her insecurity with how she'd handled her daughter than about what Olivia had made her feel. Arthur often wanted to tell this to Olivia, to make her understand that her mother possessed feelings that Olivia was capable of hurting. But of course, he could say nothing. His role was to support Elaine, and above all, to mind his own business.

"Congratulations on the wedding, Arthur," Olivia said. "Mazel tov."

"Thank you, thank you. So, shall I wear a top hat and tails to the event, do you think? Or biking shorts?"

Olivia laughed. "How about biking shorts *and* a top hat."

"You know, my dear," Arthur used the mock British accent he had often adopted to entertain Olivia when she was younger, "I think that would be lov-er-lee."

"Have you set the date?"

Arthur and Elaine both shook their heads. "Not yet," he said. "We want to have a terrific blowout, and neither of us has the cash for that just yet. We're saving our pennies for the condo in Lake Tahoe and a trip to Morocco this year."

"Morocco?" Olivia raised her eyebrows. "How mundane. What happened, you couldn't find a good tour of Kabul or Rwanda?"

"You should talk," he said. "Miss Travels-to-Chiapas." While he certainly never would have said as much to Elaine, Arthur had been secretly impressed when Olivia had packed off to Mexico all on her own. He had admired the girl's moxie. He had certainly been much more excited about her infrequent postcards and letters than her mother had been. Elaine opened each envelope with dread, sure it contained news of some latest catastrophe, while Arthur approached them with gleeful anticipation. How much would he have loved to divest himself of all his worldly possessions beyond what could fit into a backpack and take off for primitive places and untraveled lands. He was downright jealous of Olivia's adventures and had been terribly disappointed when she had hung it all up in favor of a job waiting tables at a crappy Oakland restaurant.

Olivia sighed. "I never made it to Chiapas. I never got past San Miguel. I got distracted."

"Yeah, well, you went pretty far. For a girl." He punched her lightly on the arm and was pleased when she smiled.

"Hey, Olivia, I have to show you this new camera I bought for our next trip," Arthur said. He went out to the hall and returned carrying a brightly colored cardboard box. He took the camera out of its wrappings and handed it to her. She wiped her hands on her pants and took it, holding it carefully.

"Wow. Is this digital?"

"Yup. It's the top of line. You would not believe the clarity of the image. Now I'll be able to do slide shows on PowerPoint instead of dealing with the slide projector." Olivia was one of the only people, perhaps the only one, who genuinely enjoyed looking at the slides of his and Elaine's travels. So many of their friends' responses to his invitations to a vacation slide show were decidedly lukewarm. Some even begged off entirely. But Olivia had always sat right next to him, listening rapt to his descriptions and asking questions about the places they'd gone and the people they'd seen. He had occasionally considered asking Elaine if they could take Olivia along with them on one of their trips but had always thought better of it. He enjoyed their vacations too much to risk poisoning one with the strain of Olivia's presence.

"That'll be so cool," Olivia said. "If I ever have the money to travel again, I'll have to get myself a digital camera."

"You should," Arthur said. Olivia had come over one evening not long after she had returned from Mexico and before Jorge had arrived in Oakland. She had brought the rolls of slides she had taken during her trip, and together she and

Arthur had loaded them into both carousels of his slide projector. Elaine had, as usual, found something pressing to do that precluded sitting through the slide show, and Arthur and Olivia had watched them alone. Olivia wasn't a bad photographer. Her portraits of Indian women were particularly moving, and Arthur had complimented her on her skill with the camera. She'd obviously remembered what he'd taught her about shooting portraits with the smallest possible aperture.

They didn't speak of Jorge once during the evening. Neither Arthur nor Elaine asked where he was. Elaine was surely avoiding the subject on purpose, but it simply never occurred to Arthur to wonder. They ate their dinner out on the back deck, under the shade of the fig tree. Every once in a while, when the breeze blew from the east, they could smell the jasmine growing up the side of the house. After they finished their meal, Arthur took a brown paper bag and filled it with tomatoes and green beans for Olivia. She took it and kissed him and her mother good-bye. They watched her walk slowly down the street to her car.

Elaine bustled into the kitchen and began loading the dishwasher and wiping down the counters. Arthur put the tea kettle on to boil and leaned against the counter.

"What was that about?" he said.

"What? Her visit? I haven't the faintest idea. Well, except that she announced that she might marry Jorge."

"Are you serious?"

"Yes, but *she* wasn't." Elaine wrung out the sponge and put it in the microwave. "I'm sure she just said it to drive me crazy. I mean, really. Marriage? To him? Not even Olivia would be so stupid." She pushed a few buttons, turning on the microwave. Then she wiped her hands dry on a dish towel and hung it over the bar on the oven door. "Would she, Arthur? Would Olivia be that stupid?"

Arthur was torn between his desire to comfort her and the knowledge that Olivia was one of those people who would do almost anything to prove a point. He would not have put it past her to marry the boy out of some deadly combination of political conviction and spite. Those seemed to be the blend that fueled her particular engine. "I don't know, babe," he said.

"Oh, God," Elaine moaned, resting her head in her hands.

He reached out his arm and squeezed her to him. "Don't worry. I'm sure she was just trying to get a rise out of you, in typical fashion. I wouldn't take it seriously."

Elaine leaned her head against his chest. "God, that girl."

"Why do you think she came by? When's the last time she showed up for dinner, unannounced?"

Elaine shook her head. "I don't know. A long time ago."

"Mmm," Arthur said, stroking Elaine's hair with his palm. She twitched a bit. "I know, I know. I'm messing up your hair."

"No, no. It doesn't matter."

But he could tell that it did. He stroked her cheek, instead. "I think I know something that will make you forget all about Olivia and her problems."

"What?" Elaine asked, raising her face.

"This," he said, and kissed her.

Jorge wasn't home when Olivia got back from her mother's. She took off her clothes and got into bed. She fell asleep almost immediately and awoke, much later, to the sound of pounding and shouts. She sat up in bed with a start. The noise seemed to be coming from the door of her apartment. Her stomach knotted, and she felt her bowels loosen. She reached for the telephone but had dialed only the 9 and the first 1 of the emergency number when the sharp, splintering crash of the door caused her to drop the phone to the ground. She scrambled for it, holding the sheet around her naked body. Dark forms of men burst through the door of her bedroom. There were more of them than she could count, and she began to scream, terrified beyond anything she had ever imagined she could feel. All she saw were the black of their clothes and the dull flash of their guns. The first to reach her grabbed her by the hair and forced her back onto the bed, her face pressed into the sheets. She felt his knee on her back and knew for certain what she would feel next. For an instant she imagined her body torn open by the force of him and the others as they took turns with her. She knew, as sure as she had ever known anything in her life, that they would kill her when they were done.

She lay silently, desperately trying to breathe through the sheets pressed tightly against her nose and mouth. The knee on her back was heavy, and the edge of the man's boot dug into the soft flesh of her buttocks. The quilt around her head prevented her from hearing much of anything other than the noise of the men shouting. Suddenly, the man jerked Olivia's arms behind her back, and something metal and sharp pinched her wrists.

It was only when she felt the handcuffs that Olivia realized that the man standing over her naked body, pinning her to her sheets, was a police officer.

Once her hands were securely bound, he took his knee off her back and jerked her to her feet. He forced her to her knees on the floor next to her bed and shouted at her to lie down.

Olivia lay there for a long time, slowly becoming aware of her nakedness. At one point she raised her head and saw the men tearing apart the mattress, slicing open the pillows of the couch and throwing the contents of her drawers to the ground. One of the men tossed a bouquet of dried flowers onto the floor and crushed it under his heavy boots. A rough hand shoved her face back down, and she closed her eyes again. She heard the cops jerking open the kitchen cabinets and the fridge, throwing their contents to the floor. She heard the sound of paper tearing and the crash and tinkle of broken glass and then a dry rustle that she recognized as the sound of Cheerios being poured out only after it had been replaced by the crunching noise of the cereal being crushed under feet.

Finally someone stood over Olivia and shouted to her to stand up. She got to her knees and did her best to shake her hair down over her breasts.

"I need to get dressed," she said in a cracked whisper.

The man ignored her.

She made her voice as firm as she could. "I said, I need to get dressed."

She raised her eyes to the man's face. He was young, not much older than she, with close-cropped hair and a nose that looked as though it had been broken.

He met her gaze, and then, slowly and deliberately, let his eyes drop down the length of her naked body.

"You need to shut the fuck up," he said.

A voice from across the room shouted, "Agent, tell the prisoner to put some clothes on." A few of the men who were digging through everything she owned in the world laughed. The agent with the broken nose and the dull, cold eyes smiled and said, "You heard the man. Get dressed."

Olivia stood silently for a moment, waiting. Her nipples tightened in the cool air from the open door. Her cheeks grew red and hot. The agent turned his back to her, and she could see the letters D-E-A emblazoned on his jacket.

"I can't get dressed with these handcuffs on," she said.

He turned to her again and reached out for her shoulder. She shrank back from his touch, but he grabbed her and spun her around. He freed her wrists and growled, "You have thirty seconds. Move."

Olivia scrambled through the piles of clothes strewn all over the floor. She found a pair of panties and a bra and, turning her back to the agent, slipped them on. She picked up a dirty pair of jeans and one of Jorge's sweatshirts and put those on as well. She was looking for socks when the agent grabbed her arms again, wrenched them back behind her back, and snapped the handcuffs in place.

He held her, his hand digging into her upper arm.

"I'd like to put on some shoes," she said, keeping her voice even.

"Go right ahead," he answered. He took his hand off her but did not unhook the handcuffs.

Olivia kicked through the piles of clothes until she found a pair of black clogs with worn wooden soles lying together near the end of her bed. She slipped them on her feet. The agent took her arm again, squeezing it very deliberately. It hurt as he yanked her out of her apartment and dragged her down the long alley.

The agent held Olivia with one hand and with the other reached into his pocket and pulled out a card. He read her her Miranda rights in a toneless voice.

At first Olivia lowered her head, her hair falling around her face like a criminal doing a perp walk in a TV show. But then she lifted her chin. She was damned if she'd let the officers see the mortification they had wrought. She pushed her shoulders back, steeled her face, and looked up and into the eyes of her neighbor. He stood, holding his rottweiler puppy, in the doorway of his apartment. When her eye caught his, he lifted his fingers in a barely noticeable wave. Olivia's resolve was swept away by a rush of gratitude at so simple a human gesture. This gentle recognition of her plight was from a man who had no reason to care about her at all, who might, in fact, have remembered her high-handedness toward him and responded with something other than compassion. That was when she began to cry. She stumbled alongside the agent, who seemed not to notice though her tears shook her whole body. He put his hand on her head and pushed her into the backseat of a navy blue sedan that was parked at an angle in front of her apartment building, blocking half the street. He slammed the door behind her, and Olivia was alone.

She sat for a while, crying, until she realized that she could as easily stop as continue. She leaned her face to her shoulder and wiped her nose as best she could. Her arms fastened behind her kept her from sitting back against the plastic of the seat—she had to lean on one side, angled across the length of the bench. Olivia rested her head against the seat and closed her eyes. She had an almost overwhelming urge to roll down the window and call out that they'd made a mistake, they'd confused her with someone else. She wasn't a crackhead from the ghetto. She wasn't an uneducated criminal. She'd been in all the AP classes at Berkeley High; she'd been to college. She had a mother and an almost stepfather and grandparents in New Jersey. She wanted to wave her arm in front of the agent's face like a flag and shout, "Look, I'm a white girl. See?"

Olivia wriggled around to her other side to relieve some of the pressure on her shoulder. Her wrists hurt. The sharp metal of the handcuffs dug into them. She thought about trying to step through the harness of her cuffed hands—to move them in front of her, but she doubted that she could pull off such a Houdini feat, and even if she could, the agents would yank her back the way she'd been as soon as they returned.

Olivia took a few deep breaths. It was obvious to her that the DEA had found out about Gabriel and Jorge's drug deal. The two of them were probably in custody already, along with Oreste. Somehow the police had found out Jorge's address and arrested her because she was in the apartment.

She looked out of the car. She could just make out the light from her bedroom window. She wondered how long it would be, how much damage they would do, before the agents realized that there was nothing for them to find. And then she realized that there was, of course, something there. She had been sleeping on top of the money. But was there any way they could prove that the money was from the drug deal? She could say it was her tip money, her school tuition. That she didn't believe in banks. Something like that.

She wished she knew where Jorge was. Had they found him with the drugs? The two of them would have to make sure that the police understood that Gabriel was in charge. Gabriel had set up the deal; he'd found the buyers. He'd even put the idea in Jorge's head to begin with. Once they had Gabriel, surely the cops wouldn't need a little fish like Jorge.

Olivia had no idea what time it was, but she'd gone to bed at about 10:00 and had been sound asleep when the cops came crashing into her house. She figured it was maybe 3:00 or 4:00 in the morning. She couldn't make the agents aware of her innocence until she knew how much she should or could tell them about Gabriel and Jorge. There was a good chance she would have to spend the rest of the night in jail.

At the thought of jail, saliva gathered in the corners of her mouth, and she swallowed hard, willing herself not to vomit. She had to pull it together—after all, it wasn't like this would be the first time she'd been in jail. She and a few other members of the Homeless Advocacy Council had once spent the night in the Santa Cruz county jail after someone set fire to the symbolic shanty town they had built in the middle of Hagar Drive. It was only one night—they were released the next day when the fire department determined the fire to have been caused by a malfunctioning camping stove and not politically motivated arson. Another time she'd been arrested for blocking a logging road that led to a marbled murrelet nesting area. That time she'd also been released the next morning, uncowed and firmer in her convictions than the day before. This time, though, she would be alone, not accompanied by a group of friends and fellow-protestors cracking jokes and singing songs like "Ain't gonna let Weyerhaeuser push me around, push me around, push me around."

In the morning they'd either let her out, or she'd ask to see a lawyer and have the lawyer find out who knew what and how much she should tell.

Olivia had a long time to harden her resolve. By the time the cops came back, the sky had lightened to a pale gray. The agent who'd put her in the backseat got in the driver's seat, and another agent, also a young man with short hair and an undistinguished face, got in the passenger seat. Olivia waited for them to try to weasel information out of her. They didn't. They took off without a word. The plastic seats were slippery, and she couldn't get a firm purchase on her side. For the length of the ride, she concentrated on not falling to the floor whenever they turned a corner. Once, she tumbled off the bench, and the agent in the passenger seat turned to glare at her. She clambered back up, and he looked away.

They drove through Oakland toward downtown and alongside a pair of huge, elaborate skyscrapers. Olivia recognized the Federal Buildings. She'd once participated in a demonstration against the deportation of Chinese illegal immigrants, and she remembered sitting in the plaza, leaning against a piece of abstract sculpture.

The police car pulled into a driveway marked with large signs that read AUTHORIZED VEHICLES ONLY and drove into an underground parking lot. Olivia waited in the backseat for the cops to take her out of the car. She tried to calm down by reminding herself that this was just what she had imagined would happen, but the fact that the men had not spoken to her at all, even one word, made her nervous. She had so carefully planned her refusal to answer their questions that being denied the opportunity to do so seemed not only unfair, but frightening. The agent who had been sitting in the passenger seat opened the door of the car and pulled her out, muttering, "Watch your head," as she ducked out of the open door. For this small consideration, she felt absurdly grateful.

They led her down a dark hall and into a drab, windowless room with a long Formica counter at one end. The agents walked up to a counter and called out. A man in a uniform, heavyset, his bushy moustache still wet with whatever he'd just been drinking, walked though a door behind the counter.

"All yours," the agent said, handing him a pile of papers.

She had her picture and her fingerprints taken. The ink was black and sticky, and the stiff brown paper towel the uniformed officer handed her didn't get it all off her hands. For some reason, the sight of her dirty fingers panicked her. She rubbed at them, wiped them on her jeans. She felt tears return to her eyes.

"Here," the officer said, handing her a wad of paper towels he had dampened in the sink.

"Thanks," she whispered. She scrubbed at her fingertips until finally there were only pale gray stains across the pads of her thumbs.

The officer led her by the arm—gently, not like the others had—into a barred cell. There were two long metal benches bolted along the rear and side walls, and there was a metal toilet with a sink built into the back tucked into a corner. There was no toilet seat and no toilet paper. The officer locked the cell and left the room. The door closed with a hollow thud, and Olivia was alone underneath the fluorescent lights.

She had to pee. She looked around the empty cell and then crossed to the toilet. It stank of disinfectant and something else, something foul. She pulled her jeans down and crouched over the bowl, careful not to let any part of it touch her. She urinated as fast as she could, keeping her eyes glued to the door through which the officer had disappeared. When she was done, she shook herself as dry as possible and zipped up her pants. She flushed the toilet with the toe of one foot and then walked to the far end of the cell. She sat down on the cold metal bench. After a while, she lay down, resting her cheek on her elbow.

She awoke, chilled from the metal bench, to the sound of a key turning in a lock. She had no idea how much time had passed, if it was still early morning or much later in the day. The guard with the mustache reached into the cell and handed her a tray of brown corrugated paper with a small waxed cardboard container of apple juice and a bagel. She gulped the sweet drink and took a small bite of the bagel. It was cold and hard, and the pat of margarine it came with left an oily flavor on her tongue. Olivia left it on the tray, uneaten.

She sat alone for a while, her knees hugged close. The chill of the metal bench reached up through her, along her spine, to the backs of her eyes. She felt like she was watching her own misery from somewhere far away. She wondered if she should pound on the bars of the cell, thick and lumpy with years of careless painting, and call out to the guard that she wanted to see her lawyer. But even if she hadn't recognized the futility of the action, she would not have been able to muster the energy for it.

Little by little Olivia felt herself slip into a warm, seductive bath of self-pity. Why had this happened to her? She didn't deserve this nightmare. She shook her head and forced herself to think of heroes of resistance who had undergone worse incarcerations than her own. Che Guevara. Jacobo Timmerman. Rigoberta Menchú. That was a good example. A woman, not much older than herself, who had suffered so much worse—her family had been murdered by Guatemalan death squads, her village had been destroyed. Olivia had seen her on television once. Menchú had worn a skirt of violet woven fabric and a beautifully embroidered *huipil*. She had spoken about people of all shades of brown united against oppression. Olivia had felt deeply ashamed of her pale skin and blond curls and had ached to be cloaked in the comfortable brown-ness of the people she saw on the screen.

How had Rigoberta behaved when she was imprisoned and tortured? Olivia drew herself up straighter. She put her feet on the floor.

The sudden click of the door opening startled her. She jumped, and her eyes filled with tears. She shook them away and drew her knees up to her chest, rocking slightly as she watched the guard enter the room.

"Pretrial services to see you," he said, unlocking the cell and motioning her to stand up.

"What?" Her voice came out a broken whisper. She cleared her throat and asked again, "What?"

He didn't answer. With a firm hand on her shoulder, he directed her out the door, down a short hallway, and into a tiny room. The room, no more than a booth, really, had a window on one end with a chair pulled up to it. Sitting on the other side of the glass was a woman.

Olivia slipped into the chair and looked at her visitor. The woman was busily writing on a piece of paper that Olivia could not see. She didn't raise her eyes, and Olivia could see only the top of her head. Her sparse hair was dyed jet black and teased into a bouffant. A full half-inch of dull gray roots showed clearly at the hairline. Finally the woman picked up her head and looked at Olivia. Her face was spackled with a viscous layer of makeup.

"You're here to see me?" Olivia said.

The woman pursed her brightly colored lips and tapped on the window with a violet-painted fingernail.

"Talk into the holes," she said.

Olivia looked down and saw a pattern of small holes punched into the Plexiglas at roughly mouth level. She leaned toward them. "I'm Olivia Goodman."

"Priscilla Watts-Thompson from pretrial services. I'm here to determine your eligibility for pretrial release, Miss Goodman."

"Pretrial release?" Olivia asked.

"Bail." The woman's voice was harsh and squeaky. Her eyes, tinted a strange shade of television blue and ringed with azure mascara and violet eye shadow, did not meet Olivia's.

Olivia dutifully provided information about her job, her bank accounts, her criminal history. Finally, Miss Watts-Thompson asked, "Is there someone who can provide security for your release? Your parents, perhaps?"

"Security?"

"The federal government does not generally allow the services of bail bondsmen. You'll need someone to act as a surety for you. Do your parents own their home? If they have sufficient equity, they can put that up as security."

"Why do I need that? I didn't do anything."

"That is an issue for your attorney to discuss with you." Miss Watts-Thompson tapped on her pad with her pencil. "Again, do your parents own a home?"

Olivia nodded. "My mother does."

The woman made a notation. "Would she be willing to put the house up for you?"

Olivia shrugged. "I don't know. I guess so. What does that mean, put the house up?"

"That means that she signs over the house, and if you don't appear in court when you're supposed to, we take it away from her."

"You take her *house* away from her?" The tide of panic that she had kept dammed up since the night before now began to fill her lungs.

Miss Watts-Thompson pursed her lips again. "The house would be taken only if you absconded. Is that your plan, Miss Goodman? Is that what you'd like me to inform the magistrate judge? You need to understand something, young lady; we are not required to release you. In fact, since you are a defendant in a large-scale drug conspiracy, the presumption is that we *won't* release you. If you have any interest in getting out on bond, I suggest you cooperate."

The blast of rage Olivia felt at the woman's condescending sneer pushed aside her fear. She drew herself up and narrowed her eyes. "What large-scale drug conspiracy? I don't know anything about a large-scale conspiracy."

"Again, that is an issue to discuss with your attorney, Miss Goodman. My role is simply to evaluate whether or not you are eligible for pretrial release. Quite frankly, given your attitude, I'm not convinced that you are a good risk."

"My *attitude*?"

"Your answers to my questions indicate to me that you're a poor risk for bail."

Olivia drew herself up. "As far as I know, I have a constitutional right to refuse to answer any questions at all," she said, glaring at the woman.

"Shall I call your mother to determine her willingness to post bond for you, or would you rather just stay in jail?"

The other times she had felt so proud to be arrested; she'd been glad to have the police call Elaine. Olivia had seen those midnight calls as part of her mother's political education; how else would Elaine have learned about the actions of American oil companies in Brazil or the paucity of tenured African-American women on the faculty of the University of California? This time was different. Olivia felt not heroic but filled almost to an unbearable level with shame. She didn't want her mother to know she was here. She couldn't bear to imagine her mother's horror at the sordid drug deal. *This* disappointment would be too much for Elaine to tolerate. At the same time, some part of her was wild to believe that when her mother heard what had happened to Olivia she would come and take care of it, make it all go away. She would walk into the holding cell, give the guard a piece of her mind, unlock the door, and take her little girl home.

"I suggest that you answer me when I'm talking to you," the pretrial services officer said, sharply.

Olivia wanted to scream "Fuck you!" to the over-made-up little troll and storm out of the room. Instead, she closed her eyes for a moment and willed herself to be calm. She recited her mother's phone numbers at home and work. The woman noted the numbers, gathered up her papers, and left. On her way out, she called out, "I'm done with Goodman, Archie."

Olivia waited to be taken back to her cell. Nobody came. Through the half-open door on the other side of the Plexiglas she could see only a wall painted in a muddy off-white. Suddenly, a young man with dreadlocks popped his head into the room.

"Hey! Are you Olivia Goodman?"

She nodded.

"Great." The man came inside. He was no more than twenty-seven or twenty-eight years old. His long dreadlocks were caught at the nape of his neck with a thick black rubber band. His eyes were a startling green in his café-au-lait face. He wore a nicely tailored three-button suit in charcoal gray, with a crisp white shirt and a moss green tie. He flipped the chair around, straddled it, and shot his cuffs. He was wearing gold cufflinks with large stones in the precise shade of green as his eyes.

"I'm Izaya Feingold-Upchurch—that's I-Z-A-Y-A," he said. He reached into his jacket pocket and waved a business card at her.

"Guard!" he called out. Nobody came. "Hey, Archie! I need you to pass something to my client."

"Are you my lawyer?" Olivia asked.

"Yup. I'm with the federal public defender. Know what that is?"

"I guess so," she said. She was ashamed of herself for noticing that he didn't sound like a black man, or at least like what she would have expected from a black man with dreadlocks. He spoke like her, or for that matter, like many of the black and biracial kids with whom she'd taken honors classes at Berkeley High School. But by the time they'd all started college, those students had adopted the homeboy accents of their fellows from the less rigorous academic programs. Olivia had almost forgotten what it was like to speak with a black person who sounded as white as she.

"I'm a public defender in the federal court."

The guard stuck his head in the door of the lawyer's side of the interview room. The lawyer handed him the business card and a sheaf of papers. "Give these to her, okay?" he said.

"Yes, sir, Mr. Feingold-Upchurch. Right away, sir," the guard said, and laughed. He leaned ostentatiously against the wall in the room.

The lawyer shook his head and laughed, ruefully. "Okay. *Please* give those to my client."

"That's more like it."

The guard disappeared through the door and a moment later appeared in Olivia's cubicle. He handed her the card and the papers and walked out, shutting the door behind him with a bang.

"So our first order of business is to figure out how to get you the hell out of here," the lawyer said.

Olivia sighed with relief. Finally. "I didn't do anything. I have no idea why they arrested me. I mean, I know why they did, but I didn't have any part of any of it."

"Right. We're going to have a lot of time to talk about all of that. And I even want to hear some of it right now. But first let's fill out some forms that will get me appointed as your lawyer, and then we'll figure out how to get you out on bond."

At the word *bond*, Olivia's heart sank. She knew it was unreasonable, but somehow she'd expected him to unlock the door and let her out. For good.

"I already talked to someone about bail."

"Was Cruella DeVil here already? Damn, if I've told that bitch once I've told her a thousand times to lay off my clients until I've talked to them."

Olivia felt a rush of gratitude toward her lawyer for so obviously and vociferously taking her side. "Does she work for the prosecutor?" she asked.

Izaya shook his head. "No, but she might as well. She's with pretrial services. They give a bail recommendation to the court, and then, if you're released, they supervise you while you're out. Did she get the name of any possible sureties from you?"

Olivia recounted her conversation with the unpleasant woman, and Izaya jotted down her mother's name and numbers.

"I'm going to call your mom myself. If Cruella hasn't convinced her otherwise, maybe I can get her to post bond for you. Okay, now, I'm going to ask you a bunch of questions, okay?" He flipped open a folder in front of him and began jotting down her answers to his questions. They got through the basic biographical information pretty quickly, then he asked, "Did you finish high school?"

"Yeah." She nodded.

"Where?"

"Berkeley High."

"Really? Me too."

They looked at each other for a moment, not sure what else to say. Finally he said, "Any college?"

She nodded. "UC Santa Cruz. But I dropped out in my second year."

"Okay," he said, making a few final notes in his folder. He lay his pen down. "Now, do you want to tell me a little bit about what's brought you to my humble place of employ?"

Olivia sat silently for a moment. She liked Izaya. She liked his dreadlocks and the way he had seemed to take utterly for granted that they were on the same team. She even liked his clothes. They were obviously expensive, and on a white boy with floppy hair and a prep-school accent they might have looked too slick. But they gave him an air of competence, of being so good at his job that it was only right that he should dress the part.

"This drug dealer convinced my boyfriend to carry a box for him. That's all. The cops must have arrested them, and they came and searched our apartment. They found the money under our mattress, and I guess that's why they arrested me."

"So you're basically just an innocent bystander here, right? The girlfriend. That's it."

She smiled with relief. "Exactly."

"Once we figure out who's who and what's what, we'll decide our next steps. But one thing we're probably going to need to consider is the possibility of trading information for a reduced sentence, or in your case, a walk."

"I don't have any information. I don't know anything."

"I understand, but you might surprise yourself. You've met some of the parties involved, right?"

"I suppose."

"Well, we'll have to keep all that in mind. The first thing I'm going to do is get you out on bail. After that, we'll talk to the Assistant United States Attorney and see if we can't convince him that you shouldn't be here to begin with."

"I shouldn't be. I didn't do anything."

"Right. Let's keep that as our party line for the time being at least."

Olivia opened her mouth to object. It wasn't a *line*. It was the truth. Izaya smiled at her before she could speak.

"We're going to talk a lot more about this later. Now I want to get cracking on your bail. Those papers I had the guard give you are a copy of the complaint against you. Why don't you read that while you're waiting? I'm going to make some calls. I'll try to get your mom down here for a bail hearing this afternoon. Just hang in there until then, okay?"

Olivia nodded. He reached out a hand and laid it flat on the Plexiglas. His fingers were long and tapered at the tips. They looked both strong and delicate. She put her hand up to meet his. He winked at her and left the room. A breath expanded Olivia's chest, and she imagined that she could feel her ribs nearly cracking with the force of the air filling her lungs. It was, she thought, the first real breath she had taken since her sleep was shattered all those long hours before. All she had to do was hang on for a little while longer. Izaya would talk to the AUSA. Once the prosecutor understood what had happened, she would be released.

Afterward, Elaine would often recall that her immediate reaction on learning of Olivia's arrest was a flash of annoyance. It wasn't the first time she'd gotten a call from a court clerk or police officer telling her that Olivia had been booked on some charge or other. At one time it had seemed as if the University of California campus police had an entire division devoted exclusively to arresting Olivia Goodman.

Elaine had arrived at the pharmacy, coffee in hand, a good half-hour before its 8:00 opening time. It gave her a deep sense of satisfaction to start the day with a clean desk, all the previous evening's prescriptions filled and ready for pickup, the paperwork filed, and the claim forms sent out to the insurance companies. It was as she stood, contentedly sipping her coffee and looking out over the clean-swept aisles and tidied display cases, that the telephone rang.

"Is this about the union?" Elaine asked the woman on the other end of the line.

"Excuse me?"

"Did Olivia get arrested for organizing a union? Is that why you're calling?"

The woman didn't answer, and Elaine thought she could hear the scritch-scratch of a pen on paper.

"Hello, are you still there?"

"Yes, Mrs. Goodman, I'm still here. This has nothing to do with any union. As I told you, my name is Priscilla Watts-Thompson, and I am a pretrial services officer with the United States Federal Court. I'm calling in regard to your daughter, Olivia Goodman."

"Yes, I understand. I was just asking what she got arrested for this time. Was it the union?"

"This time? Does your daughter have a history of criminal conduct, Mrs. Goodman?" There was the sound of flipping papers. "I have here a record of two prior arrests by the sheriff's department in Santa Cruz County and a misdemeanor disturbing-the-peace conviction in Humboldt County. Is there anything else I should know about?"

The woman's officious tone sent a prickle of anxiety skittering up Elaine's spine. "I don't think so. I'm sorry, if this isn't the union, then what was she arrested for?"

"Your daughter was arrested for conspiracy to distribute methamphetamine."

Elaine felt her legs give way under her. "One moment," she whispered. She pressed the hold button on the phone and gently placed the receiver in its cradle. She set her paper cup of coffee on the counter with a shaking hand. A wavelet jumped over the side of the cup. For a moment she stared at the small pool of pale brown liquid. Then the bells on the front door jangled, and she raised her head.

"Good morning!" her assistant, Warren, called out, as he unlocked the door and flipped the CLOSED sign around.

"I'll be in the back," she said, wincing at the tremor in her voice. She walked quickly to the storage area in the back of the store, sat down on a stool, and took a long, unsteady breath before she picked up the telephone again.

"Uh, yes," she said.

"Well, my goodness, I thought you had hung up on me."

"No. I'm sorry. I was just…" her voice trailed off.

The woman seemed not to notice. "Mrs. Goodman, it is my job to determine your daughter's eligibility for bail. Are you willing to post bond for her?"

"Yes, of course," Elaine said. She had bailed Olivia out before, hitting an ATM at three in the morning on her way down to the county courthouse in Santa Cruz. "How much money should I bring?"

"I'm afraid it's a little more serious than that. I will be recommending to the judge that Olivia be held on a one hundred thousand dollar surety bond secured by at least fifty thousand dollars in real property."

Elaine gasped. "One hundred thousand dollars? I don't have that kind of money. What in God's name did she do?"

"One hundred thousand dollars is a standard bond amount in our court, Mrs. Goodman, I can assure you. It is, actually, low in a case like this, where there is a presumption against release."

"A presumption against release? Excuse me, I'm sorry. I don't understand."

"In drug cases, there is a presumption that the defendant should not be released."

"Drug case." Elaine couldn't seem to stop repeating everything the woman said.

"Methamphetamine. As I said before. And because it's a drug case, your daughter is considered a danger to society."

The absurdity of those words woke Elaine from her shocked stupor. "A danger? That's ridiculous. Olivia's not a danger to anyone."

"Your daughter has been charged with dealing in methamphetamine, Mrs. Goodman. A very large amount of methamphetamine."

"Oh, God," Elaine whispered. "But I don't have that kind of money."

"We don't require or expect that the amount be paid to the court in cash. Most people sign a surety bond, with their homes as collateral. I am recommending that you be required to secure only fifty thousand dollars of that amount. Olivia says that you own your home, is that correct?"

"Yes."

"And are you willing to use that home as surety for your daughter?"

"I…I don't know. What does that mean?"

"What it means, Mrs. Goodman, is that if your daughter fails to appear in court, or if she does not comply with any of the many other conditions of her release, you will be expected to pay that sum to the government. If you cannot, we will take possession of your home."

Elaine closed her eyes and saw the bright pinks and purples of her lovely tended bougainvillea that had taken so many years to grow into the riot of color that now gave her such pleasure.

"I'm actually in the process of refinancing my house," she said.

Miss Watts-Thompson sniffed. "It's unlikely that you would be able to do that with a government lien on the home. Do I understand that you are unwilling to act as a surety for your daughter?"

"No!" Elaine objected. "It's just that I can't do this without talking to my fiancé. We're supposed to be buying a condo together. I just need to talk to him before I agree to do anything with the house. Isn't there some other way? Couldn't I sign for her or something? I did that that time she was arrested up in Eureka."

"I will inform the court that you are willing to act as surety for your daughter, but that you will not put up your home as security. Good day, Mrs. Goodman."

Elaine stared at the silent receiver for a moment. She had a creeping sensation that she had just done something terribly wrong, even unforgivable. Would another mother have simply said "yes"? She called Arthur at home and at work, leaving urgent messages that he call her. Only after did she realize that she hadn't asked the woman where Olivia was being held and if she could see her.

For the rest of the morning, every time the phone rang, Elaine rushed back to the storage area to pick it up. She was tremendously relieved when a man introduced himself as Olivia's lawyer. She interrupted him after a moment.

"Where is my daughter?"

"She's being held in the lockup in the federal courthouse in Oakland. Downtown. Do you know where that is?"

"Yes, I think so. The twin buildings by the freeway?"

"Exactly."

"Is she okay?"

"She's fine. Scared, but fine. She's going to have a bail hearing later today."

"Yes, I know. Someone from the courthouse called me."

"Ah, Watts-Thompson. She took all your information? Did she tell you what forms to bring to court this afternoon for the secured surety bond? You'll need your mortgage information—did she tell you that?"

Elaine paused, biting her lip. "Actually, I told her I wasn't sure about the house. You see, my fiancé and I are in the process of buying a second home in Lake Tahoe. I need to refinance my house in order to pay for my share of the condo."

Olivia's lawyer didn't say anything.

Elaine swallowed. "The woman said that she would tell the judge that I can't put up the house but that I'll sign for Olivia."

The lawyer remained silent for another moment. Then he spoke. "Mrs. Goodman, I'm not sure you really understand how serious this is. I can ask the court to allow Olivia out on an unsecured bond, but I doubt the judge will do it. In large-scale drug cases, there is a presumption against bond. That means the judge doesn't have to let her out at all."

"What did Olivia do?" Elaine asked, wincing at the shrillness of her voice.

"Maybe nothing. This seems to be something her boyfriend got involved with. It looks pretty likely that she was just along for the ride."

Elaine felt a rush of rage complicated by something embarrassingly akin to satisfaction. She had made her opinion of Jorge abundantly clear to her daughter. Yet, despite that, Olivia had insisted on staying with him. Elaine had certainly been proved right once again. "Why is her bail a hundred thousand dollars if she didn't do anything?" she said.

"Is that what Watts-Thompson told you? A hundred grand? Secured?"

"I think so. I don't know. I don't really understand any of this."

"Never mind. Listen, Ms. Goodman, this is federal court. That's actually not a particularly high bond. Even if Olivia really didn't do anything, it's going to take some time to convince the government of that. It's even possible we'll never convince them, and we'll end up making that argument to a jury. If you don't act as a surety for Olivia, she could spend a few weeks, or months, or even longer in jail."

"Oh, God."

"Do you think you'd be willing to put up your house?"

Elaine steeled herself against the panic that began to overwhelm her. "I don't know. I have to talk to my fiancé. Can't we just ask the judge if I can sign for her or something? Miss Watts-Thompson said I could do that."

"Will you at least come to court? If you're there in person, the judge might be more willing to consider letting her out," Izaya said.

Finally, she was presented with something specific she could do, a way to show her support without risking Arthur's disapproval. Relief flooded her, and she nearly smiled. "Yes! Yes, of course," she said.

Izaya Feingold-Upchurch set his telephone receiver back in its cradle, a puzzled frown creasing his broad forehead. He had been worried about pulling the bail package together quickly enough, but it had never occurred to him that the girl's mother wouldn't immediately step up. They almost always did, even the ones who should have known better—the ones whose child or grandchild had already proved to possess an all-consuming self-absorption impervious to even the most dramatic of consequences. In those cases he hated even mentioning the possibility of putting the house up as collateral. Knowing how it would end, Izaya sometimes flirted with the idea of protecting the woman—and it was almost always a woman—from her son's perfidy and her own delusions that her love had any hope at all of saving him. But the duty he owed was to his client, not to those exhausted women from whom, despite all reason, life had not yet drained the seductive elixir of hope. So he convinced Mama to put her house up and referred her to one of his friends in private practice when Junior skipped and the government came calling for its dire compensation.

Izaya smacked his hand down on his desk. His no-brainer of a bail hearing was fast becoming something else entirely. He considered the question of whether he should call the mother back. Perhaps the failure was his own. Perhaps he had not adequately communicated to her the seriousness of her daughter's predicament. He reached for the phone again, but instead of calling Olivia's mother, he called his own.

"What up, Ruthie!" he said, in the homeboy accent he'd been using with his mother ever since he'd realized, in sixth grade, how crazy it made her and how impossible it was for her ever to ask him to stop.

"Good morning, sweetie," his mother answered. "Are you having a good day?"

"I'm on duty," he said.

"Well that's always fun, right? Did you pick up anything good?"

"I think I might actually have gotten a tryable case," he said. Lately, it had begun to seem like he was never going to get in front of a jury again. Izaya had a caseload almost twice as big as that of most of his colleagues in the defender's office. This was no accident, but rather a testament to his ambition and to his relentless industry. Izaya loved the courtroom—the drama, the swiftness, the terrifyingly high stakes. Because only one in ten or even twenty of his cases ended up in front of a jury, he packed his schedule in order to maximize the possibility. Izaya spent ten to fifteen hours of every day, weekends included, in the office. This, too, was a choice. He was learning the family business on the government's dime, and when the day came that his father extended the inevitable invitation to join his firm, Izaya intended to be prepared. He felt absolutely sure that with enough experience he would one day rival his father's brilliance. He already had the man's natural talent for bullshit, combined with a capacity for hard work that was all his own. This fusion enabled him to win at least some of his cases, not necessarily common in a system where the decks were so completely stacked against the defense.

Still, despite Izaya's best efforts, it had been months since he'd had a client who hadn't provided the FBI with a thorough catalog of not merely the details of the offense for which he'd been arrested, but a wide variety of other crimes, most of which the cops never would have known about if it hadn't been for these confessional outpourings. "What part of 'everything you say can and will be held against you' didn't you understand?" Izaya would ask these men, none of whose cases he could hope to bring to trial when the piles of physical evidence were supplemented by a signed and witnessed confession to every last element of the crime. Now, at last, Izaya had a case that didn't feature a statement by the defendant. He had a case with a sympathetic client and what looked, at this point at least, like a decent chance of success. The nagging suspicion that he had already failed the bail hearing weighed heavily on his mind.

His mother said, brightly, "Well, that's wonderful, honey. I know you've been going a little stir-crazy lately."

"Yeah, no kidding. So, how's your day been?

"The usual. I don't have any more patients until this afternoon."

Izaya's mother was a therapist; she saw patients in the small,
sun-filled cottage in the backyard of the house where he'd
grown up in North Berkeley. As a little boy, he'd thought it perfectly normal to have a steady stream of women traipsing
through the garden past his sandbox and swingset, their faces
red, damp tissues clutched in their hands. The truth was, there
wasn't anything particularly unusual about it. Half his friends
had at least one parent who was a shrink. Berkeley was lousy
with them.

But there were other things that had always made Izaya different from those children. His name, Izaya Feingold, labeled
him neatly as what he was, the son of a Jewish woman and a
black father who had come together in the brief period in the
early 1970s when it had seemed like the civil rights movement
had succeeded, justice had prevailed, and racism was fast becoming a thing of the past. His parents' affair had lasted about as
long as those illusions of racial harmony, although their separation had more to do with his father's refusal to leave his wife than
with anybody's disappointment with the state of contemporary
politics. Izaya started using his father's name in his last year of
high school, the same time he had first sought contact with the
man who had all but disappeared from his life when he was a
small boy. He had considered dropping the Feingold altogether,
but his generally unflappable mother's tears at the prospect had
convinced him just to tack his father's name onto his own. So he
had become Izaya Feingold-Upchurch, a mouthful, but one that
served him well with feminist-minded young women, and, too,
with clients—both the ones who wanted a Jewish lawyer and the
ones who recognized his father's name.

"So, Mom, this case? The one that I think will go to trial? My
client's mother is giving me a hard time about posting bond."

"Really? Is that unusual?"

"Pretty. I mean, I didn't expect it. She's a white girl."

"And white people love their children more than other people?"

He laughed. "No. You know what I mean."

"I really don't." Ruth Feingold was, without question, the most politically correct woman Izaya had ever met. The walls of her house were hung with quotes from the Reverend Martin Luther King Jr. done in batik; in the winter she kept her neck warm with a *kaffiyeh* in Palestinian liberation red; and a rainbow-striped windsock fluttered from her front porch, even though she wasn't a lesbian.

"She's a middle-class kid. From Berkeley. I just would have expected her mother to do more," Izaya said.

"I don't need to tell you how many middle-class people abuse their children, do I?"

Izaya shook his head in irritation. "We're talking about not posting a hundred thousand dollar bond here to get your kid out of jail. That hardly qualifies as child abuse."

"Maybe there's some history there that you're not aware of. Or maybe the woman is a terrific mother, but she just doesn't understand how important the bond is."

"Maybe."

"You'll figure it out," she said. Ruth always expressed an utterly unshakeable belief in Izaya's abilities, confident that it was only a matter of time before her son rivaled his famous father as one of the country's leading criminal defense attorneys. Because Izaya had been, for as long as he could remember, as convinced of his mother's infallibility as she was of his brilliance, her certainty generally made his own self-confidence come easily. Today, however, Ruth's conviction inspired in him an unfamiliar sensation—anxiety. He had failed to persuade the girl's mother to put up bond and had thus failed his client. Still, Ruth's serene and unequivocal faith in him made him feel guilty for losing patience with her.

"Hey, maybe I'll come by after work today," he said. "We can watch a movie or something."

"That'll be lovely. How about if I pick us up a pizza at the Cheeseboard?"

"Great."

Izaya hung up the phone and debated whether or not to try Elaine Goodman again. He knew he should, but he dreaded the conversation that would, he insisted to himself, be pointless. There was no reason to devote more energy to this client than to any other. He had spoken to the mother; she had made her opinions known. There was surely nothing more he could do. He rubbed his face with his hands, sighed, and dug around in the papers on his desk, looking for the telephone number of the pharmacy. Before he could dial, the phone rang again.

"Izaya Feingold-Upchurch," he answered.

"Hey, Gee. This Jamal. I done changed my mind about that plea agreement. That shit ain't gonna work for me."

Izaya smiled ruefully, rocked back in his chair, and heaved his legs up on the desk.

"Jamal, how many times we going to play this back and forth? I've told you before, I'm only too happy to go to trial. I love making those asshole prosecutors earn their gold. But it ain't my ass that's going to end up in Lompoc doing a mandatory twenty if we lose. You plead, it's a guaranteed ten. That's half, Jamal. Now, you know and I know how strong the case they got against you. Is it worth ten years off your life just to give the government a workout? Maybe it is. Hell, it might be to me, if I was in your shoes. But it's not me that has to decide, Jamal. And we are running out of time."

"Twenty years," Jamal said.

"You know it."

"That a long time, Gee."

"Yes it is."

"Ten years ain't no vacation, neither."

"Nope."

"But it sho' ain't no twenty."

"Nope."

"Let me ask you this. I know you a good lawyer. Ain't no way you could get me off? Some kind of technicality; some shit like that."

There was no question in Izaya's mind. "Sorry, man," he said.

The buzz of the silent telephone line filled Izaya's ear, and he fought the urge to hiss back at the guards he knew taped his client's jailhouse telephone conversations.

Finally Jamal sighed and said, "Take the plea, Gee. Just take it."

By the time Izaya had put out that fire and the others that followed, there wasn't time to call Elaine Goodman again before her daughter's hearing.

When she was led back to the holding area after her meeting with her lawyer, Olivia saw two men sitting on a bench in one of the cells. The guard put her in the adjacent cell and walked out of the room. She and the men were separated only by a wall of bars. She looked at them. One, with dark hair and a thin, pockmarked face, appeared to be Latino. She opened her mouth to say something to him in Spanish when the second man spoke.

"Hey, honey. How about I stick my dick through these here bars and you blow me good?"

Olivia jumped and stared at the man. He was beefy, red-faced, and his biceps bulged out of the rolled-up sleeves of his orange jumpsuit. His arms were vandalized by blue, crudely drawn tattoos. He smiled at her, and she could see his gray, jagged teeth. A white string of saliva connected his upper and lower lips. It wobbled and broke as he stuck his tongue out at her and flicked it in and out of his mouth. Olivia heard a soft whimper. It was a moment before she realized that she had made the feeble sound.

With a bang, the door to the room opened. The guard stomped to a row of plastic chairs propped against the wall outside the cells. He sat down, took a rolled-up newspaper out of his pocket, and snapped it open. The inmate winked at Olivia, stretched out on the bench, and began to snore.

Olivia moved to the other side of her cell, stopping her nose against the smell of the chemical toilet. She wanted to close her eyes, too, but every time she did, her mind filled with the vision of a thick red tongue, a bead of saliva. She sat curled into a ball on the hard bench, afraid even to blink.

The magistrate judge's courtroom in the United States District Court for the Northern District of California had no windows. It was a small, elegantly appointed, wood-paneled room with rows of benches and a raised dais facing two wooden library tables. Elaine arrived early and sat in the rearmost row. She had gone home to change her clothes, and in her best suit, a moss green Anne Klein with a straight skirt that stopped just below her knee, she felt professional and confident. The judge would know, just by looking at her, that she was not the mother of a drug dealer. He would see Olivia for what she was, a confused young girl, the victim of some kind of misunderstanding. He would release her into her mother's care, where she belonged.

Elaine was the first person in the room other than a young black woman, her hair elaborately braided, her two-inch-long fingernails painted gold, who sat at a table immediately below the judge's bench, busy with a tall stack of papers and a highlighter. She glanced up once at Elaine, her face expressionless, and thereafter ignored her. After a few moments, the woman with the gold nails left the room through a door behind the judge's bench. A heavyset olive-skinned woman in her mid-sixties came in the rear door. Her eyes darted nervously around the room, settling finally on Elaine.

"This is court?" she asked.

Elaine nodded. The woman settled on to the bench in front of Elaine with a grunt. She turned around and said, "I here for my son." She waited for Elaine's reply. Elaine didn't provide the reason for her own presence in that room; she just turned up the very corners of her lips in something that might be called a smile. The woman's face crumpled a bit and she turned back around. Elaine stared for a while at the back of the older woman's neck. The collar of her cotton blouse gaped, and her skin looked damp and tight, stretched over a thick roll of fat.

The door to the courtroom opened, and two men wearing brush cuts and identical navy-blue suits walked in. They were leading two other men, both of whom wore handcuffs and shackles. It took a moment for Elaine to recognize Jorge. She'd only seen him a few times, and, while he had always struck her as shy and unassuming, never had he looked this cowed and disheveled. His head was bowed, and when he raised his eyes and met Elaine's his face darkened, a flush appearing under his light-brown skin. He nodded at her once, and she turned away. She kept her eyes affixed to the American flag that hung to the side of the judge's bench as the FBI agents unlocked Jorge's handcuffs and seated him in the first row behind the little wooden gate that separated the front of the court from the rows of benches.

As Elaine stared at the flag, the Pledge of Allegiance automatically ran through her mind as though she were a child standing at attention in the beginning of a school day. She closed her eyes. She opened them only when she heard Olivia's voice.

"Mom?"

Elaine snapped her head around to the door. Olivia, also in handcuffs, was walking into the room.

"No talking," said the man leading her, his voice not as gruff as his words.

Elaine nearly moaned aloud as she watched Olivia being led up to the front of the room and pushed into a seat across the aisle from Jorge. Elaine watched her daughter try to make eye contact with her boyfriend, who kept his head down and his eyes fixed firmly to the floor.

The door to the courtroom opened again, and a young, light-skinned black man with long gnarled braids loped in. One of the FBI agents rolled his eyes. The black man hustled up the aisle and leaned into the row where Olivia sat.

"Hey, Olivia. How're you holding up?" he asked.

Elaine felt a quick flash of concern, and then flushed in embarrassment. She told herself it was Izaya's youth that took her aback, not that she had expected him to be white. She felt almost irritated at the young man for having such a Jewish-sounding name, though she knew she couldn't have been the first person to have made that mistake.

Izaya looked across the courtroom at Elaine. "Ms. Goodman?" he called, his voice booming in the almost silent room.

Elaine nodded. Izaya patted Olivia on the shoulder and strode down the aisle to Elaine's seat.

"Hi," he said. "In a minute the magistrate judge will come in. Have you given any more thought to using your house as security? It would really help me to get your daughter out of jail."

Elaine's mouth felt dry, like sand. She wanted to say yes. She wanted to assure this young man that he could say whatever was necessary to help Olivia; that she was willing to do whatever it took. But she couldn't. She hadn't reached Arthur. It just didn't feel right to make this decision, one that affected him, too, without his input. Moreover, it didn't make sense to her that all this should really be necessary. Once she spoke to the judge, once he realized who she was, what she was, he would let Olivia

come home. "I want to do that signing thing the pretrial services woman talked about," she said.

Izaya sighed. "Right. Okay. We'll give it a shot."

At that moment, another group of people walked into the
courtroom, one of them a tiny woman who wobbled down the
aisle, perched on high spiky heels. Her large behind was
crammed into a black leather skirt and her breasts overflowed
out of the plunging neckline of a purple ruffled shirt. She batted her Tammy Faye Baker eyes at Olivia's lawyer.

"Izaya," she said in a squeak.

"Madame Watts-Thompson. A pleasure as always. Let's talk
pretrial release." He took the little woman's arm and walked up
the aisle and through the wooden gate, leaving a gape-mouthed
Elaine. *That* was the woman who would determine if Olivia
would be released on bail? Elaine watched the simpering Miss
Watts-Thompson arrange her files and folders on one of the
wooden tables. Izaya sat on the table, one shiny-shod foot resting on the edge of the woman's chair, and leaned over her, whispering and occasionally motioning in either Olivia's or Elaine's
direction. They were still deep in conversation when the clerk
with the gold fingernails entered the courtroom and announced
the judge.

Elaine was halfway to her feet when the judge mumbled,
"Remain seated." The fat lady sitting in front of her sat back
down with an audible groan. The judge was a younger man than
she had expected, no more than thirty-five, pink-skinned and
puffy-faced. He had cut himself shaving, and wore his black
robes with an air of self-importance somewhat marred by the
large Band-Aid stuck to his chin. As he spoke, he patted at the
Band-Aid without seeming to be aware that he was doing so.

"What do we have before us this morning, Miss Jones?"

The court clerk shuffled the papers on her table, held one up
in a gold-taloned hand, and announced, "United States versus
Goodman." The phrase chilled Elaine. All at once, it didn't seem

as certain that the judge would simply thump his gavel and let Elaine take her daughter home. It sounded as if the entire country stood in judgment and condemnation of her little girl. Olivia rose and stumbled through the gate to the podium. She stood next to her lawyer, looking impossibly small and innocent.

"Izaya Feingold-Upchurch, your honor, seeking appointment to represent Miss Goodman."

The judge glanced down at a piece of paper. "The Federal Public Defender's office is hereby appointed. Mr. Feingold-Upchurch, would you like to be heard on the issue of bail?"

Elaine could see only Olivia's and Izaya's backs as they stood facing the judge's bench. Olivia's shoulders were hunched, and she had her arms crossed over her chest. Elaine could barely resist the urge to run up and whisper to Olivia to put her arms down. She recognized that stance. Olivia always crossed her arms like that when she was feeling most vulnerable. As a child she'd stood like that whenever she was in trouble, whenever Elaine had caught her sneaking candy bars or watching television before she'd done her homework. Elaine wanted to call out to the judge that her daughter only *looked* defiant and angry; that in truth, she was overwhelmed with panic and fear.

"Your honor, my client has exemplary ties to the community. Her mother, a pharmacist who lives and works in Berkeley, has agreed to act as surety for her daughter," Izaya said.

Elaine listened closely as he described Olivia's job, her lack of a "serious" criminal record, the steadiness of Elaine's own life. The lawyer spoke fluidly and convincingly, and Elaine felt herself grow calm again. She felt a rising confidence that the judge couldn't help but be persuaded.

When Izaya finished speaking, the judge turned to a young woman sitting at one of the wooden tables. "Ms. Steele, what's the government looking for here?"

The prosecutor rose to her feet. She was a tall, angular woman with thick blond hair cut in a prim, chin-length bob.

She had a long nose and wore just a trace of pink lipstick on her unsmiling mouth. Her clothes were impeccable; a black, expensively tailored jacket worn over a silk sweater in pink so pale it was almost white. Her skirt stopped just above her knee, revealing thin legs clad in sheer white stockings. Elaine glanced down at the attorney's feet. Her mother had always said you could tell a lot about a woman by the state of her shoes. The prosecutor's shoes were black leather pumps polished to a shine. They looked very expensive.

"Your honor, Amanda Steele on behalf of the United States. The government will defer to pretrial services, but doesn't feel that bail is appropriate, given the defendant's criminal history and the seriousness of the charges."

Izaya started to speak, obviously angry, but the judge raised his hand. "Let's hear from pretrial services."

Miss Watts-Thompson leapt to her feet. "Good morning, your honor. I've made a very thorough investigation of this case, and my recommendation is in accordance with Miss Steele's view. I might have suggested a secured surety bond, however Miss Goodman's mother told me quite certainly that she is not comfortable with using her home as security."

Elaine was astonished. She had been sure that the flirtatious little woman would do whatever Izaya asked. She flushed angrily at the mischaracterization of her statements. Olivia turned her head to her mother, and Elaine was horrified to see how shocked she looked, the tears spilling from her eyes. Elaine shook her head, silenced by the enforced hush of the courtroom but wanting desperately to explain to Olivia, and to the entire court, that she *was* willing to help her daughter. Olivia turned away.

The pretrial services officer continued, "This individual has a history of political agitation and criminal conduct. She's been arrested on numerous occasions and has been found guilty of two misdemeanors. Her mother informed me that she is engaging in illegal union-organizing conduct here in Oakland."

Elaine flushed, horrified at the woman's words. She averted her eyes from Olivia's anguished stare. The woman continued, "Her employers tell me that this behavior has prompted them to consider terminating her. Her ties to the community are tenuous—she has only recently returned from extended travels in Mexico. It is my firm belief that should she be released she would immediately go underground, using her political connections to engineer an escape to Mexico or even Cuba."

"Cuba? Oh, for God's sake," Izaya interjected. "This is ridiculous, your honor. Olivia Goodman isn't a member of the Weather Underground. She's a mixed-up kid with a lousy boyfriend. I don't know what her mother is talking about, but despite what Cru— Miss Watts-Thompson seems to imagine, labor organizing is not illegal. It is, in fact, a time-honored American tradition. Moreover, none of those baseless allegations have any bearing on..."

"Counsel," the judge interrupted, "you will have your time to respond. Miss Watts-Thompson, have you anything further?"

"No, that's all, Judge," she said with a flutter of her sticky eyelashes.

"Is it in fact the case that the mother is unwilling to post bond?"

Elaine rose to her feet in protest, but sat down again under the stern eye of the courtroom deputy.

Miss Watts-Thompson said, "The mother is willing to sign for her daughter, however she does not feel sufficiently confident to put up her house as surety."

Izaya started to object, but the judge hushed him with a raised hand. "Well, if her own mother doesn't trust her, I can't imagine why I should."

Elaine could bear it no longer. She stood up and walked forward. She cleared her throat nervously. Before she could speak, she heard Izaya's voice. "Olivia's mother is perfectly willing to act as a surety for her daughter, your honor. The only problem is the house. She is in the process of getting a second mortgage in order to buy a vacation home. The surety bond would preclude that."

"Ah. A vacation home," the judge said, his eyebrows raised.

By now, Elaine stood at the little wooden gate directly behind the podium. Olivia's back was rigid, and she refused to look at her mother.

"Excuse me," Elaine whispered, tugging on Izaya's jacket.

"Are you Miss Goodman's mother?" the judge asked.

Elaine looked up. Her throat and mouth felt dry and thick. "Yes," she croaked.

"Is this true? Are you unwilling to use your home as security for your daughter's release?"

"No, sir. I mean, no, it's not true. I didn't realize…I mean, yes, I'll put up my house."

Izaya, looking over his shoulder, smiled at her.

"Your honor," he said, "it's my impression that Mrs. Goodman was simply not aware of the seriousness of this case. She was under the impression that a simple signature would be enough. Now that she understands what's going on, it appears that she's willing to act as a surety and use her home as security."

The judge looked at Miss Watts-Thompson, his eyebrows raised.

The little woman's breast heaved with indignation, and she shot Elaine a dirty look. "I fully explained all this to the mother, and she wasn't interested."

"Well, she seems to be interested now," said the judge. "Does that influence your recommendation?"

She shook her head, her bouffant trembling, one of the clips holding it perilously close to falling out. "Not at all. Not at all. There's still the criminal history, the lack of ties to the community."

The judge looked back at Izaya who said, "Olivia was a student activist. A *non-violent* student activist. This supposed criminal history consists of getting arrested for sitting in at the dean's office. Hugging trees. She's lived her entire life in Berkeley and Oakland. Her mother lives here. What more ties to the community could Miss Watts-Thompson possibly require?"

"If I might, your honor?" the prosecutor spoke in a quiet, reasonable voice.

"By all means, Ms. Steele," the judge said.

"The government might be satisfied with a surety bond secured by Mrs. Goodman's house if there were some further limitations placed on the defendant to ensure her compliance with the requirements of pretrial services and her presence in court."

"Continue."

"We might consider a bond if the defendant were compelled to reside with her mother."

"Would that be possible, Mrs. Goodman?" the judge asked.

Elaine looked away from the judge, down at her hands knotted in front of her. "Yes," she whispered, and then, embarrassed at the tentative sound of her voice, she said it again, more firmly. "Yes, of course Olivia can live with me."

"If the court is considering bond against the specific recommendation of pretrial services," said Miss Watts-Thompson, her voice tight with anger, "we ask that at the very least the defendant be placed in an inpatient drug-treatment facility."

"That's absurd, your honor," Izaya interjected, shaking his head, "There's no reason whatsoever to think Miss Goodman is addicted to drugs."

"She's charged with drug dealing!" said Miss Watts-Thompson.

"First of all, she's been *charged*, not found guilty, and second of all, that doesn't mean she's a drug user."

The prosecutor's voice was again calm and reasonable, and somehow more dangerous for all that. "The government would be satisfied with drug testing."

"Fine," the judge said. "I'm going to order a surety bond of one hundred thousand dollars, secured by fifty thousand dollars in real property, with the further condition that the defendant reside with her mother and undergo periodic, random drug testing."

Izaya thanked the court and led Olivia back to her seat. As she passed by her mother, Olivia scowled and looked away. Elaine stood for a moment, facing her daughter, then turned and walked quickly down the aisle, back to her own seat.

Neither Jorge nor the other man were granted bail. Their appearances lasted no more than a minute or two, and then the judge left the courtroom. The officer who had escorted Olivia led her back up the aisle. As she passed, Elaine called, "I'll have you out in a minute, honey. Don't worry." Olivia said nothing.

Elaine went up to the front of the courtroom and found Izaya. "Can I sign the papers now and take her home?"

"I'm afraid it's a little more complicated than that. Come up to my office and I'll have a paralegal give you all the forms you'll need to fill out. It's going to take a couple of days to get it all together."

Elaine was stunned. "A couple of *days*?" she said.

Olivia stood in the hallway outside the courtroom, tears of rage dripping down her cheeks, into the neck of her shirt. She reached up with her handcuffed hands and wiped her nose on her wrist. She tried to slow her breathing down, convinced she was beginning to hyperventilate. Why had she ever expected her mother to save her? Clearly, Elaine didn't trust her. She didn't want to put up the bail because she was afraid Olivia would abscond. And God knew the last thing Elaine wanted was to have her fuck-up of a daughter living in her house again.

Olivia wiped her tear-dampened wrists on her jeans and looked up to find Jorge being led out of the courtroom by two men in navy suits.

"Jorge!" she shouted. She'd never seen him look like this. His face was bloodless and one of his eyes looked puffy, as if he'd been punched. His hair, usually so meticulously tended, hung in greasy strings down his cheeks. His jeans were torn at the knee, and Olivia imagined that she could see blood staining the ragged fabric. She had tried to talk to him in the courtroom, but the guard shook his head at her in warning, and Jorge refused even to look at her. She assumed he was simply terrified. He had to be. The *federales* in Mexico would just as soon rob, beat, or kill you as arrest you. How was Jorge to know that things were different in the United States?

"Jorge, are you okay?"

"No talking!" said one of the blue-suited men, jerking Jorge's arm and shoving him away down the hall. Jorge turned back to look at Olivia and mouthed something. She couldn't make out what he said. She shook her head frantically to show him that she hadn't understood, but by then he'd turned back around. Olivia's own escort came over now, took her arm again, and led her down the hall in the opposite direction.

Olivia tried to figure out what it was that Jorge had had been trying to say to her. Had he attempted to communicate something about what she should or should not tell the cops or her lawyer? Or had it been an apology, a simple "*lo siento*"? She was desperate to speak to him, and at the same time she wanted to slap him in the face for his stupidity. The nightmare into which his ridiculous *machismo* had forced them both enraged her. Why hadn't he been satisfied with letting her work for the both of them? Why had he put them both in this terrifying position?

Olivia turned to her guard. "Where am I going now? When do I get out?"

He looked at her, his kindly face belying the gruffness in his tone. "It usually takes a couple of days to set up the bond. There are papers your mother's going to have to collect and file with the court. Then the judge has to review everything. While you're waiting, you'll be transferred over to the county jail in Martinez with the other female federal prisoners awaiting trial."

Olivia nodded. She wasn't surprised at the delay. In fact, it wouldn't surprise her if her mother never came through at all.

Doubtless, Elaine thought that it would teach Olivia a lesson to sit in jail until Izaya could get the charges against her dismissed.

Olivia told herself that she didn't care; she could handle county jail. She'd done it before. She could do it again.

She had not counted, however, on the smell. She had remembered the interminable noise of several hundred women, all talking and fighting and breathing, of the guards' boots clomping on the floor, of their keys jangling and the doors clanging. She had remembered the misery of trying to sleep in a cell that never got even remotely dark, the lights in the hallway intruding like the persistent reproach of a guilty conscience. She had remembered the suppressed fear that the woman in front of you might suddenly decide you'd disrespected her in some way and needed a schooling. But she had forgotten all about the smell. Or maybe, back in Santa Cruz and up in Humboldt, it hadn't been so unbearably foul. Maybe there the vile stench of poorly washed bodies, of sewage and sour food, had been better concealed by the acrid fumes of disinfectant. She spent her first morning of confinement at the women's facility in Martinez hunched over a reeking toilet, vomiting, until her dry heaves brought up nothing but a trickle of hot, yellow bile.

"Disgusting bitch. What's your problem?" a groggy voice asked, not entirely unpleasantly.

Olivia wiped her mouth with the back of her hand and stood up, leaning a palm against the sticky white tile wall to steady herself.

"I'm sorry," she said. "It's the smell, I guess."

The woman snorted. "Get used to it, girl." She was lying on her stomach, her chin propped in her hands, a large woman with dark brown, heavily freckled skin. Her kinky hair was dyed a bright maroon and hung over one of her shoulders—a mass of braids tied with black thread. Her lips were thick and perfectly shaped, her broad nose was pierced with a tiny gold stud, and her manicured fingernails were painted metallic blue with flecks of silver—all except the right index finger, which was torn and ragged. As she gazed at Olivia she chewed on the cuticle of that finger. She licked away the bead of dark red blood that appeared at the corner of the nail.

Olivia gagged again and ran for the bowl.

"Tell you what," the woman laughed. "You pregnant."

"No!" Olivia said, almost in a shout. "It's just the smell. It makes me sick."

"You pregnant, girl." She nodded. "That why you so sensitive to the smell. It might smell like a sack of granddaddies in here, but if you puking, you pregnant."

Could it be true? When had she last gotten her period? Olivia started doing frantic calculations in her head and realized with a sinking feeling that she'd missed it altogether this month. But she and Jorge had been careful—the few times they'd failed to use birth control she'd been sure it was safe. She couldn't be pregnant.

Before Olivia had left him in San Miguel de Allende, she and Jorge had played with the idea of the sweet little baby they could make together. They had compiled a list of names that would work in both English and Spanish: Carla, Sofia, and Isabel, Pablo, Roberto, and Ezekiel. It was a kind of flirtation, with only the faintest blush of possibility, enough to make it entertaining but not so much as to alarm her. On the plane home, when she'd assumed she would never see Jorge again, Olivia had found herself, to her surprise, longing for a baby. She had fantasized about stepping off the plane, a round, brown bundle hanging in a brightly colored sling from her shoulder. She had enjoyed the thought of her mother's shocked and horrified face, at how Elaine would have tried to pretend that the idea of a half-Mexican grandchild didn't dismay her. When Jorge had shown up at Olivia's door in Oakland, they'd both become too immersed in the brutal practicalities of earning a living to allow themselves even the illusory expenditures of an imaginary baby. Now, sitting in the long narrow cell surrounded by strange women, Olivia was sickened by the revived image of that fantasy child, smiling from the nest of a sling woven from rainbow-colored *campesino* fabric.

"I'm not pregnant," she said firmly.

"Shut the fuck up!" shouted an angry voice from one of the other bunks. The tiny cell held six, three against either wall. All were occupied by women huddled under light-blue blankets. Whenever one of them rolled over, or even turned her head, her vinyl-covered mattress creaked in protest. Olivia's scratchy polyester sheet had slipped off the corner of her mattress, and the discovered smell of urine from the soiled vinyl was what had first sent her tumbling off the bunk and running to the toilet.

Olivia closed her mouth, sick with fear at angering the others trying to sleep.

"What your name, girl?" The woman with the braids said, loudly.

"I said shut the fuck up!" bellowed one of the pale-blue lumps.

A chorus of groans filled the cell, and Olivia felt the gorge rise in her throat. She covered her mouth with her hand and tried to swallow the saliva that filled her mouth. Suddenly, with a clang, the cell door sprung open to let the women know that it was time to get up and out. Olivia heard howls of protest coming from the cells up and down the long hallway. A few of the women in her cell woke up, sitting up on their bunks and rubbing the sleep from their eyes. Nobody looked at her except the woman with the braids.

"Are you deaf?" the woman asked.

Olivia jumped and answered, "No. Sorry. My name is Olivia."

"I'm Queenie."

"You ain't no queen, bitch. You just a ugly old skank." The speaker jumped down from her upper bunk and towered over

Olivia. Her skin was the yellow of burnt milk, and her hair stood up from her head in twisted little peaks. Her arms were covered in thick ropy scars and open sores, the bright pink color of which was the only thing that looked alive on her sallow skin. Her open mouth revealed broken brown teeth, and the stench of her breath sent Olivia scrambling toward the toilet once more.

"Get yo' ugly white face out my toilet," the angry woman said, pushing Olivia out of her way. She sat down, screwed her face up, and with a grunt let loose a raucous, trumpeting series of farts.

Queenie snorted in disgust and leapt out of bed. "You best get out of here before that smell kill your baby."

Olivia followed the line of women to the row of sinks. She had no toothbrush, so she rinsed her mouth and scrubbed a shaking finger across her teeth. The women were talking and laughing. No one spoke to her. No one looked at her. In fact, the only time she hadn't felt like a shadow was when Queenie had spoken to her. Then, and when she had first arrived at the jail. In the intake room, she had bent over in response to the female guard's order and, gripping a buttock in either hand, spread herself open. The guard had stared at her silently, the seconds crawling by. Olivia felt her secret, soft wrinkled parts shrinking and cringing under the glare of the fluorescent lights. Finally, the guard grunted, "Squat down and cough." Olivia sank to the ground, her anus sore from the unfamiliar sensation of being stretched. When she had finally been given permission to dress, she had done so with clumsy, disgusted fingers, trying not to touch any part of herself that the guard had seen.

Olivia splashed her face, thrilling to the shock of the cold clean water. She trudged along in the line of women to the cafeteria and gagged at the sight of the mound of pale gelatinous eggs giving way to the metal spoon of the cafeteria worker with a sickening slurp. She shook her head at the offered portion and again when presented with a clot of mucilaginous grey oatmeal. She took only a piece of cold, hard toast, slick with margarine. The smell of the scorched coffee made her stomach roil, so she left her plastic mug empty. She saw Queenie sit down and almost put her tray down next to hers, but the angry woman from their cell slid quickly into the empty seat. Olivia sat alone at a long Formica table, hunched over her plate, chewing on each bite of toast for so long that it turned to thin paste in her mouth.

After a while, she followed the line of women out of the cafeteria to a large room furnished with a few rows of plastic chairs hitched together with thick metal bars. Olivia sat in a chair at the end of a row. She fixed her eyes on the television set. Sally Jesse Raphael was interviewing an obese mother and daughter who had agreed to undergo gastric bypass together on television. Olivia wished, harder than she had ever wished for anything in her life, that she were a grotesquely fat girl in an Enrique Iglesias T-shirt with lank brown hair sitting in a TV studio. She wished that she and her mother could embark together on something no more horrible than the irrevocable mutilation of their internal organs. She wished she were anybody other than herself. For hour after hour, Olivia watched television shows chosen by the other women in the room. She did not speak. She did not move. She tried to breathe as silently as possible.

When Elaine arrived home from Olivia's bail hearing, she found Arthur waiting for her in the kitchen. He had made a pitcher of margaritas and had chicken breasts marinating on the counter. Elaine buried her head in his chest for a moment, and then sat down on a stool. She gulped down her drink.

"What in God's name is going on?" he asked. "I played your message, like, ten times. Livvy got arrested for selling drugs? I can't believe it. I mean, blowing up the Federal Building, maybe, but drug dealing? That doesn't sound like her."

Elaine wiped the salt from her lips and launched into the story. When she got to the part about the security bond and the house, Arthur stood up. He crossed the room and pulled a pile of papers out from under the telephone. He looked at them for a moment, and then, suddenly, tore them down the middle. Elaine jumped and felt the tequila rise up to the back of her throat. She covered her mouth with her hand.

"So much for Tahoe," Arthur said, and crumpled up the torn pieces of the mortgage refinancing documents.

"Oh Arthur, I'm sorry. I really am. But what could I do? I mean, really, I didn't have a choice."

"Of course you didn't," he said. Something in his tone made Elaine look up. He glanced away.

"What?" she said.

"Nothing."

"No, really. Did I do the wrong thing?"

He didn't answer.

"Arthur! Please. Don't do this. Not now. What are you trying to tell me? Are you telling me I should have left her to rot in jail?"

He stood up, crossed the room, and jerked open the fridge. "Of course not," he said, then gulped down some orange juice from a cardboard container.

Elaine closed her eyes. He knew she hated when he did that.

He wiped his mouth on his sleeve. "I just can't believe that you would do this without discussing it with me, without even telling me."

"I tried to call."

"Why did you need to do it right away? You could have waited a day. Or even an hour. You know how much the Tahoe place meant to me. It would have been *ours*, Elaine. Not mine. Not yours. Ours."

"I'm sorry, Arthur. I'm so sorry."

He leaned across the counter and took her chin in his hand. "Look, it's none of my business what you do with your money, or what you do with your daughter, for that matter, but I just have to say one thing."

"What?"

"I can't stand to see you continuing to deny yourself the things you deserve. You've been incredibly good to that girl. You've bailed her out of catastrophe after catastrophe ever since she was two years old. When is it going to be your turn?"

"I don't know," she whispered.

"You've got to confront the fact that maybe that's part of the problem."

"What is?"

"That you've always been there for her to land on. Maybe if you weren't always there waiting to pick up the pieces, she might have learned to land on her own two feet. Maybe what Olivia has needed all along is a little tough love."

Elaine didn't answer. In some ways she knew he was right, but she couldn't forget the betrayal in Olivia's eyes when her lawyer had announced to the entire courtroom that Elaine wasn't willing to put her house up to post her daughter's bond.

She reached for his hand and held it tightly. "You're right. I know you're right. But this isn't the time to teach her a lesson. After this is over, I'm going to sit down with her and tell her that enough is enough. I am. Really."

He nodded and squeezed her hand in return.

"There's one more thing," Elaine said. She hesitated, watching his face. "As part of her bond, she's going to have to live here with us."

Arthur stared at her for a moment and then got up and began slicing the raw chicken meat, smacking the cleaver down on the cutting board. The force of the blows made the ice in the pitcher of margaritas tinkle and chime.

Olivia spent her four days and three nights in jail trying to make herself tiny, mute, and invisible. She refused Queenie's repeated offer of a joint, afraid that one of the many guards would see her or that they would haul her away for her court-mandated drug testing. She kept her gaze low, avoiding eye contact with everyone. Once, walking down the hall to her cell, she saw a small dark woman cowering against the cell bars. Two fat women with bleached-blond hair were leaning against her, rifling through her clothes. One had her knee jammed between the weeping woman's legs. A guard watched impassively from the end of the hall, saying nothing until the blondes had taken a pack of cigarettes away from the small woman and let her go. Only then had he shouted, "Okay, break it up, ladies."

The woman, still crying, walked quickly by Olivia. Their eyes met for a moment, and Olivia opened her mouth, wanting to offer some words of comfort and commiseration. But she could not. Instead, she looked away and hurried on down the hall.

That night Olivia lay in her bunk, her eyes gritty with insomnia and aching from the glare of the ever-present fluorescent lights. Her skin felt like a suit that had shrunk in the wash, and she was overcome by an almost irresistible urge to slice herself open, to escape from the confines of her own body. She began to writhe in her bed, tangling her legs in the coarse acrylic blanket. Suddenly she squeezed her hand into a fist and slammed it into her forehead above her left eye. The dull ache it left quieted her somehow. With an almost clinical detachment, she did it again. The urge to flee subsided enough for her to stop her tortured wiggling, and she tried consciously to loosen the contracted muscles of her legs and back. Olivia wondered if she were losing her mind.

On the fourth day she was in the common room, staring vacantly at the television, when she heard a voice call her name. She looked around and saw a female guard with lips pursed in a disagreeable scowl.

"Olivia Goodman?" the guard asked.

"Yes," Olivia said, in a small voice, hope fluttering in her chest.

"Right. Get your stuff."

"I don't have anything," Olivia said.

The guard looked at her curiously and then shrugged her shoulders. "Come on."

Olivia followed her down the hall, through a gate, and into an elevator. The guard led her into a small room where another woman handed Olivia her clothes. She changed quickly, gingerly pulling on the sour-smelling jeans and sweatshirt. The guard then led her down another corridor and through a series of interlocking gates. Finally, she stood in small passage, at the end of which was a large green steel door.

The guard stood silently, and after a few moments, the door buzzed. She pushed against it and it opened onto the street. Olivia walked through, and it clanged shut behind her. She stood, blinking in the sudden bright light. She had not been outside since the night she was arrested. She raised her face to the sun, closing her eyes against the glare. The back of her eyelids glowed red, and she breathed deeply. Standing in the street, hemmed in by the freeway on one side and on the other the jail's towering cement walls, punctuated with narrow slits, Olivia had a sensation of soaring across infinite space. She raised her arms slightly and made as if to spin around in a circle. The blare of a car horn jerked her eyes open. She looked down the block and saw her mother's Honda Accord parked on the other side of the street. As she watched, the car pulled out of its parking spot and drove slowly toward her. Olivia took another deep breath, then ran across the street to the car and opened the passenger door. She got in and slammed the door.

"Please, get me out of here as fast as you can," she said.

Her mother reached across the seat and hugged Olivia with one awkward arm. Olivia stiffened. When she was a very little girl, she would wrap her arms and legs around Elaine's neck and waist, clinging as hard as she could to her elusive mother. By the time Olivia was a teenager, however, she learned to prefer the comfort of a long string of more or less willing boys to that of the woman who had never seemed at ease in her embrace. By now, Olivia had grown as uneasy with her mother's touch as her mother had always been with hers.

"Are you all right?" Elaine asked.

"Just peachy."

"Was it horrible?"

Suddenly Olivia wanted to reach across the seat and slap her mother across the face. Instead, she said, "You don't want to know how it was. You want me to say that it wasn't too bad, that I'm fine. You don't want to hear about how the women fuck the guards in exchange for drugs or how I spent half of every day puking because the place stinks like shit and Lysol."

Elaine inhaled sharply through her nose and stared straight ahead. They rode in silence for a while. Despite herself, tears filled Olivia's eyes. She ignored them, and they streamed down her cheeks. She imagined that she could hear the plip plop as they fell from her chin into her lap.

"Did anyone hurt you?" Elaine whispered.

Olivia's anger left her in a rush, like air escaping a torn balloon. "No," she said. "It was disgusting in there, Mama. I can't go back."

"You won't have to go back."

Olivia nodded and flipped down the mirror in the sun shade. Her hair hung in grease-stiffened curls. Her face was mottled and her normally smooth cheeks and forehead were dotted with pimples.

They continued up the freeway and into Oakland in silence. When the car pulled up in front of Olivia's apartment, Elaine said, "Should I wait here while you get your things, or do you want me to come in and help you?"

It was only then that Olivia realized that she was, of course, going to her mother's house. To her surprise, she felt intense relief at not having to stay alone in the home she had shared with Jorge.

"Wait here," she said. "I won't take too long."

Olivia ran up the path to her apartment. When she got to the door, she realized that she had no keys. She tried the knob. It was locked. "Fuck," she said softly, and began searching for a rock to break a window. She was bent over, rummaging through the dirt under the front window, when she felt something cold and wet on the small of her back. She startled and turned around to find her neighbor's rottweiler puppy. She kneeled down, scooped the wriggling black dog into her arms, and buried her face in the soft fur of its neck.

"Hey," a voice said.

Olivia looked up and saw the puppy's owner. He wore baggy black cotton pants with zippers and snaps in random places, and his hair was a sea urchin of short dreadlocks.

"Hi," Olivia said.

"You okay?"

"Yeah. I'm locked out."

"I know," he said. "Mother-fucking 5-0 left the door wide open the other night. After they cleared out, I locked it for you. Your keys was on the kitchen counter." He stuck out his hand and dangled Olivia's key chain with the Virgin of Guadeloupe marble hanging from the ring.

"You went into my apartment?" she said.

The young man's face grew hard. He dropped the keys on the ground next to Olivia and backed away.

"I didn't take nothing," he said, and whistled for his dog. "C'mon 8-Ball."

"No! Wait!" Olivia struggled to her feet. "I'm sorry. I didn't mean that how it sounded. Thank you. Really, thanks for locking the door."

The man seemed to relax.

"You out on bond?" he said.

"Yeah," she said.

"Federal or state?"

"Federal."

"Yeah. Fucking DEA. My cousin's at Lompoc doing twenty years on a bullshit DEA crack bust."

"*Twenty years?*"

"Mandatory fucking minimums."

"Jesus," Olivia said. "What did he do? I mean, what was he convicted of?"

"Nothin'. He wasn't convicted of nothin'. Pled guilty."

"He pled? Why?" The young man rolled his eyes, and Olivia blushed but continued, "I mean, if it was bullshit."

"It *was* bullshit. All the fool did was *introduce* people. Ricky, meet Montel. Montel, meet Ricky. Thas it."

"And he went to jail for *that*?" Olivia began to panic. He had to have it wrong. You didn't go to jail for *introducing* people. "He didn't, like, *buy* crack or something? Or help those guys buy it?"

"Girl, the fool never *touched* the shit."

"Oh, God."

"They want you in jail, you in jail. Thas it. You don't need to do nothin'."

"Oh, God," she whispered, again.

"Mother fuckers got me for a bullshit note-drop bank robbery."

"You were in jail?"

"Three and a half years. Federal time."

"And you're out now." Olivia desperately wanted to ask him what it had been like, how he'd survived, but she was afraid he would think her question pushy, or, worse, trite.

"Yeah. I'm out. Supervised release. You want some help getting your stuff?"

Olivia started to refuse but saw his face threatening to close up again. "Sure," she said. "I'm Olivia."

"Treyvon. This 8-Ball." The puppy wriggled its entire body in ecstasy at the sound of its own name.

Together they walked into the apartment. Olivia, her mind whirring with what Treyvon had told her about his cousin, stood forlornly in the middle of the room, staring around her at the havoc wrought by the police. The belongings strewn about, torn and broken on the floors, looked absolutely unfamiliar to her. She knew, of course, that that piece of pink fabric was her corduroy shirt, but it seemed utterly strange. She nudged a can of soup she didn't remember buying with her toe, and it rolled across the pitted and scratched wood floor. It bumped into a hairbrush and stopped. She walked across the floor, bent down, and picked up the hairbrush. She weighed it in her hand for a moment, and then let it drop with a small thud.

"You gonna clean up?" Treyvon asked.

She stared around at the detritus of her life. Slowly, she shook her head. She couldn't face it now, and there would be time to do it later, when her bond was lifted and she was able to move back. Izaya had told her the case would be dismissed, hadn't he? She hadn't done anything. Even if what Treyvon told her about his cousin was true, she had done even less than that. She hadn't introduced anyone. She hadn't *known* anyone, other than Jorge and Gabriel. Olivia threw as many of her clothes as could fit into a black backpack that she dragged out from under her bed. Her wallet was on the dresser, the contents dumped out. It took her a few moments to put back all her cards and slips of paper. The money was gone.

"Cops," she said, holding up the empty wallet and wondering, despite herself, who had really stolen the money.

Olivia took a brown paper bag into the bathroom and tossed toiletries into it. She stood for a moment holding a box of tampons, weighing them in her hand. Then she put them back on the shelf, hoping that this very act would cause her period to arrive. Maybe she would put on a pair of white pants, too.

Treyvon heaved the backpack onto his shoulder and scooped up 8-Ball in his other hand. They walked together out to the curb.

As they walked down the path, Elaine popped the trunk. Olivia loaded her stuff into it and turned to thank Treyvon. He nodded and said, "Don't worry about it."

She nodded and got into the car.

"Who's that?" Elaine asked.

"My neighbor," Olivia said.

Arthur had emptied Olivia's old room of most of his things. His desk was pushed into a corner and cleared of the neat stacks of files and papers that usually decorated its maple veneer surface. His computer was gone, and he'd covered the printer and fax machine with a white sheet folded once down the middle. He'd even taken his framed Greg LeMond Tour de France poster off the wall and stuck it behind the desk. The thoroughness with which he'd erased his presence from the room struck Elaine as vaguely hostile, but Olivia didn't seem to notice. She dropped her things on the single bed, on the mirrored bedspread that Elaine had brought back from her trip to Rajasthan with Arthur. Elaine remained in the doorway, tucking her hair behind her ear.

"Honey, do you think you'll be okay if I head back to work? There are a few things I'd like to take care of," Elaine said.

"I'll come with you. I need to pick up some stuff from the store."

"Some stuff?" She had told Warren and the others at work only the barest minimum in order to explain her absences and the calls from the lawyer and pretrial services. Now she didn't trust Olivia not to blurt out all the shameful details in some misguided confessional moment. "Why don't you just give me a list of what you need. I'll get it for you," she said.

"No, that's okay. I could use a walk."

"But don't you want to take a shower?"

Olivia looked at her sharply, and Elaine blushed.

"I didn't mean that you needed one or anything. Just that it might be nice to take a hot shower…you know, to relax."

"I'll take one later." Olivia's voice was flat. Elaine opened her mouth to protest one more time, but then snapped it shut.

The women left the house and headed toward College Avenue. They walked slowly, neither particularly eager to arrive at their destination.

"You see that house?" Elaine said, trying to make her voice sound as bright and cheerful as possible. "That's my house." She pointed at a small Victorian painted in pastel pinks and blues. It was one Olivia usually claimed for her own. But this time, the girl didn't say anything.

"I'll let you live in the carriage house," Elaine persevered.

"And I'll let you live in county jail with seven smelly crack-whores," Olivia said, and then, an instant later, "Sorry."

They walked the rest of the way in silence.

At the store, Elaine bustled behind her counter and immediately got to work, but she watched out of the corner of her eye as Olivia walked up and down the aisles, grabbing things seemingly at random. Elaine looked back at her computer screen, and the next time she raised her head, found that she could no longer see Olivia. Mounted under the counter was a security monitor installed a few years back when shoplifting had become a problem. Elaine watched the fuzzy image of her daughter, crouching down in the center aisle. She was furtively slipping an EPT pregnancy test off the shelf. Olivia opened the packet and took out the foil-wrapped stick. She shoved it into the waistband of her pants, pushed the now empty box behind the others on the shelf, and stood up and walked to the counter. Elaine tucked her hair behind her ear nervously and pretended to be busy counting pills.

"All set," Olivia said.

At that moment, Warren came out from the back room. His mouth was smeared with cream cheese, and he had a bagel in his hand. "I'll ring you out," he said.

Elaine opened her mouth to object, but couldn't think of a good enough reason to insist on doing it herself. He scanned the items Olivia had chosen into the register one by one. Elaine's eyes kept drifting to the waistband of Olivia's pants. She forced herself to look away, back at the pills she'd been counting.

"Still fighting the good fight, Olivia?" Warren said.

"I guess so."

"What was it this time? The World Trade Organization? Sweatshops?"

"Excuse me?" she asked.

"Did you chain yourself to an ancient redwood?"

She looked over at her mother, who blushed and shrugged her shoulders.

"Something like that," Olivia said.

Warren put her purchases into a paper bag. "That'll be fifteen twenty-six. Should I put that on your account, Elaine?" he asked.

Olivia and Elaine answered simultaneously.

"No," said Olivia.

"Yes," said Elaine.

"I can pay for it myself, Mom." Olivia pulled her wallet out of her pocket. "Shit," she whispered, staring into the empty billfold.

"I'll take care of it," Elaine said.

"Thanks." Olivia took the bag Warren held out for her.

"Here! Don't forget the key," Elaine reached over the counter, and handed Olivia a key to the house. "I'll be home at about seven o'clock or so. Arthur should be back before then."

Elaine watched as Olivia walked out of the store. "Warren, why don't you go finish your lunch."

"That's okay. I'm basically done."

"No, really. Go on."

The young man looked at her, puzzled, and then disappeared into the back. Elaine walked quickly out from behind the counter and to the center aisle of the store. She found the empty EPT box and brought it back to the register. She rang it up, and then shoved the box down into the trash. She took the receipt from Olivia's purchase and the receipt from the EPT and scrupulously entered them under her name in the ledger where she kept the employee accounts.

Olivia sat on the toilet, the pregnancy-test kit in her hand. She ripped the foil wrapper with her teeth, took out the white plastic wand, and peed a long stream over the absorbent tip. Once she'd replaced the cap, she placed the wand gently on the windowsill and turned on the water in the shower to hot. After a few moments, the room filled with steam. Only then did Olivia strip off her clothes and get in the shower. She stood there, eyes closed against the cleansing stream that coursed over her head, fighting the nausea that seemed never to lose its grip on her, until the water began to cool. Then she took the bar of soap and scrubbed herself until her body shone pink and raw. The tap squeaked under her hand as she wrenched it shut. She stepped out into the foggy room and picked up the pregnancy test. Two dark pink lines stared back at her.

"Fuck," she said, and threw the test into the trash. Grabbing a towel off the rack, she rubbed herself dry. She reached into the garbage can, retrieved the test, and took it with her into her bedroom. For a long while, Olivia sat on the bed, staring at the pregnancy test. She didn't feel pregnant, only nauseated and exhausted. And she could not get Treyvon's cousin out of her mind. How could she be pregnant if there was even the slightest chance she'd be going to jail? Saliva pooled in the corners of her mouth. Leaping to her feet, Olivia ran, naked, to the bathroom. She made it just in time. For long minutes she spat and heaved into the toilet and cried. Finally, the spasms in her belly stopped, and she wiped the noxious combination of tears, mucus, sweat, and vomit from her face.

Olivia laid her head down on the bathroom floor, the tile cool against her flushed cheek. What had she done to deserve this particular conflagration of misery? To find herself pregnant, now, on top of everything else, was simply unbearable. It was especially grotesque to have a piece of Jorge growing inside her when, she suddenly realized, she hated him more than she'd ever hated anyone in her life. She hated him for being so fucking stupid, for getting involved in a drug deal, and for being so inept as to get himself caught. She hated him for putting her at risk, and she hated him for failing to explain her innocence. While she knew, of course, that he couldn't have done anything else, she despised him for sitting in the courtroom like some mute imbecile. Why hadn't he stood up and insisted to the judge that she was entirely uninvolved and should be let go?

Now, as if his betrayal were not enough, as if three days in jail were not sufficient punishment for the mistake of loving him, he had gone and gotten her pregnant. She placed her hand on her belly, palpating the intangible bulge. Perhaps, Olivia thought, she was being punished not for loving Jorge too much, but rather for failing to love him at all. God, that ultimate ironist, had seen what she had been too afraid to admit to herself, let alone to Jorge: she didn't love him and she never had. They were together merely because she could not figure out how to extricate herself from his embrace.

Pregnant, she was locked behind the bars of their union tighter than ever. But of course, she did not need to stay in this particular prison. Unlike the rest of the nightmare that her relationship had become, she could choose to end this. She could get an abortion.

Olivia couldn't remember a time when she wasn't pro-choice. Growing up in Berkeley, supporting the right to abortion was not only acceptable but obligatory, and a "Pro-choice Pro-family" button a required fashion accessory. Olivia and her friends had all participated in clinic counter-demonstrations, shouting down the pro-life fanatics with their pictures of bloody baby parts. Now, when faced with the decision she had always assumed would be so easy to make, Olivia longed for the youthful certainty that allowed her to adorn her car with "Get Your Laws Off My Body" bumper stickers.

Yet now, for some inexplicable reason, the contemplation of an abortion made her shoulders shake with sobs. If she ended the pregnancy, it would not be because her life was too full of other, wonderful things to complicate it with a child. She was not in school, or starting a new job, or enjoying her lack of responsibility. If she terminated this pregnancy, it would be because she might be going to prison. Almost to spite herself, she imagined keeping the baby. She saw her belly swell, her skin glow with the radiance of pregnancy. She saw a little dark-haired bundle—black eyes, pink pursed lips, miniature star-fish hands. She was startled to find herself smiling. She leaned back against the bathroom wall and let the fantasy continue. Amidst the daydreams of prenatal yoga, tiny pairs of overalls, and co-op nursery schools, a thought crossed her mind—a thought so coldly pragmatic that it frightened her. Olivia wondered if being pregnant might work in her favor—if the fact of her impending motherhood might influence the prosecutor's decision regarding the dismissal of her case.

Olivia rose to her feet, splashed cold water on her face, and rinsed her mouth. She went back to her room, pulled on some clean clothes, and stretched out on her bed. Something poked her in the back, and she reached under and pulled out the pregnancy test. She rolled onto her side and stood up. Holding the test loosely in one hand, she pulled open the drawer of her nightstand and began poking through the remnants of her girlhood. There was a bit of sheep's wool, oily and sharp-smelling, from a fourth grade field trip to a West Marin farm; a baby food jar full of bright and smooth beach glass collected in the sand at the edge of the Santa Cruz boardwalk on one of the few vacations Elaine and Olivia had taken together; a bag of dusty Valentine's Day heart candies from a boy whose name she'd long forgotten. From the time Olivia was a little girl, she had filled this drawer with things she could not bear to throw away. She dropped the plastic wand into the drawer and then slammed it shut with a rattle of bits of colored glass.

As Izaya Feingold-Upchurch bounded across the plaza of the Federal Building, he caught sight of Amanda Steele walking briskly a few yards ahead of him. Her back was to him, and he took advantage of that fact to give his opposing counsel the once over. He shook his head. Objectively, he supposed, she was attractive, but she was not his style at all. He couldn't abide that skinny, flat-assed white-girl look. Anyway, he had been white-girl-free for almost ten years—ofay clean and sober. Yes, his mother was a white woman, and he loved her ferociously, but he had long ago vowed not to make the same mistake his father had. Izaya was determined to find himself a beautiful black woman, a partner in his life, goals, and identity. A woman, he supposed, like the wife on whom his father had cheated when he'd conceived his son, and to whom he returned once the attractions of paler princesses had flagged.

"Amanda!" he called, catching her just as she was about to pass through the great revolving doors of the Federal Building.

She turned around, her face frozen in a polite mask, but when she saw him, she smiled slightly.

"Looks like we've got another case together," he said, returning her smile with his own broad, charming grin.

"Do we?" she said, and knit her eyebrows together in a confusion that he could not help but feel was contrived.

He raised a slightly sardonic eyebrow. "Goodman? Methamphetamine? We had a bail hearing last week?"

"Oh, right," she said. "I'm taking that to the grand jury this afternoon."

"This afternoon?" he said, taken aback. He should have made more of an effort to reach her right after he had picked up the case. He had left a message, which she had not returned—the prosecutors rarely felt obliged to return the defenders' calls, although he generally had some success convincing the women to pay him the attention he felt he deserved. Izaya had not really noticed when his opposing counsel had not called him back—he had put aside Olivia's case to draft a sentencing memorandum for a client facing a possible twenty years under the career criminal statute—and after that first call, he hadn't bothered to try Amanda Steele again. It was a stroke of luck that he had even run into her this morning.

"Well then, my timing couldn't be more fortuitous," he said smoothly, not letting his voice belie his shiver of anxiety at how close he had cut it.

"How so?" she said, glancing at her watch. She wore the face on the inside of her wrist and had to turn her arm to see it. Coffee splashed from the paper cup she was holding. "Shit!" She passed the cup to her other hand and shook her wrist.

"Here," Izaya said, pulling an ironed white handkerchief out of his pocket.

"It's okay. I'm fine."

"Please." He reached out and, ignoring her startled flinch, dabbed at the liquid on her cuff.

She blushed, began to smile, and then caught herself. "I'm *fine*," she said, taking a step away from him.

"Suit yourself," Izaya said. He folded the handkerchief, taking care to tuck it into his pocket so that the stained part didn't show.

"I've got a meeting," she said, turning back toward the doors to the building.

"Two minutes," he said. "Okay? Come on, Ms. Steele. I left you a message, but you didn't call me back. Not one little, tiny phone call." Izaya put just a touch of his father's smooth Mississippi tone in his voice. That dulcet drawl, combined with the sharp glimmer of the silk-shot wool of his suits, invariably set the white girls atremble. Amanda Steele was no exception.

Slowly she turned back, almost despite herself. She checked her watch again, this time being careful not to tip her cup. "Two minutes."

He smiled. "Great, thanks, Amanda. Now, we both know you don't want to indict on the Goodman case."

"Excuse me?"

"Olivia wasn't involved. This was her boyfriend's thing. She's just an innocent bystander."

Amanda Steele raised her eyebrows almost imperceptibly. "Oh, really?"

"Yeah, really. She's a good kid. She's just got a lousy boyfriend."

The prosecutor frowned at him, and there was something almost like pity in her expression. "You might want to take a look at the discovery before you talk to me about a plea."

Izaya narrowed his eyes, the softness momentarily abandoning his voice. "I'm not talking about a plea. I'm talking about not indicting her." He paused and smiled again. "Come on, you know as well as I do that the girl had nothing to do with this. Hold off on the indictment. I'll bring her in, and you can talk to her. I promise that once you hear what she has to say…"

"Oh, I've heard what she has to say."

"Excuse me?"

"I've heard her on tape. And I've seen her in the photographs. All of which I'll send you in the discovery packet."

Izaya paused, wondering if there was something Olivia hadn't told him. Was the girl sufficiently cunning to have fooled him so completely? He was not arrogant enough to believe that his judgment about his clients was unequivocally accurate, but nonetheless he felt confident that Olivia Goodman was not an artful criminal adept in the ways of deception.

"What can you possibly have her on tape saying? She wasn't involved in the deal," he said

The expression of pity on the face of his opposing counsel was now explicit, and he had to flex his fingers to resist the urge to reach out and wipe it off.

"Your client is at the center of the conspiracy. She introduced her boyfriend to the informant."

"Oh, bullshit," he said, louder and more aggressively than he'd intended.

The prosecutor's eyes widened, and he caught her unmistakable expression of fear. The same look he got when he stepped into an elevator alone with a white woman; the stiffening of the back, the trembling of the shoulders whenever he passed someone in the dark of the evening. His lip curled in disgust. This was all it took, an exclamation from a black man, a loud voice, and the apprehension, the dread that was the true nature of this and every other white woman's feelings about black men was on the surface, bubbling over.

"You take this case forward, and you're going to end up losing, just like you did in Deakins."

Her mouth formed an O of surprise. "What are you talking about?"

"You'll end up looking as bad as you did when Alvarez granted my suppression motion in the Deakins case."

A red flush crept across her throat. "You don't know what you're talking about."

"Goodman will be dismissed, just like Deakins was. You mark my words."

"Darnell Deakins was picked up by the LAPD two days after he was released from federal custody. The DA told me there's no way a state judge will rule the same way as Alvarez. He also said they're filing a three strikes case. Your client is going to end up spending the rest of his life in state prison." Her heels clicked on the stone tiles as she walked across the plaza and into the building.

Izaya grit his teeth to keep himself from throwing his eight-hundred-dollar briefcase at the woman's narrow, condescending ass. He had been so consumed with celebrating his victory in Deakins that he had never stopped to realize that they would never let his client walk away, that they would turn the case over to county. He despised losing, and the added humiliation of a loss of which he had been entirely unaware was almost more than he could stand. The consistency of defeat was the defining aspect of the job of a public defender. The U.S. Attorney's office held all the cards, and too often it seemed to Izaya that his role was just to accompany his clients as they were sucked down the drain of the judicial system and spat out in some hellhole of federal prison. Occasionally, on his bleakest days, he wondered if the real torture of his chosen profession was being forced to play the sycophant to contemptuous and contemptible prigs like Amanda Steele. The power rested entirely with those who seemed to have the least compassion, and he was compelled to prostrate himself before them and hope that this supplication would result in a decent plea offer for his client.

Izaya felt a sudden stab of guilt. He had let his temper and his arrogance get the better of him. However personally repugnant he found genuflecting before the opposing counsel's authority, he owed it to his client to do so. He took off across the plaza and bolted through the doors of the Federal Building, determined to catch the prosecutor, apologize, and try to convince her of Olivia's lack of culpability. He spotted Amanda Steele on the other side of the metal detector, waiting for the elevator.

"Amanda!" he shouted. "Amanda, wait a minute."

She turned her head away.

He dumped his briefcase on the conveyor belt, and shot through the metal arch.

"Amanda!" he called again.

"Stop right there, sir," a voice said. Izaya spun around. A uniformed court security officer held an arm out, barring his path. "I'm going to need to ask you to take off your shoes, *sir*." There was an ostentatious formality to the final word, as if the officer were making it clear to Izaya that the word applied to him not at all.

"Excuse me?" Izaya said, in the booming voice with which he addressed recalcitrant witnesses. The officer was unimpressed and unperturbed.

"Your shoes. *Sir*."

"I work here." Izaya patted his pockets and pulled out his federal identification badge. "You know me. You see me every day."

"This way, sir." The officer said, motioning for Izaya to follow him to a cordoned-off area to the side of the front doors. Once again, Izaya was the only person the court security officer had stopped. The officers, most of whom were middle-aged ex-cops, and all of whom were white, seemed to reserve for him the zealous commitment to their jobs that post-9/11 security considerations had inspired. Izaya had once complained to his boss, the Federal Defender herself, about the heightened level of scrutiny he was subject to, but she had merely reassured him that he was not alone—the officers were not fond of any of the public defenders. Despite her words,

Izaya could not help but notice that whatever they felt about the other attorneys, it was only he, the sole black man, who was routinely patted down on the way to work.

He clenched his jaw and toed off his Italian loafers, careful not to scuff the polished shoe backs. While the officer dug through his briefcase, looking for a weapon the metal detector might have missed, Izaya watched Amanda Steele step into the elevator and disappear.

The night of Olivia's release from Martinez, Elaine had presented her with a list of lawyers. Arthur had, after swearing them to secrecy, asked a few of the older partners in his firm to whom they referred clients whose troubles with the IRS demanded the services of a criminal defense attorney. Olivia had refused even to take the piece of paper on which Arthur had jotted down, in his lapidarian block printing, the names and phone numbers of the recommended lawyers.

"But why not?" Elaine said. "Why not hire the best attorney you can find?"

Olivia had pretended it was because she could not afford one of Arthur's hot shots that she was sticking with her public defender, but that wasn't really true. She might have taken Elaine up on her offer of a loan to pay for a private attorney, but she didn't want to leave Izaya. She liked him and she trusted him. And if it drove Arthur and her mother crazy that her lawyer was young and black, well, so much the better.

The next morning, Olivia took BART to downtown Oakland to talk to Izaya and check in with pretrial services. She met with Miss Watts-Thompson first and did an adequate job, she felt, of containing her loathing for the woman. She received her drug-testing instructions without too obvious a display of disgust, and made arrangements to call in once a week. Then she took the elevator up to the Office of the Federal Public Defender.

Izaya's office was small but bright, its walls hung with diplomas and a framed poster of a grim-faced Mumia Abu-Jamal. A bright purple motorcycle helmet was tossed on a bookshelf, and draped over the desk chair was a black leather jacket that looked so soft and supple that Olivia had to fight the urge to stroke it.

Olivia looked around the office and pointed at the poster. "I went to a Mumia vigil at Sproul Plaza once."

"Really?"

"Yeah. You know, protesting his death sentence. I don't think he killed that cop."

"No?"

She shook her head. "You must not, either. I mean, you've got a Free Mumia poster on your wall."

Izaya leaned far back in his chair and threw his feet up on the desk. "I don't know if he killed the cop. But even if he did, he doesn't deserve to fry. No one does. What protest did you go to?"

"Excuse me?"

"Go on, have a seat." She perched on the edge of a chair covered in a brightly colored *kinte* cloth. "Which Mumia vigil did you go to?" he asked.

She thought. "Six years ago, maybe? In, like, May or June? Right before the end of the school year. Peter Coyote, that actor, spoke. They read a letter from Jesse Jackson, and one from Mumia, too."

Izaya smiled. "I was there."

"You were?"

"Yup. I did my third year of law school at Boalt. On the Harvard-Berkeley exchange program. I was in the Black Students Association, and we organized that demonstration."

She smiled, and, for no reason that she could figure out, blushed. "Wow. Funny coincidence," she mumbled.

"Small world," he said. "So, how you doing?"

"Okay."

"I was glad your mother came through for you."

Olivia shrugged.

"You must be relieved to be out," he said.

She nodded and began picking at the fraying fabric at the knee of her jeans.

Izaya heaved his feet off the desk and leaned forward. "Martinez sucks, huh?" he said.

Olivia nodded again, not trusting herself to speak without crying.

"How long were you in for? Four days?"

"Yeah." Her voice was a hollow whisper.

"I'll bet it felt like four years."

Izaya handed her a box of Kleenex, and as if on cue, tears began falling down Olivia's cheeks. Big, fat, baby tears. She wiped her eyes helplessly and gulped.

"God, I'm so sorry. I don't know why I'm crying."

"You're crying because this *sucks*. You were in jail, and you're facing the possibility of a lot more time there. Of course you're crying."

Olivia felt her stomach twist. "Do you really think I'm going to have to go back to jail?"

"Olivia," Izaya sighed. "This is the part of my job that I hate the most."

"Oh no," she said, and buried her face in her hands. She pressed the heels of her palms into her eyes until her vision filled with an entire solar system of yellow and orange stars. It took a moment for her to realize that she'd given herself a piercing headache. She put down her hands and said, "Just tell me what's going on."

"The prosecutor filed the indictment."

Anxiety settled on her chest, and her lungs strained under its leadened weight. "What does that mean?" she whispered.

"That means Amanda Steele won't dismiss the case."

"But didn't you tell her that I wasn't involved?"

Izaya rested his elbows on the desk and looked at her intently. "I'm so sorry, Olivia. I did everything I could."

"But why? Why are they prosecuting *me*? I wasn't even part of it!"

Izaya frowned. "The DEA has you on tape talking to the informant. They have photographs of you at the pickup. Steele's under the impression that you facilitated the deal."

"That's a lie!" Olivia yelled. Then she blushed. "I mean, yes, I was in the car, but I didn't talk to any informants. And I didn't facilitate anything."

Izaya reached out. She felt the pads of his cool dry fingers pat the back of her hand. She looked up at his face, and noticed, not for the first time, how handsome he was. She was disgusted with herself—what was wrong with her? Why did she care what her lawyer looked like when he'd just told her that the prosecutor was trying to send her to jail? She slipped her hand out from under his.

"Look, Olivia, I know that it was all Jorge's idea. But there are some things we need to discuss. Hard things. This is a federal case, and the federal sentencing laws are absolutely insane when it comes to drugs."

"But I didn't do anything!"

"You and I both agree on that, and I'm confident that we'll be able to convince a jury to see things our way, but I want to make sure you understand everything that could happen, no matter how unlikely. You follow me?"

"I guess."

"The law that really has us by the short hairs here is the law of conspiracy. That law basically says that you don't need to commit a crime to be subject to criminal penalties, you just have to *agree* to commit a crime, or even just *talk* about committing a crime. Once you have that agreement, that discussion, you're as liable as if you had committed the actual crime."

"That's ridiculous," Olivia sputtered. "You mean that if you and I talk about killing someone, we can get prosecuted for murder whether or not we kill the guy?"

"Basically, yes. It's a bit more complicated—we would actually have to commit an overt act in furtherance of the conspiracy."

Olivia wrinkled her brow. "Overt act?"

"That means do something that moves the conspiracy along."

The throttlehold of fear that had gripped her began to subside, and she felt herself regain some of her composure. "Well, then we're fine. I didn't do anything like that."

"You might have. An overt act doesn't have to be anything illegal. It could be taking a phone message. Or simply going along for a ride. You took a couple of phone messages, didn't you?"

The bit of self-possession she had managed to muster slipped away. "But I didn't talk about drugs, or *anything*," she wailed.

"Olivia, this is really important, and I don't want you to say anything right now, okay? If you knew that the phone call referred to a drug deal, and if you passed the information on to your boyfriend, then that would be considered an overt act. Riding along when you knew your boyfriend was doing the deal could be considered an overt act as well."

Olivia opened her mouth to tell him that it couldn't possibly matter that she knew about the drugs, because she didn't help in any way—on the contrary, she hadn't wanted Jorge to do the deal at all. But Izaya raised his hand, "Don't say anything, okay? We're going to take this one step at a time. First, I want to explain something about my ethical obligation to you. As a criminal defense lawyer, I owe you my absolute loyalty, with a few huge exceptions. I can't help you commit a crime, I can't keep silent if I know you're about to commit a crime, and I can't put perjured testimony on the witness stand. Do you know what that means?"

"I think so."

"Let me explain it anyway. If, for example, I know that you were aware that Jorge was doing a drug deal, and you passed him important information knowing what he was going to use it for, I could not let you testify that you didn't know what was going on, that you were just an innocent bystander."

"What do you mean?"

"I mean if *I* know you did something, then *you* can't testify to the opposite."

"And if you don't know?"

"I'm allowed to put you on the stand to tell your story, as long as I don't *know* you're lying."

Olivia suddenly got it. "Okay," she said. "But none of that matters as long as I'm telling the truth."

"Right."

"And I am telling the truth."

He smiled. "I know that. I've just got to make sure you understand how it all works. You want a Coke?" He bent over and pulled a six-pack of soda out of the small fridge tucked under the credenza behind his desk. Olivia realized for the first time that her lips were dry and parched.

"I'd love one," she said.

He pried one out of the plastic ring, picked up a napkin from a pile on his desk, and wiped off the top of the can. Then he popped it open and handed it to her. "I want to talk for a moment about the worst-case scenario," he said.

She took a deep swallow and, suppressing a burp, nodded. The soda felt deliciously cold and smooth in her mouth, and she felt the turmoil in her stomach abate.

"First of all, I want you to understand that I'm easily as good if not a better lawyer than Amanda Steele. I'm not saying that to brag, but because it's true. It's true, but it doesn't matter. The government's lawyers always have the upper hand. That's because they decide what crime to charge, and in federal court, the charge is everything. The charge determines the sentence."

"What does that mean?" Olivia asked.

"It used to be that a judge could look at a defendant and make a sentencing decision based on how much time he thought the defendant deserved to serve. But all that changed under the federal sentencing guidelines. They are not guidelines at all. They are hard and fast rules under which judges completely lost their sentencing discretion. Nowadays, a judge's sole role in a federal case is to apply a series of mathematical equations to come up with the sentence required by a specific charge. A machine could do it."

"And the prosecutor decides the charges," she said. She took another swallow of soda and set the can on the table, not trusting her shaking hands to hold it.

"Exactly. Most of those fools are right out of law school. They have, like, zero real life experience. Of all the people in the system, they're the least likely to know what the hell they're doing. And depending on how they charge a case, a defendant could be looking at probation or at a long time in jail."

"So how did she charge my case?"

"Let's say that we lose at trial or you plead guilty…" Olivia began to protest, but Izaya raised his hand to her and said, "I know you have no intention of doing that. Let's just talk hypothetically. If that were to happen, you would be subject to the mandatory minimum sentences for drug crimes. Do you know anything about those?"

"No."

"Well, like I said, the judge has absolutely no discretion. The sentence is tied to the quantity of drugs at issue in the indictment. In this case, the indictment alleges fifty-five grams of methamphetamine. The mandatory minimum sentence for that amount is ten years."

Olivia gasped, "Ten years?"

Izaya nodded. "Ten years for a first-time offender. Twenty if you've got a prior. Now, we might, in your case, be able to argue that since you were so tangentially involved, you should be eligible for something called the safety valve. That would allow the judge to sentence you for slightly less time. He'd still have to go by the sentencing guidelines, which are pretty brutal, but he wouldn't be forced to sentence you to ten years, and we could then argue for a downward departure, meaning a lower sentence based on any number of things. The safety valve is available to individuals without a criminal record."

"But I *do* have a record," Olivia said, her voice flat.

"Those offenses shouldn't count against you."

"Well, what are we talking about, then? With the safety valve?"

He shook his head. "It's hard to predict. Maybe five years. Give or take. It really depends on which judge we draw at your arraignment next week. A liberal judge might allow us a downward departure. A more conservative judge might not."

Five years. Five years in that horrible place, with that vile smell, and the constant, acid wash of fear. She wouldn't survive. She would end up killing herself, if someone else didn't do it for her.

Izaya was still speaking.

"I'm sorry, what did you say?" Olivia asked.

"I said that the other thing about the safety valve is that some judges are apt to give it only to defendants who plead guilty. They won't use it if you go to trial."

Olivia raised her palm as if to stop his words, and shook her head. "I'm not going to plead guilty. I'm *not* guilty."

"Olivia, none of this is certain or even likely at this point. I'm planning on winning this case. I have a fucking awesome win record, and I'll be damned if I'll let this case screw it up. We're going to put up an innocent bystander defense, a young girl in love defense, an entrapment defense. Shit, we're going to make the jury want to take you home and adopt you, not just acquit you. But…" he paused.

"But what?"

"But I'd be remiss if I didn't tell you that there was one other way out of this."

Hope hit her like a wave of pure light. It was only when she felt the glow that she realized she'd seen nothing but the dim gray of its lack since she'd walked into Izaya's office—or even before then. She had not so much as glimpsed a glimmer of hope since she'd found herself on her knees, retching into the reeking prison toilet. "What? What's the way out?"

"Well, the only way a judge is allowed to sentence under the mandatory minimum if there's no safety valve is if the government files a 5K1.1 motion."

"What's that?"

"Substantial assistance. If the prosecutor says that you've provided substantial assistance, you are eligible for a lower sentence."

"How would I do that?"

Izaya paused and spoke a bit more softly. "By informing on someone else."

The light faded. "I'm not going to be an informant. I'm not like that. Besides, I don't know anybody. I didn't *do* anything and I don't know who did."

"Olivia, these kinds of cases often end up being horse races to the courthouse door. The first defendant out of the chute wins. If one of the others informs on you first, you'll be screwed."

"They can't inform on me, I didn't *do* anything. And I don't want to testify against anyone. I'm not a snitch."

"It doesn't often get that far. Usually it's a matter of providing information that leads someone to plead guilty."

Olivia sat silently, her mind racing. She couldn't inform on Jorge, and he would never inform on her. But he wasn't the only person she knew.

"There is one person I would give information on."

Izaya leaned forward in his chair. "Who?" he said, eagerly.

"The person who set the whole thing up. The person who got Jorge involved in the first place. I have no problem informing on him."

Izaya's face fell. "Are you talking about the guy who called you on the phone? The guy whose messages you passed to Jorge?"

Olivia nodded. "Gabriel Contreras. I would love to tell the government all about that sleazy asshole."

The look of pity in Izaya's eyes was surprising but unmistakable. "That man," he said, "is the confidential informant in this case."

Olivia sat back in her seat, stunned. "What are you talking about? It was all his idea! He was the person who set it all up. What do you mean he's an informant? What is he doing, informing on himself?"

Izaya leaned across the table and reached for her hand. "I'm sorry, Olivia. Gabriel Contreras works for the DEA. He always has."

Olivia shook her head. Suddenly she jerked her hand from his, rose to her feet, and began pacing back and forth along the length of the small office.

"I don't get any of this. How can *he* set it all up and then *we* get arrested?"

"That's what CIs do. They set up the deal, they pretend to be part of it, and then the DEA swoops in and busts everybody else."

"But isn't that entrapment?" Olivia was yelling by now. She stood behind her chair and gripped the back so tightly her knuckles ached.

"Yeah, maybe it's entrapment. Let's hope there's enough evidence for us to show entrapment, but that's a hard defense to prove. Not that I haven't won entrapment cases before," Izaya said. "It's just a hard defense to mount."

Olivia collapsed in her chair. "This is a nightmare."

Izaya nodded. "I know, Olivia. I know. Let's just take it slow. This is going to be a long process, and I'm not going to give up. I don't want you to, either. We're both going to be in this for the long haul, right?"

"Do I have a choice?" Olivia said, her voice tight and grim. The specter of the next months and years loomed over her in a reality so grim, so frightening, that it made her chest cave in with fear. At that moment, she had no confidence at all that she could survive an ordeal the likes of which she found it all too easy to imagine.

Arthur liked having his feet rubbed. He had flat, oblong feet with long, skinny toes. He complained that the specially fabricated insoles that he wore in his athletic shoes made his feet hurt, and in the evening he liked nothing better than to stretch out on the couch, watch an A's game, and have Elaine rub away the knots and aches in his soles and arches. Elaine couldn't stand having her own feet touched, let alone rubbed. It had taken her a few years to overcome her twinge of revulsion at stroking and kneading Arthur's so familiarly. Now, however, she found strange comfort in her evening attendance to Arthur's feet.

Their quiet moment was interrupted by the sound of a key in the front-door lock. Olivia let herself in and sat down in the chintz armchair that Elaine had found years ago in a dumpster on College Avenue. Elaine had spent almost as much money having it restored and restuffed as it would have cost to buy a new one, and her daughter had always claimed that the upholstery still smelled faintly of garbage. Yet Olivia always chose to sit in that chair, despite its phantom odor, or maybe because of it.

"Hi, honey," Elaine said. She pushed Arthur's feet off her lap. Rubbing them was too intimate an activity to be engaged in in front of Olivia. Arthur grunted with displeasure and plopped them back across her thighs. She let them lie, but didn't touch them. Olivia looked wan. Her eyes were puffy, and her face was pale and still marred with the blush of acne she'd acquired in jail.

"Did you see your lawyer today?" Elaine asked.

Olivia nodded.

"And?"

"And I'm going to jail for ten years."

Elaine gasped.

"Olivia, that's just ridiculous," Arthur said. "Exactly what did he say?"

Olivia described to them the intricacies of federal drug sentencing. "It's all based on quantity. The amount of drugs that Jorge sold them equals a ten-year sentence. Izaya gave me copies of the sections of the laws that deal with methamphetamine." She passed a wad of folded paper to Elaine. Elaine began to leaf through the pages, and Arthur leaned forward.

"Let me see that," he said.

She put the papers in Arthur's outstretched hand.

"Methamphetamine. For God's sake, how the hell did you get yourself involved with methamphetamine?" Arthur said, shaking his head in disgust.

Olivia didn't answer him. Elaine put her hand on Arthur's foot and gave it a squeeze of warning. He ignored her.

"I told you, we need to hire a *real* lawyer, Elaine. You get what you pay for, and nobody's paying anything for this Isaac, or whatever his name is."

"His name is Izaya, and you *are* paying for him," Olivia said. "I'm paying for him, and Mom's paying for him, and the rest of the tax-paying public is paying for him."

"Fine, Olivia. But do you know anything about his credentials? Where did he go to law school?"

"Uh, let me see. Oh yeah, someplace called, is it—Harvard? Is that any good?"

"Huh," said Arthur.

Elaine wondered if Olivia was telling the truth. They both knew that the mere mention of the Ivy League would impress Arthur enough to keep him quiet. He'd gotten his own undergraduate degree at Wesleyan University, which he consistently and embarrassingly referred to as one of the "Little Ivies."

"Anyway, he's a really good lawyer. I like him." Something in Olivia's tone made Elaine look at her more closely, and Olivia blushed under her gaze.

"Were you there all this time, honey? It's so late."

"No. I tried to pick up my car after my appointment with Izaya. The fuckers wouldn't give it back to me. They say it's *forfeited* because it was used during a drug deal."

"But that's *your* car! It's not Jorge's; what right do they have to seize your car?" Arthur sputtered.

Olivia shrugged.

"After that I tried to visit Jorge at the North County Jail in Oakland."

"Oh, honey," Elaine exclaimed. "Is that really a good idea? I mean, given everything that's happened?" She knew that Olivia was bound to get angry at the question, but she couldn't help herself. It astonished her that her daughter was still trying to have contact with the man who had so effectively and completely ruined her life.

Olivia surprised her mother by not shouting. She just slumped deeper in the chair. "I don't know. Maybe not. It doesn't matter, anyway. I couldn't get in."

Elaine sighed with relief. "That's probably for the best."

"Why wouldn't they let you in?" Arthur said.

Elaine nearly pinched him for even asking the question.

Olivia picked at a loose thread on the chair's armrest. "You're only allowed in if you're on the inmate's visitors list. And I'm not on his."

"Well, at least the son of a bitch knows enough to be ashamed of himself," Arthur said.

"Arthur, please," Elaine said, although of course he had expressed only what she herself was feeling, what any normal person would feel.

"I don't know if he's ashamed or not, but I don't have a choice. I have to talk to him," Olivia said.

Elaine wanted to slap her daughter. She wanted to get up off the couch, walk across the worn Oriental carpet, grab Olivia by the shoulders, and shake her until her head snapped back and forth. Instead, she crossed her legs and squeezed her hands tightly together. "Why?" she said. "Why do you need to talk to him? Do I really need to remind you that he's the reason you're in this horrible mess to begin with? This was all his idea, correct? Unless you lied to me before, you had nothing to do with any of this. It was *his* plan. You said you didn't even know what was happening until it was too late."

"You think I *want* to talk to him?" Olivia shouted back. Her face was red and her breath came in ragged gasps. "I don't want to *talk* to him. I want to *kill* him! But I told you—I don't have a choice. I *have* to see him."

Olivia's hysteria had the curious effect of quieting Elaine. She looked levelly at her daughter, and then, in a calm, flat voice, asked, "Why? Why do you have to see him?" Although, of course, she knew.

"Because I need to tell him that I'm pregnant."

For a moment, Arthur just sat there, his eyebrows raised, face pale. He opened and closed his mouth silently a few times, and then rose slowly to his feet. He padded out of the room and slammed the door behind him.

Elaine considered, for a moment, pretending to be surprised, but somehow she could not seem to summon the strength.

"What are you going to do?" she asked.

"I don't know. Get an abortion, I guess."

"You *guess*?" Elaine said. She was horrified by Olivia's listless reply, by the girl's seeming consideration of the possibility of doing anything other than end the pregnancy. "You just said Izaya thinks you might have to go to *jail*. Maybe for ten years, Olivia. Good God! How can you even *consider* having a baby?" Elaine tried to modulate her voice, to sound composed and reasonable, but she found, to her dismay, that she was screeching.

Olivia began to weep. "I don't know, Mommy. I don't know what I'm going to do. Please help me. *Help* me."

Olivia's cry was a familiar one to Elaine, although she had not heard it in more years than she could count. From the time she could speak, Olivia would wail those words—"Mommy, help me!"—in precisely the same tone of agonized despair that clotted her voice now. At first, Elaine would run to her, panic twisting her innards, terrified that in her moments of inattention the girl had been hurt. She invariably found Olivia stamping her foot in frustration over a lost Barbie shoe, or crying over a dried-up marker or a broken crayon, or furious with her inability to pull a doll's dress over her teddy bear's head. Elaine would kneel down, grab Olivia by her bony shoulders, and say, in as cool a voice as she could muster, given her anger at what proved once again to be an unnecessary alarm, "Don't yell for me like that when it's not an emergency. You don't need my help. You *don't.*" Eventually Olivia had gotten the message. By the time she'd started school, in fact, she had grown into a resourceful little girl, perfectly able to make her own chocolate milk, climb on a stool to pull a sweater down from its shelf in her closet, rewind and replay a video on the VCR. Elaine had always been proud of her daughter's independence and ingenuity—it was the characteristic of Olivia's for which she felt the most responsible.

But this cry rang with that same ancient, desperate need, as if those intervening years of maturity had never happened. And yet her reaction was not what it had been back then. Elaine got up and crossed the room. This time, instead of shaking Olivia by the shoulders, she kneeled down and opened her arms. Olivia sagged into them and lay her head heavily against Elaine. Elaine stroked her daughter's rough, uncombed hair. She felt the spreading damp of Olivia's tears on her shirt. She leaned her cheek against the top of her daughter's head and crooned softly to her. "It'll be all right, honey. I promise you. It will all be all right." And then, when sobs continued to rack Olivia's delicate frame, and the force of her tears would not lessen, Elaine said, "I'll help you. I promise. I'll help you."

Olivia woke on the morning of her arraignment to the sun shining through the slats of her Venetian blinds. She hadn't bothered to twirl the shades closed—the fog generally clung to the hills of Berkeley until well into the day, and there wasn't often enough sun to disturb her sleep. But last night she hadn't fallen asleep until close to dawn, and the unusually brilliant day found her groggy and nervous, her eyes gritty with exhaustion, her stomach in the grip of the now familiar nausea. It was as if the fog that had abandoned its usual post had instead taken up residence in her brain. She lay in bed for a while, her fists balled and pressed into the pit of her stomach. She didn't stir until she heard a light tap on the door.

"Olivia?" Elaine said, through the closed door.

"Yeah," she mumbled.

"You need to get up, honey. You have to be in court in a couple of hours."

Elaine walked into Olivia's room and stood uncertainly in the middle of the floor, staring around her. Olivia flipped over and attempted a smile.

"Sorry about the mess," she said, motioning at the piles of clothes and books that were tumbled haphazardly around the room.

Elaine pursed her lips, and Olivia was sure she was about to be treated to the same lecture on tidiness and order she'd received nearly every day of her childhood. Instead, her mother said, "It's your room, you can keep it however you like."

Olivia's eyes widened, and she tried not to smile. "No, really. I'm going to clean it up. I just feel kind of awful right now."

Elaine came over and sat down on the bed next to her. "Because of today? Because of the arraignment?"

Olivia shook her head. She hadn't even begun to worry about the arraignment. Izaya had promised her that it would be nothing more than a formality, and she was distracted with other, more pressing things. "No. I'm just really nauseated."

Elaine inhaled sharply, as if she had forgotten about the pregnancy and Olivia had taken her by surprise. She smoothed the blanket with her hand and then tucked her hair behind her ear. "You should get up," she said.

Olivia heaved herself up out of bed and stooped down to pick up a pair of jeans from the floor.

"You're not wearing those!" Elaine said, reaching out a hand and grabbing the jeans. "Olivia, you can't possibly go to court in jeans." She sounded almost hysterical.

Olivia hadn't actually been planning on wearing the dirty pants—she had planned on throwing them in the laundry hamper in the hall, but her mother's voice inspired in her a familiar petulance. "Why not?" she said. "Half the people there will be in prison jumpsuits. Why shouldn't I wear jeans?"

Elaine stared at her for a moment and then shrugged. "Because you have to look nice for the judge. You *have* to, Olivia. This is not a game."

Olivia dropped the jeans back on the floor and crossed to the desk chair. Before she had gone to bed, she had laid out a long plum-colored peasant skirt she had bought at CP Shades on sale the year before and a matching short-sleeve sweater. She tugged on the clothes and turned back to her mother. "Is this good enough?" she said, peevishly.

"Much better," Elaine said, rising to her feet and crossing to the door. "I'd like to leave a little early if you don't mind. I want to stop by the pharmacy and make a few quick calls before we go to the courthouse."

Olivia shook her head. "You don't have to go with me, Mom."

"What?" Elaine asked, her hand on the doorknob. "What are you talking about? Of course I'm coming with you."

Olivia swept back her hair with one hand and clipped a barrette into place with the other. "Honestly, I'd rather you didn't. It's, like, a two-minute hearing. It's no big deal. I'd just as soon go by myself." She looked at herself in the mirror and tugged a few hairs into place. She glanced over and saw Elaine's reflected expression. Her mother's mouth was pulled into a frown.

"Fine," Elaine said and walked out the door.

Olivia stood at the podium in the magistrate judge's courtroom pleating the fabric of her skirt in one nervous hand. Jorge huddled off to one side next to his attorney, a florid older man in a crumpled suit, and avoided Olivia's eye. The indictment charged her with three crimes: conspiracy to distribute methamphetamine, actual distribution of methamphetamine, and use of a communications facility to commit a drug crime. This last offense, Izaya had explained, was legalese for using a telephone to talk about a drug deal. Olivia made certain that she pronounced the words "not guilty" loudly and forcefully, so that everyone in the courtroom would understand who and what she was—an innocent person. No one in the courtroom, however, seemed to notice, apart from Izaya, who squeezed her hand.

The indictment was read to Jorge and Oreste as it had been read to Olivia, and they were asked for their pleas. The proceedings were translated for them by an interpreter, a small, pretty woman in a peach-colored suit and a helmet of blow-dried hair.

"Not guilty," Oreste said, in a thick, Mexican accent.

His voice so soft that Olivia could not hear him, Jorge muttered directly into the interpreter's ear. The interpreter's back was turned to Olivia, and when she bent over to listen to Jorge, Olivia saw the lines of her underwear straining against her tight skirt.

"Not guilty," the interpreter said, translating Jorge's whispered words into a loud and certain declamation of innocence that had something false about it, as if she were acting a part.

The judge motioned to the court clerk, who pulled a small wooden stick out of a pile. Olivia felt Izaya holding his breath.

"This case is assigned to the honorable Myron Horowitz, courtroom two."

Only Olivia could hear Izaya's muttered, "Fuck." She blanched and looked at him, but he was busily scrawling down the dates the clerk announced for motions and trial. Once they were dismissed, they walked quickly to the rear of the courtroom.

"Is that a bad judge?" Olivia whispered, wishing now that she'd let her mother come with her this morning.

Izaya pushed his fingers through his hair, disarranging his dreadlocks. "No, no. Not really. He's fine."

"But you said, 'Fuck.'"

"I was just hoping for one of the Carter appointees. They're the most liberal judges in the Northern district, but they're both on senior status and not taking too many cases."

"Who appointed Horowitz?"

"Reagan."

"Fuck," Olivia said.

"No, really, he's okay. He's not one of the most liberal guys, but he's not a conservative demagogue, either. It's really okay."

"You said that we'd only get a downward departure if the judge was on our side. Is *he* going to be on our side?"

"Maybe. Horowitz likes to say that he's tough but fair. That's true, for the most part. He's not some unpredictable wild card like some of the other judges. And it's not like he *never* gives any downward departures. He follows the rules, and that means he gives them when he thinks the law warrants it."

"Fuck," Olivia said again.

"Not so much. Maybe just a little bit fuck," said Izaya. "Come on outside so we can talk for a minute." He took her arm and started to lead her out of the courtroom.

"I thought you said you had another client entering a plea this morning."

Izaya paused. "Right, shit. Hold on a second." He hustled up the aisle and motioned discreetly at the court clerk. Olivia watched him whisper a few words to the woman, who nodded and waved him away. He then came back down the aisle, stopping to shake the hand of a young black man wearing a puffy down jacket, sitting next to an elderly woman in a felt hat with a flower on it.

"Okay, I pushed my other arraignment back to the end of the calendar," Izaya said when he returned to Olivia's side. "Let's go."

They walked out into the hallway and stood against a wall opposite the courtroom. Olivia stared at the marble floor and paneled walls. For the first time, she noticed the elegant appointments, only slightly marred by the panels of fluorescent lighting flickering overhead.

"This is a nice building," she said.

"Excuse me?"

"It's nice. I mean, it's not horrible and dingy like the ones you see on Court TV."

Izaya nodded. "Well, it's brand new. And it's federal court. More money to spend, I guess. Anyway, how are you? Are you okay?"

Olivia placed a hand on her belly. "I'm okay," she said.

"He's really not a bad judge."

"It could be worse."

"Right."

A door across the hall burst open, and two men in almost identical navy-blue suits walked out, arguing vociferously about the A's chances of winning a pennant any time in the next few years. Izaya and Olivia stood silently as the men made their boisterous way to the elevator bank.

Once they were gone, Izaya said, "Now's when we've really got to get cracking. I've already filed a discovery request with the government, and I'm going to ride them to get me the evidence sooner rather than later. I'm also going to get everything I can on the informant. We may need to go to court for that, but trust me, I'll get it."

"I trust you," Olivia said.

He nodded. "Good. We're going to need to work together on this. I'm counting on you to help me prepare the case."

"Okay."

He reached into his pocket and pulled out a small hammered-silver card case. "I'm going to give you my cell phone number. If I'm not in the office, I'm generally reachable on my cell. Call me if you think of something important, or if you just need to talk. Or anything. And my email address is on the card, too. You can always email me, although I'm a little leery of that. I know I'm probably being paranoid, but I try not to put anything in an email that I wouldn't want to hear read out in court."

He scrawled a telephone number on the card and handed it to her. As she took it, she ran her fingers across the silver case.

"This is nice," she said.

"Yeah, it was a present from my dad. When I won my first trial." He flipped it open and showed her the inscription engraved under the top. *To a Chip Off the Old Block.*

"Pretty fucking corny," he said.

"Is your father a lawyer, too?"

Izaya nodded. "My dad is Ervin T. Upchurch."

"Who?"

Izaya laughed. "I'll have to tell him you said that. He's a private criminal-defense lawyer. He's kind of famous. He's a commentator for CNN. He pretty much does only high-profile cases. You know, if the vice president's kid gets busted or if some rap star kills his girl-friend. That kind of thing."

"I think I've heard of him," Olivia said. "How come you don't work for him?"

"Because *this* is what I want to be doing. I'd rather be repre-senting somebody like you than the types my dad defends."

"What type am I?"

"The type that's getting screwed by the system. The type that deserves a lot better."

"Do I deserve you?" she asked.

"You deserve the best."

"And are you the best?"

Izaya blushed and looked down at his shoes. Olivia put her hand on his sleeve, and he raised his eyes to hers.

"Are you the best?" she asked again, not breaking her gaze.

He looked back and then smiled. "I'm pretty good. Listen, I'd better get inside or my other client will think *he* deserves someone else. I'll call you soon, okay?"

He patted her hand with his and gently returned it to her. Then he slipped inside the courtroom, leaving Olivia alone in the hall. For a moment or two she thought about their conver-sation. She was embarrassed at the thought that Izaya might think she had been flirting with him, and at the knowledge that she had been. The last thing she had time to think about now was a man, and her lawyer was the last man she should fixate on. Except, of course, that he wasn't the least obvious choice, by any means. He was young, and he was handsome. He was tak-ing care of her. That was not something she was accustomed to. He was the only person in the calamity that her life had become who both knew what he was doing and was on her side. But, Olivia reminded herself, if he was standing by her, it was only because that was his job; he was paid to be on her team. She determined to dismiss anything she felt toward him as a kind of attorney-client transference, like when you fell in love with your shrink—only more dangerous.

Olivia pushed thoughts of Izaya out of her mind and concentrated on Jorge. She didn't want to leave before she'd had a chance to talk to him. It was a long wait; the U.S. Marshals only took the line of inmates out after the judge had worked his way through the entire calendar. She stood there in the empty hallway, chewing on the fingernails of one hand, the other pressed into her belly to quiet the nausea that had overcome her again as soon as Izaya had gone. The air was redolent of a musty, not unpleasant odor, like wood chips or sawdust. In the silent, empty hallway, Olivia slowly became aware of a humming noise, a throbbing, as if the building were breathing along with her. At first the sound bothered her, but the longer she waited the more she began to find it comforting. She leaned back against the wall, and by the time the doors opened and Jorge and the other inmates filed out past her, it had lulled her almost to sleep. Olivia jerked her eyes open and grabbed Jorge's arm.

"Jorge, I went to visit you but you didn't put me on your visitors list. I need to talk to you." Her voice came out in a rush of angry Spanish.

Jorge's brown eyes looked wet, as if he were trying not to cry. He wrenched his arm out of her hand and kept walking. Olivia ran after him.

"Jorge! Stop! I need to talk to you!" she shouted.

"Move away from the inmate!"

She looked into the ruddy face of the guard who'd been almost kind to her when she'd first been arrested. He lowered his voice. "Move away, Miss."

She backed up, slowly. "I need to talk to him," she said.

The guard shook his head. "You can't, not here. And you won't be allowed to visit him. Not with an indictment pending against you."

"Oh," she said.

The guard turned back to the row of inmates and led them down the hall. She watched Jorge's back in its orange jumpsuit as he walked away from her. He did not turn around.

Olivia felt her rage ebb away, leaving behind a calm hollowness. She picked up her bag from the floor where she left it and walked to the bank of payphones lined up against the far wall of the hallway. She hauled up the torn phone book that hung by a chain from a hook in the wall and leafed through it. To her surprise, there, on the very first page of listings, was a section called Abortion Services. She looked at the large ads with the faces of smiling, relieved-looking women. She chose one called Family Choices, because the young black woman in the ad was being counseled by a woman who resembled Elaine.

To Olivia's consternation, they gave her an appointment for the following morning.

When he left Olivia, Izaya was smiling. It wasn't until he was sitting on the bench behind the defense table with the other attorneys that his smile faded, and he began to wonder what exactly was going on between him and his pretty young client. Izaya loved being in court; even the most mundane of appearances, like this morning's perfunctory arraignments, gave him a buzz, a jolt of electric vigor. He sometimes suspected that this enthusiasm often made him seem inappropriately cheerful, given the circumstances in which his clients found themselves. He could not help but enjoy, however, how women looked at him when he was in the courtroom. He knew he was a fine-looking man, and he made very conscious use of that, filling his jury with women and enjoying in particular his appearances before female judges. Female opposing counsel made for good opponents, too, although Amanda Steele seemed utterly immune to his charms.

He was, thus, not surprised at the frisson of sexual tension that had hummed between him and Olivia. What was startling, however, was his discomposure. Izaya had represented only a couple of female clients—there were, relatively, so few women arrested for federal crimes that a public defender could go his entire career representing only men. Izaya had almost certainly engaged in a mild flirtation with the other women he'd represented—it was an almost unconscious behavior on his part. He couldn't help it. But for some reason, with Olivia, it felt different: it felt wrong. Perhaps because she was so appealing and from more or less the same background as he was. They had gone to the same high school, after all. Perhaps because under different circumstances, and if he hadn't sworn off white girls, he might actually have taken her out. Whatever the reason, he felt bad about flirting with her, and he vowed not to do it again.

Izaya's other client was last on the calendar, so he had plenty of time to affirm that vow before he had to step up to the podium. Rondell Duffin stood before the court with his hands shoved into the pockets of his North Face down jacket, his chin thrust out, and his eyes half-closed. Izaya made a mental note to give the kid a lesson in respecting the judge, or at least pretending to. Gang-banger attitude didn't generally go over too well with the federal judiciary. When the magistrate announced the case assignment, Izaya had to stifle a grunt of frustration. Sure, this kid, whose open-and-shut bank robbery was going to result in a quick plea and a three-year sentence no matter which judge he got, ended up with the softest touch, while Olivia drew Horowitz, a rigid by-the-book authoritarian who seemed to delight in computing the sentencing guidelines with an inflexible precision.

After the magistrate left the courtroom, Izaya sat for a moment with his young client and the boy's grandmother.

"I'll call the prosecutor today about our plea," Izaya said, his voice sliding into the rhythms the other attorneys in his office laughingly referred to as I-bonics. He neither took offense, nor paid much attention to the teasing. Izaya spoke to his people in the way that made them and him most comfortable, and if he didn't exactly come by the accent naturally, what did that matter?

Izaya looked at the young man sitting glumly next to his grandmother. His hair was done in cornrows like fat caterpillars, tied at the ends with little red elastic bands. His lips were pooched out in an expression of tough nonchalance, but Izaya knew just how scared he was under the bluster. This young man was precisely the kind of client he'd come to the public defender's office to represent, Izaya reminded himself. He was here to help his black brothers in their struggles with the monolithic government that seemed hell-bent on incarcerating as many of them as humanly possible, not to help white kids who managed, despite every advantage, to screw things up enough to find themselves in jail.

"It's going to be all right, little brother," Izaya said.

His client shrugged his shoulders, and the old woman nodded.

"You gon' ask for that low end, right?" she said anxiously, the flower in her hat bobbing on its pipe cleaner stem.

Izaya explained once again the formula through which the court would reach her grandson's sentence. It didn't bother him that this was easily the fourth or fifth time. He knew how hard it was to grasp, and how anxious the woman was.

The old woman took his hand in hers and squeezed it. "You're a good boy," she said. "Your mama and daddy must be proud. Ervin T. Upchurch, that's your daddy?"

Izaya nodded, and saw the woman taking stock of his café au lait skin and the gold-brown highlights in his hair. He knew right away what the woman was wondering—was it possible that famous attorney, guest at the White House, winner of the NAACP image award, was yet another black man who had chosen to compromise himself and his people by marrying a white woman? There was, of course, no way that Izaya could answer her unasked question. The explanation was far too complicated, and too painful. Corinne Upchurch was precisely the upstanding, church-going, African-American woman Rondell's grandmother would have wanted her to be. Izaya had met his father's wife only once. It was at Corinne's insistence that he had *never* met his two younger half-sisters, Monique and Tamra, nor his older half-brother Ervin Jr. Ervin T. Upchurch had taken up with Ruth Feingold when he was a young man, not yet married to the woman with whom he would spend his life, but already the father of her son. He had not been living with Corinne at the time, but Izaya knew that his father nonetheless kept his relationship with the white woman a secret, even after he had fathered a son with her, and especially after he had left her and gone back and married Corinne. Izaya figured that his father had kept quiet about the child-support payments he paid with admirable regularity, too, although Corinne's equanimity when the three of them had finally shared a single, uncomfortable meal made him wonder if she had known about him all along.

"Yup, Ervin T. Upchurch is my father," he said.

His client's grandmother nodded. "He a proud man to have you as his son," she said, again.

Izaya wondered if that were true, if his graduation from Harvard, his clerkship on the Ninth Circuit, his success at the federal defender's office, had managed to dispel the embarrassment of having fathered a child with a white woman who was not his wife. He didn't think so. He saw his father every few months or so, whenever the man came to town. Ervin invariably took Izaya shopping at Wilkes Bashford, and most but not all of the thousand-dollar suits and two-hundred-dollar ties in Izaya's wardrobe had been purchased for him by his father. The man always seemed to hear about Izaya's victories almost as soon as they happened and greeted each with a congratulatory phone call and an expensive gift. But his interest seemed more avuncular than paternal, and he had never once broached the possibility of Izaya coming to work for him.

Izaya told himself that he had no interest in his father's high-end private practice, that he had become a public defender because he wanted to serve the people, *his* people. He did his best to pretend that Ervin's failure to make the offer did not cause him pain.

"That white girl—she in trouble?" the woman asked, interrupting his thoughts.

"Excuse me?" he said.

"That pretty little white girl with all the blond curls. She going to jail?"

"Not if I can help it," Izaya said.

Jorge leaned his head back against the torn vinyl seat of the bus and angled his knees to one side. In its previous incarnation, the bus had obviously ferried children, not felons. The modifications required by its rebirth had included bars on the windows and a metal grill separating the driver from his presumably dangerous cargo, but no one had bothered to consider the seating requirements of men twice the size of the pint-sized passengers for whom the bus had originally been designed. Jorge shifted his legs to avoid the similarly cramped ones of his seatmate, a tall black man whose forearms and knuckles were decorated with the ink-blue lines of jailhouse tattoos. The man grunted and glared at Jorge. Jorge bent his legs farther under his own body and pressed his palms against his neck, reflexively protecting his most vulnerable area. He felt the dull ache of the razor-burned skin of his throat. The disposable razors they gave him were worthless, the blades dull and pitted, and no matter how hard he rubbed his hands with the pale gray soap, he couldn't work up a lather. His skin was tugged and raw, and he'd cut himself at least three times. He looked worse than before he'd shaved. No wonder so many of the other inmates grew scraggly beards.

He flexed his fingers and wriggled his wrists. It depressed him that he had grown accustomed enough to the handcuffs that they no longer chaffed quite so badly. The shackles around his ankles were new, however. He supposed that he'd only have to wear those when he went to court. He wasn't sure how often that would be, however. His lawyer had come to visit him once in jail, but the man had been in such an obvious hurry, and their three-way conversation with the interpreter had been so awkward, that Jorge had forgotten to ask most of the questions that had been plaguing him since he'd been arrested. He'd tried to talk to the interpreter after the lawyer had shuffled the papers into his briefcase and moved on to another client, but the Spanish-speaking young woman had told him that she wasn't allowed to give him advice or even information. Her job was to translate, and that was all.

There were plenty of other prisoners who spoke Spanish, but Jorge was afraid to ask them about his case. Fear was too mild a word for the state of constant, soul-crushing terror in which he found himself at the North County Jail. He thanked the Virgin for Oreste, who seemed less scared, more composed. They weren't in the same cell, but Oreste had somehow worked it so the two of them were assimilated into a group of Mexican men who were from the same part of Michoacán as Oreste. Jorge was sure that without Oreste's benediction, these very same men would have turned on him, would have beaten him, or worse. He tried, however, not to think about that.

There was a lot about which he was trying not to think. First and foremost was the brief and horrible explanation his lawyer had given of the mandatory sentences for drug dealing. He was trying not to think about the letter to his parents he'd begun and torn up more times than he could count. And most importantly, he was trying not to think about Olivia. This was a constant effort of will. He had consciously to force her from his mind, because thinking of her caused him to be overcome by a humiliated panic that he knew the other inmates could smell on him. The guilt about what he'd done to her made him weak, and, while he knew very little about being a prisoner, he knew enough to understand that weakness was a fatal condition.

On the bus back to the jail from court, however, he indulged himself. He allowed himself to wonder what was happening to her. Oreste was convinced that Olivia had snitched on them; otherwise, he argued, how could she have gotten out on bail when the two of them were forced to stay inside? He'd taken to calling her *la puta rubia,* not at all worried that Jorge would object to his girlfriend being referred to as a blond whore. And Jorge did not, of course, defend her. Oreste was the only thing standing between him and utter isolation, and the last thing he could do was alienate the man. Besides, Jorge told himself, it wasn't impossible that Olivia had given information against them. The girl had a self-righteous streak that had lately grown to wear on him. He could imagine her testifying against them in the name of honesty.

It made him feel better to think her capable of informing on him, and if some voice of reason told him that he knew full well that Olivia would not have done something like that to him, or to anyone for that matter, that voice was muffled by the sounds of the prison, of men fighting, being beaten, howling with pain and rage. That the cries of anguish could all too easily have been his own, Jorge was absolutely aware, and he did whatever it took to keep those demons at bay, including making believe that Olivia was a deceitful *puta.*

The fantasy couldn't withstand her actual presence, however, and her hand on his arm had burned with the truth of his betrayal. He swallowed again, hard, to keep the tears that were hovering in the back of his throat from approaching his eyes.

"*Hombre?*" Oreste asked, from the seat behind him. "You okay?"

Jorge shook away the emotion that had threatened to overwhelm him. "*Si, si, hombre.* Just, you know, tired. Waking up at 3:00 A.M. for court sucks, man."

"Quiet on the bus!" a voice shouted. Jorge looked up to see one of the guards staring at him from behind the grill separating the inmates from the front seat. "No talking," the guard said.

Jorge closed his eyes again and pushed away the memory of Olivia's tear-streaked face. Better not to think of her at all.

"I had an abortion once, before you were born."

Elaine didn't look at Olivia when she spoke. She kept her eyes firmly on the road in front of her, and she gripped the steering wheel tightly with both hands. She had no idea why she was telling this to her daughter. Perhaps to make Olivia feel less alone; perhaps merely to fill the thick and cloying silence in the car. She had never told anyone before, not the baby's father, not even Arthur. Yet her reticence was as confusing to her as her sudden confession. She hadn't been ashamed of the abortion; she wasn't ashamed now. She certainly had never had any ambivalence about her decision. She had only just arrived in San Francisco from New Jersey, had been living in the commune in the Haight for no more than a month or so when she found herself pregnant. There had never been any question in her mind about what she should do; she didn't want a baby, and more importantly, she wasn't entirely sure who the father was. There was one man, a boy really, with a crooked beak of a nose and an oddly high-pitched and nasal voice, who Elaine thought was the most likely candidate. He had a narrow fish-white chest with black hairs sprouting around small nipples, and she didn't like him very much. She had never been particularly promiscuous, but in those first giddy days in Haight Ashbury she had done a lot of things for the first time. She took up the guitar; she dropped acid. And she slept around. Any one of three or four men might have fathered the baby who had taken up residence in her womb for so brief an instant, but Elaine was, for some reason, convinced the responsibility lay with the one she found most repugnant. She wasn't sure he would have cared about the abortion, but she hadn't wanted to find out. She'd gone alone to a clinic at the far end of Ashbury Street. Now, more than twenty-five years later, she remembered almost nothing of the experience other than that it had hurt much less than she had expected. Perhaps the real answer to the question of why she never talked about it was that it simply wasn't particularly important—it had made very little impression on her at all.

"Did you think about keeping the baby?" Olivia asked.

"God no."

"Why not?"

"That would have been a ridiculous thing to do. For one thing, I was much too young."

"How old were you?"

"About your age."

Olivia didn't reply.

Elaine continued, "The last thing I was ready to be was somebody's mother."

Elaine pulled into the parking lot of the anonymous low brick building that housed the clinic. She pulled into a spot and got out of the car. She waited for Olivia, but her daughter didn't come.

Elaine walked around to the passenger side of the car and knocked on the window.

"Olivia?"

Olivia heaved a sigh and got out of the car. She walked off in the direction of the clinic entrance, and Elaine followed.

The waiting room was decorated in a kind of shabby multicultural chic with posters of smiling black and brown women on the walls. Olivia and Elaine sat next to one another on a low lumpy couch that looked better suited to a frat house than a doctor's office. There were a few other women in the room. One, a pretty girl who looked about sixteen or seventeen, was accompanied by a nervous boy in a Bishop O'Dowd football jacket. Another girl looked about twelve, but surely she must have been older. Her mother, a fierce-looking woman with braids molded into an elaborate sculpture on the top of her head, held her daughter's hand tightly, as if afraid she would run away. The girl was gnawing the thumb nail of the hand not clasped in her mother's iron grip.

The jiggling shoe of the football player tap-tapping against the leg of his chair was the only sound in the room. Then the front door banged open and an obviously pregnant woman walked in, leaning heavily on the arm of a man who could only have been her husband. She was Asian, with thick dark hair bobbed at her chin. Her face was red and puffy and her eyes swollen almost shut. She held a soggy tissue in one hand. Her husband was a dark-haired white man with thickly lashed, dazzling blue eyes that looked out of place in an otherwise inconspicuous face. He led his wife to the receptionist's window and, holding her up with one arm, tapped the bell.

The window slid open, and Elaine could see the face of the same earnest-looking woman who had signed Olivia in.

The man tried to say his wife's name, but his voice cracked, and Elaine was surprised to see tears filling his eyes and running down his face. She hadn't seen many men freely weeping. Arthur, on the rare occasions when he was so moved, tended to screw up his face and rub frantically at the one or two tears that gathered in the corners of his eyes. This poor man, this father, wept openly, his face wet, his nose running, his luminous eyes aglow with grief. His wife put a small hand on his back and leaned into the window. She whispered something, and within seconds the young woman had opened a door for them and was leading them inside.

Elaine turned to Olivia who was gasping as though she were hyperventilating.

"Honey," Elaine whispered. "Are you okay?"

"Why are they here? She's so...so...pregnant!"

"Well, I imagine that there is probably something wrong with the baby."

"God. I never thought about that. That people would have to have abortions even when they *want* the baby."

"Poor things," Elaine murmured.

Olivia sat for a few moments, swallowing air in short gasps. Suddenly, she sprang to her feet. "I don't want to do this. I'm not going to do this." Her face was pale and her lips had compressed to a thin white line. "Do I have to do this?"

Elaine put out a soothing hand. "It'll be fine, Olivia. Sit down."

"*Do I have to do this?*" Olivia asked again. Her nostrils flared with each breath, and beads of sweat stood out on her forehead.

Elaine glanced quickly around at the others in the room, embarrassed of Olivia. Only the young girl was looking at them. All the others kept their faces averted.

"It's okay, honey. What you're feeling is perfectly normal," she whispered.

"Do I have to?" Olivia said, again, her voice louder.

"No, of course you don't *have* to do anything. But let's not be rash. They'll call you in a minute, and then you'll have a chance to talk to the counselor. I'm sure she'll be able to reassure you."

"I want to go," Olivia said. "Mom, I have to get out of here."

"Take that girl on out of here," the woman with the young daughter said, suddenly. "Take her on home."

Elaine stared at her, and the woman looked back, nodding. "Go on. Go on home," she said. Elaine felt at once that they were in a sorority of two; grandmothers whose grandchildren could not be born. Except she could see that the other woman would have, under other circumstances, rejoiced in a grandchild. That she fully expected one day to do so. Elaine knew that the other woman could never comprehend the dread with which Elaine looked forward to Olivia ever having a baby.

Elaine felt a paralyzing shame at what she was sure was her entirely unnatural horror at the prospect of becoming a grandmother.

"Go wait in the car," she whispered, pushing Olivia in the direction of the door. Then she went to the window and rang the bell. When the receptionist finally reappeared, Elaine said, "We aren't going to stay."

"Are you sure?" the receptionist said. "Would you like to reschedule?"

"I don't know."

"Don't wait too long. It's a different procedure after twelve or thirteen weeks."

"Yes," she said. "I know." She looked toward the door through which Olivia had disappeared. "Can you give me another appointment? For tomorrow?"

The receptionist pecked at her keyboard, her eyes on a computer screen that was hidden from Elaine's view. "We can do the day after tomorrow, Saturday, at nine. How about that?"

Elaine nodded, gratefully.

The receptionist paused, her fingers hovering over the computer keys. "This has to be *her* decision, you know. *You* can't make her do it, and we certainly won't."

Elaine frowned at the receptionist, but the other woman returned her gaze steadily, sympathetically, and not at all self-righteously.

In a cold, firm voice, Elaine said, "We'll be here on Saturday."

Olivia wanted to explain to her mother how she felt. She wanted to describe her disconcerting sensation that she was watching all of this happen to someone else. Someone else was going to jail, someone else was contemplating an abortion. And someone else was drowning under a creeping tide of panic whenever she stopped concentrating on keeping it at bay, whenever she lost her focus for even a moment. Olivia wanted to tell her mother, too, that the only time she felt like a real person, a single, whole human being, was when she contemplated the little blind fish swimming in her womb. When she put her hand on her belly and felt the firm swell underneath the soft roll of fat at her waist, she awoke, for a moment. She was sure that if she could explain it well enough, her mother would understand.

"I just really want to stay pregnant," she said.

Elaine, who'd been driving silently back up the freeway toward Berkeley, didn't take her eyes off the road.

"You can't stay pregnant."

"Why not?"

"Because at some point you'll have a baby, and you won't be pregnant anymore. You'll be a mother, with something absolutely dependent on you for every breath it takes. You'll never have a minute to yourself again. You'll be overwhelmed by the responsibility. *If* you're lucky. If not, you'll be in jail. And then what?"

"I can deal with it."

"Oh, Olivia. For goodness sake. You *cannot* deal with it. What do you intend to do? Even if you don't go to jail, you don't have any money. You haven't even tried to go back to work, have you? You have no idea what a burden being a single mother is. How could you possibly raise a child? You'll just ruin your life more than you have already."

"I haven't ruined my life."

"Haven't you?"

Olivia thought about that for a moment. Was her life ruined? She was twenty-two years old. Were the next fifty or sixty years going to be defined by that one night, that single moment in her car, in front of that run-down house in Oakland? If she were sent to prison, would those ten years really haunt all the succeeding decades of her adulthood? With a clarity that surprised her, given how murky everything had lately seemed, she realized that her mother was right. Her life, the fantasy of her future that she had been imagining ever since she was a small child, was irrevocably changed. Ruined. But if that were the case, then what did it matter if she had a child or not? You couldn't wreck something that was already destroyed.

"You did it. You raised a child on your own." Olivia's voice was plaintive and whining, and she saw her mother's jaw clench. For the briefest of instants, she wondered whether Elaine was going to slap her. But of course she wouldn't. Her mother had never hit her, never even spanked her.

Instead, Elaine lashed out with her tongue. "Right. I raised you on my own. And who knows what my life would have been like if I hadn't had to."

Olivia had always told people that Elaine wasn't particularly warm, that she wasn't the kind of mother who knitted sweaters or kissed owies. She had even suspected that Elaine had blamed her for the limitations, the compromises, that had marked her ultimately disappointing life. But now Olivia felt oddly vindicated by her sudden comprehension of how much Elaine resented the very fact of her birth. And yet, she also understood, at that moment, that it was not she herself who was the target of Elaine's dissatisfaction. It was not that Elaine did not want to be *Olivia's* mother. But rather, she wished she were nobody's mother at all.

"What do you want me to do, apologize for being born?" Olivia said.

Elaine scowled. "Don't be melodramatic. You know I love you. But who knows what things might have been like if I'd been smarter, if I hadn't gotten pregnant."

"I'm sorry I screwed everything up for you so badly."

Elaine sighed. "You are misunderstanding me on purpose. Nothing is screwed up. I do work that I enjoy; I'm in a relationship with someone I love. And I have you." Olivia couldn't help but feel that this last was added as an afterthought. "I'm not unhappy," Elaine continued. "It's just…it's just that I'll never know what might have been if I'd waited. If I hadn't married your father and been such a young mother."

Olivia didn't credit Elaine's excuses. For once in her life, her mother had spoken the truth about how she really felt. Nothing she said now could overshadow that, could erase those words from the air where they hung, glinting beads of pure, honest resentment.

"Well, if you're so happy, and you did so well, then why do you think it will be any different for me?"

"For one thing, I wasn't facing a criminal prosecution. And for another, I had a whole lot of help from my parents."

So. That was what really worried her mother. She would be forced to rescue Olivia as her own mother had once rescued her.

"Don't worry. The baby isn't going to be your responsibility. Even if I go to jail, I won't make you take care of it."

"Oh, really? So who *will* take care of it if you go to jail? What are you going to do, bring it with you?"

The thought hadn't occurred to Olivia. It seemed, suddenly, to be a wonderful idea. Being in prison with a baby would be infinitely preferable to being there alone. After all, the worst part was the crushing loneliness, the grim certainty that no one around you cared whether you lived or died. Her baby would depend on her, would need her, would love her. Caring for the baby would fill her days, would hold the persistent tedium of incarceration at bay.

"That's exactly what I'll do. I'm sure they have some kind of program for inmates with babies. I saw that once on TV. It's like a special prison, for moms. The baby stays with you for the first couple of years."

"Olivia, don't be ridiculous. Even if there were such a thing, what would you do after that? Izaya said the mandatory minimum is ten years. What do you think you're going to do with the child for the next eight years? Dump it in foster care? You *must* get an abortion. You don't have a choice."

Olivia allowed herself to imagine the baby in prison with her for another moment before her fantasy evaporated under the relentless sun of her mother's sensible cruelty. Of course, Elaine was right. Olivia did not have a choice. She suddenly felt horribly sorry that she had run from the clinic. If she'd only stayed, it might all be over by now.

"Can we turn around? Can we go back?" she whispered, her eyes closed.

"Oh, honey," Elaine said gently. Olivia felt her mother's hand smooth a lock of curls behind her ear and gently stroke her cheek. She didn't open her eyes. "We have an appointment for Saturday," Elaine said.

Olivia didn't realize she was crying until she felt her mother press a tissue into her hand. She swabbed her cheeks and blew her nose loudly. "Okay. Saturday," she said.

When they got home, Olivia got into her bed, drew the down quilt over her head, and submerged herself in the soft, comforting dark. She fell asleep almost immediately, waking only when Elaine knocked on the door to her room.

"Dinner's ready," Elaine said, opening the door.

"I'm not hungry," Olivia murmured, resenting her mother for having drawn her up out of the blank luxury of sleep.

"You have to eat."

Olivia didn't reply. She rolled over and buried her face in her pillow, willing her mother to go away. Elaine stood for a moment longer, tapping her fingers against the door jam. Then she sighed and left, leaving the door ajar.

Olivia seethed, knowing as she felt it that her rage was out of proportion to Elaine's crime of having failed to shut her back away in the soothing dark. She tried to fall back asleep, but the open door was a crack in the wall of her security, forcing her to cling to the misery of consciousness. Finally, she flung back the quilt and heaved herself out of bed. As soon as she stood, she was hit with a wave of nausea, and she ran for the bathroom. She bent over the bowl, trying to vomit. Only a mouthful of sour saliva came up. She wiped her face on a towel and plodded back to her bedroom. She had no sooner slammed the door and crawled back into bed when she heard her mother's voice.

"Are you okay? What happened?"

"Nothing. Morning sickness. Can you shut the door? Please." Olivia heard the door click shut. She lay in bed for a long time, miserable with queasiness, but unwilling to leave her room to get the food that would settle her stomach. Hours later, when she finally heard the door to Elaine and Arthur's room open and shut, she got out of bed and crept into the kitchen. She made slice after slice of toast, which she ate dripping with butter and jam. She didn't bother washing her face or brushing her teeth before she returned to her bed, and during the night, whenever she licked her lips, she tasted blackberries.

The next morning, she awoke after Elaine and Arthur had already left the house. She spent the day in her pajamas, watching television and eating cold cereal, toast, leftover Chinese food. She discovered that if she made sure her stomach was full at all times, the nausea was manageable. After the sun faded, and the dusk had begun to settle around the house, she heard a car pull into the driveway. She grabbed a bag of almonds and a block of cheddar cheese and ran to her room. She jumped back into bed, and lay, still and silent, listening to Arthur bustle around the house. He didn't come to her door, and she didn't leave her room. When Elaine came home, Olivia heard the rumble of their voices, but couldn't make out what they were saying. An hour or so later, Olivia heard her mother's steps come down the hall. She held her breath. The footsteps stopped just outside her door, and Olivia waited for Elaine's knock. It never came. After a moment or two, her mother walked away. Olivia fell asleep, and woke in the middle of the night to a dark and silent house. She made another midnight raid on the kitchen, this time eating the remains of a roast chicken she found in the fridge.

The next morning, Olivia woke to Elaine's hand on her shoulder. "Honey, wake up. We have to be at the clinic in an hour."

Olivia shrugged the down comforter up above her head. She buried her face in the cool softness of her pillow and concentrated on the gentle buzzing in her ears.

"Olivia." Elaine shook her. "Olivia, that's enough. It's time to get up."

"In a little while. I'm really tired. I just need to sleep for awhile longer," Olivia mumbled, her voice muffled by the bedclothes.

"No. Not in a little while. Now. You've been in that bed for two solid days. We have to leave in an hour. Get up."

Olivia sank deeper under the covers and shut out the sound of her mother's voice. It wasn't that she couldn't get up. She could very clearly imagine the steps involved in getting out of bed. If she wanted to, she could sit up, move her feet to the floor, stand up, walk across the room to the pile of clothes in the corner of the room. She could even imagine getting dressed. It was not that she was unable to leave her bed. There just didn't seem to be any particular reason to engage in such protracted activity. And the bed felt so very soft.

Olivia felt her body shift as Elaine sat down next to her. She closed her eyes against the sudden glare of light as Elaine drew the covers down from her face.

"Honey, I know what you're feeling. It's depression. I know because I've been exactly where you are. You just have to get up.

Otherwise it will get harder and harder every day until finally you won't be able to do it even if you want to."

Olivia looked up at her mother's face. Her eyebrows were furrowed in a look of concern that was entirely different from the anxious, worried expression Olivia had planted there so many times before. This time her mother looked almost compassionate. Olivia's eyes filled with tears, and she half-sat up. She fell across Elaine's lap, and felt her mother's hand softly stroke her hair.

"I don't want to have an abortion," she mumbled into her mother's lap. She hadn't thought about the words before they left her mouth, but suddenly she realized that they were absolutely true. She did not want to have an abortion. She wanted to be pregnant. She wanted to feel the baby grow and take shape inside of her. She wanted to create a little person, to make this hypothetical being real. After that, who knew. She wasn't sure she wanted a baby. She had, in fact, no idea what she was going to do after it was born, but she knew, suddenly and for certain, that she wasn't going to end her pregnancy.

Elaine sighed and said, "That's just the depression talking."

Olivia sat up, shaking off her mother's hand. "Being pregnant is the only good thing that has happened to me in all this. I'm not going to have an abortion. I'm just not going to."

Elaine bit her lip. She reached up and tucked her hair behind her ear. "Will you give it up for adoption?"

Olivia shrugged her shoulders. "I don't know." She closed her eyes and imagined holding her baby, a warm wriggling creature with its father's black hair. She felt curiously detached from the imagined infant. It was hard even to fantasize about a baby, about her baby. And yet, it was harder still to imagine the baby gone. "I don't know what I'm going to do. All I know is that I'm not going to end it."

In a soft and almost wheedling voice, Elaine said, "Have you given any thought to what you'll do if you end up being convicted?"

"I know *you* couldn't keep him. Right?" It was impossible to disguise the hope in her voice, but her mother began shaking her head almost before Olivia could finish her sentence.

"I'm sorry, Olivia. But that's just not a possibility. Arthur and I are not at a place in our lives right now where we could be parents. We're planning our wedding. We're preparing for retirement. We're beginning to work less and enjoy ourselves more. Neither of us could start all over again at this point."

Olivia wasn't surprised. She'd known from the very moment she'd seen the faint pink lines in the pregnancy test that her mother would not be able to help her, that she would be entirely on her own. She wondered for a moment what it would have been like to have a different mother, one who would have embraced the idea of a grandchild with joy, one who would have automatically assumed that it was her job to care for the baby if her own daughter couldn't. A mother, for example, like Jorge's.

Olivia had first met Jorge's parents, Araceli and Juan Carlos, only a few weeks before she had left San Miguel and returned home to the United States. One evening when he picked her up, Jorge told her they were going to a party. Olivia didn't know until they arrived at the restaurant on top of a hill over-looking the city that it was his younger sister's *quinciñeros,* her fifteenth birthday celebration. At first she had been embar-rassed, dressed as she was in nothing more elaborate than a pair of jeans and a white embroidered shirt she'd bought in the market. The other women wore shiny gowns and glittering makeup, and tottered around the room in spiked heels.

Her self-consciousness soon evaporated, however, when Jorge's mother and sisters pulled her into their tight knot of women sit-ting crowded around a table in the center of the room. Laughing, they waved Jorge away and piled Olivia's plate high with tamales and *carnitas.* Jorge's mother, Araceli, a tiny, plump woman stuffed into a pink taffeta gown like a sausage into a casing, grabbed Olivia's hand in her own and held it tightly for the rest of the evening. She stroked Olivia's hair and, after drinking two or three small glasses of tequila, made Olivia promise that when she and Jorge had babies, they would be blond like their mother.

"I'll teach you to make *birria* and *menudo*, all the food that Jorge loves. And when you two want to go away for a little romance, maybe to the beach, to Coyuka de Benitez or Puerto Escondido in Oaxaca, you'll leave the babies with me. You'll come home, and they'll be fatter than ever! Right Yolanda? Manuela?"

Her daughters and daughters-in-law smiled and laughed. "If she had her way, they'd all be round as soccer balls!" one of Jorge's sisters said. Every time Olivia tried to get up, Araceli would squeeze her close, call her *mi hija*, her daughter, and insist that she remain seated by her side. By the end of the evening, Olivia had spent more time in Jorge's mother's embrace than she had Elaine's in the twenty years since she was a baby, and had fallen more in love with the sprightly little woman than she was with the son.

"Yeah, I know you can't take the baby. I don't know what I'm going to do if I get convicted. I'm just not going to go there right now, okay Mom? I can't think about that now. I just have to trust that Izaya will figure something out. The case will go away, and then it'll be me and the baby."

Elaine heaved a resigned sigh. "I suppose you could go back to college. When you were a baby, I lived in student housing. You could do that. I could give you money to help with child care."

Olivia tried to imagine herself back in school. Almost despite herself, she could see it so clearly. She would carry the baby to her classes in a sling on her back; the baby would sleep in its cradle while she studied. She smiled for the first time in days.

"That would be great. I mean, I really should go back to school. Especially if I have a baby to support."

"That's definitely a possibility we can discuss. That and adoption. You will at least consider adoption, won't you?"

Olivia closed her eyes. She didn't want to think about that. The fantasy of carrying her baby across campus like some kind of school mascot was too appealing.

"Olivia, you will at least consider it, won't you?"

She snapped her eyes open. "Okay. I'll think about it."

Elaine smiled at her. "Good. Now, how about some breakfast?"

Olivia swung her legs across Elaine's lap and hopped over her mother and out of bed.

"I'm starving," she said.

Arthur was squeezing oranges for juice when Elaine and Olivia walked into the kitchen. Olivia was still in her pajamas. He raised his eyebrows behind the girl's back and opened his mouth to ask the obvious question, but Elaine shook her head, and he pressed his lips shut.

"Arthur, honey, will you make us some breakfast? Something special?" Elaine asked.

He wrinkled his brow. "You don't like breakfast. You never eat breakfast."

She pinched her mouth into the frown she generally reserved for Olivia. While not the first time she'd aimed it at him, it was certainly rare. He felt immediately chastened, and then resentful.

"Okay, I'll make breakfast," he said.

Within twenty minutes, he'd concocted a spread of scrambled eggs with chives and cheese, toast with butter and blackberry jam, and banana pancakes. Olivia had tucked in happily, but he could tell that Elaine was forcing down the food. In a moment of contrition, he refilled her cup with coffee.

"You don't need to finish it," he said quietly, and slid the plate away from her. She blinked at him, gratefully, and he realized with a shock that she was just barely holding it together. Her lips were clenched so tightly they were white, and her hands scrabbled at the place mat, shredding the straw fibers. He moved behind her chair and put his hands on her shoulders, drawing her head back against his taut belly. She rested there, and he thought he could feel her unclench.

"So what's the deal, Olivia?" he asked. "Aren't you supposed to be getting an abortion today?" Elaine's shoulders stiffened under his hands, and she lifted her head away from his belly.

Olivia paused, a forkful of pancakes halfway to her mouth. While he waited for her to answer him, he watched a bead of syrup gather under the bowl of the fork and then drop off. It landed on the placemat in front of her.

"Watch out. You're dripping," he said.

She looked at him quizzically and then shoved the food into her mouth. "I'm not getting an abortion," she said, her mouth full.

"I can't believe it," he said. But of course, he could. If he had sat down and tried to figure out a way for Olivia to make matters even worse than they already were, he might well have arrived at this particular scenario. Of course she wasn't going to have an abortion; that would have simplified things.

"Believe it," Olivia said, in precisely the same tone of defensive smugness she'd adopted when confronted with a bad report card or a letter from the university notifying Elaine that her civil disobedience had gotten her placed on academic probation.

"Are you okay?" he asked Elaine, leaning over to look at her face.

"I'm fine," she said. "Olivia has decided not to have the abortion, but she hasn't yet decided to keep the baby. Right, Olivia?"

The girl shrugged and nodded. Arthur felt an intense rush of relief. When she said she wasn't having the abortion, he hadn't thought of adoption. But that's what she would do, of course. She'd give the baby up for adoption. It would not be Elaine's responsibility.

"Does your lawyer know you're pregnant?" Arthur asked.

"No," Olivia said

"You should tell him. I'll bet it will help with the trial. You know, make you more sympathetic or something. No judge is going to put a pregnant woman away for ten years."

Izaya was working late when Olivia called him. His cell phone rang, to the shrill tune of "Take Me Out to the Ball Game," and it took a minute for him to find it. He reminded himself, for perhaps the twenty or thirtieth time, to change the ringer setting.

"Hey," he said into the phone when he finally dug it out of the pocket of his leather jacket.

"Um, is Izaya there?"

"This is Izaya."

"Oh, great."

"Who is this?" he asked, although he recognized her voice.

Olivia identified herself, and then, without any preamble, and not particularly gracefully, she told him she was pregnant.

"You are not serious," he said, and then frowned at his reaction. His client's pregnancy had nothing whatsoever to do with him. Why, then, had it inspired in him an emotion that felt entirely too akin to anger?

"Yes. I'm serious."

He rubbed his hands across his jaw. "What are you going to do?"

"What do you mean?"

"I mean are you going to go through with it? Are you going to have this guy's baby?" He winced at his own words and was immediately sorry he'd said anything. She didn't answer. "God, I'm such an asshole. I'm sorry. What I should have said is, congratulations."

There was a moment of silence on the line. Then Olivia said, "Thank you. I just thought you should know in case it makes any difference. You know, for my case."

He leaned back in his chair and stared up at the pocked tile of the dropped ceiling. "Right. Well, thanks for telling me," he said. "Okay."

He flipped forward and rested his elbows on his desk. "Listen, I've got to go. I've got piles of work here." He flicked at the papers lying in front of him as though she could see them.

He ended the call and then turned off his phone. Reaching one hand around the back of his head, he snapped the rubber band off his dreadlocks and ran his fingers through them, loosening them around his face. Izaya never wore his locks down at work and almost never wore them that way at all. He kept them tied back off his head in a neat band. The truth was, he was not entirely comfortable with the heavy weight of his hair. He had started growing it in high school, while in the throes of a short-lived Ziggy Marley obsession. He had not anticipated how much work it would take to grow dreadlocks, how each lock had to be twisted and waxed, meticulously constructed and maintained. While he took pleasure in the clarity of this identifiable badge of his African-American identity, it was really the thought of the years of wasted effort that kept him from cutting his hair.

He pulled at his soft, spongy locks and thought of Olivia. This particular client seemed to consume far more of his energy, of his emotions, than any other. He had no explanation for his curious devotion. It was not merely that she was pretty; the world was full of pretty girls, girls the dating of whom would not result in disbarment and the loss of his job. Neither was it entirely the fact of her dependence on him. Over his years as a public defender, Izaya had become inured to his role as champion. But Olivia possessed an adamant innocence that compelled his attention. She was so certain, so sure of her righteousness, and at the same time so vulnerable.

Whatever he felt for this young woman, when the case ended, so would their relationship. That he had to remind himself of this and of the fact that he had absolutely no business being jealous because she had gotten herself knocked up by an incompetent fool of a boyfriend who couldn't even manage to do a simple drug deal without getting the two of them busted, was troubling to say the least.

He gathered his hair in his fist and snapped the rubber band back around it. He flipped through his Rolodex until he found Olivia's number. She answered almost immediately.

"Hey, I just had a thought," he said, his voice falsely jovial. "This pregnancy is the best thing that could possibly have happened, at least from the perspective of the case."

"What do you mean?"

"It's just one more reason for the jury to love you. You're just a poor, innocent, pregnant little white girl."

He was greeted with a burst of laughter, a giggle really. And he smiled.

"I'm telling you, girl, this is going to push the jurors right over the edge. They'll be knitting you baby booties."

"I hope you're right. I could use some booties. I've never knitted anything in my life."

When he hung up the phone, he stopped smiling. He leaned back in his chair and stared up at the ceiling. After a moment or two, he grabbed his Rolodex and started flipping through it, searching for a number to call. Finally, he found what he was looking for. Patrice Lajoie, a sweet-tempered woman who had never once, since they had met in their first year of law school, turned down his last-minute invitations. Izaya left his briefcase on the desk and spent the night in her friendly, comforting embrace. It was the first time in weeks that he hadn't taken work home with him.

Almost as soon as she made the decision not to terminate the pregnancy, as if the baby had been waiting for her to make up her mind before it began to grow in earnest, Olivia found herself unable to fit into her clothes. Even the waist of the overalls that she had adopted as a uniform once she could no longer button her jeans began to cut into her burgeoning belly. After a frustrating afternoon at the Goodwill store sifting through the piles of ruffled tops and stretched-out skirts in the maternity section, she gave up and bought a few oversized T-shirts and a pair of huge men's jeans that she cut off at her ankles and belted over the top of her belly with an old webbed belt the cashier had thrown into her bag for free. She wore her "new" clothes down to breakfast the morning after she bought them. Elaine looked at her, aghast, but said nothing.

That evening, Olivia, still wearing the jeans and a vast T-shirt with a decal of Ziggy Marley that had cracked and faded from a stranger's wearings and washings, sat in the kitchen, eating a pre-dinner snack of cereal and milk. She was baking a pan of chicken enchiladas for dinner, and the tangy smell of the *tomatillo* sauce had piqued her appetite. Not that it took much to do that. She was pretty much always hungry. Elaine bustled in the front door, her arms laden with shopping bags. She raised her eyebrows when she saw Olivia.

"Is that your dinner?" she asked.

"No, this is just kind of my appetizer. I made us enchiladas and red beans and rice. I'm going to serve that with a salad. Does that sound okay?"

"Sure, honey. It's sweet of you to make dinner."

"It's the least I could do," Olivia said. "And, anyway, I like to cook."

Elaine grimaced in mock horror. "God, you and Arthur. I don't know how you can stand it. I'd be happy never to cook my own food again."

"Well, Mom, it's no wonder. I mean, if you limit yourself to macaroni and cheese and spaghetti, it can get old pretty quickly."

As soon as the words were out of her mouth, Olivia realized that her mother would mistake her jocular comment for criticism.

Elaine's smile grew stiff, and she began unpacking her bags with short, jerky gestures, not looking at Olivia.

"Sometimes I served you better food than that, I think," Elaine said.

"You did. You did. I was just kidding. Really." Olivia pushed her cereal bowl away and plastered a smile on her face. "I used to love your tuna noodle casserole, remember?"

Elaine glanced up as if to make sure Olivia was serious. "That's true. You did. Although I think that was because of the potato chips I used to crumble on the top." She pulled two trim cardboard boxes out of the shopping bag and slid them across the counter to Olivia.

"I got you something," she said.

Olivia looked at the boxes. They were decorated with sketches of pregnant bellies and the words "Pregnancy Survival Kit." She opened them up. Each box contained a complete maternity outfit: leggings, skirt, two shirts, and a dress, one in black and one in navy blue. She pulled out the black dress and held it up to her body. It was made of cotton shot through with Lycra and was soft and comfortable. She glanced down at the tattered, second-hand jeans and ugly T-shirt she was wearing.

For a moment, Olivia felt a familiar flash of irritation with her mother. It was hard not to feel that these clothes were a reproach, an expression of the disgust Elaine felt for Olivia's Goodwill purchases. But then Olivia looked up at her mother. Her face bore an expression at once anxious and wistful, as if she were waiting for Olivia to find fault with her gift, as if she knew she could expect nothing else, but nonetheless imagined some different kind of reception, even some different kind of relationship, where a mother and daughter's offerings to one another were received with ease and comfort and nothing but thanks.

Olivia reached her arms around her mother and hugged her, tight.

"They're perfect," she said. "Thank you so much."

Elaine hugged her back, briefly, and then, her face red, reached back into the bag.

"I got you a couple of silk scarves, too," she said.

Izaya had been out of the office the two times Olivia had been by the Federal Building to check in with pretrial services, and she had had to cancel an appointment with him once because it conflicted with a prenatal checkup. He had mailed her the discovery—a thick file of audiotapes, photographs, agents' statements, records and logs of surveillance, transcripts of the informant's prior testimony, and some documents of which she could make neither head nor tail, and which it made her head hurt even to peruse. It was only once she had heard her voice on tape and seen the hazy photographs snapped of her as she waited in the car for Jorge, that Olivia had finally understood that the case wouldn't simply go away, no matter how much she wanted it to. Leafing through the pages of discovery, she'd realized that she had to gird herself for battle.

She and Izaya had spoken on the phone a few times, but their conversations after the one where she had told him she was pregnant, and he'd grown so inexplicably angry, were stiff and awkward. Mostly they communicated via email. She felt more comfortable with him over the ether. He was, somehow, more easygoing, natural even, and she felt free to be as well. His notes were brief, and usually imparted some specific bit of information like that they'd been granted a continuance or had a new date for their motions hearing or trial, but they had a casual, almost breezy quality. Her replies were similar in tone and generally limited to questions about the case or specific aspects of the law that she didn't understand, but she occasionally confided her fears and anxieties to him when they grew too numerous and overwhelming for her to contemplate alone. He replied right away and was invariably reassuring and kind.

This email intimacy made her feel close to Izaya, but they had not actually seen each other in weeks.

Olivia walked into Izaya's office wearing one of the dresses Elaine had given her. The gathered empire waist accented her belly and she looked like what she was—almost five months pregnant. Izaya stared at her stomach.

"Wow," he said. "You really *are* pregnant."

"I guess I kind of popped," Olivia said. She could feel herself blushing.

"Jeez, maybe if I use you as a visual aid, Amanda Steele would consider dismissing the indictment."

"Are you serious?"

"Sorry. I wish I were. So, how are you feeling?" Izaya asked.

"Physically?"

"That, too."

"Physically, I feel kind of great." It was true. The morning sickness had disappeared suddenly one day, as if someone had flicked a switch. The crushing exhaustion had departed at more or less the same time. She no longer felt the need for at least two naps a day, satisfying herself with one long one in the early afternoon. Her appetite had, if anything, increased, and she was indulging a series of cravings of the sort you heard about only on television sitcoms. Olivia was convinced that she always hungered after salt and vinegar potato chips mixed with chocolate chip mint ice cream, even when she wasn't pregnant. It was just that now she was perfectly willing to get up in the middle of the night and drive down to the 7-Eleven, and was more than able to put away the entire bag of chips and half gallon of ice cream in a single sitting.

"And otherwise?"

Olivia shrugged her shoulders. The answer to that question was strangely complicated. Whenever she thought about the looming trial, she felt the by-now-familiar tug of panic. However, it was oddly easy to keep her mind off the case, off her predicament, even off Jorge: the baby was an all-consuming distraction. All she thought about was the creature that she had nicknamed Dragon Baby, in honor of its due date planted squarely in the middle of the Year of the Dragon. That birthday was, according to Dorothy, the midwife who was providing Olivia's prenatal care at the Temescal Holistic Birthing Center, the most propitious in the Chinese Calendar. Olivia spent hours studying the pile of pregnancy books she'd bought at Pendragon Books on College Avenue—books reflecting every era of philosophies of childbirth from Ina Mae Gaskin's spiritual approach to midwifery to the cloying earnestness of the *What to Expect* library to the modern-woman jokery of the *Girlfriends' Guide*. She had used up an entire container of white-out erasing another mother's entries into an old day-by-day pregnancy diary, and then laboriously filled in her own symptoms and emotions. Week sixteen, day three: she felt a faint tug low in her pelvis—was it a kick?; took her prenatal vitamin at lunch because she forgot it at breakfast; gained two pounds; felt mild cramping in the late afternoon; drank three glasses of milk; walked for twenty minutes; thought it might be a boy.

Late at night she would lie perfectly still in bed and hold her breath. She was sure she could feel the beat of the baby's heart deep in the center of her body.

"Well, you *look* good," Izaya said. "You know, fit and healthy." It was true. Pregnancy suited Olivia. She was good at it. Her pimples had cleared up once her nausea had abated, and a faint pinkness shone through her translucent skin. Her eyes were bright, and her hair hung in bright blond and red ringlets down her back behind the fuchsia scarf she'd used to pull it off her forehead.

Olivia smiled at him. "Thanks."

"Are you working?"

"At my mother's pharmacy. Behind the lunch counter."

"How's that going?"

"Okay. I just couldn't go back to the restaurant. You know, where I worked with…him." Olivia couldn't bring herself to say the informant's name. The thought of Gabriel Contreras sent a worm of rage wriggling through her, eating through her belly and heart. She inhaled slowly and laid her hand upon the reassuring bulge of Dragon Baby in her stomach. She closed her eyes, hoping to feel the gentle flutter that she thought might be a kick. She exhaled, counting, the way the meditation guide in her prenatal yoga book suggested. The book said that a baby could feel its mother's moods, her fears and apprehensions. Olivia wasn't sure she believed it, but at the same time she hated the idea of these dark emotions washing over Dragon Baby, bathing him in her fury and her helpless dread. She had lately, in the times when she came closest to panic, become certain that the fact that Elaine had not wanted to be pregnant, had not loved her husband, had felt trapped and desperate, had mysteriously been communicated to Olivia in utero. She vowed to protect her own child from feeling unloved and resented in its mother's womb.

"Olivia?" Izaya said.

She opened her eyes. "I'm fine. Just feeling the baby."

His eyes lowered to her belly, and she caught the faintest hint of a smile on his full lips. He leaned forward, and placing his palm against her belly, said, "Can I?" She stiffened under his touch but then willed herself to relax.

"I'm not even sure that's him. It might just be gas."

Izaya smiled and leaned back in his chair. "Pretty cool."

She smoothed the fabric of her dress over Dragon Baby's rounded form and placed a protective hand over him. "Yeah."

"Anyway," Izaya said, sorting through some papers on his desk and pulling out a single page. "I've got some news."

"Good news?"

"No."

"Oh." She exhaled gently, counting.

"Jorge is pleading guilty."

"What?" Olivia's face paled. "You said you thought he had a good entrapment claim."

"I did. I still do. But, like I told you, those cases are hard to win. The defendant has to prove that he had absolutely no pre-disposition to commit the crime. That means that without the informant, he never would have done anything."

"He wouldn't have! *I* wouldn't have. None of this would have happened if Gabriel hadn't suckered Jorge into it."

"I know, believe me. I know. But let's try to look at this from the perspective of your typical jury. What counts in your favor is that neither of you has any kind of a dope record. But, the prosecution is going to ask about drug use, too. Have you or Jorge ever used drugs…don't answer that!" Izaya squawked. Olivia snapped her mouth shut. "Remember what I told you about testifying," he continued. "I can't allow you to testify if I know for a fact that what you're saying isn't true."

Olivia nodded her head. "Jorge's never done drugs. He's never even smoked pot." She was sure Izaya noticed that she said nothing about herself, and she blushed.

Izaya nodded. "Well, the prosecution will harp on Jorge's fail-ure to find work. They'll make it seem like he was looking for easy money. Maybe Jorge and his lawyer didn't feel like it was a strong enough case. Maybe they didn't trust Jorge to testify on his own behalf. Whatever. Right now we can't worry about him. We have to worry about you."

"What does his plea have to do with me?"

"He'll be looking for a substantial assistance departure, or at the very least an agreement from the prosecutor to ask for the safety valve."

Olivia shook her head. "So?"

Izaya knotted his hands loosely in front of him and looked at her. "You understand that to get either of those things he's going to have to tell Amanda Steele everything he knows."

Olivia shrugged. "Well, that won't be too hard. He doesn't know anything."

"That's the problem. Because he doesn't know much, he's going to have to scramble to find something to tell her. He's going to implicate anyone he can think of."

She shrugged again. "So?"

Izaya's gaze was sympathetic, pitying even, and she felt a flash of impatience with him.

"So what?" she said again.

"I think we can expect him to provide testimony against you."

Olivia sat back, stunned. She immediately shook her head. "I can't believe he would do that," she said, and the words sounded, even to her own ear, hollow and false. If she'd learned anything over the course of the past few months, it was that she didn't know Jorge Rodriguez at all.

After she had finally understood that she was not to be allowed to speak to him in person, Olivia had written to him to tell him she was pregnant with his child. Long after she had stopped expecting a reply, a plain white envelope arrived in the mail. It had been forwarded from their Oakland address.

Olivia had torn open the envelope immediately, not waiting even to sit down. She stood in the front hall and read the single page of precise, beautiful script. Her Spanish was rusty, and she had to read it a few times before she was sure she had milked every possible nuance from the brief lines.

Olivia:

Time has passed, and I hope you are no longer so very angry with me. I received your letter a few weeks ago, and it has taken me until now to figure out what to say. After everything that has happened, I thought it might be best for us not to be in contact, and my lawyer thought the same. But, of course, I had to answer. Because of the baby. I don't know what to tell you, Olivia. Even if the baby is mine, I am not able to be its father, am I?

You must decide for yourself what to do. Maybe one day, when this is over, we will meet again, and you will introduce me to our son or daughter.

I'm so sorry Olivia, for everything that has happened, and for everything that will happen.

Jorge

Love is so short and oblivion so long.

The letter enraged her. Surely he knew her well enough to be certain that she had been faithful to him. She assumed the post-script was his way of telling her that he no longer loved her, and although she had long since realized that she felt the same, she was nonetheless hurt and angry. She realized that she no longer had any idea of what he was capable of, what he would do to save himself. She understood that his apology had been for this, for the betrayal that was to come.

Izaya said, "I know his panel lawyer, the lawyer appointed to represent him, pretty well. He's an old friend of my dad's. He's a decent guy, and he gave me the heads-up. He told me to expect the worst. We won't know for sure until we see Amanda's witness list, but I'd be surprised if Jorge wasn't on it."

Olivia shook her head. "*He's* testifying against *me?*" The injustice of it was so pronounced as to be almost absurd. "He decided to do the deal without telling me. He found Oreste. He figured it all out. And *he's* testifying against *me.*"

"I can't tell you how many times I've seen the same thing. Every defendant high enough on the food chain to know something can weasel his way into a lower sentence. The only people who end up getting screwed are the ones who have no information they can trade. The defendants with the least involvement, the ones who are least culpable, end up with the longest sentences." He suddenly seemed to realize what it was that he was saying and laid a reassuring hand on hers. "But I'm not going to let that happen to you."

"So what do we do now?"

"This is it, Olivia. Do-or-die time. The government's plea offer is on the table. We have to decide whether we're going to take it."

"I plead guilty to the indictment, and Steele agrees to recommend the safety valve, right?"

"Right."

"And my sentence? What would my sentence be?"

"Between five and eight years."

"And if we lose at trial?"

"You'll most likely get the mandatory minimum."

"The mandatory minimum."

"Yes."

"Ten years," she said, to herself.

"Yes."

He looked at her expectantly.

She sat very still, her palms resting on her belly. As they watched, her stomach rippled.

"Did you see that?" Olivia asked. "That was a foot, I think."

Olivia closed her eyes. She thought about five years and how long that was, and then she thought about ten. Five years ago she had been in high school; ten years ago she had been a child. Five years ago she had had her first serious boyfriend; ten years ago she had not even begun to notice boys. Five years ago she had been thinking of going away to college; ten years ago she had only just begun sleeping over at friends' houses. Olivia considered what it would mean to stand up in court and tell the judge, the prosecutor, her family, the world, that she was guilty of the crime of drug distribution. She considered the act of testifying against Jorge, how it would feel to commit such an ultimate and foul betrayal. She pressed her hands into her belly, feeling for the knob of the baby's tiny foot. Then she opened her eyes.

"Fight," she said. "I want to fight."

"Good," Izaya said, smiling. "I want to fight, too."

"So what do we do now?"

"We do what we've been doing. We prepare for trial."

Olivia nodded, and, pushing thoughts of Jorge from her mind, pulled a pad and pen from her bag. "Did you find out anything more about Contreras?"

Izaya grinned in a way that was at once playful and mean. "You bet I did," he said.

In the spring and summer of 1980, Cuba heaved open the doors of its prisons and insane asylums and vomited the scum of its society onto American shores. Or at least that's what Izaya told Olivia he was planning on telling the jury. The truth, he explained, was a little more complicated. The truth was that, by and large, those Cubans floating toward the shores of Miami in the Mariel boatlift were decent people who had somehow run afoul of Castro or were merely looking for an easier, safer life. However, amid the tide of political and economic refugees bobbed a foul flotsam of criminals, lunatics, and malcontents of every stripe and proclivity.

Gabriel Contreras was one of the scum. He'd made his living in Cuba as a drug dealer who committed no actual crimes—he sold talcum powder, baby laxative, and cornstarch to addicts too addled to tell the difference. While the crime of fraud on the junkies of Havana was not one even Castro's judicial system was able to find within its abilities to punish, it had garnered him a stay in a crumbling lunatic asylum on the outskirts of the city. That bit of good fortune had bought him a ticket on an ancient fishing boat whose motor died within sight of the Florida Keys.

The team of U.S. doctors and immigration officials reviewing Gabriel Contreras's asylum application concluded that, while he was certainly a sociopath and quite possibly insane, there was no legal reason to continue his detention, and so he was released into the indifferent arms of American freedom. Contreras did with his opportunity what one might expect. Finding actual narcotics much easier to acquire on the streets of Miami than they had been in Havana, he became an honest-to-goodness dope dealer, one who offered at least a small percentage of legitimate product to his customers. Within a couple of years, he found himself back in custody. This time, with the aid of a criminal defense lawyer who'd left Cuba only a few years before Contreras himself, he translated his arrest into a career as an informant for the Drug Enforcement Agency. By the time he had set his sights on Jorge and Olivia, Contreras had a total of thirteen convictions to his credit. He had earned more than three million dollars over the course of fewer than four years of federal employment and had been permitted to keep a hunter-green Lincoln Navigator seized by the feds during the investigation of one of his cases.

"Man, Olivia, this guy is evil," Izaya said. "I want to bring him down so bad. I'm aching for the chance to stand in front of a jury and count out every one of the millions of taxpayer dollars that despicable sponge has soaked up."

"Wow," Olivia said. "Despicable sponge. That's good. Write that down and use it in your closing."

Izaya laughed. "I already have. Gabriel is evil, and the jury will know it. He's not the problem."

"What *is* the problem?"

Izaya had been pacing the room as he recounted Contreras's history. Now he sat down in his chair and threw his feet up on the desk.

"You. You're the problem."

"Me?"

"Yup. On the one hand, you're the perfect defendant. You're a pretty white girl with a mother who cares about you and a big old pregnant belly. The jury is going to think of you as one of their own—a suburban girl who came under the sway of an unscrupulous boyfriend and went along for a ride she never should have."

"But on the other hand?"

Izaya took his feet down and sat up at his desk. "On the other hand, maybe we shouldn't even go to trial. Maybe we shouldn't be playing Russian Roulette with your life."

"We've had this discussion before. I don't want to plead guilty."

Izaya leaned back in his chair and stared at the ceiling. Then he bobbed forward again.

"Man, this would be so much easier if you were someone else."

"What do you mean? If I were who?"

He rubbed a hand across the top of his hair. "I don't know. Any one of my other clients. It would be easier if you were a smack-addicted bank robber or some punk gang-banger."

"Why? What are you talking about?"

"I don't know." He yanked the elastic out of his hair, smoothed the locks back with his palm, and snapped the band back in place. "I don't know. It's just that you're…"

"I'm *what*?"

"You're…"

"*What?*" she said, impatient and confused.

"Nothing." He jerked his chair around. "Forget it. Let's go over the transcripts of the tapes again."

She looked at him for moment, wondering what it was he'd almost said to her. Then she shrugged, and, as she pulled her chair in, she caught sight of a photograph on the desk. It was a man in a black leather jacket and a red helmet, sitting astride a motorcycle.

"Is this you?" she asked.

He looked up from the documents. "Yeah. My mom emailed it to me, and I printed it out on the office photo printer. I don't normally have pictures of myself just lying around."

"Cool bike," Olivia said.

Izaya looked at the picture and smiled. "It's a Buell Cyclone M2. I just traded in my Harley for it."

"It reminds me of the Batmobile. Or the, what, the Batcycle, I guess."

Izaya laughed. "Maybe that's why I love it so much. I was a huge Batman fan when I was a kid."

"I liked Wonder Woman," she said. "The invisible plane. The magic lasso to make people do what you say." Olivia reached out a finger and traced the rearview mirror that stuck up from the motorcycle's handlebars like a cockroach's antennae. "So where does a public defender get the money for a bike like this? Should I be slipping you a bribe under the table or something?"

"I do okay, even without kickbacks. And it's just me, you know. I'm not married. No girlfriend. No life. All I do is work. I live in a dumpy little apartment in the Mission that costs me next to nothing. Food, clothes, and my bike. That's where my money goes."

"How come a guy like you doesn't have a girlfriend?" Olivia didn't look at him when she asked the question. She kept her eyes firmly affixed to the photograph.

"A guy like me?" Izaya leaned against in his chair, his feet outstretched. "What kind of guy am I?"

She smiled faintly and reached for the picture. Her knuckles grazed his. His hand was cool, but she felt as though her entire body flushed when they touched. He jerked back as if she'd hurt him.

She shrugged and raised her eyes to his face. They smiled at one another. Suddenly he looked down at the documents on his desk.

"So, was this the extent of your phone conversation with the informant? Or was there more that didn't get taped?"

She felt suddenly let down, dragged back to earth, to the grim reality of her predicament.

"I wish I had an invisible plane," she said.

"Are you going to come for a run with me, or are you going to spend the rest of the fucking day staring at that computer screen?"

Elaine looked up. "Were we supposed to go running?"

"No, we weren't *supposed* to go running. But, in case you've forgotten, we generally do go running on Saturday mornings. Or for a bike ride. Or something. We don't usually sit glued to the computer like retarded thirteen-year-old boys."

"Arthur! I'm not glued to the computer. I'm answering my email. I have a ton of it, and I don't get much time during the week. You're the one who signed me up for this 'fucking' listserv in the first place."

A few weeks before, Arthur had called Elaine into the makeshift office he'd set up in a corner of the dining room after Olivia had evicted him from the room he had assumed as his office. He had spent some time surfing the Web and found Elaine a site maintained by an organization called Families Against by Mandatory Minimums. Elaine had ordered FAMM's book of photographs and personal essays and, with Arthur's encouragement, had joined a listserv for parents and spouses of defendants in federal drug cases. For the first week or so Elaine had not posted anything to the group, but she had logged on daily to read the fifty or sixty messages in her box. She had come to know the other posters, all of whom signed themselves by name and by the sentence imposed on their loved ones. There were six or seven women whose husbands were serving life terms for marijuana cultivation. As one of the women reminded the list again and again, in the federal system, life meant life—there was no parole. Some of the posters were parents of young men and women doing five-, ten-, and twenty-year sentences for cocaine and heroin offenses; one was the father of a twenty-year-old boy who had mailed a page of blotter acid to his eighteen-year-old sister. Both were now serving ten years.

Elaine read about parents who knew they would never see their children graduate from college or have families of their own and about wives who were afraid they would never again see their husbands outside of a prison visiting room. Her inbox was filled with calls to action, cries of despair, and rants of frustration. But the worst by far were the emails about children whose mothers were inside. Children who could not visit their incarcerated parents more than once a year because they had been moved to correctional institutions in different states. Children growing up without their mothers' presence and out of their mothers' sight.

After several days of lurking, horrified and enthralled, Elaine had posted her first message. She described Olivia's situation and her own fears. She didn't, however, tell the list that Olivia was pregnant. She wasn't sure why. Perhaps it was because she still trusted that, if the unthinkable happened, and Olivia lost her case, she wouldn't keep her baby. Or perhaps it was more simple than that. Perhaps she simply could not face the possibility that Olivia's child would grow up like the others on the FAMM list, without its mother. She could not bear even to imagine her grandchild, that lost and lonely hypothetical child, aching for a touch that was denied him.

The members of the group had welcomed Elaine as they welcomed every new member, with open arms, notes of sympathy, and compassion. Elaine felt at home, amazingly so, in the virtual neighborhood of families of tragedy. She surprised herself with the rawness of her emails, with the extent she was willing to confide in these strangers her fears and apprehensions. She asked technical legal questions about Olivia's case and the mandatory minimums and the federal sentencing guidelines. Each of her posts garnered tens of responses; all supportive, knowledgeable, and filled with information and even, although it seemed so unlikely, with love.

"When I helped you subscribe to this list, it never occurred to me that I would end up an Internet widower," Arthur said, his tone of jocularity so obviously faked that it made Elaine feel sorry for him.

"I'm sorry, honey. I promise I'm not addicted. It's just that there's so *much*. There's a ton of information out there, and I'm just starting to learn about it. There's going to be a delegation going to D.C. to lobby Congress, and we're trying to draft a series of demands for them to take with them." She didn't describe to Arthur the threads that had nothing to do with data, news, or advice—that were not about specific action but rather opportunities to rage and vent and cry. She knew that would be utterly beyond his ken.

Arthur did a knee bend and touched his hands to his toes. "Look, I'm all warmed up and I want to go. Are you coming with me or not?"

Elaine opened her mouth, about to tell him to go on without her, but the look on his face made her change her mind. She snapped the laptop closed and got up.

The two of them started off slowly, running up Russell Street toward Claremont Avenue and the hills of Tilden Park. It had been days since Elaine had had any exercise at all. That fact surprised her. Since she'd met Arthur they had worked out almost every day, together or separately. Exercise was Arthur Roth's religion. It was his favorite activity, and, other than foot massages, his only source of relaxation. Before meeting him, she had been on the plump side of normal, happy to go to a yoga class if she had time but equally eager to spend her weekends lying on the couch reading novels. Now, years later, she was fit and strong, able to run six miles up and down hills or bike for hours at a time. She'd grown to appreciate the way her body moved and worked, although she'd never achieved the euphoric endorphin rush about which Arthur so often crowed.

They pounded up the hill to the park and then turned off the road onto a marked trail. Arthur shot forward with a burst of speed, sprinted up a hill, then coasted back down. Returning to her side, he matched his pace to her slower one.

"Olivia's looking well," he said.

"She is, isn't she?" Elaine wheezed a bit with the effort of talking while she ran. They reached the top of the hill together and began the gentle descent to the other side. Breathing more easily,

Elaine looked up at the rolling hills dotted with clumps of black oaks. One of the things Elaine loved about Berkeley was how close she was to vast spaces empty of houses and telephone wires and populated exclusively with cows, deer, and even the odd mountain lion. She had fallen in love with the East Bay the first time she'd driven through a fragrant eucalyptus grove high up here in the hills. Back home in New Jersey, if you wanted to leave people behind and be somewhere that even approximated wild, you had to drive for hours down to the Pine Barrens or up to the Catskill mountains. Here, it was all so close, a few minutes' jog into the hills.

"Has she talked to you about what she's going to do with the baby?" Arthur said.

"No. Not really. A while ago she mentioned going back to school. I said I'd help her pay for tuition and child care. If she keeps it."

Arthur grunted. "That's if she wins her trial. What if she doesn't? What then?"

Elaine slowed down and came to a stop. She leaned over, propped her hands on her knees, and blew out through her mouth. "Sorry, honey. I'm out of shape, I guess."

Arthur ran in small circles around her, lifting his knees high. "What's going to happen if she goes to jail?"

"I honestly don't know, Arthur. She hasn't talked to me about that."

"Well, don't you think you should maybe ask her? I mean, will she give it up for adoption, or does she expect us to take care of the kid?"

"I don't know. She hasn't said anything about giving the baby up, and I'm pretty sure she hasn't done any research into adoption, but I made it very clear to her that we're not able to care for it for her."

He stumbled, something he almost never did, and caught himself. "Did you? You told her that?"

"Yes, Arthur. I've told you before that I told her we wouldn't be able to take the baby. I'm ready, let's go." Elaine started running again, taking the fork in the path that looped back up the hill toward the road.

They ran in silence for a while, and then Arthur said, "It's just that I've *done* the kid thing, you know? I just made my last child-support payment, like, six months ago. I'm finally free of that."

"I know, Arthur. I'm not any more interested in having a baby than you are. I told that to Olivia. She knows."

"Okay. Sprint home?" Without waiting for her reply, Arthur ratcheted up his speed. Elaine watched him as he got farther and farther ahead. For a dangerous moment she allowed herself to imagine holding a baby again, smelling its milky neck, rubbing its soft head against her cheek. The pleasure this fantasy afforded her surprised her. She hadn't felt any kind of sensual joy, none at least that she could recall, when she had a child of her own. She emptied her mind and concentrated on the burning in her thighs and chest. Slowly, she ran home, grateful for the long downhill stretch leading to her front door.

She found Arthur leaning against the kitchen table holding a small pile of papers and brochures out to Olivia. Olivia sat, her legs up on the seat across from her. She rested her hands on her protruding stomach and looked up at Arthur. Her face was blank.

"The way it works is that you get this book from the agency, full of bios and pictures. You can find out anything you want to know. You know, what kind of house they live in, how much money they have. Do they have a dog."

Olivia raised her eyebrows. "Really?" she said.

"And the beauty of it is, *you* get to choose. You get to decide who the parents will be. I mean, I imagine there might be some couples who might not be interested in your baby because of Jorge. The whole Mexican thing. But honestly, even with the drug case, you're smart, you're attractive, you went to college. You're *Jewish*, for Christ's sake. You're an adoptive parent's dream come true."

Olivia smiled ruefully. "Somehow I doubt that."

"No, really, you are. I'm sure of it. And the thing is," Arthur continued, "these open adoptions are, basically, unregulated. I mean, technically, yeah, there are state laws governing them, but we're dealing with desperate people here, you know what I mean?"

He pushed the papers toward her hands. She didn't take them.

"No, I don't really know what you mean," Olivia said. She pointed and flexed her toes. Her face was rubbed blank. She looked, if anything, bored.

"They're supposed to pay only for your living expenses and medical costs, but I can't imagine that anyone's asking for receipts. Why not have them set up a college fund for you for when you get out? I mean, if you end up losing the case. This could be a way for you to guarantee yourself some kind of future. You could come out ahead in the end. Having a baby could end up being a *good* thing, after all."

"It's already a good thing," she said, and placed her hands more firmly over her belly, as if to protect the baby from Arthur's words.

Arthur blinked wordlessly. Then he shook his head. Before he could speak, Olivia hoisted her substantial bulk out of the chair and started up the steps to her room.

"Don't you want the brochures?" Arthur called after her.

Elaine tamped down a flare of irritation and impatience with her soon-to-be husband.

"I just don't think she's ready to deal with all this," she said. "She thinks she's going to win the case. Considering the possibility of adoption means considering the possibility of losing and going to jail."

"Well, she needs to consider the goddamn possibility. She's got to be prepared. Otherwise it will be too late."

Elaine nodded her head. "You know that, and I know that. And she'll figure it out. She just needs time."

Arthur gathered the papers in a neat pile. He took a yellow Post-It note and wrote Olivia's name in large block letters. He stuck the note to the top sheet and placed the pile of papers on the counter, using an empty juice glass as a paperweight.

"I'll leave these where she can find them."

Olivia dressed carefully for her first birth-preparation class. Her midwife had given her the flyer, telling her that by now, six months into her pregnancy, it was time to start thinking about the labor. She had, however, put off calling the instructor for days. She was loath to explain that she would be coming on her own, unattended by a doting husband. But when finally she did make the call, a cheerful, friendly voice with a thick Brooklyn accent had reassured her that it was perfectly all right not to have a partner, and Olivia, relieved, had decided to go.

She pulled on her least tattered pair of black leggings, tucking the waistband under her belly—it cut into her stomach when she tried to pull it up and over. She chose a black tunic from the boxed set Elaine had given her. She shook out her curls, grown even thicker and shinier from all the hormones dancing around her body. She left her hair hanging loose down her back. She gathered up a pillow and a bottle of water, as instructed by the flyer, and headed out the door.

"Where are you off to, honey?" Elaine called from the kitchen, where she was scrubbing out the pot from the chili Arthur had prepared for their dinner. Olivia hadn't been able to eat more than a few bites. No matter how many times Elaine told him, Arthur couldn't seem to remember that spicy food gave Olivia heartburn.

"A birth-preparation class," Olivia said, her hand on the doorknob. "Is it okay if I take your car?"

"Sure." Elaine came out of the kitchen, wearing a pair of pink rubber gloves dripping in soapy water. "Is it like Lamaze or something?"

"Sort of, I guess. I don't really know." Olivia propped the pillow on her hip and reached into Elaine's purse. She pulled out the key ring. "I'll be back by nine or so." She jangled the keys against her palm.

"Where's the class?" Elaine asked.

"North Berkeley."

Elaine wiped her forehead with the back of one gloved hand. "Would you like me to come?"

"What?"

"Would you like some company?"

Olivia considered the question. While she never would have expected the baby inside her to provide her with companionship, neither could she have imagined how lonely her pregnancy would make her feel. Every time she saw a pregnant woman accompanied by a solicitous husband, she felt a twisting knot of jealousy and alienation, and a nearly overwhelming need to strike out, to wipe away the smug contentment of the couple's unity. Olivia had never considered herself a violent person, and the brutality of her loathing came as a shock. She was consumed with envy for expectant couples; she hated them. But would the companionship of her mother do anything to dissipate this despair?

"You're not busy?"

"No."

"You don't have anything else to do?"

Elaine made a show of wrinkling her brow. "No, nothing that I can think of."

"Well, okay. Sure. Come along."

Despite the instructor's assurances, Olivia had fully expected to be the only participant in the class without a husband or boyfriend. But she had forgotten that this was Berkeley. There were six couples in the birthing class, and only three were made up of the traditional husband and wife.

Frances, the instructor, a middle-aged woman with long gray hair who swaddled her substantial girth in an Indian print sarong, handed each pregnant woman a large paper cup full of lukewarm, bright-red tea.

"Berry Berry. For easing the travails of pregnancy and birth. Partners, feel free to help yourselves," she said and pointed to an oversized teapot.

Olivia sipped her tea, grimacing at the sour flavor. She looked around Frances's living room. All the furniture had been cleared out, and brightly colored pillows were scattered around the room and against the walls. The men and women in the class were leaning against the walls in a rough circle. Frances settled herself down and asked them to introduce themselves. The three "normal" couples went first. Olivia forgot their names as soon as she heard them, and almost immediately lumped them together in a category of people she would not bring herself to befriend. The next to introduce themselves were not a couple at all, but rather a triple: a husband, a wife, and the young woman they introduced, to her obvious embarrassment, as the "birth mother" of their baby. The adoptive mother gripped the birth mother's hand with a ferocity that made Olivia wonder if she was afraid that the young woman might slip away, her baby still in the custody of her womb. There was a lesbian couple, the only one of the six with another child at home; the partner who wasn't pregnant had given birth to their first baby two years before. When it was Olivia's turn to speak, she told the group her name and then said, "My baby's father is in jail on drug charges. I've also been indicted in the same case. Trial is set for a month before my due date."

The room fell silent at Olivia's words. Out of the corner of her eye she could see a red flush creep up Elaine's neck and across her face.

Frances finally spoke, "Welcome, my dear. I can't think of anyone who needs a supportive and supported labor more than you."

For two hours, Olivia and Elaine took turns deep breathing while they gripped ice cubes in their hands. They learned how to do cat and cow stretches, and watched while Frances demonstrated various labor positions. Frances encouraged Elaine to share her birth experience and tsk-tsked at her admission that she really couldn't remember much, other than that things had improved significantly once she'd been given a nice, big shot of Demerol.

Finally, Frances said, "Partners, I want to thank each and every one of you, especially, for being here. I can't stress enough how important the role of the labor partner is to a positive and satisfying birth experience. You will be able to keep your own partners comfortable. You will be able to help them focus on their breathing, not on the discomfort of the rushes. You will be their advocate and their voice with the doctors and nurses. While a pregnant woman can certainly give birth without a loving support system, she cannot birth *well*. So I thank you, and your wives, spouses, partners, mothers of your children, and," she smiled warmly at Elaine and Olivia, "your daughters, thank you."

On their way out, she handed each of them a tiny clay figure of an obese women with pendulous breasts and a swollen belly. "Your birth talismans," she said as she pressed them into their palms.

As Olivia and Elaine walked back to the car, Olivia gently tossed the little figure up in the air. "Hey," she said, holding it up so Elaine could see it. "It looks like Grandma."

Elaine laughed. "But thinner."

"Actually, it looks kind of like me," Olivia looked down at her breasts. "I'm like a forty-two quadruple D or something."

Elaine looked her up and down. "Well, I got *huge* when I was pregnant with you. And Grandma always said that she gained all her weight when she had me. So it runs in the family."

"Great."

"If you're worried about it, you could exercise."

Olivia rolled her eyes. The sensation of physical contentment that had arrived along with the second trimester had not included any desire or need for exercise. All she really wanted to do was read pregnancy books and eat. She knew she'd gotten fat. Her spreading thighs and vast rump didn't even look like parts of her own body, and she couldn't quite recognize her face in the mirror. Her features had grown thicker, somehow blurred, wobbly, and her double chin was so huge that it resembled nothing so much as a goiter. But strangely, she didn't really care. She knew it bothered her mother that she was gaining so much weight, and she could see Arthur cringe every time she ate a cookie or fried herself an egg. The two of them kept pushing carrots and celery on her, as if she were some kind of enormous rabbit.

"Don't worry. Once I have the baby, I'll be on the prison diet. Bread and water." Olivia grinned to show her mother that she was kidding. Elaine's attempt to return the smile didn't succeed particularly well, and Olivia felt guilty for having reminded her about the case. It had seemed like they'd both forgotten about it for a little while. They arrived at the car, and Olivia paused before opening the door. She wanted to say something that would make Elaine feel good, that would let her know that she loved her. Before she had time to consider what she was about to say, the words escaped her.

"So, Mom, do you want to be my birth partner?" She immediately regretted the invitation. "Your job can be to pray to the fat little birth Buddha," she continued, as if she had been, after all, only kidding.

"Sure," Elaine said. "I'd be happy to."

"Are you serious?" Olivia asked.

Elaine didn't answer for a minute; then she said, almost as if surprising herself, "I...I think so."

She looked anxious and faintly nauseated, and something about her expression made Olivia laugh. Elaine looked up, startled, and then Olivia waved the little clay sculpture at her and said, "Ooga booga, push push push." That started Elaine, and they stood there, in the cool air of the Berkeley night, laughing until the tears streamed down their cheeks.

That night Elaine lay in bed, trying to imagine the scene of her daughter giving birth. For some reason, Olivia at ten or eleven years old was the image stuck in her mind. The idea of that knobby-kneed, awkward young body birthing something not much smaller than itself was so wrong, so horrifying, that it was almost funny. Her giggles started again, and she hushed herself. She looked over at Arthur, but he hadn't stirred. He lay next to her, his head back and his mouth gaping open, snoring softly. Not for the first time, Elaine imagined dropping something into that gaping maw, an olive, maybe, or a nickel.

Elaine had worried from the beginning that Olivia would ask her to be there at the baby's birth. It was just like Olivia to request something from her mother that they both knew would make Elaine terribly uncomfortable—this type of intimacy was, of course, exactly what Elaine loathed most. She had not seen her daughter's naked body since she was ten years old, had avoided even discussions of puberty and sex, dropping pamphlets on Olivia's desk instead of making speeches and answering questions. What Elaine had not expected—and even now still could not quite believe—was how much she would *want* to be present at Olivia's labor. She would never have imagined herself not only willing, but eager to help her daughter do this overwhelmingly difficult and absolutely commonplace thing—give birth to a baby. Elaine lay in bed next to Arthur's slumbering, snoring form, running the movie of her grandchild's birth in her mind. Olivia sweating and straining. Elaine calmly suggesting new positions, gently mopping her brow. Or perhaps, more likely, Elaine vomiting quietly in a corner of the room. And the baby. The tiny yet impossibly huge creature with its soft damp skin and slippery warmth. Elaine had dozed through Olivia's birth in a drug-induced fog. She remembered nothing—not what the contractions felt like, not even how long they had lasted. She didn't recall pushing her baby out into the world, or even whether they'd let her hold Olivia before they took her off to be weighed and measured. She was sure they must have; they did that, didn't they? But she had absolutely no recollection of her daughter's newborn face. The birth of Olivia's baby would allow Elaine the opportunity to experience what she'd forgotten, what she'd never known.

Elaine imagined nothing beyond the birth itself. She closed her eyes and fell asleep with the happy scene playing and replaying in her head, without once asking herself who would care for her grandchild if her daughter was sent away.

A week before the trial, Olivia mentioned to Izaya for the first time that she had received a letter from Jorge.

"You got a *letter* from him?" Izaya bellowed.

They were in a conference room at the federal defender's office. Olivia was being cross-examined by a colleague of Izaya's, a short, red-headed woman named Giselle. They had been practicing all morning, and Olivia was exhausted. Giselle, who had been so pleasant and friendly when Olivia had shaken her hand, had, as soon as she'd assumed the role of prosecutor, asked Olivia one witheringly contemptuous question after another, giving her no time to gather her thoughts. Olivia had lost her temper more than once and found herself giving contradictory answers to Giselle's convoluted questions. Izaya had been steadily growing more and more impatient with what Olivia could only assume was her incompetence. Olivia's answer to Giselle's question about her contact with Jorge since her arrest had pushed him over the edge.

"You didn't bother to mention to me that you got a *letter* from him?" Izaya shouted, again.

"Whoa, take it easy, guy," Giselle said.

He spun around to her. "You know what? We're done. She's as ready as she's ever going to be. Which is not saying much, is it?" He turned back to Olivia. "Are you out of your fucking *mind*, you don't tell me about this until a week before trial?"

"Why? It just never occurred to me. It's not that important."

"Oh really? So now *you* decide what's important? That's just great." He slammed down the pad on which he'd been taking notes.

"You know what?" Giselle said. "Let's take a break. We've been at this for four hours. We could all use something to drink."

Izaya glared at her. "No, *you* know what? Fuck you. I don't need no fucking break."

"Okay," Giselle said, drawing out the word and rolling her eyes. She scooped up her papers and tapped them on the desk, evening out the edges. "I'm out of here." She turned to Olivia. "Don't worry. He's always like this before a trial. I wouldn't take it personally." She left the room.

"I'm sorry," Olivia whispered. She wasn't sure what she was apologizing for, her failure to tell him about Jorge's letter, or for her dismal performance in their practice cross-examination. Her eyes burned with embarrassed tears.

"Oh, shit," Izaya said. He walked around the table to her seat. He pulled a chair up next to her and leaned close, his elbows on his knees. "I'm the one who's sorry. Giselle's right. I'm always a basket case before a trial. I'm sorry I freaked out on you."

His apology made her tears come even faster. He reached an arm around her, and she leaned against his chest. It felt hard and warm under his crisp, pale-pink shirt. She sighed, hiccuping, and let her weight lean into his. It felt like a long time since she'd been this close to a man. He smelled good, like sawdust, with a thin overlay of some fruity soap. Her tears had made his shirt translucent, and out of the corner of her eye she could see where his brown skin darkened the fabric. Suddenly, she grew conscious that his hand was resting lightly on her hip. They both stiffened at the same time, and she sat up, wiping her nose on the back of her hand.

"Bring me the letter, okay?" Izaya said. "Maybe I can use it."

Inexorably, the days tumbled over themselves until it was·the night before the trial. Olivia lay in bed, her eyes open wide, staring at the ceiling. But as always, after a while, lying on her back made her uncomfortable; she couldn't breathe. She flipped over on her side, shoved a pillow under her belly, another between her knees, and willed herself to sleep. Her mind thrummed, as though she had just drunk an entire pot of coffee. She flipped over again, rearranging her pillows afresh. The baby must have sensed her agitation, because it too began to toss and turn, rolling in the space that was starting to feel too small for its increasing size. Olivia pressed on the bulge underneath her right rib, trying to force down the sharp elbow or knee that had lodged there.

She closed her eyes and tried to calm herself by imagining not her criminal trial, but the birth of the baby. She saw herself squatting and pushing, heaving out a perfectly round head, then a tiny squirming body. For a moment the image soothed her, but then it took an unpleasant turn. She saw the baby snatched by a grim-faced Nurse Ratched in a prison uniform. Olivia groaned and flipped over again.

Olivia had done a remarkable job, for a while, of not thinking about what it would mean if she were convicted. She could not bear the thought of losing her baby, so she simply refused to consider the possibility. But, as the trial grew nearer, it had become harder to pretend that nothing was wrong, that she was just another young mother about to have her first baby. For the last few days, she had been overwhelmed by the sickening fear of never getting to hold her child, of never changing its diaper, never pushing it on a swing, not taking it to its first day of school.

Olivia began to weep, and almost immediately sat up in bed, angry at herself. She needed to sleep. She needed to look and feel well-rested for tomorrow. If the jury saw her looking haggard and wan, with black smudges under her eyes, they might feel sorry for her, but they wouldn't *like* her. And Izaya said it was important that they like her. The jury was supposed to feel like she was one of them; that she was their daughter or sister or wife.

She rolled her legs off the bed with a grunt, and heaved herself to her feet. She pulled on the old flannel robe of Arthur's that he'd given her when she'd grown out of her own and headed downstairs to make herself a cup of tea. She found Elaine sitting at the kitchen table, her small square hands wrapped around a steaming mug.

"What's wrong? You can't sleep either?" Olivia asked.

Elaine shook her head. "Tea?"

"Yeah, something that'll help me sleep. Chamomile." Olivia sat down and propped her feet up on a chair. "God, my ankles. They're totally swollen. Look, I can make a dent." She pushed her index finger into the swollen flesh. The indentation lingered long after she'd taken her finger away. "At this rate I'm going to have to wear bedroom slippers to the trial. Do you think they'll let me put my feet up in court?"

"Here you go, honey." Elaine put an oversized yellow mug in front of Olivia. "Some honey for you, honey?" she asked— the same joke she made every time she made Olivia a cup of tea.

Olivia spooned honey into her cup and stirred the water.

"I downloaded some stuff off the FAMM site," Elaine said.

"Really?" Olivia murmured. Despite Elaine's encouragement, Olivia had not bothered to look through the FAMM materials or explore their website. Reading about the plight of other incarcerated drug offenders provided her with none of the comfort it seemed to give Elaine; on the contrary, it made her even more anxious.

"There's some amazing information here," Elaine said, pushing a small stack of paper over to Olivia. "Things about national rates of drug use. That kind of thing. It's just been such a colossal failure, this drug war."

Olivia leafed through the documents without reading them. "Yeah," she said.

The two sat in silence for a few moments. Then Olivia spoke. "I need to come up with a plan for the baby. Just in case."

Elaine paused, her cup halfway to her lips. She set it down on the table without drinking. "I suppose that's a good idea," she said.

"I want the baby. I mean, I know I'm being selfish and everything, but even if I go to jail for ten years, I want it to be there waiting for me when I get out."

Elaine nodded.

"Okay," she whispered.

"And you can't take it."

"No." Elaine voice was almost inaudible. "I wish I could help you, Olivia. I really do. If it were just me that would be one thing. But it's not. Just me, that is."

Olivia wasn't surprised. She had not expected Elaine to change her mind. No, she wasn't surprised, but she *was* angry. She was furious with her mother for refusing to help her, and, even worse, for pretending an ambivalence and a regret that she didn't truly feel.

Elaine sipped her tea. "Do you need more tea?" she asked.

"I still have a full cup."

"Okay."

"I thought about maybe trying to find some kind of open adoption where the adoptive parents would agree to let me have visitation or even partial custody when I got out of jail."

Elaine looked up, a glint of hope in her eye. "That sounds promising. Do you think you'll be a able to find a couple who would agree to that?"

"I don't know. Maybe. But it doesn't matter. I decided that's not what I want. I don't want to be the 'birth mother' like that girl in group. I want to be my baby's mother. In jail or out of jail, I want to be its mother."

Olivia glanced at her mother to see how well she stifled her disappointment. Elaine held her cup to her face, blowing on the already cool tea.

It was time to tell her mother what she had decided.

"I'm going to ask Jorge's family to keep the baby for me," she said.

"What?" Elaine's voice was suddenly loud in the night's quiet. "Are you *kidding*, Olivia? You're going to give the baby to the man who *betrayed* you?"

Olivia knew it wasn't really a good solution. Unfortunately, however, it was the only one. A few days before, she'd gone online, searching for some organization that could help her. She found Legal Services for Prisoners with Children and had felt an intense jolt of hope that was quickly dashed by the kind woman who had answered her phone call. Olivia had explained her situation and asked the woman what normally happened in cases like hers.

"Well," the woman had said, "generally a member of the family takes the child."

"And if there's no one who can do that?"

The woman paused. "Do you have a friend who can take it?" she asked gently.

"No."

"Then the outlook is pretty bleak, I'm afraid. If you have the baby while you are incarcerated, Child Protective Services will take custody within seventy-two hours of its birth. That means they'll come pick it up at the hospital. They'll put it into foster care, and then there will be a series of hearings establishing the infant as a dependent of the court. How long of a sentence are you facing?"

"Ten years," Olivia whispered.

The woman's voice grew even more tender. "I'm sorry. Because it's such a lengthy sentence, there will be no reunification plan. In California, a parent has only six months to reunify with a child who is removed from her physical custody before three years of age. Sometimes that's extended to twelve months, and I've even had a case or two where a mother's been given eighteen months. But not ten years. Not even two or three. I'm afraid the state will move to terminate your parental rights, and the rights of the father, and then place your baby up for adoption."

The woman sat on the phone with Olivia for a long time, listening to her cry. She didn't hang up, even when Olivia's sobs came so hard and fast that she couldn't speak. Only once Olivia had calmed down did she let her go. She made Olivia promise to call again if there was anything else she needed to know.

Olivia looked at her mother steadily and said, "I wouldn't be giving the baby to Jorge. I'd be giving it to his parents. I know they'll take care of it. They're good people. It'll have a good life with them. What's really important is that I know they'll give it back to me when it's time. They'll want the best for it. They'll want it to come to America."

"How can you be so sure? How do you know that they won't keep the baby, or give it to Jorge? If you do go to jail, you could be there longer than he will. How can you be sure that he won't go to Mexico and take the baby before you even get there?"

"I can't be sure. But I trust his parents. I have to trust them. They're the only option I've got."

Olivia thought of Jorge's mother, Araceli Rodriguez. Every time Olivia had seen the small woman, there was at least one grandchild on her hip or sitting in her ample lap. She would carry on a conversation, all the while tickling and kissing the child, tempting it with tidbits of food, wiping its nose and mouth. On Olivia's last day in San Miguel, Araceli and Juan Carlos had made her an elaborate going-away party. They'd invited their entire family—aunts, uncles, cousins. They had all eaten until they were stuffed and lazy, then they'd played music and drank beer and tequila. After she'd served a home-made peanut butter flan that Olivia had devoured with something akin to ecstasy, Araceli had pulled a massive bag of pink and white marshmallows out of a cupboard. She began distributing them to the children, pushing the soft candy into their mouths as if they were baby birds. Olivia could still so clearly see her small brown hands and the pink *O*s of the children's delighted mouths, sticky with the candy, solemn with love for their *abuela*.

At the end of the evening, Jorge's parents had presented her with a dreadful painting of the city—all pink sunsets and oddly malformed donkeys walking next to peasants who looked like little more than sombreros with legs. When she'd wondered aloud how she would carry it on the plane, Juan Carlos had pulled a long, evil-looking blade out of his pocket, and sliced it from the frame. He'd rolled the painting and tied it with a bit of blue nylon string. He'd handed it to her and kissed her firmly on the forehead. She'd carried the painting under her arm all the way to Oakland. It was still tucked away in the back of a closet in the apartment for which she still paid rent, but to which she knew that, no matter what happened, she would not return.

"His parents are great people, Mom. They're warm and loving. They would take good care of the baby. I'm sure of it. And I have no other choice. If the baby goes into foster care, they'll terminate my parental rights within six months and give it away for adoption to whomever they choose."

"Is that true?" Elaine gasped. "Are you sure?"

Olivia nodded.

"Look, probably none of this will end up being necessary. I'm going to be acquitted. I know I am. But I need to have a plan. Just in case something goes wrong."

"Just in case," Elaine repeated and poured more tea into Olivia's cup.

On their way into the courtroom, Izaya explained to Olivia and Elaine that he would try to pack as many black people onto the jury as he could. That was marginally easier to do in Oakland than in San Francisco, although since the East Bay federal court drew its juries from both Alameda and Contra Costa counties, the pool was still heavily white, weighed down with military retirees and Walnut Creek matrons. Izaya liked his own people on the jury because he knew that they were more willing to cast a cynical eye on police testimony; they were all too familiar with the ways of lying cops. Izaya warned, however, that the prosecutor would be working just as hard to keep black jurors *off* the panel. Legally, neither side was allowed to consider race in exercising their preemptory challenges; in reality, it was one of their primary concerns.

In federal court, *voir dire*, Izaya explained, was the purview of the judge—he asked the questions. What someone looked like was truly all Izaya and his opponent had time to pay attention to as the judge hurriedly grilled the members of the jury pool about their capacity for impartiality. Race, the element the Constitution precluded them from considering, was one of the few things they actually *could* rely on in selecting a jury.

True to his word, every time the AUSA tried to dismiss an African-American, Izaya would rise to his feet and proclaim, "I'm making a *Batson* objection." He had explained that he wasn't allowed to shout, "She's a racist pig and she's trying to keep the black folks off the jury." Instead, he was limited to intoning the name, *Batson*, after the case in which the Supreme

Court had ruled that an attorney could not exclude jurors based on their race, and hoping the judge would see things his way.

The morning passed slowly, with Izaya doing his best to make sure there were no middle-aged Asians selected—too "law-and-order," he explained—and the prosecutor making a preemptory challenge every time an older man came off the least bit fatherly.

One woman who looked to be in her mid-thirties, with chin-length curly hair dyed an orange-red and an expression at once compassionate and intelligent, caught Olivia's eye. She smiled, the corners of her eyes crinkling slightly, and Olivia was taken aback by the sheer normalcy of the moment they shared. When the woman announced her profession as a former defense attorney, now stay-at-home mother, the prosecutor used a preemptory challenge to dismiss her. Olivia noticed the swell of her belly as she made her ungainly way down the steps and out of the jury box.

A middle-aged African-American man seemed to cause both Izaya and the prosecutor a moment's hesitation. The man informed the judge that he had a nephew in prison for assault stemming from a failed drug transaction. Amanda Steele was quite obviously about to dismiss him when he disclosed his service as a military police officer. She nodded once, and Olivia looked at Izaya. He tapped his pencil against his teeth and narrowed his eyes at the man. Finally, he too nodded, and the ex-military cop took his place on the jury.

Finally, it all came down to one pinched spinster with a sour expression, wearing a dingy white blouse buttoned high on her neck. She held a misshapen pink purse on her lap; it was too sweet a color for a woman who looked so bitter.

"Shit," Izaya whispered.

"What?" Olivia whispered back, leaning towards him. They were sitting together at the defense table. Olivia wore one of the outfits her mother had given her. The black skirt ended at her knee and the top was cut in a generous A-line. She had tied a black-and-white-checked scarf around her neck. Her swollen feet were crammed into a pair of the sensible flat pumps that Elaine wore to work, and the puffy flesh of her feet bulged out from the tops of the shoes. Elaine, dressed in a conservative navy blue suit and a pale blue blouse, sat in the first observers' row.

"I used up my last challenge getting rid of that guy whose sister-in-law was engaged to an FBI agent."

"But you want to dismiss this one, too?"

He nodded. "Shh. Your honor?"

"Mr. Feingold-Upchurch?" the judge said.

"I'd like to have this juror dismissed. For cause."

The judge, in his early seventies with a shock of bright white hair over each ear and an otherwise entirely bald head, shook his head. "And why would that be, Mr. Feingold-Upchurch?"

"Side bar, your honor?" Izaya asked.

The judge shrugged. "By all means, counsel." He raised one pinkish hand and waved Amanda Steele over. She rose to her feet and made her unhurried way towards the bench.

"What are you going to say?" whispered Olivia, as Izaya gathered up the pad on which he'd been making his notes.

"I'm going to beg," he replied, and winked at her. It was obvious to Olivia that her attorney was enjoying himself. She wondered why she didn't resent his high spirits. She supposed it was because she knew that he cared what happened to her. If the drama of the courtroom gave him a visceral pleasure, so much the better. His obvious comfort and confidence behind the defense table and up at the podium could only help her. The jury would think he was sure of her innocence and secure in the inevitability of acquittal. They couldn't help but take their cues from him. She certainly couldn't.

Olivia watched as Izaya whispered to the judge. Judge Horowitz gripped one hand over his microphone. Olivia could hear nothing, but she could read the disgust in Amanda Steele's face as she whispered in reply to whatever it was that Izaya was saying. Finally, after a few minutes, the judge waved the attorneys back to their seats.

"Motion denied," he said.

Later, after the judge had dismissed the impanelled jury for lunch and had left the courtroom, Elaine joined Izaya and Olivia at counsel table. They waited until Amanda Steele had left the room, which she did without glancing in their direction. Then Elaine and Olivia looked expectantly at Izaya.

"So," Elaine said, "what do you think of the jury?"

Izaya nodded his head. "Overall, I think we did okay. The best we could. We scored with that acupuncturist from Berkeley."

"Why do you say that?" Elaine asked. "She seemed pretty adamant about never having tried drugs. They all did."

"Yeah, well, did you notice the pin she was wearing on her blouse? It's an AA medallion. She might not be a drug user, but she's certainly a recovering alcoholic. I'm pretty sure Steele didn't notice that."

"Do you think that's good for us?" Elaine asked. "She might be really negative about drugs."

"Yeah, but she's also liable to understand how people get themselves into situations despite their best intentions. She'll be sympathetic to Olivia. I'm sure. Also, I'm willing to bet she's a lesbian. She won't have any sympathy for a lying boyfriend."

"And the others?" Olivia interrupted.

"They're a mixed bag. I like the brother—the one who works for PeopleSoft. That young Asian girl who just graduated from Cal seems okay. The rest are the usual crowd of retirees and housewives—what you get on most juries."

"What do we do now?" Elaine asked.

"We get some lunch. I wish I could join you, but I want to work on my opening statement while I eat," Izaya said.

Elaine and Olivia wandered through the streets of downtown Oakland, passing greasy coffee shops and the ubiquitous McDonald's. Finally, they settled on a Vietnamese pho shop.

"Do you think the jury noticed I was pregnant?" Olivia asked as they sat waiting for their food.

Elaine smiled. "It's kind of hard to miss, honey."

"I thought some of the women looked sort of sorry for me."

Elaine nodded. "I think so. Especially the two older women on the far left. The one from Sonoma and the other one with the denim shoulder bag."

"The acupuncturist, too. I think it was smart to keep her on the jury. She seems nice."

Elaine nodded. "I hope she won't be too upset about missing work. I was sort of surprised she didn't ask to be excused, what with running her own business and all."

"Is that okay for you, Mom? To miss work?"

"It's fine. Warren's glad of the extra hours. He sends his regards. And Ralph says to tell you he wishes he could be here."

Olivia smiled. "I wish he were here, too. He could hand me a milk shake whenever I got hungry."

Elaine smiled and then looked down at her hands as if she were ashamed of allowing herself the moment of levity.

"You'll be acquitted, honey. I know you will." The waitress came by and plopped bowls of broth and noodles in front of them. They were both relieved at the interruption. For a while they slurped in silence. Then Elaine said, "Arthur's sorry he couldn't be here."

"Okay," Olivia said, noncommittally.

"It's just that Tuesday is one of his work days. Since he's only part-time, he doesn't like to miss the days he's supposed to be there. He'll come tomorrow. He promised."

"It's fine. I don't mind. I'm glad *you're* here, though."

Elaine looked up, gratefully. "Thank you."

"No, I mean it. I'm really glad you're here."

"I'm...I'm so sorry." Elaine's face was red and she blinked rapidly.

"Sorry?"

"If I had lent you the money when you asked..."

Olivia shook her head. "What are you talking about?"

"If I'd lent you money that day in the restaurant. Then Jorge wouldn't have been so desperate. None of this would have happened."

"It's not your fault he did the drug deal."

"But it *is*. I could have lent you the money. I should have."

Olivia patted her mother's hand. "Jorge didn't like taking money from you or from me for that matter. He would have done the deal anyway. I'm sure of it. None of this is your fault."

Elaine smiled gratefully and turned back to her soup. Olivia stared into her own bowl, feeling a strange satisfaction in having offered up to her mother such a hopeful lie.

The aroma of roasting lamb greeted Elaine and Olivia as they walked into the house that evening. The dining room table was set for three with the Umbrian pottery Elaine and Arthur had brought back from their trip to the Italian countryside. Candles flickered in the silver-plated candlesticks Elaine had received as a wedding present long ago and used only on the rarest of occasions. Arthur bustled out of the kitchen, an apron wrapped around his waist and a smear of flour on his cheek.

"Welcome home, ladies," he said. "I thought you could use a special dinner after your first day in court, so I cut out of work a little early. It's Chez Panisse at the Goodman-Roth house tonight. Our first course is seared tuna, served at room temperature with shaved fennel and radishes. We'll follow that with leg of lamb marinated in garlic, herbs, and olive oil, served with wilted escarole. And for dessert, buckwheat crepes with mangoes. That is, if I can get the little fuckers to stop sticking to the crepe pan."

"Wow," Olivia said.

Elaine attempted a smile, but she was seething. How like Arthur to leave work early to prepare an elaborate meal, but not to take time off to be at her side during the torturous first day of Olivia's trial. She had expected him to come, although when she'd informed him of the date and he'd expressed his regret that he was scheduled to work, it hadn't surprised her. She probably could have *forced* him to be there. In fact, had she asked him outright, he would likely have rescheduled his work days. She told herself that she had not made her request explicit because the desire to be present, to be her bulwark and support, should have come from him, rather than have been demanded by her. If she were honest with herself, though, she would have admitted that there was some other, perhaps more malignant, reason for her failure to ask for what she knew she needed: for some, inexplicable reason, she found her inevitable disappointment with Arthur satisfying.

"Let's eat," Arthur said. "You two can tell me how it went over dinner."

They sat down at the table, and Elaine took a mouthful of the fish. It was only once the first bite was dissolving on her tongue that she realized how hungry she was. She resolved to feel grateful to Arthur for having worked so hard on the meal. She glanced over at Olivia, who was fastidiously slicing slivers off the outside edges of her ahi.

"What's wrong?" Arthur asked, a trace of irritation in his voice.

"Nothing," Olivia said. "It's delicious."

Then Elaine remembered. "She can't eat raw fish, Arthur. Because of the baby."

"Oh, of course," he said. "Here, give me that," he snatched up her plate.

"It's really fine. I'll just eat the outside."

"Don't be ridiculous. I'll cook it through. It'll take two min-utes." He carried the plate out to the kitchen, and Elaine lay her fork down.

"It was sweet of him to make dinner," she said.

Olivia nodded.

Elaine lowered her voice to a whisper. "Are you at all hungry?"

Olivia shook her head.

"Try to eat, okay? His feelings will be hurt if you don't. And you and the baby need the food, too."

"Okay," Olivia said.

Arthur came back and put the plate in front of her with a flourish. "Cooked-through tuna for the pregnant lady. Excuse the grayish color."

Elaine smiled reassuringly at her fiancé, and they continued with their meal. Over the lamb, she filled Arthur in on the events of the day in court.

"So, Izaya's doing a good job?" he asked.

"Oh, yes," Elaine said. "Don't you think, Olivia?"

Olivia nodded.

Elaine said, "I think he's in his element in the courtroom. You should have seen his opening statement, Arthur. He scooped that jury up, held them in the palm of his hand, and took them right where he wanted them to go. It's remarkable in someone so young. It really is."

"He probably learned it from his father," Arthur said, around a mouthful of escarole. Elaine nodded. "I think he's every bit as good as Ervin T. Upchurch," she said, "and not so flashy. Well, except for the hair. And the Italian suits."

"Well, let's hope he does as well for Olivia as his father would have."

"He will," Olivia said.

Elaine ate quickly and watched as Olivia tried to choke down at least a few bites of her meal. Finally the girl rose from the table, saying that she was exhausted and wanted to take a bath and head to bed. Elaine tackled the kitchen, scouring the heavy casserole and iron skillet, up to her elbows in congealing fat and burnt, caramelized sugar. Not for the first time she wondered why none of Arthur's cooking classes had ever bothered to teach him the art of washing a dish.

"Mr. Contreras, does this figure mean anything to you?" Izaya pointed at the huge poster he'd propped up in front of the jury. The large white sign was blank, except for the number $3,560,633 printed in oversized, black letters. The dollar sign was a bright, almost fluorescent green.

"No." Gabriel Contreras sat in the witness box. He wore a dark, pin-striped suit that seemed to crumple around his body as Izaya's questioning continued. For the first few hours of his cross-examination, Olivia's lawyer had painstakingly gone through the Cuban's past, lingering over such highlights as his stint in the Havana insane asylum, his arrest and subsequent incarceration for drug dealing, his history of drug use. For almost two tedious hours, Izaya played tape recordings of contradictory testimony given by the witness in various other cases.

At the end of each bit of tape, Izaya would ask, "That is your voice, correct?"

"Yes."

"You were under oath when you made that statement, weren't you?"

"Yes."

"But the statement is false, isn't it?"

At first Contreras had objected to the characterization of his testimony as untrue, but finally the sheer number of his own contradictions seemed to overwhelm him, and he simply answered, again and again, "Yes."

Just when Olivia had grown worried that Izaya would lose the jury through sheer thoroughness, he had spun around on his heel. He lifted the poster up with a flourish and propped it on a tripod right in front of the jury box.

"This figure means nothing to you at all?" Izaya repeated.

"Objection, your honor, asked and answered." Amanda Steele had risen to her feet. She looked tired, but still as calm as when the trial had begun. Olivia had amused herself, day after day, by trying to distinguish the prosecutor's many expensive suits one from another. They were all black or navy blue and only subtly different. This one had a shawl collar, and the skirt seemed just the tiniest bit shorter than those of the days before.

Judge Horowitz looked up at Izaya. "Mr. Feingold-Upchurch, I believe Ms. Steele has a point. Why don't you get to yours. Objection sustained." The judge waggled the long eyebrows that sat atop his forehead like white millipedes. He seemed not at all irritated with Izaya, despite his rebuke. On the contrary, he seemed entertained by the young attorney.

Izaya picked up the poster and held it up. "Three million, five hundred and sixty thousand, six hundred and thirty-three. Dollars." He drawled out the words slowly, almost hissing on the final *S*. "Mr. Contreras, isn't that, in fact, the amount of money you have been paid by the DEA over the course of the past four years?"

Contreras shrugged. Olivia hoped she wasn't imagining the tiny beads of sweat appearing on his upper lip.

"Words, Mr. Contreras," Judge Horowitz said. "Use words. My court reporter has no key for the expressive shrug."

"I don't know. Maybe," Contreras said.

"You don't know?" Izaya's voice was incredulous. "Why? Too much cash to count?"

"Objection." Ms. Steele rose only halfway to her feet.

"A little less drama, Mr. Feingold-Upchurch." One or two members of the jury tittered at the judge's comment, and Olivia could see an almost imperceptible tightening in Izaya's jaw.

"Your honor, I'd like to refresh the witness's recollection with the forms establishing that he did, in fact, receive $3,560,633 dollars from the DEA in return for being a snitch."

Contreras interrupted, "I don't need to see nothing. That number sounds right more or less."

"More or less," Izaya sounded ostentatiously confused. "Oh, right!" He thumped his forehead with the heel of his hand. "The car. How could I forget the car?" Izaya reached behind the poster with the number on it and brought out another—a blowup of a photograph of a shiny green sports utility vehicle. "You were also given this Lincoln Navigator, right?"

"Yeah."

"Nice car."

"Yeah."

"It's worth, what, forty, fifty grand?"

"Not anymore."

"Not anymore?" Izaya kept his voice neutral and curious.

"It ain't worth nothing anymore. I cracked it up."

"No insurance?" This time Izaya almost sounded as if he were commiserating with the informant.

Contreras said, "No," before Amanda Steele had time to get out the objection. The judge flicked his hand at Izaya. "Let's move on, shall we?" he said.

"Of course, your honor. Mr. Contreras, you didn't pay any taxes on that three million, five hundred sixty thousand, six hundred thirty-three dollars, did you?" Again Izaya drew out the figure, saying each word slowly and clearly.

"No."

"Didn't file any tax returns?"

"No."

Izaya shook his head and walked back to the podium. He left the posters propped up on the tripod in front of the jury.

"Mr. Contreras, you've helped send thirteen people to jail, haven't you?"

Gabriel puffed out his chest. "That's right. Thirteen drug dealers."

"Thirteen drug dealers?" Izaya asked again.

"Yup."

"And how many of those drug dealers had ever committed a crime before you set them up?"

Amanda Steele was on her feet, her voice no longer calm but quite clearly angry. The judge motioned the lawyers over to the side bar, and they held a whispered conference. Olivia turned back to look at her mother who sat in the row immediately behind her. Elaine smiled at her and then reached into her purse. She pulled out a tissue, and, rising from her seat, walked over to the bar and gently rubbed a smudge from the side of Olivia's mouth. At the courtroom deputy's frown, she hurried back to her bench.

The attorneys walked back to their tables, the prosecutor's mouth tightened into a thin line and Izaya looking confident.

"Mr. Contreras, isn't it true that not a single one of the thirteen people you set up had been arrested for drug dealing before you crossed their paths?" Izaya said, facing the jury.

"I don't know."

Izaya spun back to Contreras. "You don't know? Would it help to refresh your recollection if I asked your handlers at the DEA if they'd informed you of that fact?"

"Look, none of them got caught. That doesn't mean they weren't dealing. I'm just the first guy that caught them is all."

Izaya turned to the judge. "Your honor, would you instruct the witness to answer the question posed to him?"

Judge Horowitz shook his head disparagingly, either at Contreras or Izaya; Olivia wasn't sure who. Then he looked ostentatiously at his watch, an oversized gold face on a thick, braided leather band, raised his eyebrows in a pantomime of shock at the time, and said, "Answer the question, Mr. Contreras."

"What was the question?"

"Isn't it true that none of the thirteen people you set up had ever been arrested for drug dealing before you got them involved in your deals?" Izaya repeated.

"I guess so."

"You guess so?"

"Yeah. It's true."

"Mr. Feingold-Upchurch," the judge interrupted. "Are you almost done here? It's getting late."

"I have only one more question, your honor."

"Fine."

"Mr. Contreras, what happens to Cuban immigrants who get convicted of crimes in America?"

"What do you mean? Same thing that happens to anybody."

"Really? Isn't it in fact the case, Mr. Contreras, that Cubans who commit felonies in the United States are held in permanent detention until Fidel Castro is willing to let them go home to Cuba?"

"I don't know."

"Let me put this another way, Mr. Contreras. Weren't you in fact told that if you didn't cooperate with the DEA, you would be held in indefinite detention until Castro wanted you back?"

"Objection, your honor. Hearsay." Amanda Steele was on her feet.

"State of mind, not truth of the matter asserted," Izaya said, looking disgusted.

"Objection overruled." The judge looked expectantly at Contreras.

The informant muttered, "Somebody might have said that."

"Somebody might have told you that if you didn't work for the DEA, you would spend the rest of your life in jail unless Castro said you could go back to Cuba?" Izaya asked.

"Yeah."

Izaya turned on his heel and headed back to the defense counsel. As he walked, he called back over his shoulder, "Nothing further, your honor."

Olivia sat very still in her seat as the jury filed out. She couldn't decide whether to look at them or not. She was afraid if she looked away they would think her shifty, unable to look them in the eye. If she smiled at them, they might think she was trying to worm her way into their good graces. She settled for as neutral a face as she could muster. She watched them leave, and after the door to the jury room had closed, she collapsed in her chair as though the wires that had been holding her upright were suddenly cut. She laid her head on the table for a moment, savoring the feel of the cool, smooth wood under her cheeks.

Izaya patted her on the back and, leaning over, whispered in her ear, "How you doing?"

She sighed and sat up. "Fine."

"That went really well, don't you think?"

"Yeah, I think so," she replied.

"We nailed him. We definitely nailed him. Don't you think we nailed him?"

Izaya was leaning over her seat, his hand still on her back. He looked at her expectantly, almost beseechingly. She mustered up a smile.

"We nailed him," she said.

"Come, honey. Let's go home." Elaine held open the wooden gate that separated the observers' seats from the front of the courtroom. As Olivia walked through, her back aching from the weight of her belly, her mother put her arm around her. Olivia leaned heavily against her, and inhaled the familiar smell of gardenia soap that all but covered the acrid, medicinal tang of the pharmacy. Elaine held her all the way to the car.

The next morning, after the preliminary motions and announcements that started every courtroom day, Amanda Steele called Jorge Rodriguez to the stand. Olivia felt her pulse quicken as the door behind the jury box opened, and Jorge was led into the courtroom by the U.S. Marshal. Just as he sat down, the baby kicked her, hard, and she gasped. The heads of everyone in the courtroom turned sharply toward her. She put her hands on her belly and willed the baby to settle down. Only Jorge hadn't looked at her. He kept his eyes firmly affixed to a point in the back of the courtroom. He looked pale and thin. He had shorn his hair, and it stuck up in short spikes on the top of his head. His ears looked red, unused to the exposure. His nose was even more hawk-like. He was still handsome, but he looked haggard and frightened.

A young woman who had been sitting in the back of the courtroom stood up and crossed to the witness stand. At the judge's instruction, she gave her name to the court reporter. Then she began to translate for Jorge. Olivia thus heard every question asked twice and every answer given twice. She heard the firm words of the prosecutor moderated as they were translated into Spanish by the soft-spoken young interpreter. She heard Jorge's monosyllabic, mumbled tones spoken clearly and distinctly in an impeccable English, denuded of the vague tone of guilt and dread with which they had left his lips.

The AUSA, today clad in a simple black dress under a long black jacket, painstakingly, question by question, led Jorge through the period of time leading up to his arrest. With her prodding, he described his life with Olivia, his work, her work. Jorge never once looked at Olivia. He stared at his hands, or at a spot high on the opposite wall of the courtroom. But never at her.

"Please describe for the jury how you met the confidential informant, Gabriel Contreras." Amanda Steel said.

"Olivia introduced him to me," Jorge replied.

The jurors looked at Olivia sharply. They obviously had not imagined that she'd known Contreras first. In his testimony, the informant had said only that he met them both in the bar of the restaurant in which he worked.

Slowly, almost tediously, Jorge described how he had come to discuss methamphetamine with Gabriel. He described the mechanics of the deal, when they'd agreed and to what. Then the prosecutor asked, "When did you tell the defendant that you planned to supply Mr. Contreras with methamphetamine?"

"When it happened. She knew from the beginning."

Olivia blinked her eyes, hard, refusing to allow herself to cry.

"The defendant knew from the very beginning that you'd planned to sell methamphetamine to Mr. Contreras?"

"Objection!" Izaya said loudly. "Asked and answered. And leading, too."

"Sustained on both counts," the judge replied.

"Did the defendant assist you in your drug deal in any way?" the prosecutor continued, unfazed.

"Yes. When Gabriel called, she would pass on his messages to me."

"To what did those messages pertain?"

"The methamphetamine."

"Did the defendant know to what they referred?"

Izaya leapt to his feet. "Objection. This witness can't testify about what my client knew or didn't know."

"Sustained," the judge said.

"Mr. Rodriguez, did you inform the defendant that you were dealing drugs?" Amanda Steele continued.

"I wasn't dealing drugs," Jorge answered.

"Excuse me?" Amanda Steele's voice was sharp. It was as though she jerked the leash on which Jorge was tethered.

"I mean, I wasn't really dealing drugs. I didn't sell them on the street or anything. I just did that one thing." The interpreter did a fair imitation of Jorge's confused voice. In another context, you might have thought she was making fun of him.

"Did you inform the defendant that you were involved in a conspiracy to sell methamphetamine?"

"Yes."

"Before or after she took the phone messages from Gabriel?"

"After the first call."

"When she took the second message did she know you were involved in a drug transaction?"

"Objection!" Izaya said.

"Sustained."

"Did you tell her about the drug transaction before she took the second message?"

"Yes."

"Did the defendant assist you in any other way?"

"She drove me one time."

"Where did she drive you?"

"First to pick up the drugs and then to do the exchange. To get the money."

"What did she do while you were picking up the methamphetamine and then selling it?"

"She waited in the car so we could just keep it right in front of the houses. So we wouldn't have to park."

When Amanda Steele finally sat down, she had a subtly self-satisfied smile on her face.

Izaya rose and made short work of Jorge. Within moments, Jorge had acknowledged that Olivia had not taken any active part in the drug transaction, beyond being in the car and answering the phone. He admitted that before he picked Olivia up at work, she hadn't expected to go along with him to do the actual exchange.

Izaya pulled another poster out from his stack. He angled the easel so that it faced both Jorge on the witness stand and the jurors in the jury box. On it was a sentence in Spanish from the letter Jorge had written Olivia. The English translation was printed underneath.

Izaya turned to face Jorge. "Do you recognize that line?" he asked.

"I don't know," Jorge, then the interpreter, said.

"Why don't you go ahead and read it," Izaya said.

"I'm so sorry Olivia, for everything that has happened, and for everything that will happen." Jorge mumbled. The interpreter translated in a more audible tone.

"I'm sorry, I didn't catch that," Izaya said.

"Your honor," Amanda Steele called out.

Judge Horowitz rolled his eyes. "Ask some questions, Mr. Feingold-Upchurch."

"Of course, your honor." Izaya leaned toward Jorge. "You wrote that line in a letter to Olivia, isn't that right?"

Jorge nodded.

"For heaven's sake, can you, Ms. Steele, please tell your witnesses to talk out *loud*?" the judge said.

"Yes, that was in my letter to Olivia," Jorge said quickly.

"You were apologizing to her."

"Yes."

"For everything that had happened."

"Yes."

"Her arrest."

"Yes."

"The drug deal."

"Yes."

"The entire mess."

"Yes."

"You were apologizing to her for having gotten her involved."

"Yes, I mean…" Jorge's voice trailed off, and he looked over at Amanda Steele. She looked back at him, her eyes slightly narrowed.

"Um, Mr. Rodriguez, I'm over here," Izaya said, waving his hand in the air.

"I don't know," Jorge said.

"What don't you know?"

"What you asked."

"I asked if you were apologizing to Olivia for having gotten her involved in your drug deal."

"No."

"No?"

"No."

"You weren't apologizing to her?"

"No."

"You aren't sorry?" Izaya sounded astonished.

Jorge looked confused. "No. I mean, yes. Yes, I am sorry."

Izaya sighed and sat down on the edge of the counsel table. "Okay, let's try this again. Is this or is this not an apology for having gotten Olivia involved in your drug deal?"

"Yes."

"Yes, what?"

"Yes, it's an apology."

"For having gotten Olivia involved."

"Yes."

Izaya nodded. He turned back to the poster. "And for everything that will happen," he read, almost musingly. "That refers to the trial, right? To your testimony against her. You were apologizing for testifying against her."

"*Si*," Jorge whispered. Then he cleared his throat. "*Si*." The interpreter translated it only once.

Olivia looked over at Amanda Steele. The prosecutor sat perfectly still, her hands folded on the table in front of her. There were two spots of color high on her smooth, white cheeks.

"Olivia didn't want you to do the drug deal, did she?" Izaya asked.

"I don't know," Jorge said.

"You don't *know* if she didn't want you to do it?" Once again, Izaya sounded incredulous.

"No."

"Well, she told you not to do it, didn't she?"

"No," Jorge said, staring down at his hands.

"No?"

"The money, it was for both of us. She needed it, too. She wanted it, too."

"But she told you not to do the deal, didn't she?"

"Not exactly."

"Not exactly? What does that mean."

"She said never do it *again*."

"You expect me to believe, you expect this *jury* to believe, that Olivia said, 'Sure honey, go on and do a drug deal, just never, never do it again.' Just what do you take us for?"

"Objection!" Amanda Steele was on her feet.

"Sustained," growled the judge.

Izaya didn't take his eyes off Jorge. "Olivia told you not to do the deal, didn't she?"

Jorge shrugged.

"Mr. Rodriguez!" the judge warned.

"Yes," Jorge said, softly.

"Olivia said, 'Don't do this. Don't do this drug deal.'"

"Yes."

"She begged you not to do it!" Izaya said, his loud voice reverberating through the courtroom.

"Objection!" Amanda Steele cried.

Izaya raised his hands in the air. "You know what? I have no more questions," he said, in a tone of such disgust, such derision, that Olivia felt almost sorry for Jorge.

When he was dismissed, Jorge stood up. He turned to find the marshals who waited to take him back to the jail, and in doing so, caught Olivia's eye. For a moment, they looked at one another. Without really intending to, Olivia remembered the way his face looked, staring down at her while they made love. She remembered his hand on her hip, glowing dark against her white skin. She remembered his voice, proud and angry, as he inspired a crowd of students to protest. She wondered if he, too, was imagining her in a different time, a different place. Was he remembering how she trimmed his hair with nail scissors, carefully clipping along his collar? Was he thinking of the way they'd huddle over the newspaper in the mornings, Olivia translating the headlines for him? Was he imagining her body straining under his?

Jorge blinked and ducked his head, his face bearing an expression of meek anonymity that Olivia recognized from the face that had gazed back at her in the mirror when she had been incarcerated in Martinez. Jorge walked out the courtroom door, careful to meet no one's eye.

When the jury had been excused and the judge left the bench, Izaya, Elaine, and Olivia sat at the defense table. They watched Amanda Steele gather her boxes of documents and exhibits, pile them on a cart, and trundle the cart down the aisle. The wheel caught on an edge of carpet at the back of the courtroom. The prosecutor tugged on it, and Olivia looked at Izaya, wondering if he would help her. He looked like he might be considering it, but before he could rise, the AUSA had yanked the cart free and wheeled it out of the room. When they were finally alone, Elaine turned to Izaya. "That was wonderful. You really tore him apart. The jury won't believe a word he said. That lying little pig." She seemed surprised at her own vehemence and put a hand over her mouth. A small, nervous laugh escaped her.

"Thanks," Izaya said. "I think that went alright."

"It's not his fault," Olivia said softly.

"What?" Elaine and Izaya spoke simultaneously.

"Jorge's not a pig. I mean, I'm not mad that you said that or anything. It's just that it's not his fault."

"What?" Elaine said, her voice strained to a piercing thinness.

"He's scared. He's afraid of being in jail. People get killed all the time in Mexican prisons. He's just afraid."

"And what about you? Why isn't he afraid for you?"

Olivia shrugged her shoulders. "Because he thinks I can win, even with him testifying. Or because he's a coward. I don't know. All I know is that I can't blame him for this. It's like that saying: you can't judge someone until you've walked a mile in their shoes."

"You *are* in his shoes, Olivia. You're in *worse* shoes. You're facing the same horrible predicament, but *you're* pregnant. And it *is* his fault. Every last part of it is his fault," Elaine said.

"Still. I can't blame him for this."

"Why not? Why can't you blame him? I do," Elaine said.

Olivia traced her fingers across her belly. "Because I'm responsible, too."

Elaine started to object, but Olivia shook her head.

"Not the drug deal. I don't mean that. But that he was even here to begin with. The truth is, I never wanted him to come. I never wanted him to follow me. But I didn't tell *him* that. I didn't tell him when I was in Mexico, and I didn't tell him when he showed up here. I let him move in. I let the relationship continue. And I guess I even pretended to us both that I was in love with him. I don't know why—maybe out of guilt because he sacrificed so much to follow me. In a way, it's really all *my* fault."

Elaine shook her head. "All that may be true, Olivia. But none of it makes you responsible for the choices he made."

"I know that, Mom. I just can't help but feel that none of us knows what we would do if we faced the same choice."

"*You* know, Olivia," Izaya said, his voice soft and gentle.

"What?" she said.

"You *were* faced with the same choice. You could have cooperated with the government. You could have testified against him. But you didn't. That's the difference between the two of you. You didn't betray him."

Olivia raised her eyes to Izaya's. He nodded.

"That's the difference, Olivia."

She opened her mouth to object, to explain that, perhaps, had she been as afraid as Jorge, as unfamiliar with the world in which she found herself, she might have done what Jorge did, but Izaya raised his hand to quiet her.

"I know you, Olivia. Your mother knows you. And, now, you know yourself."

She stared at him, and then, almost imperceptibly, nodded.

The first witness Izaya put on the stand to testify on Olivia's behalf was a grim little man whose bald pate shone through the three or four hairs combed over the top of his head. It was clear that he didn't want to be there. His glared at Izaya with what looked like disdain but might actually have been fear. After he swore to tell the truth so help him God, he stated his name and occupation for the record. "Oliver Stroud, Deputy Director, Immigration and Naturalization Service, Northern California division."

Izaya first established Stroud's familiarity with the Mariel boatlift and with immigration rules and regulations in general, and Cuban immigration in particular. Then he continued, "Mr. Stroud, what happens when an unnaturalized immigrant commits a felony in the United States?"

The little man shrugged, his strands of hair wobbling a bit. "That depends on the felony."

Izaya leaned forward on the podium and said, with exquisite patience, "How about the sale of cocaine? One hundred grams of cocaine, to be exact."

"Well, presumably that individual would be arrested and convicted. He'd go to jail."

"And after that?"

The INS officer pursed his lips. "Well, as soon as our office found out about the conviction, we'd put an immigration hold on him."

"What's an immigration hold?"

"It's like a warrant. It means the state can't release him when he's done serving his time. They have to send him over to federal custody."

"And why would you put an INS hold on him?"

"So that we could keep him incarcerated pending deportation proceedings."

"So someone who was convicted of selling one hundred grams of cocaine would be deported?"

"Yes, *sir*," the government official said, the sneer in his voice unmistakable. A few of the female members of the jury who had quite obviously been charmed by Izaya shot the witness reproving looks. He blushed and then continued, "I mean, he'd be deported if we had somewhere to send him."

"What do you mean by that?"

"Well, there are some countries we don't have relations with. Those countries won't accept deportees from the U.S."

"Is Cuba one of those countries?"

"Yes. It is."

"What would happen to a Cuban drug dealer then, if you couldn't deport him. Would you just let him go?"

"No, sir. We would not. We would detain him."

"What does that mean?" Izaya's tone was conversational, as if he and the jury were just there to chat with Mr. Stroud.

"We would keep him in INS custody."

"Is INS custody like, say, a hotel?"

Stroud smiled thinly. "No. I can't say that it is."

"Is it perhaps similar to home detention?"

"No, sir."

"What is it like?"

"Well, the individuals are under detention. These are *criminals*, you know. I'd have to say it's like a prison."

"In fact, these people are actually held in prisons and jails, isn't that correct?" Izaya said sharply.

"Yes."

"And how long would our hypothetical drug dealer be incarcerated?"

"Until Cuba was willing to take him back."

"Has Cuba ever taken any deportee back?"

"Not in my experience."

"In anyone's experience?"

"Excuse me?"

"Has Fidel Castro ever allowed a Cuban detainee to be returned to Cuba?"

"No."

"Isn't it, in fact, the case that a Cuban drug dealer would face indefinite detention in prison—a life sentence, in other words?"

"Objection, leading!" Amanda Steele raised her voice.

"Your honor," Izaya said, "it seems to me that this witness, given that he's an employee of the very government that's prosecuting my client, can fairly well be qualified as a hostile witness."

"Objection overruled. Continue, Mr. Feingold-Upchurch."

Izaya smiled faintly and then turned and asked his next question while facing the jury. "Mr. Stroud, isn't it true that a Cuban drug dealer would face indefinite detention in a prison-like setting until he died or until Castro took him back, whichever came first?"

"Yes, that's true."

"Can you think of any way that the prisoner might be released?"

"I guess a court could order it."

"Has any court ever ordered the release of a Cuban detainee who was convicted of dealing one hundred grams of cocaine?"

"No, not that I know of."

"And it's your job to know things like that, correct?"

Stroud sat up a bit higher in his chair. "I suppose it is, yes."

"Is there any other way that the prisoner could get out?"

"After conviction? No."

Izaya spun on his heel and exhaled loudly. "Ah. After conviction he could never get out; he'd have to serve a life sentence. What about *before* conviction?"

"Well, if the case was dismissed, then he wouldn't be a prisoner anymore, right?" The little man gave a complacent smirk, as if he'd beaten Izaya at something.

"Like, say, if the defendant chose to become an informant for the DEA, rather than serve a life sentence in prison, correct?"

The little man scowled.

"By deciding to become a DEA informant, a drug dealer could avoid a sentence of life in prison as an INS detainee, correct?"

"Yeah. That's correct."

"So if our hypothetical prisoner didn't cooperate, didn't become a DEA informant, he would spend the rest of his life in jail; but if he did, he would be released immediately, correct?"

Stroud shrugged his shoulders. A sticky strand of hair fell across one of his eyes, and he carefully spread it back over the top of his head. "Hypothetically, yes."

It was Olivia's turn. The judge had adjourned early the previous day at Izaya's request, with a lot of pointed glances at his watch, so that Olivia could go to a late-afternoon prenatal appointment. It was a routine appointment. Olivia's belly measured exactly the right size for a woman eight months along, and the baby's heartbeat was strong and regular. The midwife let Olivia spend a few extra minutes listening through the Doppler, the little machine that magnified the sound of the baby's heartbeat into something that you might hear if you put your ear to a conch shell. That night, instead of sleeping, Olivia lay in bed, hearing in her head the submarine rush-rush of her baby's heart. Once, when she got up to use the bathroom for the fourth or fifth time, she saw a light shining out from under Elaine's door. She went to the door and was about to knock on it when she heard the low hum of Arthur's voice. Olivia went back to her own room and stretched back out on the bed.

The next morning, she wore the maternity business suit that she and Elaine had bought the week before. It was deep green, with a long full skirt and a loose jacket. When she'd tried it on in the store, it had made her feel neat and well-put together, attractive for one so far along. Today, however, she felt fat and ungainly as she lumbered up to the witness stand. Her heavy thighs chaffed against one another, her swollen feet ached in Elaine's shoes, and she knew she looked as tired as she felt.

After all her anticipation and anxiety, the actual process of testifying felt almost anticlimactic. The judge had refused to allow Amanda Steele to make any reference to Olivia's criminal history, ruling before the trial that since the crimes were misdemeanors it would unduly influence the jury even to mention the fact that she'd been arrested. Olivia did as Izaya requested and looked at the jury when she answered a question. She paused in order to gather her thoughts. She answered precisely and slowly. She was a model witness.

After establishing her name, who she was, her educational background, her hometown—the recital of which was designed to convince the jury that she could have been their daughter, sister, or friend—Izaya had Olivia describe her relationship with Jorge. Only after that did they begin to talk about the crime. First, Olivia told the jurors how she had discovered Jorge's involvement in the drug deal. She recounted her phone conversation with Gabriel, how confused she'd been, how angry her subsequent discussions with Jorge had made her. Then Izaya led her slowly through the events of the night the deal actually happened.

"Did you have any intention of going with Jorge to do the transaction?" he asked.

"Absolutely not."

"Did you want to go with him?"

"No."

"Why did you?"

"Because it was late, and I didn't have a ride home. And besides, he told me that all he was going to do was introduce some people."

"Did you know he would be bringing drugs into the car?"

"Absolutely not."

"Why didn't you get out of the car when he brought the drugs back with him?"

"Because it was late at night, and we were in a really scary part of Oakland. I didn't want to be on the street alone at night. I was afraid."

"Afraid of what?"

"That I'd be attacked or something," Olivia said, looking at the jurors. The young Asian woman nodded her head.

"Why didn't you insist that Jorge take you home?"

"I asked him to, but he wanted to drop off the drugs. The truth is, I wanted him to drop them off, too. I didn't want any part of it. I didn't want them in my car, and I most certainly didn't want them in my house. I didn't want him to have them, either."

"What did you do when you got home?"

"I vomited. And then I went to bed."

"Why did you vomit?"

"I don't really know. I was afraid. And ashamed."

"Ashamed of what?"

"Of being there while he committed a crime. Ashamed of him."

"Did you ever accompany Jorge again?"

"No. I refused to."

"Were you with him when he got arrested?"

"No. He knew better than to ask me to go with him again."

"Objection, the defendant cannot testify to another's knowledge," the prosecutor said. She had risen to her feet and was leaning slightly forward, her fingertips resting on the table in front of her.

"Sure she can," Izaya said. "She's simply telling the jury that Jorge knew she didn't want to have anything to do with his drug dealing."

The judge raised one eyebrow. He turned to Amanda Steele. "And now you've given the defense a chance to tell them again, counsel. Let's move on, shall we?" She opened her mouth, but then seemed to think the better of it. She sat down again, her mouth drawn into a thin line.

Izaya turned back to Olivia, and with the solicitude that had marked his entire direct examination, said, "Where were you when you were arrested?"

"Asleep in bed." Olivia described her arrest. When she told the jurors that she'd been naked and that the agents had watched her dress, she thought she saw sympathy on the faces of the women. One older man scowled at the prosecutor.

The judge asked Olivia if she needed a recess before the prosecution began her cross-examination. She shook her head. He looked disappointed and unstrapped his watch from his wrist and rested it on the bench before him with a sigh. Olivia wiped her palms on her skirt, leaving a damp smear on her lap. She took a sip of water and then raised her eyes to meet those of Amanda Steele.

"The second time you talked to the confidential informant, you knew exactly what he was talking about, didn't you?" Amanda Steele said, her tone neutral but firm.

Izaya had told Olivia to keep her answers short, not to allow the AUSA to trick her into any unnecessary admissions.

"Yes."

"You knew that he and Jorge were setting up a drug deal?"

"Yes."

"And you assisted them by passing along information?"

"No."

"No?" The prosecutor raised her eyebrows in mock surprise. "You didn't pass along a message from Mr. Contreras to Jorge?"

"Well, yes, I did. But I wasn't trying to assist in the drug deal."

"But you passed along the message, knowing full well what it was for."

Olivia pressed her fingernails into her palms under cover of the desktop. She tried to keep her voice from shaking. "Yes."

"Before you got into the car on the night that you and Jorge picked up the drugs, you knew what you were going to do, correct?"

"No."

"You knew that Jorge was going to do the deal."

"No. I thought he was going to introduce people."

"In order to facilitate a drug deal. You knew that, correct?"

"Yes."

"And when Jorge returned with the drugs, you knew what was in the bag, correct?"

"Yes. I mean, I was afraid that was what it was and then he told me."

"And knowing full well that there was methamphetamine in the bag, you drove Jorge to the location where he was to drop it, correct?"

"Yes."

"And you saw the money he got in return."

"Yes."

"Did you insist that he keep the money out of your house?"

"No."

"Where did you put the money?"

"I didn't put it anywhere. *He* put it under the mattress."

"The mattress on which you slept for two more nights, knowing full well it was there?"

"No."

"You didn't know it was there?"

"I knew it was there, but I didn't sleep there for two nights. I slept there that night and then the next night I was arrested in the middle of the night."

"While you were sleeping on top of the drug money."

"Yes."

"Ms. Goodman, you have taken illegal drugs, haven't you?"

"Objection!" Izaya bellowed.

"Goes to predisposition, your honor," the prosecutor said. "He's given notice of his intention to argue entrapment. The defendant's history of drug use is relevant to the issue of predisposition."

"Your honor, if she had a history of drug *dealing* that might be relevant. Drug *use* most certainly is not," Izaya was just barely containing his anger.

The judge rubbed his jaw thoughtfully. Suddenly, Izaya blurted, "You know what? I withdraw my objection. My client isn't a drug user. I don't want the jury to be under the misapprehension that she is."

"Are you certain, Mr. Feingold-Upchurch?" the judge asked, obviously doubtful about Izaya's decision.

"Absolutely. Go ahead, Olivia. Answer the prosecutor's question." He nodded at her.

For the barest fraction of a second, Olivia considered the question. She thought of the times she'd smoked pot in high school and college. The line of cocaine she'd once snorted at a party. The two or three times she and her friends had taken ecstasy and spent a night contemplating their love for the universe and each other. Then she opened her mouth and spoke.

"I tried marijuana once in high school. I didn't like it. I've never done any other drugs." Her voice was firm and clear, and she was the only one who knew how her hands shook in her lap.

She felt the lie glowing white hot in front of her, a ribbon of reproach in the righteousness of her claim of innocence. She wished she could stuff the words back into her mouth and swallow them.

Amanda Steele shook her head, "Are you honestly trying to tell this jury that the only time you've ever taken drugs was once in high school?"

"Asked and answered, your honor." Izaya was crowing.

The judge, who had been preoccupied with shaking his watch and holding it to his ear, looked up. "That's enough, Ms. Steele. You've got your answer. Let's move on."

The prosecutor leafed through her notes for a moment. "I'm done, your honor."

"Mr. Feingold-Upchurch, redirect," the judge said.

"I'm done, too, your honor."

"The witness is dismissed," the judge said. Izaya leapt to his feet and made a great show of leading Olivia back to her seat. She needed his arm. The trembling that had begun with her hands had spread now to her entire body, and her back was sticky with sweat. She sat down heavily and turned to look at her mother. Elaine smiled, and Arthur, who sat next to Elaine wearing one of his accountant suits, gave her the thumbs-up.

Judge Horowitz dismissed the jury, informing them that the next day they would hear closing arguments and begin their deliberations. Elaine, Arthur, and Olivia walked with Izaya to the elevator bank. Amanda Steele was waiting for the elevator, pushing her metal cart full of exhibits, rule books, and notebooks. They all stood together in the narrow hallway, silently. At one point, Arthur opened his mouth as if to say something, but Elaine silenced him with a hand on his arm. When the elevator finally arrived, the AUSA motioned for them to take it.

"I'll wait," she said.

"No," Olivia replied. "You go ahead." Those were the first words she'd ever spoken to the attorney for the government, outside of her cross-examination. Olivia was sure the woman knew she had lied on the stand. How could she not? What person Olivia's age could really claim such inexperience with drugs? Olivia was confident, in fact, that the prosecutor herself must have tried them. What did she make of this dishonesty? Olivia wondered. Perhaps she considered it justification for her prosecution of Olivia. Olivia wished she could tell her, now, away from the jury and the judge, that yes, she had lied on the stand, but that didn't make her guilty of the crime.

She was innocent. For some reason it was important to her that the blond woman with the thin lips and expensive clothes know that.

"Go ahead," Olivia said, again.

Amanda nodded her head and wheeled her cart into the elevator.

"Bitch," Arthur said as the elevator doors closed behind her.

"Amen to that," Izaya said.

"She's just doing her job," Olivia answered.

Elaine, Arthur, and Izaya looked at her, stunned.

"Let's just hope you keep doing yours so much better than she does hers," Olivia told Izaya. The elevator arrived, and she stepped inside. After a moment, they followed.

Izaya stalked through his living room, wearing nothing except for a pair of purple silk boxer shorts he'd gotten for a long ago Valentine's Day from a girl whose name he could no longer remember. This room was the perfect place to practice a closing argument. He'd never bothered to buy furniture, and the long empty space was ideal for pacing and orating. His words bounced off the pale, dusty walls and echoed from one end of the narrow railroad apartment to the other.

He had just convinced an imaginary jury to acquit Olivia of all charges when his telephone rang.

"You ready, boy?" his father asked

"How did you know I was closing tomorrow?"

Ervin T. Upchurch's deep guffaw made the telephone receiver buzz in Izaya's ear. "You *ready*?" he asked again.

"I think so."

"You *think so!* What you mean you *think so*, son? You better do more than *think so*."

"I'm ready!" Izaya said, in the tone of confident excitement he knew his father expected of him.

"You want to try your closing out on me?"

Izaya laughed. "Why don't you come on up and watch me. Maybe you'll learn something."

For all the gifts and acknowledgments that arrived at the end of every trial, his father had never once come to see Izaya in action. With every new trial, Izaya had invited him, at first with a tentative shyness—hoping he would have the opportunity to strut his stuff for the man he had spent most of his life trying to impress. By now, though, he made a joke of the invitation he knew was certain to be rejected.

"I just might, one of these days," Ervin said. "You going to win this one, son?"

Izaya considered the question. The possibility of losing, of failing Olivia, made the almost manic buzz of anticipation he experienced with every trial turn into an anxious dread. Olivia was, he realized, the first of his clients, in his nearly five years of practice, whom he genuinely believed to be innocent. Virtually everyone he met, at some point or another, in a tone either of hostile confrontation or prurient interest, asked him what he would do if he found himself representing someone who was guilty. What they never realized was that that was the constant state of affairs.

A criminal defense attorney's job is, by and large, to represent the guilty. If Izaya took a case to trial, it was not because his client was innocent; it was rather because he thought he could win or because the cause was so completely lost it made little difference. In the latter case, he figured that the government might as well work a little for the privilege of prosecution. In the former, while he knew that his client had committed the act of which he'd been accused, the government's case was, for some reason having nothing whatsoever to do with the truth of the accusation, weak.

All this was not to say that Izaya believed his clients deserved the punishment meted out to them. One of his clients had been a father who lied on a mortgage application in order to borrow enough money to renovate his home so that it could accommodate his severely disabled daughter's wheelchair. That man had received two years; the daughter had been institutionalized. Izaya had had mentally ill clients who had tried to rob banks as part of addled plans to assuage the voices in their heads. And, more times than he could count, he had represented minor participants in drug offenses who received ten- or twenty-year prison terms. He was inspired, first and always, by a righteous indignation at the extent of the government's mean-spirited prosecution of these people, when it was so clear to him that it should have been providing them with the care and services that would allow them to live more productive lives.

He had, thus, often felt that he was on the side of justice, but never before had he held an innocent person's future in his hands. And never before—it had to be confessed—had he been so personally involved with a client. The irony of this did not escape him. It was pretty, white Olivia, so clearly not the kind of person he had ever expected or intended to represent, so clearly not one of those he thought of as "his people," who aroused in him an unprecedented intensity of devotion. He knew that any mistake he made could spell disaster for her, and he felt a grim apprehension at the thought of losing the trial. He told himself that this was because of Olivia's vulnerability and dependence on him. The truth, he knew, was much more complicated. Olivia was, of course, much more like him than he wanted to acknowledge. They were from the same place and of the same time. Reflected in her was his own devotion, however naive, to social justice. More importantly, he recognized her as another child whose identity had been forged in the absence of a father. They had this in common, and for both of them it had defined their lives. It was, perhaps, why he found himself in love with her.

"I have to win," he said. His father didn't reply, and Izaya wondered if he had noticed his son's vehemence. "I just have to," he said.

"You got something going on with this girl?" Ervin asked.

"What?"

"You heard me, son. You two got something going on?"

"She's my client!"

"Give me a break, boy. Who you think you're talking to?"

"I'm not sleeping with my client, Ervin," he said.

His father chuckled.

"I'm *not*," Izaya said.

"Good thing, son. I been there, and it ain't no place you want to be."

"You've had affairs with *clients*?" Izaya asked, wondering why he felt so shocked. His father's proclivities were fairly notorious. Izaya knew that his own mother was by no stretch of the imagination Ervin's only conquest, although he was fairly confident that she was the only one of his mistresses to have borne him a child. There was a steady stream of attractive female attorneys second-chairing Ervin's high-profile cases, and on more than one occasion, Izaya, watching his father and his associate on Court TV, had felt a jealous admiration of the older man's ability to seduce such young and accomplished women.

Ervin chuckled. "Oh Lord. And it was one hell of a mistake, too. Don't do it, son. That's all I'm saying. Don't do it."

"I would never sleep with a client. I'd never even think of it," Izaya lied.

"Good boy."

Izaya sighed. "Hey, Ervin. Dad. I'd love if you would come tomorrow. I mean, if you're going to be up north."

"I might just do that, boy. I might just."

Amanda Steele's closing argument was much like the rest of her case—like her—dry, cool, and convincing. She approached the podium with a neat stack of bright-yellow index cards and set them out tidily on the polished wood surface. She laid her silver pen down next to the cards and took a single step back from the podium. Then she turned and faced the jury.

"Ladies and Gentlemen of the jury, on behalf of the government of the United States of America, I thank you for your participation in this case, and for your attention over the course of the past week. The role of the citizens in the criminal justice system is the most crucial of all. It is more important than that of the investigators; it is more important than that of the prosecutors. It is even more important than that of the judiciary. Your role, as a jury, is to evaluate and make a judgment about the evidence presented against the defendant. I am confident that you will find that evidence to be overwhelming in support of a conviction on the charge of distributing methamphetamine, conspiracy to distribute methamphetamine, and using a communications facility, to wit, a telephone, to facilitate the distribution of methamphetamine."

As Amanda Steele went on to describe the events leading up to Olivia's arrest, she looked scrupulously from one member of the jury to another, making eye contact and speaking clearly and dispassionately. She reminded the jury of the tapes they had heard of Olivia speaking on the phone with Gabriel. "The defendant herself has admitted that she knew full well that the topic of that conversation was the distribution of methamphetamine. The defendant herself has admitted passing the information on to her accomplice, Mr. Jorge Rodriguez, so that he could exchange the drugs for the money. The defendant herself has admitted that she knew the money was hidden underneath the mattress on which she slept."

The prosecutor then held up the photograph of Olivia waiting in the car for Jorge. "Ladies and Gentlemen, I remind you as well of the photographic evidence against the defendant. Here you can see the defendant, the owner and driver of the vehicle that transported both the drugs and money, waiting for her accomplice. Her presence was necessary in order to make an expeditious getaway. The defendant herself has admitted that she knew full well that Mr. Rodriguez was effecting the exchange of drugs for money while she waited behind the wheel of the getaway car."

During the course of the trial, the prosecutor had never once referred to Olivia by her name. She called her only "the defendant." As the closing argument progressed, Olivia began to feel that phrase, that word, like a sharpened, poisoned dart, piercing her, reminding her that she was not an ordinary person who could leave the courtroom and go home to a life unexamined by the government, unsupervised by the police. She was a criminal with an arrest record. Someone who would, even if she were acquitted, always be different from the rest of the world.

Amanda Steele next turned to Jorge's testimony. She went through it, item by item, and then she paused. "The idea of a man testifying against his own girlfriend and accomplice may be troubling to some of you." Olivia looked at the members of the jury, one of whom, the black businessman, was nodding his head. "I ask you, however, to view this from another perspective. Mr. Rodriguez realized the error of his ways. He confronted his own culpability and determined to take responsibility for his actions. He confessed his crimes to the investigating officers and offered to do what was necessary to make up for his misdeeds. Testifying honestly and forthrightly was what was necessary. Describing the entirety of the events was what was required. That includes implicating his accomplices, including the defendant."

Olivia looked back at the juror who had seemed to condemn Jorge for turning on her. His face was blank. Olivia licked her lips, her mouth suddenly sticky and dry. She reached for the pitcher of water sitting on the table and poured a few inches into a paper cup. She drank it down in a single gulp. Then she felt Izaya's hand on her arm. He patted it gently, and, when she looked at him, nodded very slightly, as if to remind her that everything was going to be okay. She exhaled with a sigh, conscious for the first time that she had been holding her breath. She wasn't sure for how long.

Amanda Steele ended her closing argument by thoroughly rehashing Gabriel Contreras's testimony. Then she said, "The world of drugs and drug dealers is a murky one, hidden from the light of law-abiding, decent society. In order to infiltrate this society, our law enforcement officers must make use of individuals like Mr. Contreras, whose own pasts have put them in contact with the underworld. There is, unfortunately, no other way to fight these crimes. Mr. Contreras is a valuable and trusted informant for both the FBI and DEA. Again and again, he has participated in sting operations that have uncovered crimes and criminals that otherwise would have gone undetected."

Finally the prosecutor paused, picked up her stack of notecards, and tapped them together. She replaced them on the podium and said, "Ladies and Gentlemen of the jury, I am confident that you will find that the government of the United States has proved, beyond a reasonable doubt, that the defendant is guilty of the crimes of drug trafficking, conspiracy, and the use of a communications device in the commission of a drug crime. Thank you for your time and your consideration."

She returned to her table and sat down, crossing her legs primly at the ankles.

Judge Horowitz shook his wrist with the heavy watch strapped to it at Izaya. "Counsel, you want a break before you start?"

"No thanks, your honor. We're ready to go, aren't we, Olivia?" he smiled at Olivia, and she nodded back. He put his hand on her shoulder and squeezed it. She could not figure out if he did so to reassure and comfort her or to show the jury that she was someone he cared about and thus someone they should care about, too. Perhaps he meant to do both.

Izaya didn't take any notes up to the podium. In fact, he didn't use the podium at all. He loped up to the front of the courtroom, his tripod tucked under his arm. He set it up directly in front of the jury, walked back to the defense table, and picked up the poster with the dollar figure.

"I'm going to set this right here," he said. He placed the poster on the tripod and stood back for a moment as if to admire it. Then he turned to the jury.

"Three million, five hundred and sixty thousand, six hundred and thirty-three dollars." His voice managed to be both conversational and confiding, and booming at the same time. "Let me say that one more time, because, honestly, I don't think we can repeat it often enough. Three million, five hundred and sixty thousand, six hundred and thirty-three dollars. In four years. That's about twenty times what I earn. How about you? And let's not forget that that's *tax-free* dollars.

"Now, you and I, we pay taxes on our money or we're looking at a little thing called an IRS audit. Not so for Mr. Contreras. He just doesn't bother with things like tax returns. I guess if you've got a free pass from the DEA, well then, tax returns seem pretty silly. As long as Mr. Contreras can find some poor sucker to buy his line and do his deal, he can do pretty much what he wants. He spends his piles of cash on whatever it is he desires. He drives his beautiful SUV, courtesy of the DEA, the FBI, and you and me, the American taxpayers. He doesn't bother to insure the car, because what the hell, the laws don't apply to him. He doesn't even have to go to jail like the rest of us when he deals cocaine. He's got a get-out-of-jail-free card." Izaya reached behind the poster with the dollar figure and pulled out a blowup of a *Monopoly* get-out-of-jail-free card. A few of the members of the jury laughed.

"*This* is what you need if you're a coke-dealing Cuban. Because without this here get-out-of-jail-free card," Izaya whacked the card with his hand and Olivia jumped at the sharp noise, "our Mr. Contreras would be looking at indefinite detention. *Indefinite.* A life sentence. Like, until he dies. Or Castro dies. Whichever comes first.

"Let's put ourselves in Gabriel's shoes for a moment, as despicable a thought as that might be." Izaya gave a little shudder. "You're a drug-dealing Cuban. You bust out of an insane asylum, come to America, and start living the cocaine high life. But you're not too bright, and you get yourself arrested. We all heard from our friend at the Immigration and Naturalization Service what happens to coke-dealing Cubans.

"Remember what happens?" He gazed at the jury for a moment and a few of them nodded. "They go to jail. Forever. Why? Because we don't want them here. We don't need any more coke dealers in our country. We want to send them back where they came from." Izaya shook his head and sighed. "But we can't. We can't send them back to Cuba. And we don't want to inflict them on the rest of decent society. So we put them in jail, where they belong, and we hold them. We hold them until they can go back to their own country. Now, Fidel Castro may be a dictator, but he isn't a fool; he doesn't want these drug-dealing criminals any more than we do. He won't take Gabriel Contreras. So Gabriel goes to jail. For the rest of his life.

"Except he doesn't, does he? Because the FBI and the DEA get this bright idea. Let's take this mental patient, this drug-dealing criminal, and let's *hire* him as an *informant*. Let's promise him that if he sets people up, he can *get out of jail*. Hell, let's fill his pockets with gold and give him the good life, as long as he keeps setting up folks.

"And do the DEA and the FBI care who he sets up? Nope. They do not. Do they care if he sets up people who would never have considered doing a drug deal if it weren't for Gabriel? Nope. Hell, it's another notch in the belt, a conviction on the board. Who cares if the person we arrest is a young girl with no criminal past who's never done anything like this in her life. Go for it, *hombre*. Set up an innocent girl. Here's your free pass." Izaya lifted the get-out-of-jail-free card up, shook it, and set it back down.

"And do you know the saddest thing, my friends?" Izaya said, shaking his head. He paused, and the courtroom was silent for a moment. Olivia watched a few of the jurors lean forward in their seats. "The saddest thing," Izaya said, finally, "is they don't even care if he *lies*. And man, oh man, does this guy lie. He lies to the folks he sets up. He lies to the cops. Hell, he lies to the judge. And worst of all, he lies to you. We sat in this courtroom for hours, very *long* hours," he smiled at them ruefully, "and we played tapes of this criminal's perjury." Izaya reminded them of a few of the more egregious examples. "But does he care about committing perjury? No, he most certainly does *not* care about committing perjury. He couldn't care less. And do you know why not? Do you know why he doesn't care?" He turned to them and spread his arms as if waiting for an answer. Then he said, "What has he got?"

The jurors looked at one another and then back at him.

Izaya pointed at the poster of the *Monopoly* card. "He's got a get-out-of-jail-free card." The young Asian woman on the jury mouthed the words along with him, and Olivia felt something akin to delight shiver through her. She clamped her lips together to keep from smiling.

Izaya then moved on to talk about Jorge, "the pathetic and dangerous boyfriend." "My friends, that miserable excuse for a man wants *his baby* to be born in jail just so that the prosecutor over there will carve a few years off his prison sentence. And she is only too willing to do it. Because to the *government*," Izaya spat the word as if it left a bad taste in his mouth, "it doesn't matter *who* goes down for the crime, as long as *someone* does. And the more time the better. If the real culprit will agree to testify against an innocent bystander, by all means! Give him a deal, by all means, and let's drag as many other people along as we can, by all means! Let's get us the poor girlfriend. You know the one? The one who didn't call the cops on her boyfriend when she should have? That one. The pregnant one, whose crime consists of answering the phone and getting a ride home after a hard day at work. Let's get her!

"Answering the phone and taking a ride home. That's what Olivia did, folks. When the father of her unborn baby suddenly decided that standing on a street corner looking for an honest day's work wasn't good enough for the likes of him, that he was going to go into the drug business, she did her best to convince him to stop. She yelled, she screamed, she cried. Hell, the creep

himself admitted that she tried to make him stop. But he would-
n't listen to reason. He wouldn't listen to her. There was nothing
she could do to make him stop. Nothing short of calling the
cops and turning him in. And she didn't do that. Maybe she
should have. But she didn't. What *did* she do? She took a phone
message. And she went along for the ride late one night. She got
in the car, because it was late, and she was tired, and she wasn't
sure how else to get home from work. From working at a job, by
the way, that she used to support the good-for-nothing. A job
that let *her* earn the money he was too *good* to earn.

"The prosecutor is asking you to convict this poor, young
mother-to-be of conspiracy because she committed the crime of
love. She loved this man. Was it foolish? Probably. Does she
have lousy taste in men? Most certainly. But what was it that she
did? She took a phone message and a ride. Yet her most egregious offense was one of omission. She didn't call the police. She
didn't turn the father of her baby in to the cops. And for that,
the prosecutor wants you to send her to jail.

"Jorge? He's getting a sweet deal in return for setting her up.
Gabriel? He's walking around with three and a half million of
your dollars. But Olivia? What's going to happen to Olivia?"

Izaya looked over his shoulder at Olivia, his eyes damp as if he
were about to cry. He was carefully positioned so that the jury
could see both his face and hers. He smiled at Olivia tenderly and
shook his head. Then he heaved a sigh and turned back to the jury.

"The prosecutor wants you to send Olivia to prison. What
do *you* want to do?"

Amanda Steele's rebuttal argument was a brief restatement of
her case against Olivia. Then it was the judge's turn. For once, he
managed to keep his eyes off his watch. He described the offenses
in the indictment and told the jury what they would have to find
in order to convict Olivia. He instructed them as to the meaning

of reasonable doubt. The jury finally filed out of the courtroom shortly before noon. Izaya told Olivia, Elaine, and Arthur that the jurors would most likely order lunch before even beginning their deliberations.

"I don't expect to hear from them before three at the earliest. And they might stay out longer than that. Or even until tomorrow, although I doubt it. Juries like to go home at the end of the day. It's a powerful incentive to compromise. So, I'd suggest you stay close, but not too close. Go get some lunch."

"Would you join us, Izaya?" Elaine asked. "I think we should all go out somewhere special. Like Marcel's. The French place? It's right around the block."

"I'm afraid I can't let you take me out. Federal public defenders aren't allowed to accept anything from clients. Not even lunch." He smiled apologetically.

"Oh, that's a shame," Elaine said.

"Will you join us, anyway?" Arthur asked. "We'll let you pay for your own lunch."

"Sure, why not?" Izaya said.

Olivia turned away from them and began walking down the hall.

"Olivia?" her mother called.

"Um, I have to use the bathroom," Olivia said.

"Why don't Arthur and I head over and get a table, and you two can follow. Do you mind waiting for Olivia, Izaya?"

"Not at all. I've got to run my stuff up to my office, anyway."

Olivia took a long time in the ladies room. She desperately had to pee, but the baby seemed to be sitting on her urethra or bladder, preventing the stream from being anything more than a trickle. She hoisted up her belly in her hands and, after a moment or two, felt the relief of a rush of urine. She sat for a while, even after she was done, thinking about Izaya in the courtroom. His performance had been impressive; had it been on someone else's behalf, she might even have burst into applause at the more dramatic moments. But his oration had been on her behalf. It was for *her* that he had strode around the courtroom impressing the jury with his honest outrage, his concern and tenderness. It had *seemed* so real, felt so real; yet she knew that it was also contrived.

Olivia was interrupted in her reverie by harsh sounds of gagging and spitting coming from the neighboring stall. She rose and tugged her maternity panty hose up into place. She left the stall, went to the marble sink, and splashed cold water on her face. She took a paper towel out of the holder and pressed it against her cheeks and eyes. As she was tossing the crumpled towel into the trash, the door to the other stall opened, and Amanda Steele walked out. She stopped suddenly when she saw Olivia and raised her hand to her mouth, dabbing with the back of her wrist at her lips. The two women stared at one another for a moment, and then the prosecutor lowered her eyes to Olivia's bulging belly. She brought a hand to her own stomach, as if involuntarily, and Olivia glanced down. She thought she could see the faintest roundness.

"Are you pregnant?" Olivia asked.

"What?" the prosecutor said, looking trapped.

"Are you pregnant?"

"I…I don't think we should be talking to each other," she stammered.

Olivia nodded.

The prosecutor walked to the sink, turned on the faucet, and gulped some water from her cupped palm.

Olivia turned to go, and stopped with her hand on the doorknob. "Well, congratulations. If you are, that is. The first trimester is the hardest. It gets better once the nausea passes." She walked out of the bathroom.

Olivia found Izaya waiting for her in the hall, his hands shoved into the pockets of his jacket. As they walked out of the building, she said, "I just peed with Amanda Steele."

"No kidding." Izaya sounded distracted.

"I think she's pregnant."

"Really?"

"Well, she didn't say she was, but she was throwing up, and she looks like she has a little belly. So I asked her."

He raised his eyebrows. "What did she say?"

"She said she didn't want to talk to me. Or, rather, that she didn't think she *should*."

He gave a disgusted grunt. "I really can't stand that woman. If she is pregnant, she'll probably give birth to a replicant. Robobaby."

Olivia smiled. They walked for a few more steps, and then she said, "You were amazing in there."

"Thanks."

"No, really. That was an incredible closing argument."

"It was all right."

"I was just wondering…" she paused.

"What?"

"Nothing."

"No, what?"

"Well, how much of it was *real*." She lifted up the hair from the nape of her neck and let it drift down in what she knew was a cloud of red and gold. She could see him watching her from the corner of her eye.

"How much of what was real?"

She wrinkled her brow. "Well, like at the end, when it almost seemed like you were going to cry. Was that real? Or was it for the jury?" She looked at him, forcing her face into an expression of neutral curiosity.

He laughed uncomfortably, and Olivia thought she could detect a flush glowing under the brown skin of his throat and face.

"Both, I guess," he said. "I mean, yeah, I definitely try to make the jury feel like I care about my clients. I try to make the jury like me, first. The idea is that if they like me, and trust me, then they'll care about the people I care about. Namely, you."

"So it doesn't *really* make you cry."

"What doesn't?"

"This whole thing. The trial. The possibility that I'll go to jail."

He stopped in the middle of the sidewalk. "I care what happens to you, Olivia."

"Do you really?"

"Of course I do."

"Like you care about all of your clients?"

He inhaled suddenly. She watched him, waiting for what he was going to say next. She knew what it was that she hoped he would say. In her fantasy of this moment, he spoke the truth of the intensity of his feelings toward her. Olivia knew that Izaya would never act on his emotions, but she wanted to hear him acknowledge them. She wanted him to admit that he wanted her, even that he loved her.

"Yeah, like I care about all my clients. Which is a lot, Olivia. A whole lot." He started walking again. "Come on. Your mother's going to wonder what's taking us so long."

What Elaine really wanted was to wrap her daughter up in cotton batting and put her somewhere where no one could ever harm her again, but, for now, a decent lunch would have to suffice. When Olivia and Izaya finally joined them, looking out of breath from their walk, the four of them sat down at a table in a corner of a cavernous room paneled in pale wood with French posters decorating the walls. Elaine watched the solicitude with which Izaya treated Olivia: the way he pulled back her chair, the way he leaned forward to talk into her ear. Not for the first time she wondered if the young attorney wasn't a little bit in love with her daughter. Olivia did look remarkably beautiful. Her hair had escaped its knot and curled in delicate tendrils around her face. Her pregnant belly did nothing to diminish her attractiveness; on the contrary, it lent her an air of serenity and gravitas that she'd never before possessed.

Arthur, almost as if he were taking his cue from Izaya, paid special attention to Elaine. He ordered something for himself that he knew she liked, and when it came he offered her half his plate. He even stood up when she left the table to use the restroom, something he hadn't done since their first dates. Elaine felt a rush of gratitude for his attentiveness, although it did make her feel even guiltier at how little he'd been in her mind of late.

They were sipping coffee—all but Olivia, who limited herself to herbal tea—when Izaya's beeper went off. He glanced at it and said, "They're back."

"But you said it wouldn't be until three at least. It's not even two." Olivia's voice was panicky and almost hysterical. Elaine got up from her chair and walked around the table. She knelt down next to Olivia and put her arms around her.

"It's okay, honey. It's okay. You're going to be okay." She murmured into Olivia's hair, inhaling deeply and smelling the lavender of her daughter's shampoo. Olivia gulped once or twice, but then pulled herself together.

"I'm all right. I just got scared for a minute."

She rested her hands on the table in front of her, then pushed herself to her feet.

"Let's go," she said.

Elaine and Izaya paid the bills, and they walked quickly back to the courthouse. Amanda Steele was already in the courtroom, waiting. She sat at her table, pursing and unpursing her lips. She, too, looked worried.

The judge entered, and they all rose. He motioned them to their seats and instructed the courtroom deputy to bring in the jury. Again they rose as the members of the jury filed in, one by one. Elaine stared at them, willing them to look at Olivia. The Berkeley acupuncturist did, for a moment, and then looked quickly away. Elaine felt her bowels clench. Arthur squeezed her hand in his. The commingled sweat from their palms felt slick and greasy.

"Madame Foreperson, have you reached a verdict?" Judge Horowitz intoned.

"We have, your honor," said the older woman with the pink purse.

"Please give the verdict form to the courtroom deputy."

The forewoman handed the form over the rail separating the jury box from the rest of the courtroom. The deputy walked it over to the judge, who opened it slowly. Elaine felt dizzy, her sight telescoping until the only thing she could see was the white page with her daughter's future written on it.

The judge looked at the form for longer than Elaine thought possible and then handed it to the deputy.

"Please read the verdict," he said.

The woman cleared her throat and began to read.

"For the crime of distribution of narcotics, to wit, methamphetamine, we, the jury, find the defendant not guilty."

Elaine sagged against Arthur, tears pouring down her face. "Oh, thank God, thank God," she whispered.

"For the crime of conspiracy to traffic in narcotics, to wit, methamphetamine, we, the jury, find the defendant not guilty."

Arthur clenched his fist and pounded it on his knee. "Yes!" he said, aloud.

"For the crime of use of a communications facility, to wit, a telephone, in the commission of a drug offense, we, the jury, find the defendant guilty."

The room was absolutely silent. Elaine stared at the jury. She had no idea what that meant. Would Olivia go to jail? What did that mean?

"Is that your unanimous verdict?" the judge asked.

"It is," the forewoman said.

"Counsel, would you like the jury polled?"

"Yes, your honor," Izaya replied. One by one, the jury members recited their verdict. When it was the acupuncturist's turn, she began to cry. Her heavy chest heaved, and she could barely get the word "guilty" out of her mouth. Elaine glanced down at her hands, away from the streaming eyes. The pinched and sour-faced woman who had so troubled Izaya during jury selection announced her verdict loudly and sternly, as if to reproach the crying juror beside her.

Finally, after the jurors had all been obliged to pronounce their belief in Olivia's guilt to the courtroom, the judge dismissed them. He turned back to the courtroom.

"The case is put over for sentencing in thirty days. Ms. Steele, I assume you have no objection to a continuation of the bond."

"No, your honor. The government does not object."

"Your honor," Izaya interrupted.

"Yes, Mr. Feingold-Upchurch?"

"Ms. Goodman is due to give birth in more or less thirty days. Would it be possible to continue the sentencing for an additional month to allow her both to give birth and recover?"

The judge looked at the prosecutor. "Any objection from the government?"

Amanda Steele stood silently for a moment, looking at Olivia, her hand resting lightly on her own belly.

Elaine glanced at the woman's hand, wondering for a second what was the meaning of that protective palm, before she was once again distracted by her own and her daughter's agony.

Then prosecutor said, quietly, "No, your honor. I have no objection."

Olivia had been breathless with fear when the jury had walked in the room, afraid to look at them, staring instead at her hands clasping and unclasping each other in her lap. Under cover of the counsel table, Izaya reached for her. He held her hand the entire time the verdict was read. When the words "not guilty" echoed in the otherwise silent room, he squeezed her fingers so hard she almost gasped. Then, when the third verdict was announced, his hand went limp, and it was she who gripped him.

As soon as the words were spoken, she began repeating to herself, "Not so long, not so long." When they had discussed the indictment and the various sentences, long ago, Izaya had explained to her that the "telephone count," using a communication facility to commit a drug offense, had a maximum sentence of four years. She repeated her mantra again and again, to remind herself that she could have gone to jail for ten years, or even longer. So long as words kept up on a continuous loop in her head, she was calm; if she stopped for even a moment, the vile, caustic taste of panic rose in the back of her throat.

But she did not cry, not when the verdict was announced, nor in the car on the way home. She did not cry while Arthur made his inevitable calculations, informing her that she would be twenty-six when she was released, and the baby four years old. She did not cry when she listened to the telephone message from Izaya that was waiting for her when she arrived at the house. She did not cry when he apologized for having failed her, nor when he promised to do whatever he could to minimize her sentence. She did not cry while she lay on her bed, imagining a prison cell instead of her room.

It was only when she began to write the letter to Jorge's parents that she finally broke down. It took Olivia a long time to write the letter. She tried at first to write with pen and paper, but she kept scratching things out until finally the page was a mess of blue smears. It was her inability to find the words that brought her to tears for the first time that day. At last, frustrated by her clotted sobs, stuffed nose, and the ruined pages, she went out to the dining room and sat down at Arthur's computer, hoping that the businesslike click of the keys and the presence of Arthur and her mother would inspire in her the necessary detachment. She wrote in Spanish, leaving off the tildes and accents that the keyboard hid behind a labyrinth of option and control keys. Because she did not know whether Jorge had even told his parents about what had happened, her first charge was to break the horrible news. She did so briefly, telling them only that she and Jorge had been arrested because someone got Jorge involved in a drug deal; that Jorge had pleaded guilty; and that she had been convicted of a lesser sentence but one that would require her to spend as much as four years in jail. She told Jorge's parents that she was pregnant, due soon, and that her own mother was unable to care for the baby. She asked them to take the baby in just for as long as she was in jail. Then she called to Elaine.

"Mom, can you come in here?"

Elaine looked through the door from the kitchen where she'd been hiding since they got home from court. Her face looked drawn and almost gray.

"Yes?"

"There's something I need you to do."

"Anything, honey."

Anything but keep my baby for me, Olivia thought.

"I'm going to need you to take the baby to Mexico. To, you know, deliver it."

"To deliver it?"

"To Jorge's parents. I told you, I'm going to ask them to take the baby."

Olivia and Elaine had not spoken of her plan since she'd first mentioned it. Neither, however, had they spoken of adoption, nor of any other alternative for the baby's care. Olivia assumed that, like her, her mother had been counting on an acquittal making any other plans superfluous.

"But you might not have to go to jail. I mean, the judge might decide to let you go. Or he might just say that you have to wear one of those ankle bracelet things."

Olivia shook her head, wondering at her mother's transformation. Elaine had always been so practical, and her own optimism had, she knew, always struck her mother as a particularly frustrating sort of naïveté. As a child, when Olivia had expressed a belief that something—a test, a problem, a conflict—would somehow work itself out, Elaine had always admonished her. Far better to prepare for the worst than to wish helplessly that the best might happen. Yet now, when pragmatism seemed most called for, her mother was hanging on to pipe dreams of home detention and ankle bracelets.

"Mom, he can't sentence me to anything other than what the sentencing guidelines call for. You know that."

"But there's always a downward departure. He could grant you a downward departure, couldn't he?"

"Maybe. I mean, I hope so. But I have to be prepared in case he doesn't. I have to make sure my baby is going to be okay. I need you to agree to take it to Mexico."

"Of course. Of course I'll take it. I mean, that's allowed, right? To take a baby out of the country?"

"I'll get a passport for it after it's born. I don't think it will be a problem."

"Oh. Okay."

"And something else."

"Yes?"

"Money."

"Money?"

"Jorge's parents are poor. Having an extra mouth to feed is going to be hard on them. But even what seems like a little bit to us will help them out. I was hoping you'd send them a hundred dollars a month. I'll pay you back as soon as I get out. With interest."

"Don't be silly, Olivia. You don't need to pay me back. I'll send them the money every month."

"Thank you."

Elaine came up behind Olivia and rested her hands lightly on her shoulders. Olivia sat absolutely still at the unfamiliar touch.

"I wish…" Elaine began.

Olivia was afraid to breathe.

"I just wish things were different. I wish Arthur…No. I wish *I* was different."

Olivia felt her mother's weight more heavily against her shoulders. "It's okay, Mom. I understand."

"Do you? Do you really? Because I'm not sure *I* do." Her voice trailed off.

"It's okay, Mom." But was it, really? Olivia understood that it was impossible for Elaine to take the baby; the necessary sacrifice—of losing Arthur—would simply be too great. But it seemed to her that her mother was asking for something more than understanding. Elaine sought, rather, absolution, and the reassurance that this failure was not an ultimate betrayal. That, Olivia could not give her.

Elaine suddenly left Olivia's side, pulled out a dining room chair, and sat down. She stared out the window, smoothing her hair behind her ear over and over again. Olivia turned away and looked back at her letter.

Olivia finished writing and then dug through her address book for the telephone number of the hotel where Jorge's older sister worked as a desk clerk. She called the hotel and asked to speak to Aida. She told her nothing, just let her know that she was sending a fax for her parents, and that Aida should pull it out of the machine before anyone else at the hotel saw it.

"What is this about, Olivia? We received a letter from Jorge saying that he is in jail. What is going on? My parents are hysterical."

"The fax will explain everything. I have to go now." Olivia hung up the telephone before her tears could overwhelm her.

She stood over the machine watching the paper feed through, feeling like she was sending her baby farther away with every inch that slipped beneath the roller. Elaine came up behind her and stroked her hair. Olivia shrugged away her mother's hand.

"Honey, I promise I won't just drop the baby off. I'll make sure everything is okay. And I won't just send money. I'll go visit the baby. I'll make Arthur swap years with me, and instead of taking that trip to Morocco we put off until the fall, we'll go to Mexico instead. I promise. I'll write them, and call, and go see the baby. I promise."

"You can't call. They don't have a phone."

"I'll get them a phone. How much could a phone cost? How about that? I'll get them a telephone when I go to Mexico, and I'll even pay their phone bills. That way you can call them yourself. How about that?"

"It takes years to get a phone installed."

"What about a cell phone? They must have those in Mexico. They've got them all over. I'll get one of those international cell phones and give it to Jorge's parents."

"Okay." Olivia tried to feel the gratitude she knew her mother deserved. Instead she felt numb, blank. She let her mother hug her.

"It was a compromise verdict," Arthur said. "It has to have been. Some of them probably wanted to convict her. And the others wanted an acquittal. So they settled on the telephone count."

Arthur had a way of making Elaine believe he knew what he was talking about even when the chance of that was relatively slim.

They were lying in bed, neither of them able to sleep after the tumultuous and devastating day in court.

"It was that woman with the pink bag," Elaine said. "The one who looked so mean. I never liked her. And Izaya didn't either. Remember, he wanted to throw her off the jury?"

"Did he?"

She nodded vigorously. "It was a mistake. He had used up all his challenges. It was her. I just know it was."

"It could have been any of them."

Arthur punched his pillow a few times, fluffing it. Elaine flinched at the dull thuds.

"I'm not really surprised," he said.

"What?"

"Well, she was technically guilty, Elaine. We all know that."

Elaine sat up. "What do you mean?"

He reached under the bed for the specially fabricated neck-support pillow he used when his head was hurting him. He tucked it under his head. "She took that phone message and passed it on to Jorge. She was guilty of *that*."

Elaine felt her face begin to burn. "Are you saying she deserves this? That Olivia deserves to be convicted?"

"No, of course not. I'm as outraged about it as you are. The whole prosecution was a farce. It's ridiculous that that telephone count thing is even a crime. But you know what they say."

Elaine gritted her teeth. "No, Arthur. I don't know. What is it that *they* say?"

"Ignorance of the law is no excuse."

And so saying, he closed his eyes, and without another word, fell soundly asleep.

Elaine slipped out from under the blankets and padded in her bare feet into the dining room. She had wanted to get online, to tell her friends on the FAMM list what had happened to Olivia, as soon as she had returned from court. She had been desperate to spill her story, to howl her anguish to people who would understand, but she had been afraid that Arthur would have gotten angry. He hadn't grown any more understanding of her need to participate in the online community. On the contrary, he seemed more resentful of it than ever. She felt better getting on the computer when he was asleep, although the truth was that at this moment she was so furious with him that she might have logged on even were he not snoring in the bedroom.

Elaine posted to the group. She had been giving daily updates since the trial began, and there were already messages waiting, asking her how the closing arguments had gone and whether the jury had reached a verdict. She didn't bother with the good news about Olivia's acquittal. The joy she had felt at hearing the words "not guilty" had by now been almost entirely overwhelmed by the misery of the single count of conviction. After she had posted a short and bitter message, she clicked over to the chat room, hoping there would be someone to talk to. There usually was, even late in the night. The wives, mothers, husbands, and children of convicted drug offenders had a hard time sleeping. When the bustle of the day's business gave way to the familiar loneliness of the dark hours, they congregated online, anxious for any contact, no matter how virtual. An imaginary room full of recognizable voices was a significant improvement over a forlorn bed.

Once again, Elaine posted her story, and this time the responses were immediate. She was congratulated on the counts of acquittal, as if she, and not Izaya Feingold-Upchurch, had engineered what felt to her to be a terribly minor victory. More importantly, she was inundated with messages of support for the conviction. Elaine didn't need to explain what the telephone count meant. These truck drivers, librarians, ministers, teachers, waitresses, and others were all experts in the intricacies of the federal laws, drug offenses, and sentencing guidelines. They knew just how long a term Olivia was facing.

DEAR ELAINE, wrote a woman, also the mother of a daughter who had followed a boyfriend to prison. THIS IS SO HARD FOR YOU. THE NIGHT OF BRITTANY'S CONVICTION I THOUGHT I WOULD DIE. REALLY I DID. HUGS TO YOU.

Brittany, Elaine knew, had just finished the fifth year of a twenty-year sentence for the importation of ecstasy; her boyfriend, and the father of the three small boys she had left behind in her mother's care, had served two years in a Danish prison and been released. Some of Brittany's mother's postings were expressions of rage at the inequity of her daughter's sentence, especially when compared to that of the man who, as even the prosecutor agreed, was the kingpin of the smuggling operation. Most, however, were about how difficult it was to care for children who both missed their mother terribly and could barely remember her face.

AT LEAST YOU'LL HAVE YOUR GRANDBABY, Brittany's mother wrote.

After weeks of silence on the subject, Elaine had finally confided to the group about Olivia's pregnancy. She wasn't sure what had made her tell them at last. Perhaps it was something as selfish as wanting to become the focus of their outpourings of support once again: within a week or two of her first post, other voices had joined the Internet support group, and Elaine was no longer the only new person to whom everyone sent messages of encouragement. It was at this point that she had told them about the baby, and for another week or so had basked in a flood of sympathetic emails so plentiful that it took her hours to reply to them all.

Elaine's fingers hovered over the keyboard for a moment, and then she typed a few words about Olivia's plans to send her baby to Mexico. Just then, another line of chat tumbled across the screen.

HONESTLY, IF IT WEREN'T FOR BRITTANY'S THREE BOYS, I DON'T KNOW HOW I'D GET THROUGH THE DAYS.

AMEN TO THAT, someone else wrote. JACK JR. IS MY HEART AND SOUL.

Before she even realized what she was doing, Elaine deleted her unsent line and typed out another. YES, THANK GOD FOR THE BABY. FOR OLIVIA'S SAKE, BUT ESPECIALLY FOR MINE. IT WILL BE A TRUE COMFORT TO ME.

Elaine sat looking at the words she had written. She knew she had, in fact, absolutely no intention of keeping the child. She wanted it no more than she had before Olivia had been convicted, no more than before she had gone online. And God knew that Arthur wasn't going to let her keep it.

She hit SEND.

A rush of solicitous chat followed, messages filled with advice on raising a baby whose mother was incarcerated, which she graciously accepted, pretending to jot down the visiting rules at different women's prisons. She stayed up long into the night, lying.

It was only after the others had all gone to bed, and she was the last member of a now-empty chat room, that she understood what her dishonesty had wrought. She would never be able to face these people when she sent Olivia's baby away. Neither could she lie for the next however many years, pretending to be caring for a child who was in an entirely different country. She had cost herself the only support she had left.

She stared at the screen, her back hunched, and her fingers twisted on the keyboard. And then she sent another message, this time to the list manager, asking him to unsubscribe her from the list.

The next morning, Aida called.

Olivia's fingers trembled while she held the telephone receiver. Her voice caught in her throat, and her greeting sounded to her own ears like the croak of someone very ill.

"We have been so worried about Jorge, and about you," Jorge's sister said.

"I know," Olivia answered. "I'm so sorry."

"It's okay, Olivia. You need not apologize."

"Will they take the baby?" she whispered.

"Yes. Yes, of course. We are all so grateful to you for allowing us this chance, for letting us do this for you, and for Jorge."

"They understand that it will only be for a few years, that I'm going to want the baby back as soon as I get out of jail?" Olivia said.

"Yes, Olivia. They know. They promise they will give the baby to you."

"And what if Jorge comes back? What if *he* wants the baby? What will happen then?"

"We promise to you on the blessed Virgin that we will give the baby back to you. My father is a man of his word."

"Thank you," Olivia said. She hung up the telephone and wished that she felt reassured. She knew that Juan Carlos and Araceli meant what they said, that they were not lying to her. And yet, what guarantee was there that they would feel the same after four years? After they had raised her child, cared for it, and watched it grow, would they still be so willing to give it back? And what if Jorge was released? What if he came home before she did? Would he take her baby away from her?

Olivia hugged herself, covering her belly with her arms.

Olivia was trapped. There was no other way she could keep her baby, no other person who would care for it. She determined, at that moment, to believe that Araceli and Juan Carlos would return the child to her. It would take all of her energy to survive the years of her incarceration; she could not face them weighed down by the anticipation of Jorge's family's betrayal. She had to muster every ounce of hopefulness and optimism of which she was capable.

Olivia put her hands on her belly and imagined, for the first time but by no means the last, what it would feel like to hold her four-year-old child in her arms after so many years had passed.

She shook her head before the tears could come again and hoisted herself to her feet. She'd taken Aida's phone call in her bedroom, and now she walked out to the kitchen where her mother sat, warming her hands around a cup of tea.

"It's all set," Olivia said.

"They'll take the baby?"

She nodded.

"And they've agreed to give him back when you get out?"

She nodded again.

Elaine sighed. "Well, I suppose that's a relief," she said.

Olivia caught her lower lip between her teeth and bit down, hard. "I suppose so," she said, once she could trust her voice not to betray her.

part three

part three

Olivia woke one morning, a week before her due date, feeling a dull ache in her back. She tossed from side to side, trying to get comfortable, but finally got up to pee. She sat on the toilet, staring down at her distended stomach with its line of darkened skin leading from her protruding belly button to the top of her pubis. She wiped herself and was startled to see a clump of something, streaked yellow and red, on the toilet paper. She stared at the paper for a moment or two and then smiled. The baby was coming.

Olivia spent the rest of the day by herself. She didn't tell Arthur or her mother what was happening, and the two of them went to work, leaving her alone in the empty house. She sat down in her favorite chair with her legs drawn up under her and her knees spread wide. At some point she realized that the dull ache in her back had traveled around to the front of her body. She looked up at the clock on the wall the next time she felt the tug of pain and noted the time. Twenty minutes later, it came again.

Olivia slipped on a pair of her mother's old running shoes and tied the laces very loosely over her feet. She went out for a walk, stopping every few blocks or so to lean against a tree or telephone pole while her belly tightened in spasms that were slowly growing stronger and more intense. When it seemed as if the pains were coming closer together, she walked slowly back home and drew a bath. She tentatively lowered herself into Elaine's oversized tub and lay there, breathing through the contractions until the water grew cold. Only then did she call her mother.

Olivia felt as if the very moment after she hung up the phone her mother was there, standing next to her. By then Olivia was on all fours in the living room, doing the cat stretches her birthing instructor had taught her.

"What time is it?" she murmured as Elaine crouched down next to her.

"Almost five. Are you okay? Do you need anything? Do you want some water? Ice chips? Are you hungry? Remember, Dorothy said you'd need to eat to keep your strength up."

"Five? Wow. It felt like just a couple of hours."

"How long have you been in labor?"

"More or less since this morning."

"Oh my God! Olivia are you out of your mind? Have you called Dorothy?"

"I'm okay, Mom. Really. You call her."

Elaine rushed to the telephone where she'd prominently tacked up a piece of paper with the midwife's phone number. She punched in some numbers and then hung up. She hustled back to Olivia's side. Olivia, meanwhile, was crouched over, her knees bent and spread under her, her belly hanging between them, her cheek resting on the carpet. Every time she felt a contraction begin, she began a deep, slow inhale. She felt the pains; in fact, she sank deep into each painful wave, but she almost didn't mind them. She welcomed them, imagining her body gently pushing the baby out.

In the middle of the next contraction, Olivia was distracted by the sound of the telephone ringing. She shut her eyes and ears to the noise and tried to catch hold of her breath to think of softening and opening. Elaine began tapping on her shoulder, trying to hand her the phone.

"C'mon, honey. Dorothy wants to talk to you. Just take the phone."

Elaine held the phone to her ear, but Olivia batted it away. Finally she gave in to Elaine's insistence and listened to Dorothy's voice. She tried to answer her the best she could, describing her contractions, how they felt, how long they'd been going on, but another one came just then and she began to breathe, shutting out the sound of the midwife's voice.

At the end of the next contraction, Olivia felt her mother pull her to her feet. "We're going to the hospital, honey. Dorothy's going to meet us there."

Olivia began to protest. She didn't want to go to the hospital. What she wanted was to get back into her mother's tub, to give birth there. Elaine grabbed an old afghan from the couch and wrapped Olivia in it. She pushed and pulled Olivia to the door, and finally Olivia gave in. She let Elaine settle her in the front seat of the car, but when they had driven no more than half a block, another contraction overwhelmed her, and she desperately tried to get on top of it. She started fighting the contraction, beginning to cry as the pain became unbearable.

"Stop! Stop the car!" she screamed. "I can't get comfortable here!"

Olivia felt that if she didn't get out of the car in a minute she would die. She began to cry harder, so hard she didn't even notice that they'd pulled up in front of Alta Bates Hospital, which was mercifully close to the house. She saw Elaine toss her car keys at the parking attendant, and then felt her mother half-carry her to a wheelchair that was parked in front of the entrance. Another contraction clutched at her belly as they rolled through the doors of the hospital, down the hall, and to the elevator. She began crying again in the elevator, begging her mother to take her home so she could give birth in her own bed.

She was sobbing, and saying over and over again, "I don't want to be here, I don't want to be here," when they arrived at the labor-and-delivery floor. A nurse in a pair of pale yellow scrubs took one look at Olivia weeping and writhing in the wheelchair, smiled, and said, "Looks like someone's in transition here."

When Olivia's panic abated, she found herself in a small, dark room, lying on a bed. She was naked, and her mother was standing next to her, talking to the midwife who had her hand up inside of Olivia. Olivia had not passed out; she had simply been too caught up in her fear and her dread to notice what was happening to her. Now, as though a lightness had overcome her, her fear was gone.

"I want to push," she said, surprised at how calm her voice sounded.

"So push," Dorothy said.

After what felt like moments but was actually closer to two hours, the midwife said, "Okay now, Olivia. One more."

Olivia tucked her chin into her chest and pushed one last time. She felt a slithering and a pop, and then Dorothy held something up and put it on Olivia's chest. She reached out her hands and stroked the pink and white creature with the shock of black hair. Its huge brown eyes were wide open and it stared at her, its mouth an *O* of surprise. Olivia picked it up and looked at the baby's kicking legs and its little gray feet.

"It's a girl," Elaine said. Olivia looked at her mother, who was smiling and crying at the same time. "A beautiful girl. A perfect girl."

Olivia brought the baby up to her face and inhaled deeply, smelling her strangely familiar scent, like the smell of her own body, yet sharper and more pungent.

The baby began pushing her head against Olivia's chest, and she took one of her breasts in her hand and guided the nipple to the baby's mouth. At first the tiny girl didn't seem to know what to do. She kept her mouth closed and rubbed blindly against the nipple. Then, suddenly, she opened her mouth impossibly wide and Olivia slipped the nipple inside. The baby gulped once and began to suck, voraciously, as though she'd been waiting for this moment for every minute of the nine months she'd been hidden inside her mother's body. Olivia felt a current run from her nipple down through the center of her body and into her womb.

Elaine stroked the baby's head and smoothed Olivia's hair away from her eyes. "What do you want to call her, honey?" she asked. "What's her name?"

"Luna," Olivia said. "Her name is Luna."

"Luna Goodman?" Elaine asked, doubtfully.

Olivia nodded, laughing, and after a moment her mother joined in. Olivia picked up the baby's hand and kissed her soft palm.

Olivia slept deeply, propped in the hospital bed. Elaine rocked in the glider, holding Luna and crooning to her. The room was dim—the shades were drawn and the lights were off. Elaine had spent the night on the pullout armchair, waking when Luna woke and helping Olivia get the baby on her breast. Now, mother and daughter were quiet, and only grandmother was awake. Elaine traced a finger along the baby's downy cheek. Her skin was softer than anything Elaine had ever felt, softer than silk, softer than fur, as smooth as water.

Luna's pursed lips made sucking motions as she slept, as though she were dreaming of nursing. She frowned, and Elaine slipped a pinky into her mouth. The baby sucked hard on it, harder than Elaine had imagined such a tiny mouth would be capable of, and settled again. Elaine stared into the baby's face, looking there for signs of her own self, of her genes and family history. Luna's dark hair was clearly her father's, and her nose had the faintest arch that looked as if it might grow into her father's hook. Elaine remembered how proud her own grandmother had been of Elaine's "shiksa nose," insisting that its pert bluntness was a testament to the family's successful assimilation, although Elaine's father had always said it was more likely the legacy of a Polish pogrom. Olivia's, like her mother's, lacked the defined curve of caricature. The irony of Luna inheriting a Jewish nose from a Catholic father made Elaine smile.

Carefully, so as not to wake the baby, she unwrapped the end of the tightly swaddled blankets. She took one tiny foot in her hand and played her fingers lightly along the pearl-like toes. Olivia's own foot stuck out from under the covers of the hospital bed, long and thin with the sparkly blue toenails that she had asked Elaine to paint a few days before. The polish on the big toe was slightly chipped. Now, for some reason, Elaine was startled at the sight of that large, adult foot. It seemed like only moments ago she'd been able to fit baby Olivia's entire foot in her mouth. Moments, days, weeks, years; along the way, that baby had turned into a woman, and Elaine couldn't help but wonder if she had paid the slightest attention to the time as it passed. She could remember almost nothing about Olivia's infancy and early childhood. Brief flashes of memory were all that remained, and Elaine had little confidence even in those; they all seemed to coincide with the photographs she had snapped.

Elaine was startled from her reverie by a soft knock at the door. She raised her eyes and met Izaya's as he peeped in. She nodded, and he entered, laden with a ridiculously large bouquet of spring flowers in a cut-glass vase, a stuffed moose that must have been three feet long under one arm, and a dozen Mylar balloons tied to his wrist. Elaine burst out laughing when she saw him, and Olivia woke to the sound.

"Oh, no," he said. "Did I wake you up?"

"No, no. It's okay. What did you bring?" Olivia asked, her voice languid.

"Um, a moose."

Elaine laughed again. She gently laid the still-sleeping baby in her bassinet and held out her hands to Izaya.

He gave her the flowers and the stuffed animal and then untied the balloons. They floated up to the ceiling. Half of them had dancing blue bears and read, "It's a boy." The other half had the same picture in pink and announced the arrival of a girl.

"Arthur called and told me you were in labor. I didn't know if it was a girl or a boy."

"This is Luna," Elaine said, picking up the baby and handing her to Izaya. Izaya looked startled at his burden, but then his face softened. He rocked back and forth on his heels, holding the baby in his arms.

"She's as beautiful as her mother," he said, and then blushed. Luna woke with a soft cry and Izaya quickly handed her over to Olivia. Olivia settled the baby in the crook of her arm and pulled down the shoulder of her hospital gown. Elaine watched Izaya's face as the baby nuzzled her mother's full breast, rooting around until she found the long pink nipple, and then gulping greedily. Olivia smiled serenely down at Luna. Her hair was full and wild and caught the light shining though the slats in the window shades with a glint of gold brightness. Her cheeks were flushed, as was the full, round breast pressed up against the baby's face. She *was* beautiful. Izaya stared and then, suddenly seeming to realize that perhaps he shouldn't be looking, glanced quickly away.

Elaine pulled the rocking chair up to the edge of the bed. "Why don't you sit down," she said. Then she walked to the other side of the room and busied herself arranging the flowers and gathering the balloons into a bright bouquet in a corner. She listened to the low hum of Olivia's voice describing her labor to Izaya, in perhaps more detail than Elaine thought was strictly necessary.

Elaine ached to see the almost timid longing she recognized in Izaya's face. She wondered, again, about the extent of his feelings for Olivia. His eagerness, his tenderness, gave him away. Elaine smiled ruefully to herself at the thought that Olivia might finally have found a man of whom even her mother could be proud. She couldn't decide, however, if she was really seeing something that was there, or if it were only her own desperate hope for a future for her daughter that led her to imagine a connection that did not exist. Lawyers were not allowed to fall in love with their clients, and if Izaya had, by some accident of chemistry or fate, then surely he would never act on it. Olivia was going to jail. What was the point of this impossible newborn love?

Elaine leaned heavily on the windowsill, closing her eyes against the tears that threatened to begin again. She, a woman who never cried, who had remained dry-eyed at the birth of her own child, in the courtroom where her marriage was dissolved, at her father's graveside, had wept so often and so freely since Olivia's conviction that sometimes she wondered whether the tears would ever stop flowing. She felt like a faucet whose washer had given way with a final groan, allowing a constant stream of water to come pouring through the tap. She didn't like anything about her tears. She didn't like the hot prickling in her eyes. She didn't like the red ache in her nose after her eyes finally dried up. She didn't like the pitying glances of those who saw her crying. She brushed angrily at her face and got up.

"I'm going to go get some breakfast," she said.

Luna had fallen off the breast and lay in the crook of Olivia's arm. Olivia leaned back on her pillows, her breast still exposed, the pink nipple spilling a clear stream down onto the sheet.

"Honey," Elaine said. "You're leaking."

"She really is beautiful," Izaya said, after Elaine had left the room. He was staring not at the baby, but at Olivia. She moved to cover her breast. She paused for a moment, her hand resting lightly across her nipple. She looked directly into his eyes, and her mouth softened, almost into a smile. He blushed, and she tugged her nightgown into place.

Olivia made a nest of blankets for the sleeping baby next to her body. She lay Luna down.

"She's so tiny," Izaya said.

"I don't know, she felt pretty big to me when I was trying to get her out," she said, and he laughed. "I don't think I ever really said thank you."

"Thank you? For what?"

"For everything. For the trial."

"How can you thank me? I screwed it up! We lost."

"We didn't lose. I got acquitted of everything but the phone count."

Izaya leaned back in his chair and rubbed his hands roughly across his face.

"You're going to jail," he said. "That means I lost."

"Well, then, thanks for the moose."

He smiled thinly. Conscious of the faint absurdity of having to comfort her lawyer for her own misfortune, Olivia said, "Four years isn't so long. I mean, it's a lot less than ten, isn't it?"

Izaya sighed. "Man, I'm such a dick. I should be the one telling you that."

She shrugged. "It's okay. We can tell each other." She closed her eyes. The birth had drained her of all her energy and strength, and then the baby had woken up every ninety minutes or so during the night, nursing desperately, occasionally bursting into tears of helpless rage at the mere trickle of colostrum that was all Olivia's breasts were producing. Olivia knew that her milk would come in eventually, but she still felt a kind of distressed inadequacy at this, the first of many ways she would disappoint her little girl. She could not even allow her mind to contemplate the horrible betrayal of abandonment that was to come.

"You're tired," Izaya said, rising.

She nodded. "I am. But thanks for coming. And for everything. Really."

He nodded and then grabbed at the string of one of the pink balloons. "I'm going to take this one, okay?" he said. He left the room, the balloon bobbing in his wake.

She picked up the baby and unwrapped her from the swaddling blankets. She pulled her hospital gown aside and held Luna's nearly naked body to her own bared breasts and belly, and she took comfort in the warmth that spread between them.

Olivia and Luna were easiest with each other at night; Olivia felt none of the anxiety that sometimes overtook her during the long days of caring for the baby. When Luna cried, Olivia would nurse her without really waking, fitting a nipple between her daughter's mewling lips in a kind of somnambulant haze. The baby slept nestled in bed against Olivia, not in the ivory wicker bassinet that Olivia had found waiting in her room when she came home from the hospital. In the mornings, before she came downstairs, she would muss the lace bedding in the bassinet so that Elaine would think the baby had passed the night there, rather than in her mother's arms. Olivia did this in part because she was sure Elaine wouldn't approve of the baby sharing Olivia's bed, that she would argue that Olivia might crush the tiny girl, that it was important for Luna to learn to sleep alone, in her own bed. Olivia had no energy for the argument, which she knew with a kind of weary self-foreknowledge would devolve into a lecture by her of the sleeping patterns of indigenous people the world over. But there was another reason for the charade—Olivia didn't want to hurt her mother's feelings. Elaine had been so proud of the gift she had presented to her new granddaughter, one that was so unlike her in its fundamental frivolousness. An opulent bed for a child who would sleep in it for no more than a couple of months was so extravagant, so indulgent, that it was something Olivia had a hard time even believing her mother had purchased.

The first days home from the hospital were the worst. Olivia's milk came in almost as soon as she walked in the door of the house. Her breasts swelled to the size of bowling balls and were just as hard and unyielding. Luna, who had been so hungry, seemed horrified at the transformation of the objects she'd so clearly come to view as her own. She had screamed for hours, refusing to nurse, unable to be comforted, and her tears were soon matched by her mother's. Olivia found herself more grateful to her own mother than she had ever been before. Elaine had appeared with a head of cabbage, four icepacks, and a page of instructions she had downloaded off the Web. For some reason that neither of them could figure out, stuffing Olivia's bra with raw cabbage leaves relieved the engorgement, and Luna was soon nursing peacefully again.

Arthur, to no one's surprise, absented himself from this and all the other everyday dramas associated with the baby's arrival. When Elaine had come home from the hospital the night after Luna's birth, he'd happily informed her of his decision to begin training for an Iron Man competition. She'd greeted his invitation to join him with a dull shake of her head. He spent his days at work and his evenings training for the two-and-a-half mile swim, the one hundred-twelve–mile bike ride, and the twenty-six–mile marathon.

When Luna was a week old, Elaine went back to work. Olivia had at first been panicked at the thought of being entirely alone with the baby, but she soon found their isolation pleasurable, even blissful. She would drag the baby's three-hour cycles of sleep and nursing out until the mid-morning. Then she would fill Elaine's deep tub with warm water and a squirt of lavender soap. The two would float in a fragrant steamy haze for a while, until Olivia grew hungry enough to begin the day. At first she'd simply heat up whatever was left over from the previous night's dinner, but soon she began bundling Luna up in her Baby Björn, the infant carrier she had found at the resale store down the block from the pharmacy, and walking over to the lunch counter, where Ralph would serve her a pile of scrambled eggs, toast, and potatoes large enough to feed her twice or even three times over.

In the afternoons, she'd keep the baby attached to her chest and do her best to prepare for her sentencing hearing. Periodically, Izaya would call or email, making sure she was gathering letters to be submitted to the court on her behalf. Elaine and Arthur each wrote a letter, as did Ralph and one of Olivia's high school teachers—her favorite, with whom she had stayed in touch. A couple of the families for whom she'd been the baby-sitter of legend also wrote, although there were others who greeted her request with something akin to horror.

On Izaya's instructions, Olivia drafted a statement to the judge, which Izaya then edited heavily and returned to her. They emailed the statement back and forth for a while, pulling out and putting back various lines and sections until it satisfied both of them.

Izaya sent her a copy of the brief he wrote to the judge, asking for a downward departure from the applicable sentencing guideline range. His request was audacious, to say the least. The fact that Olivia had been convicted only of the telephone count meant that her sentence was capped at four years. However, the judge was still obliged to use the sentencing guidelines and make his calculations based on the fifty-five grams of methamphetamine at issue in the trial. When Olivia had expressed confusion at how she could possibly be sentenced for a crime of which she'd been found not guilty, Izaya had shrugged his shoulders in disgust.

"It's unbelievable; I know," he said. "But the Supreme Court has said it's the law. You get sentenced even for conduct of which you've been acquitted. Basically, it means that all the government has to do is get a conviction for one small count. Then you go to jail as if they'd won on every count."

"But that's not *fair!*" Olivia had howled into the telephone, waking the baby lying in her arms.

"Tell me about it," Izaya said, over the resultant sound of Luna's wails. "You're lucky. The phone count statute limits your sentence to four years. I've had clients end up serving ten, or even twenty, for crimes for which they'd been acquitted, all because they got convicted of some minor, lesser included offense."

In the absence of the statutory maximum for the telephone count, the sentence required by the guidelines in Olivia's case was sixty-three to seventy-eight months. Izaya was not content, however, to accept the four-year sentence prescribed by the statute. Izaya's brief asked the judge to make use of the safety valve to bring her sentence down to forty-one to fifty-one months, and to depart even lower. The sentence he requested was home detention—the ankle bracelet of Elaine's fantasies.

"Will he do it?" Olivia had asked.

"I don't know," Izaya had replied. "I've never asked for anything like this. We'll have to wait and see."

The morning of her sentencing, Olivia woke early and forewent her usual lazy bath. She fed Luna, then hooked herself up to the breast pump Elaine had rented for her. She sat at the kitchen table, sleepily rocking to the rhythm of the suction whooshing through the tubes of the pump. She had begun pumping breast milk as soon as she had gotten home from the hospital. Over the past five weeks, she had filled her mother's freezer with three hundred ounces of pale yellow milk packed in tiny Ziploc bags. Her nipples were cracked and sore from all the pumping, and the smell of the lanolin she used to relieve the ache made her nauseous. But she wanted Luna to have breast milk as her only nourishment for as long as possible, and she was determined to leave enough for at least a month, in case Izaya's hopes went unrealized and she had to go to prison.

The sound of Elaine's voice caught Olivia's attention.

"I just can't get used to seeing you hooked up to that machine. Are you sure it doesn't hurt?"

"It's not too bad. Well, once when I had the power amped up all the way it sucked my nipple in about three inches. That was awful. But normally it's pretty bearable."

"Ralph will be here in a few minutes. Do you want to get dressed?"

Ralph had become Luna's greatest fan. It was all Olivia and Elaine could do to keep the man from dribbling spoonfuls of Rocky Road into the baby's mouth. He had been only too happy to watch her on the day of Olivia's sentencing hearing and had even decided to close the soda fountain for the day. It would be the first time in thirty years that milk shakes wouldn't be available on a Tuesday on College Avenue.

Olivia went upstairs to dress. In the month since Luna's birth, she'd lost some weight, but nowhere near enough to fit into her pre-pregnancy clothes. She sifted through her wardrobe, loath to wear the maternity dresses that she'd grown so sick of, but unable to find anything else. She knocked on her mother's bedroom door.

"Come in," Arthur called. He was standing at the mirror, tying his tie. "Check this out," he said, delightedly. "I got sick of tying my ties in the same lame way, so I went online and found directions for tying *this*. It's a new kind of knot, called a Pratt. What do you think?" He was holding a printed sheet with diagrams and instructions in his hand. He held up the picture next to his own tie. "Does it look right?"

"It looks fine," Olivia said, without looking at either the paper or Arthur. "Are you coming today?"

"Sure. I mean, Elaine told me that she wanted me to come. That *you* wanted me to come. Right?"

Olivia nodded. "Thanks. It'll be good for Mom to have someone there." She opened the door of Elaine's closet and began to go through the hanging clothes. She pulled out a navy dress with an empire waist and held it up to herself. Then she found a white blouse with a floppy bow at the neck. After Arthur walked out of the room, she pulled on the shirt. The top buttons strained over her pneumatic breasts, and she couldn't even close the shirt over the thick roll of her belly. Still, it was good enough; the voluminous dress would hide it all. She gazed into the mirror hanging on the back of the closet door, turning this way and that. She looked, to herself, like an overgrown schoolgirl. Perfect.

Olivia stood silently next to Izaya as he argued to Judge Horowitz that she deserved a downward departure. Izaya told the judge that they all knew that if he looked only at the sentencing range demanded by the charts and graphs that dictated his decision, he would have to sentence her to the full four years. However, this case, Izaya argued, mandated a different outcome. He talked at length about how tangentially involved Olivia was, about her naïveté, and about her lack of a serious criminal history. He argued that her minimal role in the offense justified a much lower sentence range.

Then he asked the judge to depart even further. "Your honor, Olivia is, as you know, a new mother. Her baby girl is five weeks old. Just five weeks. If you sentence this young mother to jail for four years, she could lose her child."

Izaya had called up one night soon after the trial and asked Olivia what she planned to do with the baby. He quickly explained that he had begun thinking through his sentencing strategy as though he wanted to be sure she didn't assume there was some more personal reason for his concern.

"I'm sending her to Jorge's parents in Mexico."

"Are you serious?"

She didn't feel the need to reply.

"What about your own mother?" Izaya asked.

"She can't take it."

"Why not?"

Olivia opened her mouth to explain about Arthur and about Elaine's own unwillingness to begin again the chore of raising a child but could not bring herself to say it all. "She just can't."

"Okay," Izaya said, softly. "Is foster care out of the question?"

"I'm allowed only a six-month window," Olivia said, and then described to Izaya what she had learned from the attorney at Legal Services for Prisoners with Children.

"Jesus," he had said when she was done. "And there's no one else?"

"No," she had said.

Olivia had expected him to use this information in his argument, but it still came as something of a cold shock, now, to hear the dangers she and Luna faced expressed so clearly.

"If she puts the baby in foster care, she will lose it," Izaya said, and then described the intricacies of the California adoption policy. "Her mother is unable to care for the child." The judge glanced up sharply, looking at Elaine. Olivia wasn't sure if the expression that flitted across his face was one of puzzlement or disgust. Elaine seemed not to notice his look. "Thus, poor Olivia's only option is to send the baby to Luna's other grandparents, the parents of the boyfriend who got her into this mess, the man who testified against her. Honestly, your honor, what do you think the chances of them giving the baby back are? What if Mr. Rodriguez gets released before Olivia? He could take Luna, and Olivia would never see her again."

Olivia swayed. Had she not been sitting, she might have fallen. She pressed her hands into her thighs, firming the muscles of her legs and arms, willing herself not to topple off her seat.

"I believe I sentenced Mr. Rodriguez last month, counsel," the judge said. He turned to Amanda Steele. "What did I give him?"

She opened a file and leafed through it. "Approximately three years, your honor." Olivia looked over at Izaya. His face was red; he was clearly embarrassed at having failed to find this information out before today.

"You see, your honor, he will be released before her. Olivia has no choice but to take the terrible risk that she might lose her baby to the man who involved her in this drug deal to begin with. Unless you do something else. Something dramatic. The only way you can keep this young mother and infant together, the only way you can guarantee that Luna will grow up here in the United States with the people who love her, is if you depart far below the range and sentence Olivia to home detention."

During Izaya's speech, the judge had not once looked at his watch. He stared from Izaya to Olivia, and Olivia tried to convince herself that in his eyes she recognized the softness of compassion.

Amanda Steele got to her feet. She was obviously pregnant now, her belly a tiny round ball under the black silk of her dress. She told the judge that Olivia's refusal to plead guilty and her persistent denial of her own responsibility for the offense warranted a sentence of four years, the most allowable by the statute. She denied that Olivia was a minimal participant and told the judge that even if he considered her role to be minor, a four-year sentence was still what the guidelines required. She also reminded the judge that Olivia had at the time of the offense been "harboring an illegal alien."

When it was Olivia's turn to speak, she rose and made her way to the podium, clutching the statement she'd prepared over the course of the previous weeks. Izaya had been satisfied that they'd achieved the precise tone of supplication and apology to which he felt the judge would respond. He had been pleased with the final draft, which begged the pardon not only of the judge, but of the prosecutor, of the police, of Olivia's family and friends, even of the theoretical users of the methamphetamine she had never actually seen.

Olivia cleared her throat and began to read. "Before I say anything else, I want to apologize. I want to apologize to my mother, to my friends, and most of all to my daughter for what I did, and even more importantly, for what I didn't do. I'm ashamed and sorry that my actions have caused them pain.

"This whole experience has been a terrible lesson in the price of staying silent, of going along with things I knew were wrong. When I got the very first phone call from Gabriel Contreras, I should have insisted that Jorge go to the police. I should have gone to the police myself. I shouldn't have watched as things moved forward. When I heard Gabriel's voice on the telephone the second time, then, too, I should have gone to the police. I now understand that passing on that telephone message was a crime. I should never have done it. I should never have gotten into the car with Jorge. I should never have gone along for the ride. I should never have allowed it all to continue."

Olivia paused and looked up at the judge. When he looked back, his expression one of mild, detached interest, suddenly she realized that he had already made his decision, had made it even before he stepped up to the bench. Nothing she said today was going to make the slightest bit of difference. She looked down at the paper in her hand and then crumpled it up. Izaya inhaled sharply and her mother gasped. She ignored them both and looked up at Judge Horowitz. "But I did all those things, and I never called the police, and I never turned in my boyfriend and his friends. If I had, I wouldn't be here today. But the truth is, your honor, I still don't believe that I deserve to be here today. My judgment was bad, and maybe I deserve to be punished, but I still don't accept that this is the right punishment."

Olivia felt Izaya's hand on her arm.

"Your honor," he said. "Can I have a word with my client?"

She turned to him, and, gently but firmly, shook her head. "No, Izaya," she said, and turned back to the judge. "What kind of a justice system is this, where because I was the only member of a conspiracy who didn't know anybody else, who didn't even sit down with the members of the conspiracy, I was the only one who ended up facing trial? What kind of a system rewards those who are *more* culpable with downward departures for assisting the government and punishes those whose very lack of culpability prevents them from having information to exchange? I don't think this is justice, your honor.

"I know if I just do what my lawyer wants and look pathetic, you might be willing to sentence me to what my lawyer asks, to home detention. But, honestly, I think you're going to abide by the guidelines and apply them as they're written, no matter what I say. That's what you're *supposed* to do, isn't it? But this is my only opportunity to make my voice heard and I want…I *need*…to do it.

"I need to tell you all," she looked around the room, "I need to ask you all, and particularly you, Ms. Steele, if this is what you think is *right*. Is locking me up for four years serving some greater purpose? Is taking my baby girl's mother away from her going to win a battle in the war on drugs? As far as I can tell, you all keep putting people like me in jail, and drugs are still out there. This group my mother is involved with, FAMM, they have all this research that shows that the price of cocaine and heroin has gone down every single year for the past ten. And the drugs are getting purer. I don't know much about economics, but it seems to me that if you were winning this war, drugs would be getting more expensive and harder to find instead of cheaper and more plentiful.

"You know what? I think this war you're fighting isn't against drugs at all. I think it's a war against *people*. People like me and people like Jorge and all the other people in jail for ten or twenty years or however long. And your soldiers are people like Gabriel Contreras.

"Your honor, I hope you sentence me to what my lawyer asked for because I want to stay home and be a mother to my baby. But, I'm sorry. I won't stand here and tell you I think I deserve the punishment in order to get you to give me a lower sentence. All my life I've demonstrated and spoken against injustice. This is the first time the injustice has been at my own expense. I won't be silent now. I can't."

There was no sound in the room except for Elaine's jagged breathing. Olivia turned to her mother. They looked into each other's eyes, and then, after a long pause, Elaine nodded, once. Olivia smiled gratefully and turned back to the judge.

Judge Horowitz was leaning forward in his chair, his fingers drumming silently on the smooth expanse of polished wood in front of him. "Ms. Goodman, this may surprise you, and it is certain to surprise your lawyer, Mr. Politically Correct, but it is my considered opinion, based on my twenty years of experience on the bench, that to a very great extent, your doubts about the fairness of the federal sentencing guidelines and the mandatory minimums are justified. In fact, over the years, I have come to share the opinion of many other judges that they do not serve the objectives of deterrence, rehabilitation, and just punishment that are the goals of our judicial system. I find myself, now more than ever, concerned that my role in meting out fair and reasonable sentences has been usurped by, forgive me Ms. Steele, young, naïve, and ambitious prosecutors concerned less with ultimate justice than with winning their cases and improving the records of their offices.

"Nonetheless, I must do the job for which I have been appointed. It is my belief that this case warrants a four level adjustment due to minimal role. The appropriate sentencing range is, thus, forty-one to fifty-one months, limited to forty-eight months by statute. I hereby sentence you to forty-one months of detention to be followed by a two-year period of supervised release."

Olivia stood still, unable to speak or even to move. She had expected this—in fact she'd feared worse. However, hearing the words still stunned her. Forty-one months of her daughter's life—lost to her.

Izaya, who had not so much as flinched at Horowitz's insulting nickname, thanked the judge. Then, he said, "Your honor, I'd like to ask that Ms. Goodman be allowed to self-surrender, and that this self-surrender not take place for a few months, to give her more time with her newborn daughter, whom she is breast-feeding."

Judge Horowitz said, "Mr. Feingold-Upchurch, is there really any reason to postpone the inevitable?"

"Your honor?" Amanda Steele's voice was as cool and calm as ever. Olivia turned to the prosecutor, who had risen to her feet. Amanda Steele did not return Olivia's gaze. Her eyes on the judge and no one else, she said, "The government would not object to a sixty-day delay."

"What was that line from the boyfriend's letter?" Ruth Feingold asked. She was leaning back on her overstuffed Victorian sofa, her bare feet stretched out in front of her. She rubbed the arch of one foot with the toes of the other. She had been listening to her son's agonizing postmortem of his most recent trial for almost two hours. Izaya was obsessively, even compulsively, describing to his mother every way he imagined he had failed. He had just launched into a diatribe about Jorge's duplicity when Ruth interrupted him.

"What line?" he asked. He had recited to her from memory the letter Jorge sent to Olivia. Neither he nor his mother was surprised that he remembered it. As Ruth often said, that was just the way Izaya's mind worked.

"The last one. The postscript."

"Love is so short and oblivion so long," he said.

"I know that line. It's from a poem. Hold on a sec." She got up off the sofa and went over to the wall of books separating the living room from the rest of the house. She scanned the shelves and then pulled out a thin paperback volume. She flipped through the pages, then said, "Pablo Neruda. It's called 'The Saddest Poem.' Here, look." She handed Izaya the book. He read aloud, slumping lower and lower in his chair.

I can write the saddest poem of all tonight.

Write, for instance: "the night is full of stars,
And the stars, blue, shiver in the distance."

The night wind whirls in the sky and sings.

I can write the saddest poem of all tonight.
I loved her, and sometimes she loved me too.

On nights like this, I held her in my arms.
I kissed her so many times under the infinite sky.

She loved me, sometimes I loved her.
How could I not have loved her large, still eyes?

I can write the saddest poem of all tonight.
To think I don't have her. To feel that I've lost her.

To hear the immense night, more immense without her.
And the poem falls to the soul as dew to grass.

What does it matter that my love couldn't keep her.
The night is full of stars and she is not with me.

That's all. Far away someone sings. Far away.
My soul is lost without her.

As if to bring her near, my eyes search for her.
My heart searches for her and she is not with me.

The same night that whitens the same trees.
We, we who were, we are the same no longer.

I no longer love her, true, but how much I loved her.
My voice searched the wind to touch her ear.

Someone else's. She will be someone else's. As she once
belonged to my kisses.

Her voice, her light body. Her infinite eyes.

I no longer love her, true, but perhaps I love her.
Love is so short and oblivion so long.

Because on nights like this I held her in my arms, my
soul is lost without her.

Although this may be the last pain she causes me,
and this may be the last poem I write for her.

He put the slim book down on the leather ottoman at his
mother's feet.

"It's beautiful, don't you think?" she said.

"Yeah, it is." But he didn't think so. Or rather, the beauty of
the words was entirely irrelevant. What Jorge meant by quoting
them and what Olivia would think when she read them, if she
hadn't already, was all he cared about.

"I imagine he was trying to tell her that despite everything,
he remembered their love."

"Bull*shit!*" Izaya exclaimed, and leapt to his feet.

"Izaya?" his mother asked, unruffled by his outburst. "What's
going on here? Are you jealous? Are you sleeping with this girl?"

"Man, you and Ervin. Is that all the two of you think of me?"

"What does your father have to do with this?"

"He asked me if I was fucking her, too."

Ruth rolled her eyes. "Nice, honey. Nice language."

"Give me a break, okay? No, give me a *fucking* break."

Ruth sat forward and took her grown-up baby's face in her hands.

"What's wrong, sweetheart? What's going on with you? Are you in love with Olivia?"

He rested his hand against her familiar palm for a moment and then shook her off. "I don't know. And don't start!" he barked. Ruth closed her mouth. "I know exactly what you're going to say. She's vulnerable. Her life was in my hands. I feel responsible and guilty. Blah blah blah. No, I'm not sleeping with her. But I can't stop thinking about her."

Ruth nodded. "Well, maybe you should talk to her."

"What good would that do?"

"Maybe she feels the same way."

"So what? I'm her *lawyer*, Mom."

"I know, Izaya. I know you are. But is that what's most important? Really?"

"I don't know anymore," he said, and lay his head in his mother's lap.

Olivia stopped her work for a while. She rested against a half-packed box and lifted Luna to her breast. At eleven weeks, the baby was round and chubby, almost fat. She was a cheerful child who rarely cried, except when she was hungry. Her favorite activities were sitting in her bouncy seat, flailing ineffectually at the toys strung along the bar just out of her reach, and, of course, nursing. Luna nursed for hours every day.

Olivia held Luna's hand in her own as the baby drank. Her tiny fingers were impossibly strong, and she gripped her mother's index finger as if she knew that all too soon it would be taken from her grasp. Olivia inhaled deeply, smelling Luna's odor, so familiar that she was sure it was just like her own, like the smell of her own sweat or even the almost rank sweetness between her legs.

"Hi."

Olivia raised her face to the sound of the voice, squinting at the light shining through the open door of the Oakland apartment she had shared with Jorge. In the doorway, silhouetted against the light, was the form of a man holding a large dog by the collar.

"Treyvon?" she said.

"Hey, Olivia. 8-Ball! Sit."

"Wow, is that the puppy? He's so big!"

"He over a year old now. That your baby? She beautiful." Treyvon walked into the room and knelt down next to Olivia. 8-Ball hung back, obedient in his sitting position. Treyvon was wearing a rugby shirt and baggy jeans and had buzzed his hair nearly down to the skull. A silver lightning bolt hung from the lobe of his left ear.

Olivia gently took her breast from Luna's mouth and covered herself. The baby began to protest, but Olivia lifted her to her shoulder and patted her on the back. Soon, she was cooing.

"You leaving?" Treyvon said.

"Yeah. I can't believe I kept the apartment for so long. I guess I just couldn't face packing it up."

"Can I?" Treyvon said, holding out his arms. Olivia passed him the baby and he bounced her gently on his lap. The dog nosed his hand and he pushed it away. "What happened to your case?"

"I was convicted."

"Fuck no!"

"Yeah. I mean, I was acquitted of the drug charges, but they got me on a phone count. Four years."

Treyvon shook his head and looked at the baby. "What you going do?"

"About Luna?"

"Yeah."

"My boyfriend's family is going to take her. They live in Mexico."

Treyvon nodded. "That's good. She'll be with family."

Olivia nodded.

He lifted Luna's T-shirt and buzzed her belly with his lips. She giggled. 8-Ball barked as if in reply. Treyvon turned to Olivia. "Uh, yeah. Look, it ain't my place to give no advice, but you don't look like somebody used to getting by. Inside, I mean."

Olivia shook her head. She had never really spoken to anyone about her experiences waiting to get out on bail. She hadn't wanted to, and even if she had felt like talking, there would not have been anyone who would have understood.

"I'm really scared," she whispered.

"I know. I was scared every goddamn day I was there. But you know what? That's why I'm here now. I'd ever of stopped being scared, I'd of ended up dead. Being scared kept me, you know, awake. Kept me on my *toes*. Kept me alive."

"I couldn't stand it in Martinez. I'd lie in my bed thinking I was going to die if I didn't get out, like I'd explode or something."

"Yeah. It passes. It do. I mean, don't get me wrong; you don't never feel good. You don't never sleep like you do outside. But that feeling—like you gonna jump on out your skin?" Olivia nodded. "It might not ever go 'way, but it get easier." Treyvon leaned back on his heels and looked at her. "It's like at some point you, like they say, hit bottom. You get so scared, you lie awake at night in your cell, and you thinking, shit. You going to die. Either explode, or slice yourself up, or someone else going do it for you. That the moment could be what saves you. The moment you start to *survive*. What you got to do is figure out what you care about, fix it in your scopes. For me, it was getting the fuck out of there with something to show for it— my GED. For you, it be getting back to this pretty little baby. Just keep that in your mind, and start walking toward it. At the end of all the years, you be there."

Then Treyvon gave Olivia what he called his tips for federal inmates. He told her to bring a toothbrush and toothpaste and to wear her sneakers when she turned herself in. He explained how she could go about having money put on her account.

After a while, as he spoke, the sheer mundaneness of all the details began to calm her. She began to see the next three and a half years as a horrible time that would depress and dismay but not destroy her. She felt something almost like a tranquility seep over her, and she held out her arms for Luna. She squeezed her baby close to her chest and inhaled her sweet smell.

Treyvon helped Olivia load the car full of boxes. She secured Luna in her seat and hugged her neighbor close. Then she drove home.

As she pulled in, she had to stop short to keep from hitting the large motorcycle crouched like a shiny black and chrome beetle in the middle of the driveway. Izaya was sitting on the front steps, his long legs outstretched and crossed at the ankle. He waved at her. She smiled in return.

"Hi," he said when she got out of the car.

"Hi. Have you been waiting long?"

She wrestled Luna's car seat out of its base and carried it to the steps.

"Not long." He looked over at the car stuffed with boxes. "Were you packing up your apartment?"

"Trying to," Olivia said. "This one didn't make it particularly easy, though." She gently swung Luna's seat, and the baby laughed.

"Can I help you unload?"

"Sure." Olivia sat on the steps while Izaya hefted the boxes out of the car and stacked them neatly against the back wall of the garage. When he was finally done, he collapsed on the step next to her and groaned.

"Not used to physical labor, are we?" she asked, laughing.

He wiped the beads of sweat from his forehead. "What makes you say that?"

"Do you want to come in and get a drink?"

He followed her inside and leaned against the kitchen counter while she poured him a tall glass of ice water. He drained the cup and then held his arms out for the baby. Olivia handed Luna to him, and he raised her up in the air above his head.

"You are so big, baby. You are so *fat!*" he cooed.

"She is, isn't she?" Olivia said. Although she knew it was somewhat ridiculous, she felt like every pound added to Luna's plump frame was her doing, a testament to her mothering, to her nurturing of the baby. Each pound was like savings she was stockpiling for the day when she could make no more deposits.

Izaya sat down on the floor in the living room, next to a pile of baby toys. He stretched out his legs and balanced the baby across his thighs.

Olivia joined them, sitting cross-legged on the carpet.

"So, what's up?" she said. "Is there something I forgot? Something we need to do?"

Izaya hoisted himself up on one side and reached into the back pocket of his jeans. He pulled out a folded piece of paper and handed it to her. "I just wanted to bring you this."

"What is it?" she asked.

"A poem."

"A *poem?*"

"Not from me!" he said hastily, and she blushed at the assumption they both knew she'd made. She raised her eyebrows at him.

"Read it," he said.

She skimmed the lines, stopping short at the one she recognized. Then she backed up and read the rest. She wondered what Jorge had meant by quoting this particular poem. Had he intended to tell her that his soul was lost without her, or that he no longer loved her? Perhaps both were true, or perhaps the poem meant nothing at all. Perhaps he had quoted the line because it alone seemed apt. Love *was* short. Oblivion, and a prison sentence, were very long. Olivia puzzled over Neruda's words for a little while, and then suddenly realized that she did not care very much what Jorge had meant. What had been between them was now long over. Only Luna mattered.

Izaya cleared his throat. "So, Olivia. I have some news."

She glanced up at him. "News?"

"About your appeal."

"My appeal? I thought you said that there weren't any appeal-able issues in my case."

He shrugged. "There aren't any, really. But we might as well file an appeal. Hell, let's make the government work for their money."

"Okay."

"There's a woman who does most of my father's appeals when he loses, which isn't often. She's a private criminal appellate lawyer, and she's one of the best in the country. She's agreed to represent you, if you're interested."

"I can't afford someone like that, Izaya. Particularly if there isn't any real chance we'll win. Why can't you do the appeal? I mean, do you not *want* to do it?"

"It's not that I don't want to. It's just that she'd be better. And she's going to represent you *pro bono*."

"Why?"

"She gets most of her high-profile cases from my dad. I guess she figures that doing me a favor is a good way to pay him back for all of his referrals."

Olivia picked up a rag doll and smoothed its dress. "I don't get it. Why is representing *me* doing *you* a favor?"

Izaya picked Luna up off his lap and put her over his shoulder. "Because I don't want to be your lawyer anymore."

Olivia bit her lip. She'd cried enough today.

"Oh," she said and reached her arms out for the baby. "Okay, that's fine. But I don't need you to find me another lawyer. I'm sure there's someone in your office who can take over the case."

"You don't get it," he said, ignoring her hands and kissing Luna on the cheek. The baby began to squirm and he put her back down in his lap. "I don't want *anyone* at the Federal Public Defender's office to represent you."

Olivia scooped up Luna and hugged her tightly. The baby began to cry.

"Fine. Whatever. I'll find my own damn lawyer."

"Olivia. Hey, Olivia." Izaya leaned over and smoothed her hair away from her eyes. "I don't want my office representing you, because if we do, then I wouldn't be allowed to do this." He kissed her, gently at first and then harder. She felt her body begin to grow limp, and then, with a rush of warm dampness, her milk began to flow, soaking her shirt.

"Oh, Christ," she said.

He leaned back on his haunches. "Oh, my God! I'm sorry," he said and began to get up.

"No! No, don't be sorry. Just wait a second. It's just, I'm—I'm leaking." She pulled her shirt up and put Luna to her nipple. For a few minutes they sat silently while the baby sucked and grunted, kneading Olivia's breast with her fists. At last, in stages, Luna drifted off to sleep. Olivia slipped her nipple, shiny with milk and spit, out of the baby's mouth. She tugged her shirt back into place and gently laid Luna on a baby blanket on the floor. She looked at Izaya. He was so beautiful. So strong, and so gentle.

She gazed at his soft, full lips and imagined pressing her own against them, darting her tongue into his mouth, tasting him. She felt an ache in her groin and crossed her arms against her breasts to keep the milk from flowing again. She closed her eyes and saw the length of his naked body wrapped around her own. And then, unbidden, Luna's face appeared. Olivia opened her eyes and turned back to her daughter. The baby's mouth was pursed in the shape of Olivia's breast, and she sucked at the empty space her mother had left behind.

"I want to kiss you so much," she said.

Izaya began to smile, but stopped. "But you're not going to," he said flatly.

She shook her head. "No, I'm not going to."

"You're not interested in me *that way*."

She laughed. "No, I'm interested. I'm interested. I'm very—interested. I mean, you're smart and you're gorgeous..." she lifted her hand to silence his protests. "No, you really are. At any other time in my life, I'd probably jump at the chance to be with you. Just not now."

"Is it because of him? Because he sent you that poem? Because you know he loves you?"

Olivia smiled ruefully. "Is that what you think? No. It has nothing to do with Jorge. I told you. I don't love him anymore. I'm not sure I ever loved him."

"So why then?"

She sighed. "I just can't. Not now. Your timing is just, well, really bad, Izaya."

Izaya sat back heavily, swinging his long legs out in front of him.

"Do you know what a *b'shert* is?" he said.

Olivia shook her head.

"It's a word in Yiddish. My grandmother used to tell me when I was a kid that every person had a *b'shert*, like a soul mate. And she said that just before you're born, an angel takes you around, shows you this person, and then smacks you hard, right here right under your nose, where this little thing is." He reached out and tapped her philtrum. She jumped. "And that makes you forget what the angel told you. So then you get born, and you grow up, and you spend the rest of your life searching for that person you once saw that you don't quite remember." Olivia stared at her hands. She couldn't bear to look at him. "Here's the thing, Olivia. What if you're my *b'shert*? What if I'm yours? Are we really just going to let that slip through our fingers because of something as stupid as *timing?*"

Olivia wanted desperately to accede to Izaya's gentle, tantalizing persuasion. She could tell he was absolutely serious, that he was, or thought he was, in love with her. To disappear into the horror of prison with Izaya's photograph in her pocket, with the security of his love, real or imagined, in her heart—wouldn't that make it all easier? Or would it? She had spent her entire life going from one boy or man to another, looking for someone who would take care of her, would provide her with the sensation of ease and security that she imagined other girls, daughters of actual, present fathers, took for granted. Here was a man willing, eager to give her that refuge.

And yet, even though she thought she might be in love with him, it was suddenly clear to her that there was no way she could be with him. While it might seem like the easiest thing to allow him to save her, or at least to make her feel like being saved was even the remotest of possibilities, she could not do it. The fantasy of a relationship that might or might not outlast her incarceration would not provide her with the specific goal she knew she needed to survive the next years. More importantly, it would distract her. She knew herself well enough to understand that she could not fix both Izaya and Luna in her scopes at the same time.

Olivia looked down at her sleeping baby. Luna was on her side, her legs curled up and her arms flung wide.

"I don't know if I'm your *b'shert*, Izaya. I know I like you a whole lot. I admire you. I might even love you. But I have Luna now. I have to spend every moment with her. I have to fill my eyes, and my mind, and my heart only with her. There isn't room for anyone else, not now. There can't be." As Olivia spoke the words, she realized that they were the absolute truth. The only person she wanted was Luna; the only focus for her attention, her love, her devotion, was her baby. By bringing Luna into the world, Olivia had abdicated the right to retreat to the security of yet another man's arms and attention. Her own anxiety, her own loneliness, could no longer be the motivating force behind her behavior. It was Luna's security that had to be her primary—her only—concern. What Olivia had lacked as a daughter was no longer important—it was what she had to provide as a mother that mattered now.

Izaya opened his mouth, but something about her expression must have made him realize there was no point in arguing, that she had made up her mind.

He nodded. They sat in silence for awhile, and then Izaya said, "Well, what about later?" he asked.

"Later?"

"You know, when you get out."

Olivia imagined a scene some three and a half years hence. Izaya waiting for her at the gates to the prison, Luna in his arms. "I don't know. It's a long time away. Why don't we just wait and see," she said.

Olivia held her coffee in one hand, away from her body and the arm where the baby rested. She sipped carefully and set the cup down far from Luna's grasping fingers.

"Are you ready?" Elaine asked.

Olivia nodded. She had packed the contents of her apartment into a storage container and had the container picked up and taken away, having prepaid three and a half years of storage fees. She had boxed up Jorge's belongings and mailed them down to his parents in Mexico. She had packed Luna's tiny jumpers and T-shirts, her toys, pacifiers, and bottles, into an oversized duffel bag.

"I was wondering," her mother said. "Would you like to do something special today? Since it's your last day."

Olivia squeezed Luna a little tighter. "Like what?"

"Maybe Point Reyes? We'll drive out and take a hike along the beach, eat some barbecued oysters?"

When Olivia was ten years old, she and Elaine had spent one Sunday driving along the Pacific Coast Highway in West Marin. At one point, they had strayed off the main road and stitched their way along the quilted seam of road between the rolling hills and dairy farms. They had stumbled upon a gas station with a picnic table set up on the grass behind the pumps. A charcoal fire was burning in half of an oil drum propped up on sawhorses, and rows of oysters on the half-shell bubbled on top of the makeshift grill. A hand-lettered sign leaning against the table read BBQ OYSTER 50 CENT. Olivia and Elaine had pulled over and spent an hour shoveling the oysters into their mouths, slurping up the briny liquid and wiping up tomato sauce with slices of Wonder Bread.

For a couple of years afterward, they had taken Sunday drives up to Point Reyes in search of the gas station with the perfect barbecued oysters. But they hadn't paid attention to the name of the road, and they disagreed about whether it had been north or south of Inverness. They'd stopped at countless oyster shacks and eaten hundreds of barbecued bivalves, but nothing had ever come close to that first perfect mouthful of vinegar, tomato, and sea. In a lifetime of misremembered accidents, affronts, and hurt feelings, each held a joyful memory of that day that was both precise and identical to the other's. The last time they'd gone in search of their legendary feast had been the year Olivia started high school.

"Point Reyes! That'd be great! We can take our bikes and do the entire spit," Arthur said as he came walking through the kitchen on his way to the laundry room, a pile of fetid bike shorts and Lycra T-shirts in his arms.

Elaine looked up at him, startled. "Oh, but what about the baby? I mean, what would Olivia do?"

"She and Luna could take a little hike while you and I bike," he said.

Elaine's voice was soft and almost wheedling. "That's a wonderful idea, but why don't I keep Olivia company. *You* bike and we'll walk."

Arthur looked at Elaine for a moment, his brow slightly wrinkled, as if he were trying to figure out what it meant that she was choosing to spend the day in her daughter's company rather than his. Elaine smiled blandly back.

"Sure," he said, after a moment. He adjusted the load of dirty laundry in his arms and walked back to the laundry room.

The road to the Point Reyes National Seashore ribboned over and through the lolling West Marin hills. To Olivia, sitting in the backseat next to Luna, the hills looked like a woman's not-quite-spread legs and thighs, with patches of black oak nestled in the valleys like mats of mossy pubic hair. Fields dotted with the black and white spots of grazing dairy cows and draped in a gentle gray mist rolled by her window. She inhaled deeply, smelling the ocean's sharp tang. The hills gave way to trees and then again to smooth brown mounds of waving grasses, and finally the road dead-ended in a little parking lot at the Tomales Bay trailhead.

Arthur leapt out of the car and wrestled his bike off the rack attached to the trunk. He clamped his bullet-shaped helmet onto his head and shrugged a neon green windbreaker over his taxicab-yellow top. He clomped in his bike shoes over to Elaine.

"Okay, I'll bike back. We'll meet in two hours in Point Reyes in front of that gourmet market."

"Perfect." Elaine gave him a kiss on his cheek. He mounted his bike and rode away.

Olivia strapped the Baby Björn to her chest, lifted Luna out of her car seat, and slipped her into the carrier. She adjusted the straps, and Luna kicked, delighted to be facing outward, looking at the world and, at the same time, snuggled tightly against her mother's breasts and belly.

Elaine led the way through the gate and they began walking down the hill. The path wound through a valley with gentle slopes rising on either side. The ground was soft and sandy, and their shoes left sharp-edged prints in the dirt.

Olivia hiked carefully, placing each foot squarely so that she would not stumble and crush her tiny burden. She bent her head and pressed her lips against the top of Luna's head, feeling the feathers of the baby's soft hair and the delicate skin underneath. Olivia closed her eyes and willed herself to remember everything about the moment. The feel of Luna's feet resting in either one of her palms. The heavy heat of the baby's back pressed against her chest. The brush of her hair against Olivia's mouth. And her soft velvet smell, with just the barest hint of sour musk, like apricots that had begun to rot on the tree, or sweet, thick cream at the moment before it turned.

"Coming?" Elaine called from farther down the path. Olivia inhaled once more, then began walking again, catching up to her mother. They strolled in silence for a while, watching the gulls drift by overhead, and stepping cautiously to avoid the snails creeping slowly across the path.

They came upon a sign and stopped. Elaine read it aloud.

"Beware of sharks and sneaker waves."

There were two pictures—icons, simplified to their essence. One, the shark, was all fang and jaw. The other was really two images in one. The first showed a man and a woman enjoying a picnic on the beach under an umbrella. In the next frame, a wave had reached out and snatched at them, upending the umbrella, and sending the woman tumbling off into the surf. The man reached out for her, helplessly.

They stared at the sign for a moment, and then, without speaking, continued along the path.

In another fifty yards, the valley opened up to the sea. The path ended at the beach. It was suddenly cooler, and Olivia hugged Luna to her body. She zipped her jacket around the two of them, and walked closer to the water's edge, heedless of both sneaker waves and great whites. The water lapped at the toes of her boots, and Olivia stared at the ocean. She could see only a few hundred yards ahead of her. Beyond that, the sea wore a veil of mist and fog. Although she knew the Pacific went on and on for thousands of miles, she saw nothing but the nearest little edge of water. She contemplated walking into the ocean. She had not, since her trial and sentencing, been plagued by fantasies of escape—neither in the form of flight nor in that of suicide. It had never really occurred to her that she had a choice other than to go to prison. At the edge of the sea, for a brief moment, Olivia imagined taking Luna, sliding into the cold water, drifting off to a secret place hidden in the blanket of mist, and disappearing without a trace.

Elaine came up beside her and gently touched her. They stood there for a few minutes, Elaine's hand warm on Olivia's back. Then they headed up the path toward the car.

About halfway to the parking lot, Elaine suddenly stopped and motioned to Olivia. Olivia followed her mother's pointed finger and gazed up the side of the hill banking the path, directly into the eyes of an elk. The elk stood impossibly still and stared at the human interlopers. Her fawn, its tiny white bottom snuggled tight against its mother, looked at the them curiously. Olivia and the elk stared at each other for a long while and then, with a flick of her ears, the elk led her baby up the slope and away.

Olivia turned to smile at Elaine and found her crying, tears streaming down her cheeks. Olivia opened her arms and embraced her mother. Luna wriggled, trapped happily between them, laughing at the game.

Prison was where Jorge was finally learning English. It was not particularly necessary; the guards at the Federal Corrections Center at Lompoc spoke enough Spanish to make their orders and insults understood, and the only inmates with whom Jorge associated were Mexicans, like himself. Nonetheless, he was slowly beginning to pick up bits and pieces of the language that had always eluded him when his only motivation for learning had been to make Olivia happy.

Life was by no means good or easy in the prison, but the pervasive misery was somehow more manageable than it had been when he had been in county jail. The uncertainty of his future had, then, been an excruciating element of his fear. Now he knew exactly how long he would be incarcerated—thirty-five months, less good-behavior credit if all went well and he could keep himself out of trouble. He knew, too, what would happen to him upon his release. His lawyer had explained that he would be transferred to INS custody and deported. The prospect of deportation, of leaving behind the country that had treated him, he believed, with a cruelty he could not have imagined before he had crossed the Rio Grande, filled him with nothing but relief.

Jorge had received one letter from home, written by his father. Juan Carlos had contained his anger, inquiring about his son's well-being without once writing the true disappointment and fury Jorge knew he felt. Only when he wrote about the baby and their agreement to care for it in Olivia's absence did something of his chilly disgust for his son come through on the page. Juan Carlos had always been a man who took full responsibility for his children, and he instructed Jorge that this behavior was the least of what would be expected from him as well. Upon his release, Jorge would be expected to work with his father to support his child, and even once it was returned to Olivia, Juan Carlos would require that Jorge continue to send money and maintain contact, both for the child's sake and for his entire family's, who were sure to come to love it in the meantime.

Jorge had written a letter replete with apologies and assurances, filling four pages with the words he knew he should have written to Olivia, not to his father. He knew, however, that he never would write to Olivia what he was afraid she deserved to hear. He satisfied himself with making his regrets known to his parents. Jorge then put from his mind all thoughts of the baby whom he could not bring himself to expect with anything other than guilt and despair. Having failed its mother so completely, he imagined it would be only a matter of time before he did the same to the child.

Jorge concentrated on learning English, getting by as quietly and unobtrusively as possible, and marking the days until he would be released and his time in America would fade to nothing more than a bitter memory.

Olivia self-surrendered on a Monday. Instead of having the federal marshals come and put her in handcuffs, she drove with Elaine, Arthur, and Luna to the women's Federal Correctional Institution at Dublin. The prison's barbed-wire fences cast long, spiky shadows over the parking lot, and as they crossed toward the gate, they walked deeper into the gloom. Olivia clutched Luna in her arms. She had dressed the baby as if for a party, in a pale-yellow dress with tiny white rabbits embroidered at the neck and along the ruffle. Izaya was waiting for them at the front gate, and he greeted Olivia with a short hug and a kiss to the top of Luna's head. They walked through the gate together and down a path between the cyclone fences. Elaine and Arthur followed them into the prison, through a surprisingly small steel door.

Elaine could hear her daughter's breath rasping in her lungs as they entered a narrow office. At one end of the cold, empty room was a window behind which a uniformed man stood. Olivia approached and whispered her name, and Elaine saw her daughter's back begin to tremble. Within seconds, her entire body was shaking. Luna began to fret and whimper. Elaine, who had been standing back from her daughter and holding Arthur's hand, rushed forward.

"Okay, okay, darling. Okay," she mumbled in a monotone at once quiet and desperate. She threw her arms around Olivia, and the two women began to cry. Luna, sensing their panic and fear, joined in with an agonized wail. Arthur and Izaya looked at each other and then stepped forward. Arthur gently led Elaine to a bench across the room. Izaya took Olivia's hand and, bending over her, began whispering into her ear.

As soon as Elaine found herself alone with Arthur, she calmed down. She leaned her head against his arm and willed her tears to stop. She looked across the room at where Olivia was now resting in Izaya's arms, Luna fitted snuggly between them. Elaine could not hear Izaya's words, but she watched as her daughter slowly calmed down, her breath becoming obviously more measured and slow. Finally, Olivia smiled, tremulously, and Izaya leaned his face to hers. His lips grazed Olivia's and then clung for a breath of a second. And then almost before it had begun, the kiss was over, leaving Elaine to wonder if she had actually seen it.

"Mom," Olivia called. Elaine walked over. Now she was trembling, and Olivia stood firm and tall.

"You'll write as soon as you get back from Mexico?" Olivia said.

"Tomorrow. I'll write tomorrow," Elaine answered, doing her best to imitate her daughter's measured tones.

"Okay." Olivia reached her free arm around Elaine's waist and squeezed. She leaned over and pressed her cheek against Elaine's. Her skin felt overwarm, and Elaine pressed her lips to her daughter's forehead, checking for a fever as though Olivia were still a little girl. Olivia let go of her mother and turned to Arthur. She kissed him briefly, almost briskly, and then held Luna out at arm's length.

"Mama's going bye-bye, Luna," she said.

Luna kicked her fat little legs in their yellow terrycloth socks and smiled a wide toothless grin. "I'll be back for you. Do you understand me? My baby girl. I will be back for you." Tears rolled down Olivia's face, but her voice was gentle and steady. She hugged the baby to her and inhaled deeply. She pushed her lips into Luna's yielding cheek, burying her mouth in her silken neck. Then she handed Luna to Elaine and looked toward the door that the guard held open for her. She turned back to her mother and daughter.

"Good-bye," she said, and stepped through the door.

The week before, Elaine had bought a plane ticket for León, a city not too distant from San Miguel, the town in which Jorge's family lived. She had found the ticket on a travel website. On the same site she'd come across a list of San Miguel hotels. Her eye had been caught, inevitably, by a bed and breakfast called "Casa Luna." She had emailed a reservation request, deciding after much thought that she would stay for five nights. That would give her enough time to meet Jorge's family, to make sure they were set up to integrate the baby into their lives, and also to let the consulate know of Luna's presence. Elaine wanted some representative of the United States to understand that Luna was to be a visitor in her Mexican grandparents' home. She wanted there to be an official record of Olivia's intention to return and reclaim her baby.

The morning of her departure, she checked and rechecked the contents of her suitcases, her ticket, and their passports. She ran into the kitchen for some large Ziploc bags to stuff into the diaper bag to hold any clothes Luna soiled during the flight, and found Arthur standing in front of the freezer, dumping bags of frozen breast milk into the trash bin.

"What are you doing?" Elaine screamed, her shrill cry reverberating through the kitchen.

"What?" he said, turning around, a plastic baggie in his hand.

"You can't throw that away!" She rushed to the trashcan and hauled out the bags that had already begun to defrost. She wiped the outsides clean and set them back upright in the freezer.

"Didn't you already pack as much as you could fit?" Arthur asked. Elaine had filled a cooler with dry ice and breast milk, desperately hoping that the ice would keep the milk from defrosting. She had crammed as much as she could into the cooler, but she'd nonetheless left a freezer full of rock-hard baggies.

"Yes."

"Then why are we saving the rest?"

"Because…" Elaine swiped away the tears that had begun to roll down her cheeks. "Because you don't throw away breast milk, Arthur! You just don't."

He backed away from her and leaned on the counter.

"Why not?" he asked, gently.

"Didn't you see her pumping with that god-awful machine? Didn't you see how much time, how many hours, days, it took to get all this?" She waved at the stacks of frozen milk. "We can't just throw it away."

"Honey," he said. "You're being ridiculous."

Elaine shoved the freezer shut and leaned back against it. "I'm being *ridiculous?*"

He shrugged. "Irrational, then. I mean, what are you planning to do with it? Make ice cream?" He laughed at his own joke.

Elaine pressed her back into the cool metal and crossed her arms in front of her chest. She dug her fingers into the soft flesh of her inner arm, hoping the pain would distract her enough to prevent her from reaching and slapping Arthur across the face.

"My daughter is in jail," she said.

He didn't reply.

"Olivia is in *jail!*" she shouted, and then snapped her lips shut around the words.

He walked over to her and touched her shoulder. She jerked away, but didn't leave the fridge. He stood awkwardly in front of her.

"I know, Elaine," he said. "I know."

"No. You *don't* know. You don't know anything about this. You don't know how I feel. You don't *want* to know."

"I do. I do know."

She laughed, grimly. "Oh please. She's my daughter, Arthur. Mine." Hot tears ran down her cheeks, and she swiped at the mucus dripping from her nose with the back of her hand. "No one else's."

He shook his head and made as if to touch her again. He stopped his hand before it reached her. He lowered it, awkwardly, and said, "This isn't your fault."

"What?"

"It's not your fault. Olivia made her own choices. You had nothing to do with this."

Elaine stared at him. "Do you think it helps me to hear that?"

"It should."

"Should it? Why? Why should it help me to feel absolved from responsibility?"

He scowled. "Because I know you, and I know you're probably feeling guilty. And you shouldn't."

The tears dried on Elaine's face. "Oh, Arthur. Do you really think you know how I feel?"

In a single step he bridged the gap between them. "I do," he said, and hugged her.

She stood stiffly in his embrace and then sighed. "How can you? How can you, when I don't even know myself?" She said the words into the soft cloth of his T-shirt, and she was not entirely sure that he had heard.

Then she leaned back, out of his embrace. "Just don't touch the milk," she said.

Elaine arrived at the airport laden like a pack mule. In addition to her own small suitcase, she had an overflowing duffel bag filled with Luna's clothes, toys, bottles, blankets, and all the bright plastic apparatuses of American babyhood. Luna sat in her car seat, which was itself nestled in a rolling stroller. Elaine dragged the cooler out of the trunk and let Arthur heave out her two oversized suitcases.

Elaine eyed the line of people waiting for the curbside check-in. "You'd better not stay," she said. "You're liable to get a ticket."

"Right." He leaned over and held her chin in his hand. "I love you, Elaine."

She looked up at him. He smiled at her, and she realized, with some surprise, that it had been some time since they'd said those words to one another. She had been so involved with Olivia and Luna, focused so exclusively on this trip and what it meant. She did love Arthur. He was the one man in her life with whom she'd ever felt comfortable, secure—they were two parts of one well-matched whole.

"I love you, too," she said.

Arthur smoothed her hair behind her ear with his index finger.

"Elaine, I know what you're doing for me. I understand the sacrifice you're making."

"It's not a sacrifice," Elaine said. "We can't handle it. We both know that. Luna will be safe and happy with her other grandparents."

But as she spoke, she realized that of course it *was* a sacrifice. She was sacrificing her second chance at motherhood, her chance to do it right, on the altar of her relationship with Arthur and of her own selfishness and fear.

Arthur hugged her. She stood stiffly for a moment, then wrapped her arms around him and squeezed him back.

"I'll see you in a few days," she said.

Elaine and Luna arrived in León late in the evening. She and Luna were waved through customs with barely a glance from the official. As soon as she walked out the door, she saw a young man with a sign that read "Good Man." She waved him over.

"Miss Good Man?" he asked.

"Yes," Elaine smiled and followed him to the pristine Ford Explorer he'd pulled up to the curb. She settled herself and the baby in the backseat, and she watched the lights of the roadside markets and houses as they passed. At some point, she fell asleep. Elaine was woken by a gentle clearing of the driver's throat.

"Casa Luna," he said. "I put your bags in the room. You go in now." Elaine stood for a moment in the doorway of the hotel, looking up and down the silent street. The dim bulbs from the streetlights illuminated rows of houses strung together directly on the curb. The windows were shuttered and the doors were shut tight. The open door of the hotel cast a glow on the cobblestone street and looked like the only open eye in a row of sleeping faces.

Elaine carried Luna, in her car seat, into the silent lobby. She stopped, enchanted. The hotel was made up of a few old stone buildings around a patio, with a bubbling fountain embedded in one wall. Creeping vines, full of flowers, climbed the walls and dangled from the roofs. There was a fragrance of jasmine and roses, and the night air was alive with the buzz of cicadas and the distant barking of dogs.

The night watchman led Elaine to a room at the far end of the courtyard. The wide doors were leaded glass, covered with a white curtain. She carried the car seat and the sleeping baby in and found her bags already laid out on the oversized oak bed. She kicked off her shoes. The tile floor felt cool and smooth on her stocking feet. She quickly and quietly unpacked her things. Diane, the American innkeeper, had provided a basket for Luna to sleep in. Elaine neatly lined the long, oblong basket with Luna's baby blanket and considered moving the sleeping baby into the makeshift crib, but in the end she left her in the car seat. Elaine stripped off her travel-worn clothes and stood for a long time in the brightly tiled shower, letting water course over her body. When she finally turned off the water, she heard Luna stirring. She wrapped herself in a thick white towel and went to the baby.

Twenty minutes later, when Luna finished the bottle Elaine had heated under a stream of hot water in the bathroom sink, Elaine gently laid her in the basket and climbed into the bed. The lumpy mattress was oddly comfortable; Elaine fell quickly asleep. She was awakened soon after by Luna's wails. The baby cried for a long time, refusing milk, uncomforted by rocking. Every time she quieted and Elaine tried to place her back in her basket, she began to scream. Elaine found a small stuffed bear in the diaper bag and nestled it in the baby's arms, but she merely howled and tossed it aside. Finally, Elaine took Luna into her bed. She settled the baby into the crook of her arm. Luna wiggled for a moment and then fell still, her warm breath ebbing and flowing against the side of her grandmother's breast. To her surprise, Elaine, too, fell asleep, and they woke, hours later, sun streaming into the room, in a warm, damp embrace.

Elaine telephoned Jorge's sister, who gave her directions to their house in the hills above the city. Aida told Elaine what the carfare should be and instructed her to arrive that afternoon at five. Araceli and Juan Carlos would be expecting her. With the entire morning and early afternoon to kill, Elaine decided to take Luna out and explore the colonial city. They'd gone about a block before she stopped, frustrated. Cobblestones and narrow sidewalks made it virtually impossible to maneuver the bulky stroller. Luna squawked indignantly at the rough jerks and fitful stops and starts. Then Elaine remembered the Baby Björn and dragged the stroller back to the hotel.

They spent the rest of the day strolling through the main square and the churches, staring into the beatific face of *La Virgin de Guadeloupe* on every corner and in every building. Luna seemed happy, cuddled up against Elaine's chest. The heavy warmth of the baby gave Elaine a sense of well-being that surprised her. She nestled each of Luna's bare feet into one of her palms and ambled through the city, tickling the tiny toes and placing periodic kisses upon the baby's soft head.

In the late morning, Luna began to fuss, and Elaine realized that she, too, was hungry. She ducked into a storefront *taquería* and sat on one of the high stools. She unsnapped Luna from the carrier, and, balancing the little girl on her hip, dug through the diaper bag until she found the bottle she'd put there before they had set off on their tour of the city. The milk had defrosted during their walk, and Luna began drinking noisily. The woman behind the counter wandered over and smiled at the baby.

"Su hija?" she said, leaning over the counter and stroking Luna's head. *"Que guapa."*

"My granddaughter," Elaine said. *"Hija de mi hija."*

The woman let loose a torrent of Spanish and reached into the pocket of her apron. She laid a photograph of a small girl in an elaborate white gown on the counter. *"Mi nieta,"* she said.

Elaine looked at the photograph of the other woman's granddaughter. She traced her finger along the edge of the picture. *"Muy bonita."*

"En los Estados Unidos. Tejas. Houston." She put her hands over her heart and mimed the ache of being separated from the child. Elaine shook her head sympathetically, and the woman shrugged as if to say, "What can you do?" She smiled and motioned to the pots of food bubbling on the gas rings in front of her. Elaine ordered two tacos with chicken, but found that she couldn't finish them. She had lost her appetite.

When the time came to head up to Araceli and Juan Carlos's house, Elaine's peaceful calm began to drain from her, replaced by an anxious dread that gripped her deep in her bowels. She packed lightly for the excursion, with just a single change of clothes for the baby and a few diapers, wanting to make it clear by her paucity of belongings that Luna was not going to remain there that night, that she was going to stay at the hotel with her grandmother for at least another day.

Elaine held Luna in her lap as the taxi meandered through the cobblestone streets and up into the hills surrounding San Miguel. They left behind the large gracious colonial homes and passed into neighborhoods of little houses behind wrought-iron gates. The barks and howls of dogs greeted them at every turn, ratcheting Elaine's anxiety up another notch. Luna gazed out the window, her eyes wide, almost as if she knew that she was going to her new home. The small, neat houses gave way to more ramshackle ones with corrugated tin roofs, and the taxi bumped along uneven pavement and finally pulled to a stop in front of a narrow two-story house. A tiny market took up the first floor. Elaine had passed what seemed like hundreds like it during her walk through the city. Every corner had one—its narrow shelves stocked with dusty cartons of unfamiliar foods and coolers of soda and ice cream.

"Is this the right place?" Elaine asked the driver, showing him once again the scrap of paper with Jorge's family's address.

"*Si. Familia Rodriguez,*" the driver said, motioning her to disembark from his cab.

Elaine looked up and down the long crooked street, miles away from the center of town. "Can you come back for me later?" she asked, as she handed him the money for the fare. The driver shrugged ambiguously, and Elaine clambered out of the cab, clutching Luna in one arm and her bag in the other. A curtain hung in the doorway to the *tienda*, with beads that formed a mosaic image of the face of Jesus. Elaine pushed aside a few strands of beads and found herself face to face with a small wrinkled woman with black hair held back with two pink barrettes.

"Araceli Rodriguez?" Elaine asked, trying to roll her *R*s the way Olivia did.

The woman's face cracked into a huge smile, and she bustled out from behind the counter, a stream of Spanish greetings flowing from her lips. She wrapped Elaine in an embrace and then held out her arms to Luna. She tickled the baby on the neck and tried to take her from Elaine. Elaine resisted, and for the briefest of moments, the two held the baby between them, each tugging on whatever yielding limb she could reach. At last Elaine let her arms fall, and Jorge's mother squeezed Luna close to her chest, beaming gratefully at her opponent in the grand-mother tug-of-war. She called out loudly to someone in the back of the market and motioned for Elaine to follow her behind the counter and through another beaded curtain, this one of St. Michael with his sword, treading on the chest of Satan Defeated. They clambered over crates of laundry soap and plastic flats of Blimpie Bread, pushed aside the dusty cur-tain, and walked into what looked like the family's living room. The market appeared to take up the front hall of the house and was separated from the rest only by the St. Michael curtain. In the living room, there were two daybeds pushed into opposite corners of the room and a brightly colored rug on the floor. A long, narrow table stood against one wall, and an open door let out into a courtyard. Araceli rushed out through this door, and Elaine followed her much more slowly. The courtyard was full of people. It was dark but for the light of the television flicker-ing from its perch on a metal stand against one of the walls. A group of men, some old, some young, sat on chairs and on the floor watching a soccer game. There must have been five or six children zooming tiny cars around and playing house with an oversized cardboard box. The courtyard was loud with the sound of men's voices and the children's happy cries. When Elaine walked in, it fell silent for a moment, and then one by one members of Jorge's family came over and greeted her.

Juan Carlos, a tall man with Jorge's Mayan features but a far readier smile, took Luna from his wife. The baby seemed per-fectly willing to be passed from stranger to stranger, and grabbed hold of Juan Carlos's nose. He laughed delightedly and said something in rapid Spanish to Elaine that was beyond her rudimentary skills. He motioned to a young woman who had come out into the courtyard from a small room that looked like it might be the kitchen.

"Hello, Elaine. I am Aida. My father say thank you for bringing the beautiful Luna to us."

Elaine smiled faintly, and in a voice that surprised her with its tremulousness said, "Thank you, too, but I think I'd better take her now. She's not used to so many new people." Aida murmured something to her father, who dutifully handed the giggling infant to Elaine.

"Please, sit down." Aida led Elaine to a chair in the courtyard. Moments later, two of the young men had dragged the long table out into the darkness. They set it before Elaine, and Araceli appeared with a bowl of steaming soup.

"Please, eat," said Aida. "My mother's *sopa Azteca* is delicious."

Elaine sipped from the proffered bowl and nodded her agreement. "Wonderful." She ate self-consciously, watching the others watch her. Only once Araceli had placed before her a plate laden with *carnitas*, beans, and rice, did she ask, "Aren't you all eating, too?"

"Yes, yes," the girl said and called to her mother. Plates and bowls and heaping stacks of tortillas began materializing from the kitchen. Soon, everyone was eating. Some people sat at the table, but they left Elaine a large space to herself. She ate with one hand, holding Luna in the other. She knew that she should allow Luna's family to hold the baby and play with her, but she was unwilling to let her go. After they'd eaten, Juan Carlos pulled a chair up to Elaine and leaned forward, his hands resting on his knees. He drew his finger along the length of his moustache and motioned to his daughter to step forward. Aida translated as he spoke.

"My father say he so sorry that Jorge and Olivia be so trouble to you and to him. He say he is shamed of his son. He say a man should protect his woman, not bring problems to her and to her family. He say can you forgive him for this."

Juan Carlos held his hands out to Elaine. "I so sorry," he said, in thickly accented English.

"I am, too," Elaine replied. She spoke slowly to give Aida time to translate. "My daughter is innocent. I think your son was tricked by evil people, and I think he grew frightened, and that is why he brought Olivia into his troubles. I understand his fear, and while I am terribly sad my daughter has been punished for something she didn't do, I am grateful to you for your apology."

Juan Carlos frowned as Aida spoke and shook his head, almost reprovingly. He spoke again, and Aida translated. "My father say, let's not talk about who is right and who is wrong. They are both in a sad situation now, and we must help them. Right now we must think about Luna and how to care for her. He say thank you for bringing the baby to him. He say I promise we will care for her and that you will be proud of her."

Elaine stifled her flash of anger at any implication that what had happened was Olivia's fault in any way. She reminded herself that Juan Carlos knew only what Jorge had told him and what Olivia had written in her letter. "Aida, please ask your father if he understands that Olivia will want Luna back in a few years, when she's released from prison. Does he promise to give her back, even if Jorge wants her as well?"

Juan Carlos nodded vigorously as Aida translated. "My father understands that of course Olivia is afraid to send her child so far away. My father say a child belongs with its mother, and when Luna's mother is free she will have her baby."

Elaine nodded. She looked around at the sea of serious, thoughtful people. The room was simple, spartan even. Many of the toys the children played with were broken—their dolls had hair worn to a frazzle or rubbed off completely. Most of the toy cars seemed to be missing wheels, and the children wore clothes that had clearly been handed down from older siblings or cousins. But they looked content and well fed. Juan Carlos and Araceli seemed, as Olivia had promised, to be warm, loving people who would take good care of their granddaughter. Luna would be safe; she would be comfortable, she would be happy. Elaine believed the man when he said he would return Luna to Olivia when she was released.

Araceli came out from behind Juan Carlos's chair where she'd been hovering and took Elaine's hand. Aida translated her mother's words. "My mother say you keep Luna for another night, so that you can say good-bye. Tomorrow, maybe you come and sleep here with her. After, you must promise you will visit many times, so Luna will have both her grandmothers to take care of her."

Elaine smiled and began to cry. Araceli rushed to hug her, and they rocked back and forth together, Elaine bent over awkwardly in the small woman's embrace.

The line for the pay phone was long and the women huddled under a miasma of gray cigarette smoke. Olivia leaned against the cold tile wall whirling her hair with a raw-looking finger. Chewing on her cuticles and playing with her hair were two of the habits she'd developed in the two weeks she'd been confined at Dublin. From the moment she'd arrived, Olivia had crept through the prison, hoping to slip undetected by the grim, angry inmates who ran the place. On her first day, a bleached-blond with a jagged purple scar across her throat had lifted a lock of Olivia's hair as they stood side by side in the meal line.

"Sexy," she had said, and Olivia had cringed under her foul-smelling breath and the threat she was sure was implied by that single hissed word. From then on, Olivia had scraped her curls back into a braid so tight it made her temples ache. She shared a cell with two other women, both as silent as she. After she'd dumped her blanket and sheets on the bunk, she'd mumbled her name to the women. They'd told her theirs, but had said little else in the weeks they had been sleeping side by side.

The line moved sluggishly forward, and Olivia did her best to tune out the whining voice of the woman at the front. She was speaking Spanish with what Olivia thought was a Guatemalan accent and was berating the person at the other end of the telephone for not putting money in her prison account. Olivia closed her eyes, and Luna's face swam into view behind her eyelids. She was desperately afraid that her daughter's image would grow cloudy in her memory, or, worse, that the living, breathing face would be replaced by the static likeness in the single photograph Olivia had been allowed to keep with her. She lingered over her daughter's brown eyes, so round they seemed like circles fringed with velvet lashes. She held tightly to the memory of her daughter's soft pink lips pursed around a nipple. Just as she traced a finger across an imaginary downy cheek, she felt a sharp poke in her back.

"Move it or lose it, girl."

Olivia turned and saw a tall dark-skinned woman with long, kinky hair done up in a mass of braids. Her lips were berry-red and shiny with contraband lipstick. The woman motioned to Olivia to move a few steps forward in the line and then looked at her with narrowed eyes.

"Do I know you?" the woman asked.

Olivia ducked her head, shaking it at the same time, and stepped forward. She turned her face away, wrapping her finger around a strand of hair that had pulled loose from her braid. The woman leaned over her and peered into her face.

"I know you, girl. You have your baby already?"

Olivia looked up, startled, and then it dawned on her. She'd met the woman in lockup when she was awaiting trial.

"Queenie?" She was surprised at the hoarse croak of her voice, then realized that she had not spoken a word in days.

"That's me. What your name again?"

"Olivia."

"Right. O-Livia. You get rid of that baby, or you have it?"

Olivia paused. "Both, I guess. I had her, but…" Her voice trailed off.

"But you can't keep no babies in here." Queenie nodded. "You had a little girl? What her name?"

"Luna."

"That's pretty. That's moon in Spanish, am I right?"

"Right."

"My girls are Cassandra and Deandra. They twins."

"How old are they?"

"Six. Six tomorrow. I'm calling them today in case I don't get the phone tomorrow. You calling your baby?"

Olivia shook her head. She felt the tears rise in her eyes. "My mom's taking Luna to Mexico, to her grandparents. She's going to live there while I'm here. I'm calling my mom's boyfriend to see if she made it okay."

"Oh, baby," Queenie reached out a sympathetic arm and drew Olivia in to her ample bosom. "That so hard. You so far away from her. She can't even visit you. You poor baby."

Olivia began crying in earnest, but had to dry her tears quickly. It was her turn for the phone.

After leaving the Rodriguez home, Elaine took Luna back to her hotel room for their last night alone together. She changed the baby's diaper and prepared a bottle. She stretched out on the bed, nestled Luna in the crook of her arm, and watched her. The baby's lips moved vigorously at first, and she stared into Elaine's eyes as she drank. When she was awake and wriggling, Luna felt small and light in Elaine's arms. But as her eyes drooped, she seemed to gain weight, grow dense and heavy. Elaine rubbed her face gently against the top of Luna's head. The baby's dark hair tickled her cheek, and she took a mouthful of it. She tasted just a hint of salt.

Careful not to wake the baby, Elaine reached across the bed and picked up the telephone.

Arthur sounded pleased to hear from her and launched into a long description of a new cross-county trail he had found. Elaine listened to the hum of his voice, but, busy stroking Luna's soft cheek, paid little attention to his words. It was only when she heard Olivia's name that she focused on what he was saying.

"What? What happened?" Elaine asked anxiously.

"Nothing happened. She called, that's all."

"How did she sound?"

"She sounded fine."

"Fine? I find that hard to believe. She hasn't sounded fine in any of her previous calls. Why should she sound fine now?" Elaine's voice was sharp and pitched higher than normal. She cleared her throat and lowered her voice. "Sorry. I didn't mean to bite your head off."

"Apology accepted. How are things going? Do Jorge's parents seem like nice people?"

"Oh yes. Lovely. Very sweet. They don't have much money, but it seems like a happy home."

"Thank God. I was worried. What a huge relief."

Elaine felt a sinking in the pit of her stomach. Nothing was going to make what she had to say any easier.

She knew that Arthur was, simply and absolutely, not interested in having Luna move into their home; he had barely taken an interest in his own children. He had moved across the country when they were very young, and had seemed more than satisfied with their twice yearly visits. Although he had scrupulously paid child support for as long as the courts had obliged him to, the last thing he would do was raise someone else's child.

Elaine put her hand on Luna's belly and felt it rise and fall with her breath. The baby pursed her lips and mewed softly in her sleep. She wrinkled her forehead at some troubling baby dream. Elaine smoothed it with a gentle finger. Then she gathered herself together and sat up in the bed.

"I'm bringing her home, Arthur."

"What? What are you talking about? You just said everything is fine. They're nice people. What could possibly be wrong?"

With the weight of Olivia's daughter nestled in her arms, Elaine allowed herself, as she never had before, to confront the fact that she had failed as a mother. Somewhere along the line, very early on, she had decided that she would give Olivia only so much and no more. She had withheld herself, providing for her daughter, dressing her wounds, accomplishing the required routine tasks, as if mothering were itself a kind of mandatory minimum sentence, as if there were some minimum amount of love you were required to give your child, some minimum responsibility you were obliged to assume. Elaine had resented the vast extent of even that minimum and had tried to limit it in any way she could. Her life as a mother had been a series of calculations, of estimations: what was required of her, what she could get away with, what she might avoid. Motherhood was a language that Elaine did not speak and had never bothered to learn. She had viewed it as a series of tasks, of duties, that would pass as soon as her child reached adulthood. The ultimate standard of behavior for her was and had always remained the responsibilities incurred by and the freedoms granted to a woman who was nobody's mother at all. She had never understood, until now, the fundamental truth: that the sentence of motherhood had no limit. There was no cap. There was no maximum amount of love you were compelled to extend, no point at which you would have served your full sentence.

Elaine had never allowed herself to experience the infinite love a mother felt for her child. She had not realized that it was possible, nor felt ashamed of its absence in herself. Though she had certainly been plagued over the years by a kind of amorphous guilt, she had always dismissed it without understanding it as a message that, somewhere deep within, even she recognized her own failure. Now Elaine wondered at the source of her limitations. Why had she been such a pinched and constricted mother? Perhaps it was because she had not been ready when

Olivia was born—the responsibility came too soon and was so unlooked for. But plenty of mothers rose to that same unexpected occasion. Why had she failed to do so? Perhaps, she thought, it was because the father of her child had deserted her. Yet many women loved children of absent fathers, loved them all the more *because* of their abandonment.

Now Elaine recognized that, while she might never understand the reason for her failure, she *had* been offered an exemplary model of a mother who reveled in the maximum sentence of motherhood: Olivia. Like her, Olivia had been surprised by a baby that came when she was too young and even worse off materially than Elaine had been. Jorge's abandonment was so much more profound than that of Olivia's own father that it seemed hardly logical to compare them. Yet with no example to follow, Olivia loved Luna effortlessly with immeasurable, bottomless devotion, celebrating the terms of her sentence, seeing it not as a confinement but rather a form of liberation. Lying there, in a Mexican hotel, Elaine determined to learn from her daughter. She vowed, now that she had been granted a second chance, to take care, completely and finally, of her own child. She would care for Olivia by loving Luna.

"This is wrong. All of it," she said. "Luna belongs with me. She belongs with me because I'm the only person who can take care of her and make sure she visits Olivia as often as they'll allow it. She belongs with me because she's my responsibility." Elaine cupped the top of Luna's head with her hand and felt the beat of the child's pulse in her palm. "She belongs with me because I love her."

Elaine heard nothing but the crackle of the phone line.

"Arthur," she asked. "Did you hear me?"

"Yes," he said.

"I'm bringing her home."

"I heard you."

"Well?"

"Well, what? It doesn't sound like you're asking me if I agree with your decision. It doesn't sound like you're giving me the opportunity to object. It sounds like you're telling me what you're going to do."

Elaine stroked the baby's hair. "Yes. That's right. I'm telling you that I'm bringing Luna home. I'm going to take care of her until Olivia gets out of jail."

"And what about us?"

She inhaled softly. She imagined Arthur's face, his back, the muscles of his legs. She pictured him in their kitchen cooking dinner, running ahead of her on a wooded path, posing for her camera with his effortless, automatic smile.

"I think that's up to you," she said, softly.

"I can't hear you. This line sucks. What did you say?"

She cleared her throat and spoke louder. "I said that's up to you."

Luna's face wrinkled, and she wriggled closer to Elaine.

"I suppose it is," Arthur said.

"I love you, Arthur. I really do."

"Do you?" he asked.

"Yes."

He sighed. "I love you, too, Elaine."

Arthur didn't meet Elaine at the airport, of course. She was not sure why she had not told him she had arranged to come home a few days early. It certainly was not because he appreciated a surprise. She didn't know what she had expected to greet her on her arrival, but it was not an immaculate house. Carrying the baby on her hip, she wandered through the empty rooms. The first she entered was Olivia's. It looked much as she had left it, with the bassinet set up in one corner, and diapers, baby wipes, and a changing pad laid precisely in the middle of the desk. It was only after a moment that she realized that there was an extra bag of diapers and another box of baby wipes on the desk. New bottles of baby shampoo and bath soap stood next to the changing supplies. Arthur had done the shopping.

She walked down the hall to her own room. The top of Arthur's dresser was empty. She pulled open a drawer. Nothing. His side of the closet was abandoned but for a row of empty wire hangers; he had taken the wooden ones. She wandered out to the dining room. His computer had disappeared, as had the stacks of papers and folders from the table. The printer she had bought him sat in a corner of the room, on the floor, covered with a folded sheet. In the kitchen, his basket of vitamins was gone, as were the boxes of nonfat soy milk from the cupboard. Arthur had replenished the baby's supplies and then erased all trace of himself from the house.

Elaine wondered why she wasn't crying. Perhaps the morning's emotions had drained her of any further capacity for tears. On her way out of San Miguel, Elaine had stopped at the hotel where Aida worked. She had presented Jorge's sister with a cell phone, prepaid with enough time to call the United States every couple of weeks for a year. Luna slept in her car seat at Elaine's feet.

"I'm going home," she had said. "I'm taking Luna with me."

"But Olivia wants us to take Luna. She said so," Aida had said.

At the young woman's insistence and because she knew herself that the confrontation was unavoidable, Elaine had waited in the lobby of the hotel until Araceli and Juan Carlos could be fetched. They rushed through the arched doorway. There had followed much weeping on all sides, but finally the grandparents had agreed that the baby should live in the United States, within visiting distance of the prison where her mother would spend the next few years.

"And Jorge?" Araceli asked through her daughter. "Will Luna visit her father?"

Elaine didn't answer for a moment. She did not want to lie to Araceli. Neither did she want to carry out that particular promise. And yet, how could she refuse? "If Olivia wants me to, I'll take Luna to visit him," she said.

Araceli opened her mouth to object, but Juan Carlos shook his head at her. "*Es justo,*" he said. No translation was necessary.

Araceli and Juan Carlos promised to call, and Elaine promised to send photographs and to come visit the following year. Elaine left San Miguel as she had arrived, with her granddaughter sleeping in the carseat, next to her.

Feeding, changing, bathing, and putting Luna to sleep kept Elaine too busy to cry on her first night back at home without Arthur. Her dry eyes made her believe, incorrectly it turned out, that she would never weep for the loss of the man who had shared her life for such a long time, that the gap he left would be filled by Luna's needs and her blossoming love for the baby whom she reminded herself never to think of as entirely her own.

Arthur saw Elaine only once more. A few weeks after he left their home, he came into the pharmacy. He paused in the doorway, watching Elaine in her white coat, her hair shiny and impeccably colored, her face bearing its professional mask of interest and concern as she patted the wrist of an elderly man clutching a small white bag filled near to the bursting with bottles of pills.

Arthur heard his name and turned to greet Ralph, who was staring at him with frank surprise. At the sound of Ralph's voice, Elaine raised her head, and even from across the store Arthur could see her face pale. He raised a hand, and she smiled tentatively. He crossed through the aisles of cold remedies, diapers, and shampoos until he reached her counter and waited patiently while she finished with her customer.

Once the man was gone, Arthur said, "Hi."

"Hi," Elaine said, softly.

"How are you?"

"Good. Good. And you?"

"I'm okay," he said, not bothering to hide the heaviness in his voice. "I'm dealing with it, I suppose."

A red flush crept up Elaine's neck. She reached up a hand and tucked her hair firmly behind her ear.

He leaned against the counter. "I needed a refill of my Ambien prescription," he said.

Elaine raised her eyebrows. "What?"

"My Ambien? I still have one refill left on my old prescription." This was, of course, the truth. Arthur had a single refill left, and he hadn't wanted to explain to his doctor, a cantankerous old man with rather Puritan opinions on the efficacy and necessity of sleeping aids, why he needed an entirely new prescription. It was also true, however, that Arthur had wanted to see Elaine. He missed her, and he wondered if she missed him. He was not confident that she understood the extent of their mutual loss. It was important to Arthur that Elaine fully comprehend what she had given up in choosing to indenture her life to Olivia's once again.

"Are you seeing anyone?" he said, suddenly.

Elaine laughed, a single short bark. "Of course not," she said. "I have Luna."

Arthur nodded and knew that the moment had arrived for him to ask about the baby. He could not bring himself to.

"Are you?" Elaine asked.

He shrugged. "No. Soon, I suppose. But not now. Not yet." She nodded.

Warren poked his head around from back behind the counter. He was holding the telephone in his hand. "Elaine? It's Ana."

Elaine jumped. "I'll be right there." She turned back to Arthur. "It's Luna's nanny. She probably can't figure out what to give the baby for lunch."

Arthur nodded. "Anyway, my prescription?" he said.

She reached her hand out for the phone. "Warren, will you refill Arthur's Ambien prescription? And any others he's got left?"

Arthur stared at Elaine, wondering if he would always remember her as the woman who had finally, irrevocably, broken his heart.

She smiled at him blandly, the phone tucked under her chin. "I'm pretty sure there's a Zantac, too."

epilogue

Even in FCI Dublin, Mother's Day is a holiday. The volunteer organization dedicated to helping incarcerated mothers makes a big deal out of Mother's Day. And it's a good thing, too, because were they not there, if they did not arrange for the single red roses and the visiting children, it would be a long, lonely day, and lonely women might be more disposed to do things like hurt themselves or the other women next to whom they were crushed and crowded.

Elaine and Luna visited Olivia regularly, as often as every weekend. They were used to the drive; they had their favorite truck stop along the way. Luna was a fan of the fries in gravy.

Elaine always dressed the little girl in something nice for the visit—something Olivia would have chosen if she could have, like overalls and a bright-colored top, or a hat knitted in the shape of a strawberry. But today, Mother's Day, the baby was even more adorable than usual, in grape-purple pants and an Indian print shirt in complementary shades. She also wore purple high-top sneakers, a new addition to her wardrobe bought to celebrate a recently acquired skill—walking. Her shoulder-length hair was held off her face with a lavender ribbon. She was, at thirteen months, much the same as she'd been at three, cheerful and good-natured, and newly loquacious. She spoke both English and Spanish, thanks to the Honduran nanny who watched her while Elaine was at work.

They arrived early, standing in line with the other grandmothers, aunts, and foster mothers. There were no fathers in the line.

Elaine had never once seen a father there escorting his children to visit their mother. She wasn't sure why. Maybe the men were in jail, like the women. Or maybe they weren't the ones caring for the kids. Or maybe they just couldn't bear to visit the prison.

Luna sat on her grandmother's hip, chattering in her just barely unintelligible language. She stuck her tongue out merrily at the children running under her grandmother's feet. She put one hand on either side of Elaine's cheeks, looked deep into her eyes, and said, "Down."

"No honey, not yet. When we get inside and see Mama you can go down."

They waited their turn to empty their pockets and enter the visiting room. Elaine, by now absolutely familiar with the drill, had left her purse in the car and carried only a small bag with two diapers for Luna, a packet of baby wipes, and a plastic bag filled with quarters. When they'd first begun visiting, she'd been surprised at the way everyone in the visiting room crowded around the vending machines, feeding in an endless supply of quarters and eating packets of Fritos and chocolate, drinking can after can of Diet Coke. By now, she too rushed over to the machines, glad of an excuse to give Olivia the illusion of privacy with her baby, if not the reality, surrounded as she was with other mother-and-child reunions. The machines were also a way for Elaine to give Olivia treats; candy, soda. Things she couldn't buy for herself inside.

This time, as she carried Luna through the metal detector, a young woman handed them a long-stem red rose.

"To give to Mom," she said, her voice determinedly sprightly.

Elaine murmured her thanks and walked to the first set of double doors. She passed through with a small knot of other visitors. They waited silently in the hallway and were finally buzzed through the second set of doors. As she walked down the hallway to the visiting room, Elaine made out the group of women waiting behind the final set of glass doors. They were dressed in their regulation green and khaki shifts, but it was painfully obvious how much care they'd taken with their appearances. The hairdos were elaborate, and their homemade cosmetics were thickly applied. Some had ironed decorative fans and pleats into their clothing. Others wore earrings and necklaces fashioned from bits of aluminum foil. Every woman behind the door stared at the group of visitors, eyes darting to find the longed-for face. Elaine quickened her step and saw Olivia.

The two looked at each other through the glass. Olivia had her hair in the braid she always wore. She, unlike the other women, wore no makeup, and her pallor would have concerned Elaine had she not become accustomed to it. Olivia smiled at her mother and began waving at Luna. Elaine looked down at her charge. At first she was happy to see that Luna was waving back, but she soon realized that the child was looking not at Olivia, but at another woman entirely. Elaine turned Luna in her mother's direction, trying not to draw Olivia's attention to Luna's mistake. The momentary faltering of Olivia's smile gave away the fact that she had noticed.

The door buzzed, and the little crowd surged forward. Elaine and Olivia found each other's arms and hugged, hard, Luna squashed between them.

"Mama!" Luna announced, and Olivia beamed with relief.

"Come, let's grab a table," she said, taking Luna from Elaine's arms. Only once Olivia turned to lead the way did Elaine notice that her right cheek was swollen and bruised.

"Oh my God, honey, what happened?" she said, touching the abrasion.

Olivia flinched. "Nothing. I just had a little difference of opinion with one of the guards. It's nothing."

"Nothing? It doesn't look like nothing. Did you report it? Did you call Izaya? Maybe you should file a lawsuit or something?"

Olivia smiled ruefully, "Mom, it's really nothing. Honestly, if I reported everything, I'd end up in segregation for the next three years. Never mind, okay? I don't want to spend our precious time talking about this."

Elaine pressed her lips together. She'd call Izaya herself when she got home.

"Have you heard from him?" she asked.

"He was here yesterday."

"Again?"

Olivia blushed. "Yeah, well, he's a lawyer; he can come whenever he wants. There's no limit on legal visits."

"And are things between you…" Elaine's voice trailed off.

Olivia shook her head. "There's nothing between us."

"Oh really?"

"Nothing romantic, that is. I've got another thirty-one months in here, Mom."

Elaine nodded. "Well, he came by to visit the baby again. He brought her that outfit." Elaine pointed at Luna's purple ensemble. Olivia tugged the label from inside the collar of Luna's shirt and read it. She smiled.

"What?" Elaine said.

"I'm picturing him shopping for little purple clothes at Sweet Potatoes."

"You should see him change a diaper."

Izaya had fallen into the habit of coming by Elaine's house every once in a while to take Luna for an outing to the park, to the zoo, or just for a walk around the neighborhood. At first Elaine had always tagged along, but she quickly realized that Izaya wanted the baby all to himself, and once she'd reassured herself that he was adept at diaper changes and the other mundane tasks of parenthood, she'd backed off and let the two of them have their time together. The last time they came back from Willard Park, Izaya had been wearing an unusually large smile, as if there was something he was dying to tell Elaine.

"What happened?" Elaine said.

"Nothing," he said. "Just, one of the moms complimented me."

"What did she say?"

"She said she wished her husband was as good a dad as I am."

He bent down and nuzzled the top of Luna's head. "She said that. Didn't she, Moon-pie?"

"Hmm," said Elaine, feeling a little catch in her throat.

He looked up, and she could see that he was trying to gauge her reaction. "What?"

"Well, what did you say?"

"What do you mean, what did I say?"

"Did you tell her that you aren't Luna's father?"

He shook his head and kissed the baby on the cheek. "Nope."

"Why not?"

"It was none of her business." He smiled softly.

Though this exchange had pleased her, Elaine had decided not to tell her daughter about it. Olivia was right, it would be a long time until she was released. Why raise hopes that could end up being false?

Olivia sat down in a chair at an empty corner of one of the long tables bolted to the middle of the room. She began talking to Luna in Spanish, kissing her on the face and tickling her belly. The girl looked at Elaine for a moment, and then, reassured by her grandmother's nod, smiled at Olivia. Once again, Elaine breathed a sigh of relief. Each time they visited, she was terrified that Luna would cry or otherwise reject her mother. It was their good fortune that the girl was easy with strangers. Luna was always perfectly happy to go to Olivia, and if she didn't seem to remember her mother from one visit to the next, that was something Elaine was confident only she really recognized.

Olivia balanced Luna on her lap and reached into the pocket of her dress.

"Happy Mother's Day, Mom," she said, and handed Elaine a small envelope made of a piece of red construction paper folded in on itself. Elaine opened the envelope and found a card with a drawing of two women and a baby. One woman, with chin-length brown hair, was holding the fat little baby in a sling of brightly colored woven fabric. The other women, with long blond and red curls, had her arm around them both.

"It's us!" Elaine exclaimed. "Did you draw it yourself?"

Olivia nodded. "That's why it doesn't look anything like us. Except for the hair, I guess."

Elaine smiled at the picture. "You drew me holding the baby."

Olivia nodded again. Elaine opened the card and read the inscription.

Happy Mother's Day. Love, Olivia and Luna.

"I made the card from both of us," Olivia said.

Elaine smiled at her. "Thank you, honey."

"Because you're really like Luna's mother right now."

Elaine shook her head. "*You* are her mother. I'm her grand-mother."

"No. I mean, I know I'm her mother. It's just hard, in here, to feel like anybody's mother, you know?"

Olivia looked around the room, and Elaine followed her gaze as it alighted on woman after woman, holding tight to children who seemed to wriggle uncomfortably in their arms.

Olivia turned back to Elaine. "You're *being* a mother to her. You're doing everything for her I could ever do, and more. I'm so grateful to you, Mom. I just want you to know that. I'm so…so …" Olivia's voice trailed off. Elaine looked at her daughter's mottled face and brimming eyes.

"I know you are, honey. And I'm grateful to you, too."

"You've always been a good mother," Olivia said, her voice low.

The two women stared at each other for a moment. They both knew exactly what kind of mother Elaine had been.

"Do you want a soda? Or something to eat?" Elaine asked.

"Thanks," Olivia said.

Elaine excused herself and wandered over to the vending machines, exchanging pleasantries with the other grandmothers, some of whom she'd come to know. Suddenly, they were distracted by raised voices at the other end of the room. A tall black woman with a swirl of elaborately braided hair rising high off the crown of her head was trying to break up a fight between twin girls who looked about seven years old. They were rolling on the floor, punching and kicking each other, while the mother and an older woman tried to pull them apart. The girls ignored their mother and grandmother, raising their voices to shrieks. The grandmother began shouting, too.

"I'm going whup you both senseless! Stop it, now!" she screamed.

The mother tried unsuccessfully to pull the girls apart, backing away when one of them kicked her viciously in the stomach. Elaine looked over at Olivia, who had risen to her feet and walked quickly over to the writhing girls. Luna was balanced on her mother's hip, her eyes round and staring.

"Queenie?" Olivia said, "Need some help?"

"Listen, you break this up or I'm going to toss your butts right on out of here," a guard said, marching over to the group. "Break this up right now."

Olivia stretched her mouth into a smile, and said, "Hey, we're sorry. You know kids. We'll have them quiet in a minute."

Queenie reached into the fray and grabbed one of the girls. Suddenly, she howled, jerked back her hand, and cradled it to her chest. "She bit me!" she said to no one in particular.

"That's it," said the guard. "I'm throwing the little animals out."

"No! Please no. Please," Olivia cried. "Please, she hasn't seen them in almost four months!" She turned to the grandmother. "Mrs. Swain, can't you make them stop?"

The grandmother put her hands on her hips and shook her head. "I been telling Queenie. I can't make these hellions do nothing. Nothing. They don't never listen to me."

The guard was joined by another. Each of them grabbed one of the girls and wrenched them off each other.

"No!" Olivia cried again, to no avail.

The girls, stunned into silence by the guards' touch, stared at their grandmother with wide eyes. They both began to cry as the guards started walking them toward the exit door. Queenie ran along behind them, begging, "Please, see, they're okay now. See? They'll be quiet. Please! Goddamn you! Stop!"

Olivia followed her friend, running as quickly as she could while simultaneously trying to comfort a now-crying Luna.

The guards motioned for the grandmother to follow them, and she did, shrugging her shoulders at her daughter. The group passed through the double doors and away. Queenie fell to her knees, her faced pressed against the glass. Her sobbing voice was just barely audible as she continued to plead with the guards who had disappeared from view. Olivia kneeled down next to the weeping woman and embraced her, Luna between them, her face pressed into Olivia's shirt, and her arms wrapped tightly around her neck. The three sat there for a moment, and then one of the guards took Queenie's arm and led her away.

Elaine met Olivia and Luna back at their table. The little girl's tears had dried, and her customary smile had even made its appearance.

"Will your friend be all right?" Elaine asked.

Olivia nodded. "I hope so. I'll write her mother and ask her to bring the girls again in a couple of weeks." She reached an arm around her mother's shoulder and squeezed. "She'll be fine, Mom. Tell me more about what's going on with you guys."

"Why don't you put Luna down," Elaine said. "She's been cruising on the furniture. She's so close to walking."

Olivia set the girl on her impossibly small feet and watched her as she smacked her hands on the plastic bench. The baby turned around and, wobbling a bit, set off down the aisle, her arms raised in the air.

"Oh, my God! She's walking," Olivia said, laughing. She ran out in front of her daughter and caught her just as she stumbled and sat down on the floor, her padded rear end hitting the rubberized flooring with a soft smack. "When did she learn to do that? How long has she been doing that?"

Elaine smiled at her daughter and lied. "This is her first time. She's been getting ready, but this is the first time she's really walked on her own."

Elaine protected Olivia with her dishonesty. She protected her from the agonizing irony that the mother's redemption, hers, had come at the daughter's expense. Elaine, who had contracted and constricted herself until what she had offered her daughter was something barely recognizable as a mother's love, had been given a second chance. She had been given the opportunity to atone for her neglect, but this very act of contrition was itself a betrayal. She had replaced Olivia in Luna's affection. It was Elaine who was now the center of the little girl's world. And yet, even so, Olivia loved her child with every bit of the generosity and fidelity she had felt during the months they had passed their nights tangled in each other's arms. Such was the depth of her love that it could survive both separation and the little girl's disregard.

They spent the rest of the visit standing ten feet or so apart as Luna stumbled and staggered between them. Finally, a loud voice informed them that their visit was over. Olivia scooped the baby into her arms and buried her face in her neck, inhaling deeply. Elaine looked around the room and saw the mothers all doing the same thing. They were all smelling their children, breathing their aromas, memorizing their particular and unique fragrance. Olivia stood up and handed Luna to her mother. Elaine leaned over and kissed her daughter on the cheek.

"Write as much as you can," Elaine said.

"Don't forget your Mama," Olivia said, tracing a finger down Luna's cheek.

"Wave bye-bye to Mama," Elaine said, and the little girl obediently lifted her hand, adding her voice to the chorus of children all saying the same thing. The grandmothers, aunts, and foster mothers guided their charges through the glass doors, leaving behind a crowd of women, each gripping a single red rose in her hand.

about the author

Ayelet Waldman graduated from Harvard Law School and clerked for a federal judge prior to becoming a criminal defense attorney for the Federal Public Defender's office in Los Angeles. Currently, she is an adjunct professor at Boalt Hall School of Law at the University of California. She is also the author of a successful mystery series. Ayelet lives in Berkeley, California, with her husband, author Michael Chabon, and their four children.

acknowledgments

This book benefited from the patience and attention of many talented and generous readers. Ed Swanson and Katya Kamasaruk's expertise in criminal law and the prison system was invaluable. The attorneys and staff of Legal Services for Prisoners With Children provided information critical to the plot and story. Amanda Coyne's essay, "Lockup," was an inspiration, as was the work of Families Against Mandatory Minimums. Elaine Petrocelli not only read this book and supported it early on, but also corrected a glaring error. I'm grateful to Vicki Carter of Elmwood Pharmacy for her expertise. Kathleen Caldwell read draft after draft, and was both critical and supportive, not an easy balance to strike. I also thank Mona Simpson, Vendela Vida, Dorothy Allison, Daniel Handler, Gail Tsukiyama, Susanne Pari, Kim Chernin and the other women of Edgework Books, Heidi Julavits, Rabih Almaddine, Elizabeth Joyce, Saundi Schwartz, Michael Barnard, and especially Amanda Davis, Daniel Mendelsohn, and Dave Eggers.

Megan McDonald, Melinda Johnson, and Carmen Dario did the work that gave me time to write.

Mary Evans championed this book with a devotion typical of her, and unique in the world.

I am grateful to Jennifer Fusco for her kind editorial guidance, Megan Dempster for a beautiful design, and to Dominique Raccah, Barbi Pecenco, Todd Stocke, and the entire Sourcebooks family. I am lucky to have fallen into their talented and generous hands.

I thank my children, Sophie, Zeke, Ida-Rose, and Abraham, my sweet jailors in the life sentence that is motherhood, and their father, my editor, critic, champion, and b'shert, Michael Chabon.

There is no way to acknowledge the debt I owe to the victims of the federal mandatory minimum sentences.